PRAISE FOR
COMPLICIT

New York Times Book Review Editors' Choice
Best Crime Novels of 2022 and Best Noir
Fiction of 2022—CrimeReads
Best Crime Novels of 2022—*The Irish Times*
Best Books of 2022—*Glamour*

"Like the best filmmakers, Li draws you to the edge of your seat and keeps you there."
—*The New York Times Book Review*, Editors' Choice

"*Complicit* is an amazing examination of the film industry. . . . This timely and thrilling book raises tough—and necessary—questions about justice and revenge in the twenty-first century. Don't miss it."
—David Heska Wanbli Weiden, Anthony and Thriller Award–winning author of *Winter Counts*

"*Complicit* is immensely powerful, compelling, and enraging. A feminist thriller set in the workplace that feels all too real."
—Harriet Tyce, author of international bestseller *Blood Orange*

"A compulsive read—Winnie M Li's powerful and beautiful writing immediately immersed me and kept me furiously turning the pages. . . . I loved it."
—Sarah Pearse, *New York Times* bestselling author of *The Sanatorium*

"Page-turning . . . An utterly compelling read."
—Liv Constantine, internationally bestselling author of *The Last Mrs. Parrish*

"Winnie's skill as a writer is to forge out of a familiar film story one that is beautifully unique. It haunted me when I was away from it. . . . Utterly compulsive reading."
—Sarah Winman, internationally bestselling author of *Still Life*

"A masterful example of the slow-burn thriller, highlighting the still-all-too-true fact that often the real terror for women is simply existing in a man's world. Also an ode to the power and beauty of storytelling. I loved it."
—Araminta Hall, author of *Imperfect Women*

"Compelling, courageous, and brutal in the best possible way."
—Liz Nugent, #1 internationally bestselling author of *Little Cruelties*

"Like John Grisham did with the legal profession in *The Firm*, Winnie M Li's *Complicit* provides an insider's look at the film industry that is full of suspense."
—Peter Swanson, *New York Times* bestselling author of *Nine Lives*

"A sharply written and absorbing dive into a dark and glamorous world. As timely as it is entertaining, this spectacular novel hooked me from the first page. Winnie M Li is a remarkable talent."
—Cristina Alger, *New York Times* bestselling author of *Girls Like Us*

"A shattering and morally complex portrait of power, ambition, guilt, and the toxic culture that enables entitled men to do as they please."
—Robin Wasserman, PEN/Faulkner finalist and critically acclaimed author of *Mother Daughter Widow Wife*

"A propulsive page-turner, Winnie M Li's *Complicit* is a glittering story of ambition, regret, corruption, and ultimately hope. Sarah Lai is an unforgettable protagonist."
—Vanessa Hua, author of *Forbidden City*

"Bold, brilliant, dazzling, and devastating. Winnie M Li writes with pure heart and effortless style, and in *Complicit* handles the sharpest of stories with such compassion and skill."
— Chris Whitaker, *New York Times* bestselling author of *We Begin at the End*

"Skillful, engrossing, and timely."
— T.M. Logan, #1 internationally bestselling author of *Trust Me*

"A must-read for anyone who's sat in a movie theater, watched an entertainment show, or followed their favorite celebrity on social media. It's a harrowing explanation of how powerful men are able to get away with so much for so long—as seen through the eyes of an unforgettable heroine whose dream to make movies becomes a nightmare."
— Kellye Garrett, Edgar-nominated and Agatha, Anthony, and Lefty Award–winning author of *Like a Sister*

"With slick, addictive writing and characters that feel so real and relatable, *Complicit* is both engrossing and completely enraging!"
— Allie Reynolds, author of *Shiver*

"Winnie M Li gives us an insider view of the intoxicating and corrupt world of the movie industry, which often places women in a no-win situation. . . . A page-turner for our times."
— Naomi Hirahara, Edgar Award–winning author of *Clark and Division*

"Simply brilliant. Beautiful writing, a compelling story, an intriguing structure—I was captivated from the first paragraph to the last. . . . Like the fallout from the #MeToo movement, this story will resonate for years to come."
— J. T. Ellison, *New York Times* bestselling author of *Her Dark Lies*

COMPLICIT

A NOVEL

WINNIE M LI

EMILY BESTLER BOOKS

ATRIA

New York London Toronto Sydney New Delhi

EMILY
BESTLER
BOOKS

ATRIA

An Imprint of Simon & Schuster, Inc.
1230 Avenue of the Americas
New York, NY 10020

First Emily Bestler Books/Atria Paperback edition June 2023

EMILY BESTLER BOOKS/ATRIA PAPERBACK and colophon are trademarks of Simon & Schuster, Inc.

For information about special discounts for bulk purchases, please contact Simon & Schuster Special Sales at 1-866-506-1949 or business@simonandschuster.com.

The Simon & Schuster Speakers Bureau can bring authors to your live event. For more information or to book an event, contact the Simon & Schuster Speakers Bureau at 1-866-248-3049 or visit our website at www.simonspeakers.com.

Manufactured in the United States of America

1   3   5   7   9   10   8   6   4   2

The Library of Congress has cataloged the hardcover edition as follows:

Names: Li, Winnie M, author.
Title: Complicit / Winnie M Li.
Description: 1. First Emily Bestler Books/Atria Books hardcover edition. | New York : Emily Bestler Books/Atria, 2022. |
Summary: "After a long-buried, harrowing incident, a woman whose promising film career was derailed has an opportunity for revenge in this visceral and timely thriller about power, privilege, and justice."—Provided by publisher.
Identifiers: LCCN 2021050592 (print) | LCCN 2021050593 (ebook) | ISBN 9781982190828 (hardcover) | ISBN 9781982190859 (ebook)
Classification: LCC PR6112.I22 C66 2022 (print) | LCC PR6112.I22 (ebook) | DDC 823/.92—dc23
LC record available at https://lccn.loc.gov/2021050592
LC ebook record available at https://lccn.loc.gov/2021050593

ISBN 978-1-9821-9082-8
ISBN 978-1-9821-9084-2 (pbk)
ISBN 978-1-9821-9085-9 (ebook)

The writing of this novel was supported in part by Arts Council England.

*Dedicated to all those whose lives were affected,
whose careers were diverted, whose voices went unheard*

Prologue

SEE IT NOW.

I look at the free newspapers I collect on my commute, so much detritus abandoned on the seat of a subway car. In these crinkled pages, I recognize names from my earlier life. Faces I saw at a private club, or an after-party, or an awards ceremony where I sat wearing borrowed jewelry and a borrowed gown, like all the rest of that vaunted, posturing audience.

Now, in 2017, I sit among a different audience. The ordinary folk, who commute on the shuddering subway through Brooklyn, already counting down the hours to when we will leave our offices and ride this same way back, in the opposite direction. We who pick through the papers to catch a glimpse of that celebrated life—what do we really know of these marquee names, these reputations now ground into the dust?

Deep down, I am quietly ecstatic—and enthralled. What latest studio head or screen icon will find his past circling back on him? In horror films, there is the silent horde of the undead, dragging the villain down to a well-deserved fate.

Some things we cannot bury, no matter how much we obscure them with gift bags and PR statements and smiling photographs. The truths live on, even though their traces can only be found if we're looking: in the comments that were edited out, the glances in unpublished photos, the meetings that took place behind closed doors but were followed by strange silences. Or one-way messages, never returned.

So we are all seeing it now.

I saw it then, too. But I pretended I didn't.

I look at the life I thought I led, and what I see now: projected as if from a missing reel, newly rediscovered. The two images flicker, shift into focus.

I still can't make sense of it, but I'm trying. I squint into the light, and I hope I haven't been blind this entire time.

In some way, I know it is coming, even before I hear from the outside world. When it happens, it is through slow, old-fashioned, respectable email.

Not through the fast-firing synapses of social media, because I am difficult to find on those channels. I am no one of note, and no one would particularly want to follow me, this stale thirty-nine-year-old woman. I lead a simple life now, riding the subway to my office and my classroom at an unremarkable local college. And then, back in the evenings to my silent apartment.

But this morning on my computer screen, an email appears. Unbidden yet demure, an uninvited guest waiting to be noticed.

A name that has never appeared in my inbox before, but which I recognize right away.

Even now, I know what it is about, though the subject line is so neutral, seemingly harmless: Some questions related to a New York Times investigation.

My heartbeat vaults within a millisecond, and I force my eyes to the rest of my emails. A blip of excitement in my otherwise dull day-to-day. For a moment, I am reminded of what it had been like to get dramatic emails in my inbox by the hour, even the minute. An office buzzing with activity, the forgotten thrill of being there, in the middle of things.

And then just as promptly, a wave of some other buried emotion takes over. A ghost I wish I'd never summoned.

I choose not to open the email. There are other, soothingly

humdrum matters to attend to: student assessments, a utility bill to pay, the department's autumn barbecue.

When I leave to teach my first class, that email remains un-opened. But it hangs somewhere at the back of my mind, like some dusty, disused tool at the darkened far-end of a shed.

As much as I try to ignore it, I know it is there.

It sits in the gloom, waiting for me.

1

SCREENWRITING 101 IS literally called Screenwriting 101 at the fine institution where I teach. That's how original the place is.

I have three classes this semester: two sections of Screenwriting 101 and another one, also innovatively titled, Advanced Screenwriting.

My students aren't any more innovative, although I suppose it's my job as their lecturer to try and encourage them to be. But at this college, most of the students have ambitions that significantly dwarf their actual talent. Of course, I can never really tell them this. I have to humor them, indulge their own doomed fantasies of a Hollywood future, while gently guiding their screenwriting to show a little more nuance, to stray ever so slightly away from a slavish devotion to formula.

Still, the job pays me a salary I can live on. I get to teach the classics, fine, Syd Field and Robert McKee, but also to add my own twist on them. I introduce the kids to "the canon," then throw in a few weird ones. Let's watch this dreamlike, head-scratching enigma of a film by a Thai director whose name none of you can pronounce. Here's a ninety-minute black-and-white film documenting Berlin in the 1920s, set entirely to music, no dialogue. Stomach that, millennials.

Today, in my ten thirty a.m. Screenwriting 101 class, we are talking about character.

"How do you know when you have a truly memorable film

character?" I ask, as my first provocation to twenty hungover college students, who stare at me, zombie-like.

Radio silence.

Sometimes it helps to ask the same question again, but rearrange the words in a slightly different order.

"What makes a film character memorable?"

This time I train my eyes on a specific student, as if willing him or her to utter anything—a sentence, a sound, just show some sign of intelligent life. I look at Claudia, a bespectacled, brown-haired girl known to occasionally make an insightful comment. That does not happen today. She looks at me wordlessly.

For god's sake, I'm thinking. I'm not even asking about the assigned reading. It's literally just a question about the movies. *Kids, say something!* I want to shout.

Instead, I repeat my previous question verbatim.

"What makes a film character memorable?"

Finally, a boy—of course, a boy—speaks up. It's Danny. Dirty-blond hair, with a few piercings in his face, he's one of the more talkative students in class.

"Uhh . . . because you remember the character?"

Then he breaks out in a short, sharp rip of laughter. I'm unsure if he's laughing at the sheer stupidity of his own answer or the rhetorical way in which he upended my question, but I let the giggles ripple around the classroom and die down. Okay, work with these kids.

"And what makes you remember a character?" I ask.

"If they're funny?"

"If they do crazy things?"

"Because they're really hot."

More giggles after the last comment, but I ignore them.

"So . . . who are some film characters that you really remember?" I attempt eye contact with the students, as I stroll between their desks. "Come on, name a few."

"James Bond," someone shouts out.

"Luke Skywalker," another guy says.

"Thor."

"Robert DeNiro in *Taxi Driver*," some kid says, and I know he thinks he's showing off his film knowledge, because he just referenced a movie made before 1980.

"Hannibal Lecter."

"Any characters who haven't *killed* other people?" I ask. This generates some laughs among the students, but no one seems to be able to name one.

Until one kid says: "Dumbo?"

Fine, I'll take Dumbo. I then pose my second provocation, one I hadn't planned. "Any female characters who are memorable?"

Another awkward silence.

"Julia Roberts in *Pretty Woman*?" a girl says.

She played a prostitute! I want to shout. Instead, I say: "Okay, that's a start. She was Oscar-nominated for that performance.

"She also had great hair," I add. The kids reward me with some laughs.

It churns on, this interminable game, but I want to plumb the alarmingly shallow depths of my students' film knowledge. They name female superhero sidekicks. They name Disney princesses.

Finally, I say: "How about Scarlett O'Hara in *Gone with the Wind*?"

The students look at me blankly.

"After all, tomorrow is another day?" I offer, quoting Scarlett O'Hara's iconic phrase of survivalism. Still nothing. "Sweeping Civil War epic, set in the American South?"

I nearly shout at them. "Have none of you seen *Gone with the Wind*?!"

"Uh, I think I saw the poster once," Danny offers.

"I might have to add a screening of that to the syllabus," I say, trying to hide my disbelief. "It was a game-changing film in Hollywood, back in the day. Not so great on representing race, but then again, it came out in 1939."

"Oh my god, that is like, *so old*," Avery, blue-haired and lip-glossed, gasps.

"It's the same age as *The Wizard of Oz*," I say, to mitigate her shock. "They came out in the same year."

"I never saw *The Wizard of Oz*," Avery admits.

This makes me want to cry, literally, that there are kids in America taking film classes who haven't even seen *The Wizard of Oz*. Still, I struggle on.

"So film characters are memorable—should be memorable—if you can get a sense of their interior life. If you can imagine their hopes and their fears, what their past was like, their insecurities and weaknesses."

The kids are nodding, but I have no idea if any of this is actually percolating into their brains.

"Yes, a lot of this emerges through the performances of the actors, but the actors are working off what's written in the script. So it all comes back to the importance of the script. Of crafting memorable, believable, three-dimensional characters."

I've finished my perambulation around their desks. As I reach the front of the classroom, I look at them as a group.

"So your challenge, as a screenwriter, is to write a character who isn't just a cliché because she's pretty or because he . . . fights well. But a character who could have started out as someone you knew in real life. Someone believable."

They're still paying attention to me, so I continue on.

"Movies are about the suspension of disbelief. People can fly, cities can get blown up. Sure. But in order for the movies to work, you have to believe in the characters first."

My students gaze back at me, an inscrutable herd.

Danny raises his hand. "Sarah?" he asks.

"Yep, what is it?"

"Speaking of believability, what do you think about all these accusations going around?"

I look at him, and I feel my pulse increase, even though I doubt my students suspect anything.

I stay silent, giving him space to continue.

"You know, all this stuff about Bill Cosby and that Weinstein guy . . . All these women accusing them of assaulting them over the years. Do you believe all those stories? I mean, it's crazy, isn't it?"

I am careful about how I craft my words, careful to maintain a teacherly tone. "What do you think is crazy about it?"

"I mean, why's this all coming out now, when they were quiet about it before? It's kind of suspicious, isn't it?"

And I am stuck, wishing for one moment to launch into a real lesson for the students: how the industry really works, all the improbabilities and the hierarchies and the crushing desperation of wanting that career. But there are limits to what I can teach as their lecturer.

"I don't think . . . Just because they've waited so long to tell these stories . . . I don't think that necessarily means these things *didn't* happen. Maybe we listen to them first before forming an opinion."

Danny has an odd, unsatisfied look on his face, but before I can say anything, Claudia pipes up, her hand raised hesitantly.

"Um, Sarah? I saw on the IMDb that you and Holly Randolph worked together on a film. Is that true?"

"Whaaaaaat?!" one of the kids chokes. "No *way.*"

If they weren't already paying attention, now every single student is staring at me, waiting for my answer.

Ah yes, the Internet Movie Database. Online archive of every film ever made, and every person involved in every film ever made. I could have, if I really wanted, tried to remove my name from the IMDb, but some remaining shred of pride has stopped me. The IMDb listing is my lasting proof that I had once been a person of note, a mover and shaker (or so I'd thought), someone who once had done more impressive things than teaching Screenwriting 101 to a bunch of kids at a no-name college.

Nothing really dies, in this day and age.

I can't lie about it, of course. It's spelled out right there on the IMDb, which any student could bring up this minute on their phone.

"Yes," I say after a pause. "I worked on one of her early films." I do not mention that was the film which sent her career stratospheric, or that I was associate producer on it.

Avery gasps again. "Oh my god, what was she like? I absolutely *love* her!"

"Holly Randolph was great to work with." I nod. "I'm really happy for her success."

I'm aware of how superficial my answer sounds, rattled off as if I were a brainwashed soldier from *The Manchurian Candidate*. But a shadow of nausea tugs at me. I know that if you were to examine that same IMDb listing, you would find another name located not far from Holly's and mine. A name credited as executive producer of that film. A name which I'd rather forget.

I glance at the clock, thankful I only have two minutes of class left.

"Listen," I say, regaining control. "I think we're getting off-topic here. For homework this week, I want you to find a compelling character in a film—not a superhero movie, please. Watch *all* the scenes with that character, take notes on why you find him or her particularly compelling. What about that character is believable? What makes you want to keep watching?"

The kids grumble. Just when things were getting interesting, I have to steer them back towards homework.

The irony is not lost on me, as I pack up my papers at my desk, my head down, my face frozen in an emotionless expression.

What about that character is believable?

The characters that live on in our memories, the ones that were real. All their weaknesses, all their special skills and talents, all their hidden sides.

That email sits unopened for the entire day, but late that afternoon, when I can no longer procrastinate, I finally click on it.

Thom Gallagher of the *New York Times*. What do you have to say?

Dear Ms. Lai:
I hope this email does not come as an inconvenience,
but I am investigating some past events regarding the
film producer Hugo North for an important piece in the
New York Times. I believe you used to work with Mr. North
at Conquest Films in the mid-2000s. I was wondering if
you might have some time to talk on the phone or meet
in person to answer a few questions. Please do know
that whatever you say will be treated with the utmost
confidence, if you wish it to be so. . . .

There is that name I'd been trying to avoid for a decade, spelled
out right in front of me. Hugo North.

I sit confronted with it for a few minutes, then re-examine the
email.

If you wish it to be so. What strange wording. Like some in-
cantation proclaimed by a genie from a lamp. None of the hard-
hitting, fast talk you might expect from a newspaper reporter. But
these matters are delicate. People are inclined to silence. And just
sending an email about this to a stranger, out into the ether, requires some element of flattery and artfulness, if you're hoping for
a response. Even if your name is Thom Gallagher and you write
for the *New York Times*.

I wonder if his job is so different from what mine had once been,
back in the day. The strategy of asking, slowly connecting one person to another, to build something meaningful. But whereas a film
producer toils to fashion an entire production—an illusion—from
where there had once been nothing, the investigative reporter per-
forms a work of excavation. Scraping the dirt from what had once
laid buried, until an entire picture emerges.

But he can't do this on his own. He needs people like me to
show him where to dig. And there are many like me out there. He
just needs to find them.

I try to ignore Thom Gallagher's email as I ride the subway home. Even the unusual spelling of his name marks him as rarefied, elite. Because he is not just any journalist, but heir to the beloved Gallagher dynasty, generations of blue-eyed statesmen who stood in the Senate and blustered for the rights of the oppressed. Yet instead, Thom chose journalism, as if he already knew politics is a diseased beast. And only the fickle, untrustworthy media can bring us any semblance of justice.

I muse on this as I chop a salad for dinner and then confront a pile of student screenplays of ten to fifteen pages each, most likely of mediocre quality.

Deflecting any thoughts of Thom Gallagher, I forge my way through the scripts. A hard-boiled noir about Dominican drug dealers in the Bronx. (*Gritty and atmospheric*, I write. *But can you let us see the humanity of your characters?*) At the same time, I am thinking: Who would ever green-light that? Unless you attached three of the biggest Latinx stars ever, maybe a crossover from the music industry.

Next, a heartfelt drama about a dysfunctional New England family on the verge of a crisis. (*Your characters are great*, I write. *But I'm having difficulty seeing what your plot will be.*) Again, nobody cares about these kinds of films. Not unless they star a certain iconic, multiple-Oscar-winning actress as the matriarch.

I work my way through eight assignments and finally call it quits. I consider watching something, a TV episode or part of a movie, given how late it is. But I will most likely get frustrated by whatever I see. These days, it's only ever nature documentaries that can calm me down, that truly transport me to another world.

I brush my teeth, climb into bed.

That email glows on an imagined screen in my mind.

Dear Thom . . . I imagine typing.

Or would I write *Mr. Gallagher*?

There is a weird power structure here, one which I've navigated around before, but never in the context of a celebrated journalist trying to unearth information from *me*.

No, you have a story, I remind myself. Put him on the same level as you.

Dear Thom—Thank you for getting in touch. I might be interested in speaking, but I would prefer if it were very discreet. Would you have time to speak this weekend?

Make them wait. That whole game.

But to be perfectly honest with myself (which is not something I excel at), I'm not even sure if this is a story I want to tell.

2

T IS AN October morning, unusually hot, when I finally climb on an L train to meet Thom Gallagher. Bright sunlight shines down on Times Square, which throbs with the same ridiculous surge it always boasts, twenty-four hours a day, seven days a week. Tourists walk agape, staring up at the never-ending churn of video screens and neon lights. Sign-holders dressed as oversized chickens and Roman centurions and Statues of Liberty flail to catch their attention. A shell-shocked woman, wearing a jumble of mis-matched clothes, wavers on the corner of Forty-Second Street and Eighth Avenue. She gestures into the intersection, muttering at no one in particular, her hands trying to convince an invisible audience.

"They ain't never listening to me. I'm telling them always, but it's always the same. A pack of lies, complete pack of lies . . ."

I want to linger and listen further, but then I am drawn mag-netically to the glassy fortress that rises up near the steaming maw of Times Square, its provenance stamped across the second-floor facade in that unmistakable Gothic font. Floor upon floor of in-dustrious journalism climbing high into the polluted ether, while the homeless and the preoccupied swarm at its feet, oblivious.

I approach the dark revolving doors of the Times Building. The Gates of Heaven. Or Hell, depending on who you are.

And just like that—a single swish, and I am transported.

=

From the heat and grime of the heaving city, to the calm, pristine sanctuary of this lobby. I breathe in the anodyne scent, which smells of security and a certain prestige. This newspaper, educating an entire country for over a century. I probably know people from college who work here, but I pray I will not run into them on a weekend. I am just an average visitor, nothing more.

I sign in, nervous I might not be on the guest list. But I am issued a security pass by a bored receptionist. The digital camera captures a distorted image of my face, like a portrait from a fun house mirror.

I take it with some relief (and amusement), and sit down on the cushy gray couch. I wait for Thom Gallagher to arrive.

He is remarkably punctual, striding in mere minutes later. There is a warm smile on his boyish face, and his hands are clasped in a deferential way. I have to admit, I am impressed with the display of humility, given how famous he is.

Thom is wearing horn-rimmed glasses, as if in some homage to the old newspaper movies. Or to hide his youth or his hereditary handsomeness, which cannot be disguised—the same noble features we recognize in his male forefathers.

"Sarah, I'm so pleased to see you. Thank you so much for coming in."

A swift but welcoming handshake as I stand up.

It is a Saturday, and still he is making an effort in his dress. Button-down shirt (light green, not white) and dark jeans.

I gather my bag. "Sorry for insisting we meet on a weekend. I just had a busy week and I . . . needed some time for this chat."

That is both a lie and a non-lie. Busy hardly describes my current life. But it is true I needed time to prepare. I needed at least ten years.

We are sitting in a secure meeting room on the twenty-fifth floor, the door closed, just Thom Gallagher and myself. An enviable view of Midtown and the Hudson River stretches beneath us, the autumn sunlight glinting off scattered windows and waters below. There is a table: round, squat brown glass, it becomes the nondescript altar for the digital recorder.

"I hope you understand," he explains courteously. "We need to record this for accuracy, and the last thing in the world I want is to misquote you."

"So you might directly quote whatever I say at this point?" I ask. I am more nervous than I expected, and this rookie question reveals my naivete in the world of journalism. I secretly curse myself for asking it.

"Oh please don't worry." He gestures with his palm out, reassuring. "I won't be making those decisions just yet. At this point, let's just start by having a chat. I want to make sure you are comfortable with all of this."

Comfortable. It's been a while since anyone cared about my comfort.

"But . . . the quoting. I don't want to say something that you'll take out of context." I glance at the recorder as if it were a ticking bomb, red automated numbers counting backward. "Or something I might regret saying later."

"I won't. I promise I won't. For this story, context is everything." His hands are now clasped in a semi-prayer position, his blue eyes earnest. I wonder if the Gallagher family upbringing taught him to demonstrate sincerity so well, so . . . convincingly.

"Listen," he continues, leaning in slightly. "At this stage, I'm just gathering information. Gathering context, if you will. It'll be weeks, maybe even months before I start to write up my next piece on this. So when the time comes, *if* I want to quote you directly, I will absolutely get in touch and make sure that you are happy with what you've said. In the meantime, you have all the time in the world to think about it."

I nod. "You promise?"

"Absolutely, Scout's honor." He holds up his palm vertically and grins, those white teeth flashing in a goofy, ironic smile.

You were born in the '90s, I want to say. *Were Boy Scouts even a thing when you grew up?*

But somehow, the combination of that familiar face, the horn-rimmed glasses, the evocation of wholesome, white-boy-next-door-ness works.

"Okay." I nod again. "You better."

I point a finger at him, gun-like. Now it's my turn to grin.

Thom continues. "It's not standard *Times* policy to double-check on quotes, but it's such an important and sensitive topic for . . . you, possibly, and for others. The most important thing is your own story. I want to make sure your perspective is respectfully told."

His final comment is maybe too much. *It's not standard* Times *policy, but . . .* I am reminded of salesmen, greasing their usual wheels, reeling you in. "*I don't normally do this for other customers, but just for you, I'm throwing in a bonus gift . . .*" My cynicism returns just in time, brings me to my senses.

We're all trying to sell each other something, aren't we?

This time, I wonder if the price is even negotiable.

Thom presses the Record button, and the red light on the machine blinks alive.

We lean back on our respective couches. Next to me, there's a *New York Times* mug full of coffee, the famous newspaper motto emblazoned on the side. *All the News That's Fit to Print.*

Thom takes a sip of his water.

"Why don't you tell me a little bit about how you got involved in film in the first place? Even before you started working with Hugo North."

Where do I even start with that one? With the first time I ever saw a film? (*Peter Pan* re-release in 1982, then *The Return of the Jedi*, in its original theatrical run.) Or with those Sunday nights, religiously watching the Oscars each year? Even though my parents and grandmother shouted every time about staying up that late, and I had to turn the volume down and creep up close to the TV screen to hear what the presenters were saying while the rest of my family dozed away, uninterested.

I didn't care. For one night a year, that was my magical Technicolor dream, shimmering beyond the black-and-white threshold of my drab home. The glamor and the fantasy. These were the movie stars, the filmmaking legends, shedding tears and gratitude when they ascended to receive their golden statues. They glittered from the other side of the continent, impossible beings in an impossible realm.

I didn't think I could ever be a part of that world. But somehow, I found my way in.

3

IMAGINE THE STANDARD movie with a frame story. We know what it looks like: one character talks to another, leaning back to reminisce, and the image on-screen goes blurry, fades into a scene which we instinctively know is the past. *All About Eve*, *Citizen Kane*, nearly every Hitchcock film has this flashback device. It is a complicit agreement between the filmmaker and the viewer.

Well, that's what's happening here. Of course, I do not tell Thom Gallagher every single detail from these moments of my life. There is a constant negotiation inside me: How much do I reveal? How much do I *want* to remember? But in the telling, I am necessarily transported to a time when I was younger—an immersion in the past I cannot avoid.

I'll need to start with that younger me on the outside, looking in. Otherwise, the rest of it won't really make sense.

I studied English at Columbia. I am your quintessential middle child, overlooked and left to her own devices. So stories have always been my escape. Whether on-screen or in books, it didn't matter. Through the English department, I discovered classes on film studies, and I frequented as many of them as I could.

My parents weren't happy about my choice of major. My older sister Karen had gone into accounting, and they hoped I'd do something equally practical. But in the end, as long as I got good grades, they couldn't really complain. I mean, what more did they want?

I didn't have that much time for extracurriculars in college, because I had to help my family with their business.

"And what business is that?" Thom asks, seemingly genuine in his curiosity.

I glance at his aristocratic white face and I suppress a grin. *Nothing as worthy as your family business.*

"My family runs a Chinese restaurant in Flushing," I say, looking straight into his eyes. "Well, owns and runs. My grandfather started it when he came over from Hong Kong, my father took over a bit, before my great-uncle arrived. My parents both work as computer programmers, but they also help with the restaurant. We all do."

"Ah," Thom says.

He is chastened, I think. What was he expecting, a family law firm? All oak-paneled offices and oil paintings of patriarchs? Hardly.

"So you worked at the restaurant even throughout college?"

Yes, on weekends especially. Those were the busiest. When my friends were hungover, recovering from a Saturday night party and enjoying long, convivial brunches of custom-made omelets in the campus dining hall, I would be back in Flushing, staving off a swarm of noisy Chinese families, all desperate to be seated for their Sunday dim sum.

My adored younger brother Edison was exempt from working at the family restaurant, but Karen and I were both assigned weekend shifts. I'd developed more of a knack for wrangling the crowds, keeping customers entertained, as tables were hurriedly cleared behind me. So while Karen graduated to calculating the restaurant accounts in the back office, I was on my feet for twelve hours on a Sunday, my voice constantly raised. Then I'd be back on the 7 train in the late evening, heading to campus for the week, exhausted, my hair and clothes reeking of stir-fry, with a few hours of homework still to finish.

"And then when was your first involvement with the film industry?"

Yes, Thom Gallagher wants to cut to the chase. But all good filmmakers know to provide a bit of backstory first. Get your audience engaged in your characters and their plight. What are their wants and needs?

I *wanted* to work in film. I was *needed* in my family business. Assigning table numbers, doling out menus, ensuring teapots were filled, stomachs sated. Our hierarchy of needs, of course. Appetite before art.

After I graduated, I didn't have any employment figured out. No one was there to guide me through that whole senior year of college, when you're meant to be lining up your metaphorical ducks in a row, gunning your way towards a coveted offer from a consulting firm or an investment bank or a graduate school. I was supposed to have spent the previous summer interning at the place where I eventually wanted to work. But I couldn't plan that far ahead. My great-uncle had just survived a heart attack, so I had to step in and temporarily run the restaurant—a fucking twenty-year-old still in college, running the family business—while he recuperated. So no, I didn't ingratiate myself into corporate culture in that pivotal moment before my senior year.

A year later, I graduated in a sweltering Manhattan summer—and all my friends shot off to their respective new jobs in prestigious offices. And I was just kind of there, with nowhere to go.

"But surely, graduating from Columbia, there would have been alums you could have networked with—" Thom starts, then stops. Realizing perhaps he's overstepped a line as a journalist.

"I didn't really understand networking at the time," I explain.

What I don't say is that it's an immigrant thing. If your parents aren't born here, or maybe if they aren't Westerners, you don't really learn that game. You don't have those family contacts to get you started, you don't fully grasp that self-assured American way of striding forth with your intentions, building a path of connections toward your desired profession. . . . That's not something we're taught by our parents. Or certainly I wasn't.

Sure, my family had contacts. In the Chinese restaurant industry. But the whole damn point of immigrating is so your kids don't have to keep smelling of stir-fry their entire lives.

"Oh, I see," Thom says. A single nod of understanding.

We both laugh.

And that's enough. That admission from Thom Gallagher, that not everyone has the world handed to them on a silver platter. *"What'll it be, Tommy? A shining career in politics, like the ancestral clan? Or show business? Or maybe, to be a true knight in shining armor . . . journalism?"*

I didn't have that kind of choice. Certainly not back then. And not even now, in my late-thirties.

So that business of networking I only picked up later, working for my first boss Sylvia—and then from Hugo North. There's a lot I learned from them. I'll give them that.

Because I graduated Phi Beta Kappa, my parents (in a rare show of clemency) gave me the summer off. Meaning, they weren't on my back the whole time. So long as I still did my weekend shifts at the restaurant, they said I could spend a few months relaxing, to figure out where I would go next in life.

I like to think they were accommodating, but in reality, I suspect they were anxious about my lack of direction. That I was some kind of failure to have graduated from Columbia with no foreseeable income. (Unlike my sister, who had graduated straight into a trainee program with one of the Big Five accountancy firms.)

Maybe all parents are anxious, but mine were especially so. It might be a Chinese thing, or an Asian thing. To use a politically questionable food metaphor, anxiety is like the hidden spice that undercuts all our dishes. It's there in every report card, every dinner conversation, every time they watch us walk out the door. Perhaps it comes of living in a culture that's not our own.

So my parents were relieved when I had to move back in with them after leaving the dorms at Columbia. Back into that three-bedroom apartment in Flushing where I'd grown up. The clear plastic covering on all the furniture, the Chinese scrolls hanging on the walls, the perpetual smell of grease wafting up from the street below, or the apartment next door, or our own kitchen. It was like being forced back into a cage, one I had grown too big for. The bars of that cage dug in, and I could feel every single one pressing inward on me.

In the summer, it was nearly unbearable. To save money, my mom rarely turned on the air-conditioning, and inside that apartment, I would melt into a lethargic amoeba, devoid of higher thinking.

So I escaped by going to the Queens Library. There, I was irked by the throngs of families who, like me, were seeking refuge from the city heat, saving money on their own electricity bills by retiring to the air-conditioned stacks and the free reading.

Eventually I went farther afield. I found myself crossing back into Manhattan, back to Columbia. I frequented those redbrick buildings again and miraculously found some paid summer work for an assistant professor in film, whose classes I had taken before. I had that all-important Columbia ID card, which allowed me to swipe back into those familiar hallowed spaces: the yawning libraries, the department hallways with their bulletin boards full of brightly colored flyers. These spaces now largely empty in the summertime, with the AC on full blast. There were summer courses on film studies, only it was too late for me to work as a teaching assistant. But the professor let me audit her lectures, sit in on the film screenings, and most importantly, organize those screenings.

Let me tell you a little bit about my love affair with the movies. Between two people, love at first sight may be a myth—and it leaves many of us sorely disappointed. But between a person and the movies, love at first sight is real and it is always satisfying. From the minute I entered a darkened movie theater at the tender age of four, I knew it. I sat, gazing up at the screen, dwarfed by the story that unfolded above me, larger than life—and for ninety minutes, more important than life itself. This world would always be more fascinating than my own mundane existence.

From that moment onwards, I loved the movies. But my family rarely went to see anything. Going to films cost money, while TV was virtually free, minus the electricity bills. So our trips to those sacred temples of cinema-viewing were limited to a few times a year, my mother conscientiously scanning the reviews to ensure we only spent our money on three- or four-star films. Still, I watched TV shows about the movies: Siskel and Ebert, Rex Reed, these expert white men telling me which films were worth seeing, even if I knew I would never get to see them. I watched the Oscars, and all the end-of-year, best-movie retrospectives. I read all the reviews and behind-the-scenes features in the newspaper, eagerly searched for the box office reports on Mondays.

If it was a very one-sided love affair for most of my childhood, I can tell you it has since blossomed into the most reliable relationship for me thus far. Because movies don't let you down. They will always be there, ready to provide you solace, to relieve the loneliness you might feel in your real life, provide more drama and fear and joy than you will ever know outside of the cinema. More perfectly crafted stories, more satisfying endings than you will ever experience.

Back then, at the age of twenty-two, anything having to do with the world of film was sacred ground for me. And when that assistant professor asked me to organize her screenings, I felt a certain awe, realizing I would actually be dealing with real, living people who worked in the film industry.

I remember the first time I picked up a phone to call a film distributor. They were only in Midtown, a few miles south of where I was sitting in the department office.

"Cinebureau," the person said, sounding so efficient and professional.

"Oh hi, is this Cinebureau?" I asked. I immediately hated myself because that question had already been answered.

"Yes, it is." The woman was not impressed by my stupidity.

"Oh hi, yes, I'm calling from Columbia, on behalf of Assistant Professor Kristin Bradford, who is running their summer film studies course. We are teaching *Vagabond* by Agnès Varda, and I just wanted to organize a screening of it for our students."

"So, an educational screening, then? Let me run through our educational screening fees."

And just like that, I suddenly had purpose. A legitimacy in this world. I didn't really name myself (not until the end of the call), but I had a reason for calling, and they didn't laugh at my reason. I could order a 35 mm print of a film and a screening license. It was a verifiable transaction within the film industry.

I realized it was no different from ordering bean sprouts and sesame oil in bulk from our food supplier. Do the deal, agree on the price (and with Columbia's budget, I didn't even have to haggle), arrange the delivery.

Ah, those breakthrough moments when we are young and start to realize how the world works. That everything in this world is just a series of transactions, a sales pitch for the unique product we have to offer, ourselves, our talent. Our story, which is never as special as we think it is.

As I carried on a conversation with Cinebureau over the next few weeks, Stephanie, the employee on the other end of the line, tried to sweet-talk me into hiring more of her "titles." Was it French New Wave we were interested in? Or New Hollywood in the '70s? They had a particularly good selection of cinema verité documentaries.

I realized she was being deferential to me, and only because I was the one with the money, the supposed ability to decide which films to screen, and whether to hire them through her company. In reality, I didn't have such decision-making powers. I was following orders from a pre-determined syllabus, already decided by the professor, but something about me enjoyed the illusion of having that power, at least when I spoke to Stephanie.

Maybe that's how the seed was planted in me. The illusion of power, or at least the thrill of having that illusion in place.

And that, Mr. Gallagher, is the ethos which governs the entire film industry.

But I bet you already knew that.

4

F ROM ORGANIZING SCREENINGS, I gradually realized that companies like Cinebureau were only unspectacular distributors who peddled already-made films for money, like the produce-sellers on Flushing Street, impatient to shift their morning's haul of bok choy or lychees: 2 FOR $3! 2 FOR $3!

It was disappointing, indeed, to learn that these companies weren't the ones *making* the films, the creative forces behind these cinematic masterpieces. *That magic* took place within production companies—where genius and artistic collaboration thrived. But how could I possibly enter that Promised Land?

I found a directory of New York production companies and spent several late nights in the department office, carefully crafting the perfect cover letter to convey my passion for film, my balance of academic excellence and real-world skills. *For the time being, I am also willing to work for expenses only,* I added, hoping that might show my dedication. These I printed out with my résumé (also painstakingly curated). I filched a few Columbia envelopes to send them in, guessing their branding might make more of an impression, might give that extra nudge for the contents to be taken more seriously.

But I paid for the stamps myself.

I sent out about sixty letters, some in plain envelopes, some in Columbia envelopes. And waited eagerly.

"Sixty letters?!" my sister repeated over dinner at her apartment later that week. "Well, I'm sure you'll hear back from *someone*."

And for a while I imagined an email might appear in my inbox, or my phone might light up with an unrecognized number. But a month went by, and I heard nothing. A cloud of hopelessness settled over me.

I went to the Columbia libraries and religiously read film books and screenplays. I checked out DVDs—everything from slow foreign films to blaxploitation flicks to recent blockbusters—and watched them on my laptop, in my family's sticky apartment. The summer stretched on, unbearably humid, and at the end of it, there was sure to be a sit-down discussion with my frowning parents. A radical decision made which would probably result in me enrolling in accounting classes or being shipped off to Hong Kong to learn the higher art of Chinese restaurant expansion. Something that would crush any possibility of me entering that distant realm of screenplays and headshots and issues of *Variety* magazine, fanned out on a table in an air-conditioned lobby.

I considered taking the subway downtown to where these production companies hummed—I knew all their addresses anyway, from the cover letters I'd sent—and hovering around, presenting myself as a willing and eager disciple. But I figured that might label me as crazy. Desperate. Not nearly cool enough to be a part of that world.

In the end, it was a bulletin board posting that provided my entry ticket in. I saw it in the second-to-last week of summer school. A nondescript white page tacked on the right side of the Events & Opportunities board. No hot-pink or electric-blue paper, like the student groups advertising '80s-themed mixers or radical feminist spoken word nights. Just plain white, with a single paragraph printed in Times New Roman.

Busy Film Production Company Seeking
Intern for a Few Months

We are a busy film production company near the West Village. We make short films, with a few feature films in development.

We are seeking a smart, enthusiastic, hard-working individual
to help us get our company into the next gear. This will be an
unpaid internship, but expenses can be covered. In return, you
will learn a lot about the day-to-day of making films and further employment may be possible, depending on performance
and circumstances. Please email your cover letter and résumé to
fireflyfilms@aol.com. Thank you.

In retrospect, it was such a generic, blandly described job posting, that any normal person would have found it sketchy. Who
were Firefly Films? Were they even legit? How could I know this
wasn't just a scam?

I saw that white sheet of paper and read it twice. Three times.

I don't know when it had appeared there, but I passed this bulletin board multiple times a day, and surely I would have noticed
it before. Who put it up? I looked around, but the department was
empty aside from me. Vacant desks and the nondescript hum of
the air-conditioning, posters flapping in the current from an air
vent.

I took out a notebook and scrawled down the email address,
started to walk away.

Then I turned back. I stepped closer to the bulletin board,
scanning the paragraph one more time. My heartbeat rose when I
tried to imagine myself in the thick of that busy production company office, the phones ringing around me, scripts piled high on a
desk for me to read.

Did anyone else really need to see this?

I glanced around me again, to ensure I was alone. Then I re-
moved the printout from the board, folded it up, and slipped it
into my bag.

I sank the thumbtack deep into the cork with a silent, satisfying
push.

The space underneath it was blank again, just as it had been
that morning.

I omit that one small detail in my retelling to Thom.

Me, pocketing the bulletin board posting, keeping it safe from other eyes. After all, it's not central to the story *he's* interested in. But that's how it starts. This shielding of opportunities, carefully crafting your own way forward, jealous others might get there before you.

So a queasy cocktail of guilt and elation roiled in my stomach as I walked away from Columbia that day. I felt nominally bad, in a good way. Like a young child who has stolen a piece of candy from a corner shop. Thrilled you've somehow gotten away with it, guilty because you've taken from Mr. Kim or Rahman or Lopez, that shop owner you've known all your childhood.

But in this case, I reasoned with myself, I wasn't really stealing from anyone. The posting had been up there publicly, it was there for whomever in the Columbia School of Arts to see. I just happened to take it down a bit early.

Looking back on it now, I am amused at my twentysomething moral quandary. To be so young, to read such ethical significance in every single action we take.

But really, how different is it from the way the entire industry works? Most of the time, there isn't even a bulletin board. It's a phone call, a text message sent from one person to another. Find someone young, someone eager. And there are so many of us, thronging the edges of that world, pressing our noses up against the window, that we become disposable.

Even here, how many starry-eyed cub reporters and vloggers wouldn't kill to enter these hallowed fifty-two stories of journalistic integrity?

I don't ask Thom Gallagher, because it is a moot point with him.

He has already staked his claim, at the young age of twenty-seven. Pulitzer Prize nominations are probably winging their way to him, and an offer to host a TV news magazine or pose for the cover of *GQ*. But for every one of him, there's thousands of us.

Hoping to be a young hotshot, one of the 30 Under 30, or 40 Under 40.

There are no lists for 50 Under 50. Because if we haven't made it by then, we probably don't belong in this world.

But how, then, did I manage to enter this blessed realm, a child of Hong Kong immigrants, from the heaving, grease-tinged streets of Flushing?

One morning I stood on a sidewalk in the Meatpacking District, close to the West Village, and buzzed up to the Firefly Films office on the third floor. I climbed the stark concrete stairs and emerged into a repurposed industrial space with natural light pouring in. A network of exposed metal pipes snaked beneath the high ceiling, while leading ladies in giant framed posters of 1950s films smiled down from the brick walls. Marilyn, Rita, Grace.

A middle-aged woman, slim, very polished, walked towards me, her heels clacking in the cavernous space. "You must be Sarah," she said warmly.

"Yes, that's me," I replied, trying to strike the right note of enthusiasm, without sounding too juvenile.

"So nice to meet you. I'm Sylvia Zimmerman. Please, have a seat," she gestured to a couch in the corner, what looked like three carrot-colored cushions perched precariously on a geometric metal frame. She sat across from me in a globular armchair.

We exchanged pleasantries and talked about film. What had I seen recently? What had I liked about these movies?

I had thought she would ask one of those painful questions designed expressly for job interviews ("What is your greatest weakness?" "Describe a time you had to overcome an unforeseen obstacle," etc.). But there was none of that. Just what sounded like general chitchat, and what was expected of me. Come in every day at nine thirty. Be prepared to do a variety of different work tasks, and we'll reassess after two weeks. No pay, but she would cover my MetroCard. So when could I start?

I looked at her, somewhat agape. She had at least printed out my résumé and made a passing reference to it ("Looks like you have a lot of good, practical experience in other industries and a strong interest in film")—but was that it? Was I allowed into the club so easily?

Evidently I was. As long as I didn't expect to be paid.

"Uh, how about Thursday?" I asked, literally picking a random day of the week.

"Oh fantastic, why don't you come in at eleven?"

"That could work . . . I just need to check on a few things before I can confirm," I said.

There was one thing I had forgotten, and that was mentioning this internship—especially this business of working for no pay—to my parents.

"So . . . I got the job!" I told Karen breathlessly over the phone, as I navigated my way under the abandoned rail track that would, years later, become the High Line. I knew she was at work, but I shouted with excitement, my voice echoing under the steel platform above me.

"No way. Congratulations!" Karen chirped. In the background, I could hear the bleating phones and general hum of an open-plan office. My heart sang. Soon I, too, would be installed in a thriving workplace, my purpose on this planet affirmed. "See, I told you something would come through. Do they seem like cool people?"

"Cool? Yes." Certainly cooler than an accountancy firm. I plugged my other ear as I skittered past the painfully loud drilling at a construction site. Why was Lower Manhattan constantly under construction? The city was never finished rebuilding itself.

"But um, they're not exactly paying me. So it's not *really* a job in that sense," I added. "More like . . . an opportunity."

"An opportunity, huh," Karen mused. It probably sounded so sketchy from her world of regular paychecks and corporate training programs. "Well, as long as *you're* happy, that's what counts, right?"

"Yeah, I'm happy." But I stopped in my tracks for my next question, uneasy. "Only . . . how do you think Mom and Dad are gonna react?"

I heard her intake of breath. "*That*, I'm not sure."

Of course she wouldn't know. Because unlike me, Karen always did what was expected of her. Anything I did was destined to disappoint my parents.

"It's a what? Unpaid internship?" My parents looked at me uncomprehendingly across the dinner table.

It was a stifling hot night, the air hung motionless between us, and I was trying to suppress my usual annoyance at my frugal mom for never turning on the AC.

"She'll cover my MetroCard," I offered.

My mother was not impressed. "So she wants you to work there full-time, and not get paid?"

"It's called work experience," I said.

"Work means you do work for someone, and you get paid by them. You don't need other type of experience."

"I've been working *how* many hours at the restaurant for how many years, and I'm not exactly getting a living wage for that, either." I put forward my opening gambit. For some reason, the Living Wage Campaign at Columbia flickered through my head, students camping out on the main building steps in support of university cafeteria workers and janitors.

"That's different," Mom said. "That's within the family. Plus, you live with *us*. No need for living wage."

I tried another tack. "I've been doing homework since kindergarten. I don't get paid for doing homework."

"Also different. That's for when you still learning, so you get a degree and then graduate with a good job. A job that actually pays." My mother frowned.

"Well, this is also learning," I countered. "Just learning how the film industry works."

My mom narrowed her eyes and issued an indistinct, but clearly judgmental, growl. I realized how, in that moment, she was such a caricature of the irate Chinese parent, with her accent and her stern attitude. I became even more inwardly ashamed, more outwardly angry.

"Wai-Lin." My dad tried to reason with her. "This is a different world, it's run by Americans. They have their own ways of doing things, you can't expect them to hire Sarah right away if she's never spent an entire day working with them?"

"Why you want to learn about the film industry anyway?" my mom asked. "All so many entertainers. That is not a respectable job."

Are you kidding? I wanted to ask her. *Did you miss my entire childhood, when I watched the Oscars every single year? Did you notice all the film books I checked out from the library, stacked up on the coffee table? How I recorded nearly every movie that aired on TV and carefully labeled each VHS tape?*

But I stayed silent, and instead, Dad spoke up.

"Wai-Lin, you are too old-school. Kids these days . . . no one wants to be an accountant. They want to be movie stars."

This alarmed my mom even more. She dropped her chopsticks, irritated.

"You want to be movie star? Why'd we send you to Columbia to be movie star?"

"I do *not* want to be in front of the camera," I tried to explain.

"Then what you want to do? What you want to learn in your 'internship'?"

"Everything else," I answered. "Everything that happens behind the scenes. How movies get made. How they go from script to—to what you see on-screen."

My mom still shook her head, confused. "That's no real profession."

"Yes it is," I answered. "The film industry employs millions of people."

"That's not a profession *I* raised you to have."

She exhaled loudly. Two lines appeared above the bridge of her nose, the ones that always indicated her frustration.

I shifted in my seat, peeling my leg from the plastic chair cover, where it had been stuck by the humidity.

"Listen," I said. "How about we make a deal."

And this was me, dealmaking with my own parents. How many of us haven't done it? Negotiating our way around their rules and our desires. It's our first foray into adulthood, inching closer to what we want. If we somehow manage to maneuver our way past that obstacle, then maybe we have a shot at an individual life we can call our own.

So I offered to work at the restaurant every weekend, all day Saturday and Sunday *and* alternate Friday nights, for the next three months. I was their best crowd-wrangler, and they knew it. Normally if I worked for them this much, I would at least get paid something. But this time, I would forfeit half that pay, so our staff costs would go down.

"This is not about the restaurant's profits, Sarah," my dad said. "This is about your future."

"Well, we're only talking about the next three months of my life," I argued back. "Just a temporary arrangement."

In the meantime, I would intern full-time, Monday to Friday at Firefly Films. I'd get to learn about the film industry, to see if this was a career I really wanted. The restaurant wouldn't have to find someone to replace me on weekends, and our margins might even go up. We'd reassess in three months' time, I said, borrowing a phrase I'd heard from Sylvia that morning.

My parents looked at me perplexed, as if they found themselves negotiating with a new vendor. They'd never heard me utter that phrase before. I knew they wanted me to start a real career (doctor, lawyer, accountant, banker, professor), but I also knew how much the restaurant needed me on weekends.

Already I was learning from Sylvia. Make them an offer they can't refuse.

5

A ND WHAT WAS it like, finally working in film?"
It was slow at first, just me and Sylvia in that yawning
industrial office. But we grew busy quickly. And within a year,
things were really happening.

I'll spare you the details. Few people care about the trials and
tribulations of a small, independent film production company.
There are hundreds of such aspiring outfits across our planet, and
the stories of how they formed, developed, and usually died are
only ever interesting to the people involved.

I threw myself wholeheartedly into the company, feeling every
small victory or advance as if it were my own. True, I wasn't earning a salary in those first few months, and when I asked Sylvia if
we should sign some sort of contract, she would gloss over the
issue, as if it were an unnecessary formality. What mattered most
was the work itself, and whether I was any good at it. I set out
eagerly to prove that I was, investing my sense of self in the responsibilities that were handed to me: the answering of phones,
the memorizing of Firefly's business contacts, even the unlocking
and locking of the office, when I was handed a set of keys a few
weeks into my internship. I wanted to be part of the wonder of
making films. And through these small, mundane tasks, I hoped to
inch just a little closer to learning that magic.

I absorbed every experience greedily, like a sponge placed in a
vast ocean. That first day at Firefly, I was tasked with organizing
all the scripts Sylvia had been sent from various agencies, writing

the titles in black marker across the side of each screenplay, stacking them on shelves so all titles were visible.

I marveled that these were actual film scripts, sent from the big, shiny agencies in their gleaming glass towers. Words which one day might be transformed into moving images projected onto a cinema screen at the Tribeca Film Festival, or a Kansas multiplex, or a distant mall in Japan, wringing laughter or tears or adrenaline from multitudes of strangers.

I was tempted to spend all day reading script after script, but unfortunately that wasn't my job. The majority of these screenplays, piled up and labeled, were just excess "dross" sent to us by agents or writers in the hope we might randomly pick them up and find something worthy in them.

No, to start, I was only needed for purely administrative work. Organizing, filing, diary keeping. Printing scripts, binding and labeling them. I hardly needed an Ivy League education, or even a college diploma. I could have done this straight out of high school. But I read scripts during my lunch break, or borrowed a few each evening and read them on the express train back to Flushing. And in a few months, I read nearly all the scripts in our office, all the "excess dross." Most of them, I realized, had been ignored because they weren't very good.

The significant scripts were the titles Sylvia would mention to me after a meeting with an agent or another producer. She'd forward me an email, with a typically brief instruction (*Pls print & bind for me to read*)—and I'd know there was something about this particular script we should take seriously.

Once, I made the mistake of telling Sylvia I had read one of these screenplays. She snapped at me, sharp and angry. "I didn't *say* you could read that script. It's confidential."

"Oh, sorry." I was taken aback, unsure of what I'd done wrong. Surely, printing and binding a script would have given me access to also read it. It didn't seem to make sense. But after that, I stayed silent. I still kept reading the scripts that came in, I just didn't mention it to Sylvia.

That's the tricky business of being an assistant. You have to learn the boundaries of your duties. You're responsible for XYZ, but you can't visibly cross the perimeter around them, no matter how eager you are. And you can't ever upset your boss.

Around that time, I read a book on being a Hollywood assistant, and rule number one was to quietly make yourself indispensable. Once your boss realizes she can't function without you, then you're in a position to do more interesting work.

So eventually, after I'd sat in her office for forty hours each week, answered the phones, organized all the files and her online database, greeted all the various people who came in for lunch meetings—after I'd earned her trust, after she noticed I might be good for something more than just simple admin work, Sylvia asked me to look at a script. One had just come in from Xander Schulz's agent, and she requested the usual printing and binding.

I had heard Sylvia mention Xander so many times in conversation. I was curious about this one.

"Do you mind if I read it?" I asked quietly.

Sylvia said, so nonchalant: "Sure, read it. Let me know what you think."

The next morning, I had two pages of typed script notes, which I'd zealously written on my laptop at midnight. Now, as jaded professionals, we might laugh at how eager-to-please I was back then. But it wasn't just about wanting to impress the boss or earn her good favor. For me, it was something more genuine than that. It was about a love of the craft, wanting to learn it that badly, wanting to make some kind of substantial contribution, and be recognized for it.

"I think that is what drives most of us in the end, isn't it?"

I glance at Thom Gallagher sidelong as I ask this rhetorical question. But there is no noticeable reaction from him, just a cursory nod.

After three months, I was doing more interesting things. I still had to take care of all the admin, the tedious details which made me want to cry out of boredom (sorting all of Sylvia's receipts, explaining them to the bookkeeper). But in addition to script notes, I got to draw up casting ideas, research funding opportunities, draft emails to agents and potential co-producers.

I was also, finally, earning something of a wage. Not enough to actually cover my living expenses if I were to move out of my parents' apartment in Flushing. Yet enough to keep my parents from fully voicing their displeasure about my choice of career. By the end of the year, I managed to avert whatever drastic parental intervention they may have been planning. Karen and I breathed a sigh of relief. I was also allowed to stop working at the restaurant, save for the odd weekend shift.

In the meantime, Sylvia surprised me with a generous holiday present: a year's membership to the Lincoln Center Film Society and a one-hundred-dollar gift certificate to Saks Fifth Avenue, a department store I'd wandered through many times but had never purchased from, on account of their terrifying prices.

Buy yourself something nice for the winter! Sylvia had written in the accompanying card, in her sloping, elegant script.

Amazed by this unexpected charity, I waited until the after-Christmas sales to purchase a luxurious cashmere scarf, hand-knit in a thick golden weave, which elicited compliments whenever I wore it. I still wear it to this day.

My parents were impressed with Sylvia's generosity. I didn't tell them I'd seen our company accounts, and my Christmas presents had been included as an expense.

I was also invited to Sylvia's annual holiday drinks, which took place in her Upper East Side brownstone on a chilly December evening. I'd helped her compile the guest list and mail out the hundred or so invitations, aided by her ten-year-old daughter Rachel, who happily licked the envelopes shut, as she sat next to me chatting about the latest books she'd read. The party guests were a mixture of friends, acquaintances, and Sylvia's chummier business contacts: filmmakers, advertising execs, actors, publicists, photographers, production managers. When I met these professionals in person, I was surprised how easily I could converse with them, how smoothly the conversation flowed, especially after I had drunk my third glass of rum punch.

"Ah, you must be Sylvia's right-hand woman. I heard you just graduated from Columbia," various people said.

I nodded with a certain pride: simply working with Sylvia verified me as someone with a worthy opinion.

Amidst the crowd, I'd glimpsed Xander Schulz, the hotshot director and photographer whose commercials and music videos Sylvia had produced for the past few years. He'd been away for much of the autumn on an extended vacation, combined with a few fashion shoots in Bali, Australia, and the Fiji Islands. But now he was back and ready to dive into a feature film script he'd been developing.

He glanced my way once that evening; I doubt I registered in his mind.

In the new year, I had my first real encounter with Xander. Until then, I'd heard Sylvia gush often about his "striking visual style" and his "intuitive sense of storytelling." I'd watched all his previous work, read the script he'd written and was hoping to direct, with Sylvia as producer. The script was okay. Gripping enough, but nothing mind-blowing. I kept that opinion to myself.

I'm not sure what I was expecting, but when Xander walked into our cavernous office, he seemed like just another thirtysomething white guy, not particularly tall or noticeable. Expensive sunglasses sat atop his narrow forehead. Yet he was the first film director I could observe for longer than fifteen minutes, so there was a particular awe for me. Surely that level of talent and success must shine through occasionally, it couldn't stay hidden the entire time.

"Is this the Xander Schulz who later won the Golden Globe in—"

"Yes, that's the one." I am brusque, a sudden flash of anger. I chafe even thinking of Xander and his Golden Globe. "I'll get to that later."

Thom Gallagher raises his eyebrows and jots something on his pad, perhaps noting my outburst.

I remind myself to calm down.

"What was he like to work with?" Thom asks.

I sidestep the question somewhat. "He had a very clear image in his head of how he wanted things to be. And he didn't really take on any advice or suggestions otherwise."

I stop. "Hold on," I say. "Let me tell you a little bit about film directors."

This is the lecture I've always wanted to give my students but haven't, for propriety's sake.

What is your stereotypical image of a film director? A bad-tempered but visionary man with a dark beret on his head, shouting, "Cut! Cut! Cut!"

Now, in reality, he's more likely to wear a baseball cap, and the first assistant director does the shouting, but we won't get into details. It's as if all male film directors have the prerogative to be cranky and demanding, because that's what we expect of them. (I never had a chance to work with any female directors, which is another conversation in and of itself.)

But ask the American public why they go see a particular film, and it's usually not because of the director (unless that's someone like Spielberg). It's because of the stars: those familiar, photogenic faces on the poster or in the trailer. So while directors are the "artistic eye," the creative force behind a film, they're dependent on famous actors to get their film seen. And undoubtedly there is envy when the actors attract all the publicity shots on the red carpet, the guest spots on the talk shows, the centerfolds in magazines.

It is a complicated miasma of egos that drives filmmaking. Because directors are also very dependent on financiers to fund the making of their movie (but financiers are only interested if there's anyone famous in the cast). Now, private financiers are a unique breed unto themselves. They generally care little about the art of filmmaking, but they've made good money over the years, in real estate or the stock market, say, and they now imagine themselves movers and shakers in this sexy, glamorous industry.

Then take that whole jumble of egos and add a producer into the mix. Well, the producer is the one who's *really* responsible for a film coming into existence. But no one ever cares about producers. We're those nameless entities who only emerge out of the crowd to receive a Best Picture Oscar each year, and then vanish again. *No one* goes to see a film because of who's producing it.

So you have all these tensions of who's stroking whose ego, who sees themselves as most responsible for the film's success, and who's getting recognized for their contributions. It's messy.

"And the interns and assistants?" Thom Gallagher asks.

No ego allowed. We're lowest on the pecking order. Completely expendable.

But I didn't know any of that when I first observed Xander Schulz in our office that afternoon. He reclined on the couch, discussing potential financiers and actors for his project, *A Hard Cold Blue*. Xander sat stock-still and assured in his physicality, hardly moving, as if he couldn't be bothered to waste energy on small, unnecessary exertions. He hadn't once glanced my way, just kept talking to Sylvia.

"I mentioned the project to Joaquin Phoenix's manager the other day—"

"Xander, first things first," Sylvia was telling him. "We don't have enough finance lined up yet to be approaching cast."

"Well then, get it lined up," Xander said firmly. He left it at that, a single command.

There was a pause, as I continued filing away, trying to pretend I wasn't listening. In my months at Firefly so far, I had only witnessed meetings where people were pleasant or even deferential to Sylvia. I'd never heard someone give *her* an order, assume that kind of authority over her.

"Xander, I can't just do that." Sylvia was stern. "You know what it takes. Meetings meetings meetings, and those meetings are more effective when you're there. Since you're the one who's going to be directing the film."

A note of resentment, barely noticeable, had crept into her voice.

"I know," Xander said. He sounded oblivious to Sylvia's point.

I glanced up at them during this exchange. Xander caught me looking at him, and a scrutinizing light crept into his eyes. Then, without any acknowledgment, he turned back towards Sylvia.

"So how long do you think it'll take?"

"I have no idea, we can't predict these things—" Sylvia started.

"Well I can't wait forever, I have all these music videos I'm being asked to direct, and then this gallery's bugging me about a potential exhibition."

"You *have* to make room for meetings, if you want this film to happen." Twenty years older than Xander, Sylvia had taken on a maternal but disciplinary tone here.

"Isn't that *your* job? And Andrea's?" Andrea was Xander's agent, who inhabited a big, shiny office a few blocks uptown.

"If you want Andrea to go to bat, you also have to play their game. Show some interest in those other projects they're packaging. Did you read those scripts she gave you?"

Xander didn't answer right away. He gulped down his coffee. He scanned the room again, settling on me.

"Hey," he said, raising his voice.

"This is Sarah," Sylvia reminded him. "She's been working here since the summer."

"Hey Sarah."

I looked up, surprised to be called out. Aware that my cheeks might be flushed from—from what? From being recognized as a human being?

"Hi," I said hesitantly.

"D'you read these scripts?" Xander gestured to the three scripts

Sylvia had put in front of him. *Closing Time. Serious Measures. A Hidden Shade of Anger.*

I glanced at Sylvia, unsure if I should reveal how many of the office scripts I'd been reading. But she was awaiting my answer too, with some curiosity.

"Yeah, I read them last week," I said.

Xander raised his eyebrows as if impressed, looked at Sylvia. "Wow," he said to me. "You probably like reading a lot, huh?"

I'm not sure what he meant by that. That I was Chinese, therefore nerdy, therefore I read a lot? Or just that . . . I liked reading? Which was true of course.

"I guess I do," I replied.

"Were they better than my script?" he asked.

I was shocked he asked me that directly. Was it a rhetorical question? In all honesty, his script, *A Hard Cold Blue*, was engaging enough, but not any more remarkable than the three he'd just mentioned. But I wasn't about to tell him that. Besides, I'd only been reading scripts for a few months. I couldn't be sure my opinion mattered much at this point.

"No," I lied. "I found yours more original."

Xander nodded, satisfied. "Good answer."

"See?" he turned to Sylvia. "I'm not directing anyone else's script. Only mine. So go find that financing. Because I don't want to waste any more of my time looking for it."

Sylvia's face was an unreadable mask. "But you will at least *read* those three scripts, right? We need to show your agency we're being cooperative."

Xander seemed to ignore her question.

"Hey Sandra." He snapped his fingers at me, his face alight with a new idea. "That's your name, right?"

"Sarah," I corrected him.

"Sarah, what's your favorite Polanski film?" he interrogated, suddenly serious.

For a second, I panicked. But there really was no contest. "Uh, *Repulsion*," I blurted.

Xander grinned. It was the first time I'd seen him smile. "Nice choice."

He snapped again. "And your favorite Kubrick?"

Kubrick's filmography swam before me, his output all so different, it seemed impossible to choose.

"*Paths of Glory*," I finally said.

Xander reacted with surprise. "Hey, look at that. A purist."

"What, did you think I was going to say *2001*?" I asked sarcastically.

"Only amateurs say *2001*." Xander winked at me. I glowed inside; I must have passed the test.

"Sarah, do you have time to write a quick report on these three scripts tonight?"

My eyes widened in shock. Was he asking me to assess those scripts for him? *Instead of* him?

"Um, I mean, sure." I mumbled uselessly. I'd have to scan the scripts again, which would take a couple hours, before I started writing. I would be up past midnight, even if I started on the train home.

"Could we get some comments on them by first thing tomorrow?"

"Uh . . ." I was a young deer in headlights, uncertain if the blinding glow in front of me was going to transport me to a higher existence or to a bloody, painful death.

I glanced at Sylvia, and she scowled at Xander.

"For god's sake, Xander. You're *that* lazy?"

"I'm not being lazy. Just efficient. I don't want to direct those scripts, and Sarah wants to learn. I mean, it's just a formality, right? Me reading them isn't going to help anyone."

"Yeah, but Sarah's not *you*."

"No, of course not." Xander smirked at the obvious. "But *you* trust her script notes, right?"

"Sure . . ." Sylvia's gaze softened and alighted on me. By now, she'd been asking me regularly to assess any incoming screenplays. "Sarah's good with scripts."

"Then what are we paying her for, if not to read scripts for me?" Xander finished his argument.

Then he added, *sotto voce*: "We *are* paying her, right?"

I was more amused than offended by this latest exchange. I piped up.

"I can do it," I said loudly. "And yeah, I'm being paid."

They both swiveled their heads in my direction, their eyebrows arched high like marionettes. A look of relief on Sylvia's face.

"I can read the three scripts," I asserted. "And write some notes on each. I'd be happy to."

"You sure?" Sylvia asked. She didn't doubt my ability or enthusiasm. The unease in her voice had to do with something else, a subtle shifting of interactions, moving slightly out of her intended grasp.

I shrugged. "Yeah, you know me. I like reading scripts."

Xander beamed at his ingenuity.

"Well, well, well. My kinda gal." It was a phrase I would often hear him use with women, trading it around like a well-worn coin. But it had its effect. He glanced approvingly at Sylvia, jerking his head at me. "I can imagine it must be useful to have her around."

And that was my introduction to Xander Schulz.

6

I WAS INDEED USEFUL to have around, as Xander soon discovered. Of course, I wasn't like the other women he was accustomed to. As the months went by, I noticed he was often accompanied by some type of very pretty, slender girl, sometimes a model. I didn't have elegantly defined features or wear immaculate makeup or designer outfits. I never positioned my rail-thin figure around him in a certain way, cooing at his comments, instantly laughing at his jokes. Nor was I like Sylvia or his agent Andrea, both older women, hard-nosed and businesslike, bathing him in compliments but unafraid to call him out on his ego—and all of it, still, with the singular aim of elevating the pedestal on which Xander already stood.

I was young, but not stupid. That much was clear. And *gradually*, Xander came to value my opinion on scripts, even though he would never say that outright to me.

There was something almost reptilian about Xander Schulz. If you studied him for a period of time, he would appear to hardly move, save for an occasional, necessary blink of his heavy eyelids. He could remain poker-faced, revealing little of his emotions, observing you and the room around him. And then—like a lizard suddenly skittering into action—he could light up, a disarming grin breaking across his face, an expertly deployed flash of charisma warming you to him. He had a sharp and entertaining sense of humor when he chose to use it. And oftentimes he did this to great effect, winning over financiers, actors, agents whom he hoped to convince of his artistic vision. But he could just as easily sit wordless at the back of the room, contributing little to the conversation, while you labored to make everything possible for him.

The more I worked with Xander, the more I grew to begrudgingly respect his single-mindedness, his laser-like intensity to bring his own vision—and no one else's—to the screen. Whether you encountered the engaging, animated Xander or the silent, morose version, his behavior always seemed strategic, calculated on whether you were important enough to merit an expenditure of energy.

But behind those observant eyes churned a mind that had memorized the shot sequences in every Polanski and Peckinpah film, every editorial quirk of Nicolas Roeg. His visual vocabulary was astonishing. It seemed he was always envisioning how a camera could move through a space, capture it, transform it into something dynamic and riveting for the viewer. Perhaps he saw people and situations in the same way, imagining how to position them for optimal usage. I suspected when he was having sex with a supermodel girlfriend, half his brain was still preoccupied with how to best frame her naked body in a camera shot—the only way to satisfy his cinematic eye.

But always, *his* was the perspective that mattered most: his imaginary camera manipulating light and angles to show you the world the way *he* wanted you to see it. I suppose that was the modus operandi of a man who had spent at least twenty years working towards being a film director. Knowing that one day he would ascend to that iconic canvas-backed chair and command an entire production with a single nod of his head.

Xander would often ask me to read a script for him, and I jumped at the chance. These were not the kinds of offers you turned down in this industry.

If you're trying to forge your way ahead in this world, you never say no. You always say yes.

See how early the traps are set for us?

Artistically, Xander knew his weaknesses, even though he would never voice them to anyone. Despite his visual talent, he maybe suspected he wasn't good at writing about emotions and relationships. His characters tended to be two-dimensional, lacking in anything interesting to say. This was especially the case with his female characters, who in his first few scripts, functioned solely as a romantic interest. They were inevitably described as "early-twenties and beautiful," leaping fiercely in action set pieces while wearing scanty clothing.

Few people have read his very early screenplays, but I discovered a file named XANDER SCRIPTS, saved on the bubble-shaped, translucent iMac I inherited from Sylvia. When I opened the file and saw the date on it, the name on the cover pages, I realized they were Xander's early attempts at screenwriting.

After reading them, I realized why those scripts were never mentioned. They were, simply put, very unoriginal. I was puzzled by the gap between his extreme confidence and their lackluster quality.

Since then, his screenwriting had improved vastly, but was still far from perfect.

I clocked this the first time I read a draft of *A Hard Cold Blue*, which I printed out, along with our company's boilerplate, a biography of Xander, and included with a VHS showreel of his work as a commercials and music video director. This was the same pitch package we'd been sending around to financiers for months, with little luck.

"I don't get it," Xander grumbled one afternoon. "I mean, everyone seems like they're really excited, and then they come up with some excuse not to come on board. *Oh, it's not for us.* Do you think they've even *read* my script?"

Come on, Xander, I thought. *As if you always read the scripts you're supposed to.*

Sylvia perched her rimless glasses on top of her head, tapped the burgundy nail of her index finger to her mouth. "Well, maybe the synopsis can use some redoing."

She looked to me. "Sarah, what do you think of the synopsis for Xander's script? Do you think it really captures the story well?"

"It's a bit . . ." I searched for the right word. I didn't want to insult whoever had written the synopsis, in case it was one of them. Generic? Bland? Like you could just be describing the latest video game pitch from Sega Genesis?

"It's not working, is it?" Xander asked.

"I guess there are ways to rewrite it," I suggested diplomatically.

"Do you want to try retooling the synopsis?" Sylvia asked.

"Me?" I stammered, just to be sure. I was delighted with the opportunity but didn't want to appear too enthusiastic. I also—at twenty-three—wasn't sure I had it in me to improve the existing writing.

"Xander, do you mind if Sarah tries a rewrite? Of the synopsis?" Sylvia asked in her most accommodating voice.

He shrugged and glanced over, bored. "Sure, whatever."

A synopsis is meant to hook financiers, agents, actors, industry players into reading an actual script. There's an art to writing one, just as there's an art to writing the cheesy taglines you see on movie posters. (*One man. One mission. One impossible deadline.*)

The problem is, if you have a really zippy synopsis and the actual script doesn't live up to the promise . . . well, then you have some disappointed readers. And players who ultimately decide not to fund your film.

So from retooling the synopsis (which was a success), I somehow ended up retooling the script itself. I didn't go so far as to actually open the file on Final Draft software, delete Xander's lines, and type in new ones of my own making. Such meddling would be enough to infuriate any filmmaker, let alone one as bigheaded as Xander.

But in the grand tradition of underappreciated script editors, I typed up detailed notes, ten-page manifestos on all the ways the screenplay could be improved, suggestions cushioned wisely between flattering praise about what impressed me, and how the character arc and plotline could be made even better if you just made these *slight* adjustments.

They weren't slight adjustments, in truth. They were major changes to the story, proposing a darker, more realistic conflict grounded in societal corruption and indifference. Perhaps I was being too bold in suggesting this to Xander. I squirmed with misgivings when I hit Send in my email to Sylvia.

"Let me look at your notes first," she had said. "You know what Xander's like. He can get sensitive about his work, even though he'd never say so himself."

So Sylvia was the first test. What if she hated them? What if she called me up in a blind fury, accusing me of needless cruelty towards her prize horse—or worse yet, poor judgment, an inability to really appreciate good scriptwriting?

I mulled around in the office the next morning, trying to keep busy, stapling Sylvia's latest receipts onto blank pages, filing the latest résumés and showreels to come in. When that was done, I flipped through a catalog of office supplies and started an order for more printer ink cartridges, script binders, reams of paper. Oh, the safety that resided in such banalities. Why aspire to anything higher than this?

When Sylvia burst in, she had a mysterious air about her, a schoolteacher about to spring a pop quiz on her nervous students.

She'd been to the coffeehouse around the corner and carried not one, but two cardboard cups, balancing them against the weight of her plum-colored Mulberry bag.

I guessed that meant Xander was coming in shortly, and my heart sank. But to my surprise, Sylvia set one of the steaming cups in front of me.

"Double cappuccino for you, right?" she asked.

I was shocked. "Uh . . . yeah." I imagined she'd forgotten I was lactose-intolerant, but I didn't ask if it was with soy milk.

She leaned back on the ridiculous orange cushion, and a wide, lipsticked smile spread across her face. "Sarah."

I looked up, anxious.

Sylvia's hand sliced towards me in a single chopping motion. "You need to know: your script notes were fantastic."

I fixed Sylvia with an incredulous stare. "Really?"

"Honestly, stop being so humble. If Xander had a fraction of your humility, he'd be so much more bearable to work with."

I didn't say anything, just hid a smile behind a mouthful of frothed milk.

"These notes are exactly what he needs. They're really on point, they're really well-written, very convincing. It's just about making sure he's receptive to them."

"Do you think he will be?"

"Well, Xander's coming round at twelve. I'll talk through the notes with him. So it may be best to have you out running an errand during that time. Go buy yourself another coffee or something."

It was an early spring day, and while my script notes were being either trashed or lauded inside the office, I found a rare pleasure in wandering outside on the streets of Chelsea, the sun warm on my face. I could see the shoots of young flowers pushing up through the dirt by streetside trees—and wondered if this might be the start of something a little more meaningful in my day-to-day work at the company. What if I became the go-to script fixer in the company, and what if—one day, I might actually write a script that they'd look at and produce? I'd read about it in that same book about being an assistant. Make yourself indispensable, establish your expertise in something, and then . . . maybe, you can casually hand over that script you wrote on the side.

But I hadn't birthed a screenplay yet. The sheer freedom of writing, the blank-paged nature of it all, was too daunting to me. Every day I was confronted with an entire wall of unspectacular scripts—practically haunted by the specter of the mediocre.

I couldn't think of an idea at the time, but standing on Seventeenth Street between Eighth and Ninth, I told myself that one day I would.

Or am I adding a flattering filter to that particular moment in my life, fifteen years on? Perhaps my goals were not so clear at the time. In our twenties, we seem to stumble around, thinking the world will magically clarify at the right moment, like a dense thicket of brambles lifting back to reveal our true path. But generally, that flash of epiphany never happens. We have to bash our way through, and we suffer our injuries and our wrong turns along the way.

Sylvia, true to her word, convinced Xander to work with my script notes, and the three of us sat that afternoon, discussing ways forward on the screenplay. Rework the characters, introduce a plausible new conflict rooted in a societal issue that could set this project apart from other, more standard suspense fare.

Over several more rounds of script notes and rewrites, I kept mentioning the need for significant female characters. Later, I impressed upon Xander the importance of having a smart, female-led thriller, and I'd like to think that contributed in some small way to his next film, *Furious Her*.

He'd never deign to give me such credit, of course.

With the new draft of *A Hard Cold Blue*, we started to attract significant interest from financiers, and within another year, we were moving into pre-production on Xander's first feature film.

"You're pretty good at this script work," Xander said once, after reading another set of my notes. It was the closest he'd ever get to thanking me.

Sylvia asked me if I'd given any thought to what I wanted to do in the film industry. I told her I liked working with scripts, but I was interested in learning more about producing. This was true at the time: there was a definite appeal to being the person in charge of it all, driving a project forward. It was a fine line between flattery (since she herself was a producer) and minimizing any sense of threat (since I didn't want her to think I was after her job). Which was impossible, anyway, as she owned the company.

"So what do you think producing is really about?" she asked me. "Don't take me through all the stages of filmmaking, but if you had to say it in just a few words."

"Making things happen?" I suggested.

Sylvia nodded. "But things don't happen right away. First, you have to build your network and nurture your projects. Then, you see a good opportunity. And when the moment's ripe, remember your worth. And negotiate."

I made a mental note of all these things and told myself I could learn to do them.

"Well," Sylvia continued. "Stick around. I think you could really go far. And in a few years' time, I could see you as head of development here."

That single statement, proffered out like a thin, dry Communion wafer, was enough to sustain me through the next few years of harried multitasking and inadequate income.

I didn't think to ask for more. Nor did I ask for any kind of official credit for my work on Xander's script. At the time, I just was grateful to be part of the team.

7

"SO CAN WE skip ahead?" Wait, why am I asking you? It's my story.

If this were a film, a single card title would now come up on-screen: *Four Years Later.*

Four years on, and *A Hard Cold Blue* was about to reach theaters. We'd settled into a comfortable triangular relationship at Firefly: Xander and Sylvia at the top, me at the bottom. Following Sylvia's lead, I'd been learning the art of networking, and of negotiating—both of which only worked if you wore a sufficient mantle of confidence. And this, too, I was developing. My reputation as a script whiz was gradually spreading throughout New York's wider film scene, thanks in part to Sylvia's praise. I could have, if I wanted, leveraged this to meet other producers, other industry players, to "build my network." As usual, it didn't occur to me at the time.

Instead, I spent long hours at Firefly, playing backup to whatever Xander and Sylvia needed me for: prepping marketing packages for financiers, reviewing contracts with our lawyer, researching sales agents and distributors. I was also running the office by then, overseeing our rotating stable of interns, who came in to work for free. Thankfully, by that point, I myself was earning a passable salary. Nothing compared to my Columbia friends who had gone into the corporate world or were now fresh out of law school or medical school. I still gravitated towards ordering the cheapest item on any restaurant menu, but I was earning enough to move out of my parents' apartment and rent a two-bedroom in Williamsburg with a friend-of-a-friend. I finally felt like an adult.

I was in my late-twenties by then. I had dated a few guys, but there'd been nothing lasting. Karen, on the other hand, had married her longtime boyfriend the year before and was now expecting a baby. (As always, neatly fulfilling our parents' expectations.) But for me, romance—and everything that came with it—wasn't really a priority, because I poured my heart and soul into work. Men seemed infinitely less interesting than movies, and the unpredictable process of flirting, waking up next to someone, texting, possibly never hearing back, often proved more disappointing than the satisfaction of watching a good movie. Instead, I envisioned a long and exciting career as a film producer. That seemed like the most rewarding character arc my own life could follow.

And the job could be convivial, too. Sylvia sometimes asked me to work from her brownstone, where she always opened a bottle of excellent red wine later in the day, and her three kids (Nathan, Rachel, and Jacob) were often friendly and curious. Over the years, I'd watched Rachel grow from an eager ten-year-old into a sulky, skinny fifteen-year-old. But despite her grumpy struggles through adolescence, I got the feeling she liked having me around, this long-haired, twentysomething woman who seemed very different from her own mother.

"What're you working on now?" she'd ask me, as I sat in their living room, waiting for Sylvia to finish a phone call.

I'd explain the current script I was reading.

"Your life is so cool," Rachel would pronounce, her teenage eyes ringed with too much liner.

I doubted I could ever really be "cool," having grown up living above our Chinese restaurant in Flushing. But Rachel probably never suspected my origins.

With her family and busy social schedule, Sylvia often passed on to me the invites she got for film premieres and receptions. In time, I myself started getting invited. A couple nights a week, I found myself at screenings or industry events, meeting other film-makers, talking avidly about cinema, what projects we were work-ing on, what movies we'd recently seen. There were always drinks, and amidst the open bars and free-flowing wine, I circulated among rooms of attractive and witty industry professionals—most of them well-educated and white, but all of us drawn together by our abiding passion for film.

The socializing was as much a part of the job as the office work. That, after all, was how you built your network. And at that age, I thought nothing of staying out until one or two a.m., meeting di-rectors and actors and acquisition execs, and then blearily unlock-ing the office at nine the next morning, hungover but exhilarated. Hangovers were the necessary consequence of good networking. And we were the blessed few, were we not? We who earned a salary (albeit a meager one) from doing what we loved: making films.

Our own film productions were always an opportunity to meet a new range of cast and crew members, every person on the rolling end credits: from runner to key grip to director of photography. I often befriended the cast, and realized that actors were just like normal people, only better-looking and more charismatic. And perfectly friendly, especially if they wanted a role. Of everyone in the industry, actors were maybe the most dedicated to their craft, but usually the most insecure—and the least lucky.

So I was no longer a starry-eyed newcomer to the industry by the time Hugo North arrived on the scene.

And yes, ominous drumroll now. We have reached the point in the story when Mr. North enters the frame.

Thom Gallagher leans forward in anticipation. This must be the moment that makes investigative journalists salivate.

"Can you describe the first time you met him?"

As much as I've tried to obscure the thought of him all these years, the moment is very clear in my mind. The influential figures in our lives always get a noteworthy entrance, don't they? Or perhaps that's just our memory, preserving that specific encounter in a selective kind of formaldehyde, when so many other encounters in our lives fade away, forgotten.

Hugo North, of course, is someone whose reputation has always preceded him. By the time you meet him, the reality of the encounter merely fulfills an existing expectation—and a predetermined outcome.

What struck you immediately was his British accent. In this industry, people just want to stand out from the crowd, to be seen to offer something unique. Hugo's accent did it for him. Americans hear a British accent, and we picture the Queen of England and all her royal descendants having tea in a garden. Hugo's accent granted him a patina of refinement, his voice promising a world of impossible privilege.

But beyond his voice, there was that supreme self-assurance. That ability to command attention through his sheer reputation, that implicit awareness of his wealth. I have never met someone who, simply by speaking, could make you feel fortunate to be next to him, in his orbit.

Yet just when you'd write him off as another silken-voiced Brit who only ever frequented private clubs and five-star hotels, Hugo would confound you. He would chat to homeless people, bemusedly giving them the time of day, but rarely any change. I once saw him chomping on a slice from a grungy pizza place on the Lower East Side, cramming the cheese and the crust into his mouth as quickly as he could chew.

Remember what I said?

Appetite before art. And Hugo had a lot of appetites.

But he was also an expert at sensing other people's appetites, knowing how to feed them, knowing when to keep them hungry.

When I met Hugo North, it was at the Cannes Film Festival, my third year there. I knew what to expect; I was no longer the unsuspecting novice floored by the spectacle of it all. I tried describing Cannes to Karen the first time I went, but I doubt she'd ever experienced anything like the utter madness of that scene, the frenzied hustling and posturing beneath the Mediterranean sun.

This is what Cannes is like: You step onto the Croisette, the famous street that runs the length of the waterfront. The pavement is heaving with people, most of them film industry professionals, or wannabe professionals, with their business card cases, their phones and BlackBerrys and accreditation badges swinging from their tanned necks. Everyone rushing from one meeting to another, following a packed agenda of screenings and lunches and drinks. How many people can you meet, how many contacts who could possibly get your film script read or your project funded or sold or distributed?

To one side, the Mediterranean sparkles in the sun. The beach is covered with the white peaks of pavilions erected along the sand, each of them the home of some national film commission trying to lure filmmakers to spend their production budgets shooting in *their* unique country, with its stunning locations and favorable tax incentives.

On the other side, the waterfront luxury hotels lounge next to each other: the Marriott, the Majestic, the Carlton, the Martinez. Their indolent architecture sits swathed in massive film advertisements, some of them five stories high, which distributors have paid thousands of euros for, endeavoring to make a splash at the world's most famous film festival.

Everything, of course, is about making a splash.

The launch of a new film necessitates elaborately themed parties in distant villas in the hills, or on the rooftops of palaces, or on yachts docked in the marina—or more exclusively, on yachts anchored out in the bay, requiring a mysterious motorboat ride to reach them. I'm sure the budgets of some of these parties easily exceeded that of our entire feature film.

Who can throw the biggest party, on the biggest yacht? Or mount the biggest advertisement, draping the Hôtel Martinez with an eye-catching image of its leading lady and the film's imposing title? Which new film gets talked about in the trades the following day, or discussed in breakfast meetings or inter-screening chats, everyone wearing their giant sunglasses to conceal their epic hangovers?

At one end, the Croisette culminates in the Palais, where each evening for a new premiere, the vast red carpet welcomes the glitterati, the white-hot flashbulbs augmenting the intensity of the Mediterranean sun. Off to the side, desperate French teenagers stand in rented tuxedos and ill-fitting secondhand evening gowns. They hold up signs begging for unwanted premiere tickets (because screenings aren't open to the public and can only be attended in black-tie attire).

The first year I went, I hadn't packed properly. I mean, what Chinese kid from Flushing knows how to pack for the Cannes Film Festival? I was generally confident enough about my looks to not worry about them. But Sylvia hadn't warned me that just to be a functioning professional in Cannes, I was supposed to dress glamorous in a manner I'd never dared before. Cannes was a catwalk in its own way, and if you were a woman, no one would take you seriously if you weren't slim and glossy-haired, wearing a flattering dress and the requisite sunglasses. Thankfully, I fit the first two criteria. The second two I could easily acquire. So my first time in Cannes, I took one look at the people on the Croisette, headed for the nearest affordable clothing shop, and felt justified spending one hundred euros on a dress, so I didn't look like a fool to people we were trying to do business with. It was the cheapest dress I could find, but that was a lot of money for me at the time. It still is.

It must have worked somehow, because two male tourists stopped me on the Croisette and asked for my autograph. I paused, momentarily surprised. Did they mistake me for someone else? Did they think I, Sarah Lai, was a celebrity simply because I wore the right type of sunglasses and looked the part?

I wondered if I should sign someone else's name—Lucy Liu or Gong Li or . . . well, there weren't that many actresses I could choose from—but instead, I just scrawled *Sarah Lai* in big, illegible script on their free tourist map of Cannes. They'd be disappointed if they could actually decipher my name and realize I wasn't anyone famous.

But what mattered was the illusion. For them, that they'd met a movie star at the Cannes Film Festival. For me, that I was somehow famous, worthy of recognition.

Now, "doing business" at Cannes for the most part means endless meetings. Some people are there to actually buy films, and there is a whole arena of screenings and buyers visiting sales agent suites and bidding on distribution rights to different titles. It sounds sophisticated, especially when set against a backdrop of white-washed terraces overlooking the Mediterranean. Yes, people drink rosé while making their deals, but remember what I said? It's still about sales—no different from crusty street hawkers peddling bean sprouts on the sidewalks of Flushing. Films are products to be sold. Just products with more glamorous packaging.

The one thing I wasn't allowed to do in Cannes was actually see movies. That naive first year, I mentioned going to a screening, and Sylvia stared at me with a sort of muted outrage.

"I'm not paying for you to go to Cannes so you can see *films*."

Her voice took on that sharp tone, the one I always dreaded and sometimes still ran up against unexpectedly.

"Really?" I asked, out of sheer confusion. It was a film festival. Surely, somewhere in there, the point was to see films.

"Sarah, you can watch films to your heart's content right here in New York. I'm paying for you to go to meetings. To make contacts, expand our network, meet talent, find people with money. This is *not* a vacation."

I stood there, shocked. Trying to grasp the concept of attending Cannes and *not* settling into a hushed silence in the audience, waiting for that ripe moment as the first reel breaks across the screen . . .

No, that was the illusion. The product.

The business of making said product took place elsewhere, in meetings, over phone calls, through emails and negotiations and contracts. The film world had drawn me in, like it does so many of us, through its promises of escape and wonderment. But it was work, plain and simple. And Cannes was a work trip.

So by my third time in Cannes, I knew the drill. Sylvia and I usually planned at least a month in advance, pinpointing the people we wanted to meet, emailing their office to set up a thirty-minute slot sometime over the course of four days. I drew up a schedule of parties and sent in our RSVPs. We had dinner gatherings and drinks appointments and after-parties planned out in our diaries. I saved our scripts and marketing materials onto a flash drive that I carried with me at all times. And I made sure to pack enough business cards, my name embossed, dark gray on pale yellow: SARAH LAI. FIREFLY FILMS. ASSOCIATE PRODUCER.

That was when I knew I had arrived. I had my own business card. I belonged.

That third year in Cannes, there was an exception, and I was allowed to attend one screening: our own film, *A Hard Cold Blue.*

Xander's feature debut had been selected to play in Un Certain Regard, the official Cannes festival program for emerging filmmakers. It was an enviable honor, and one that any director or producer would have gladly murdered for. Twelve feature films by novice directors from around the world, with the global film industry paying attention. It had swelled Xander's head to unbearable proportions, but Sylvia and I tolerated it because this was a step up for our production company and our other projects. We could capitalize on the attention Xander now attracted as a director. We had Xander's second film project lined up, the script done and dusted, conversations with cast already happening, 60 percent of the financing in place.

Everything was ready. The film could go into pre-production the minute we sourced the rest of the funding: another $4 million or so. Not a petty amount, but it was out there somehow. We just had to find it.

Which is where Hugo North came in. When we met Hugo in Cannes, Xander's film had just had its first screening earlier that day, and the buzz was good. A glowing review in *Variety* ("heralds an ambitious new virtuoso talent"), a fairly positive one in *Screen International* ("clever and daring"), and a photo in the *Hollywood Reporter* of Xander and the two leads had boosted our profile. If you perused the fine print of the reviews closely enough, you could find Sylvia's name and mine, listed as producer and associate producer, respectively.

I had probably seen the film about forty-two times in various stages of post-production. Sitting in edit suites, then later alone, watching the time-coded DVD to take notes on visual effects, sound effects, sound recording, music. But watching it for the first time, with a full audience of strangers at the Cannes Film Festival was a quasi-religious experience. When they laughed at the jokes, I felt relief. When they clapped enthusiastically at the end, I felt joy.

I had witnessed my name on a single card at the end credits. My name, Sarah Lai, had the screen all to itself, for three entire seconds. I realized that amidst this whole crowd of professionals, no one sitting next to me had any idea who I was, that I had spent years of my life working on the film they'd just seen. In that room full of people, I could have been a nobody. But I wasn't. I smiled to myself in the darkness, knowing that for the first time, I could actually claim to be a somebody.

I filed out of the screening, a few steps behind Sylvia, who was chatting animatedly to someone I didn't know. I tried to hear what people were saying, hums of approval or muttered disappointment. Turning to the man next to me, I noticed he was young-ish, pleasant-looking, and American, so I asked him what he thought of the film. He said it was a really unique take on the genre, with a great twist at the end.

"That's good." I paused, then went on. "Because I'm one of the film's producers."

That little line was all it took.

The man did a double take. Maybe he didn't expect me, this young Asian American woman, to be a film producer—and maybe he thought I was a publicist or wannabe actress or someone's assistant. But his attitude changed in an instant.

"Oh hey, congratulations. It's a great film. Really, I mean that."

I grinned. "Thanks."

For once, I genuinely felt proud of what I'd done for the film, and yet, it had taken a stranger to prompt that.

"I'm Ted, by the way." The man smiled warmly and extended a hand. "I'm a producer too. What are you up to now?"

In Cannes, any interaction can sound vaguely flirtatious. This is, after all, a week of business taking place amidst copious alcohol, nearly-as-copious drugs, where women parade in low-cut dresses and men lounge with their shirts partially unbuttoned. Seduction is part of the game. Because in film, if you don't have the charisma to charm people, you're never going to convince them to fund your film, or buy it, or star in it. And more importantly, at Cannes, you never know who you might encounter at the next party.

But just then, Sylvia came up to me. She didn't bother to introduce herself to Ted.

"I'm headed to our next meeting now with Xander. Check your email, and don't forget our drinks at the Carlton. There'll be someone important you should meet."

8

SYLVIA'S EMAIL SAID this: 10 p.m. drinks are with this British guy Hugo North. He liked the film a lot and might fund us. Be nice to him.

Looking back on that email now, one might be tempted to read between the lines. But Sylvia meant this at face value and nothing more. "Be nice to him" wasn't code for "shower him with sexual favors." In this industry, we are all transactional, but we're not that blatant. And what I liked about Sylvia was that she was a straight shooter. She saw a business opportunity or a potential project, and she went for it, based purely on its qualities. She wasn't swayed by things like partying or sex or drugs or even fame, beyond their practical functions. She *could* be swayed by money, though.

So I left my dinner with Ted rather sober and made sure to arrive at our ten p.m. drinks on time. The Carlton is certainly the grandest and most elaborate of the waterfront luxury hotels that dominate the Croisette. This is where Grace Kelly met Prince Rainer III before she became princess of Monaco in 1956, where Hitchcock filmed her in *To Catch a Thief*. Even after three years at Cannes, I was still mildly elated when the security guards allowed me to step onto its marbled terrace and penetrate the glittering crowds that spilled out under the starry night.

I am trying to reimagine that scene from ten years ago, on that particular balmy spring evening. If I were to direct it for a movie, how would it unfold?

It would be me, twenty-seven years old, unsure of what to expect as I arrive at the Carlton terrace alone. Of course, it would be shot on a Steadicam, the camera following my own point of view. So the viewer walks with me too, and together, we would enter this hive of buzzing revelry, entranced.

To the right is the tinkling of laughter as a stunning woman in a sleeveless gown perches atop a table, surrounded by a cluster of male admirers.

I turn left, and see a champagne-addled bald man, grinning merrily at a cluster of young women. He drops a glass in his drunkenness, and it shatters to the sounds of feminine squeals.

But still I push on, the camera following me towards a definite, unseen target, somewhere farther in the room.

Then the crowds part—a couple crosses our line of sight to momentarily obscure things. I drift through a knot of laughing partygoers, and there—previously hidden but now in plain view—sits the figure towards whom I have been moving all along, though I do not yet realize it.

The figure looks up, straight at me, and grins.

He is a middle-aged man, past his prime, but still with the dark, assured magnetism that defined him throughout his charmed youth. His girth is now wider, his shoulders broader, and this gives him more presence, more heft in any interaction. He no longer moves with the quickness of youth, but he no longer needs to, because everything and everyone in the room now moves around him, to accommodate him.

He stands to greet me. His skin is tanned to the point of leathery, and his heavy, distinguished brows gather above a hawkish nose. Beneath them, his eyes are a striking green, indulgent, perhaps teasing. As if he had been studying me long before I finally meet him.

This may arouse some suspicions; perhaps I seem ill at ease, aware already of his latent power. But these suspicions vanish the moment he chooses to smile. A flash of his preternaturally white teeth draws me into his confidence.

The teeth of Hugo North must have been artificially bleached; I can think of no other explanation as to how he got them so white.

And yet, like most Brits, he hadn't bothered to straighten them, so they gleamed out at me: blindingly white amidst his tanned face, but slightly askew.

"Hugo," Sylvia said. "I want you to meet Sarah Lai."

Hugo's greeting took me by surprise. I was expecting a straight-forward handshake, but he leaned in, drew me towards him, and delivered a moist kiss on my cheek, in the European style of greeting. Unaccustomed to intimacy like this, I froze awkwardly. Then he kissed my other cheek.

"So very pleased to meet you, Sarah. I've heard wonderful things about you."

Even though I knew he was British, I was still momentarily startled, hearing that English accent directed at me. There was something arresting, even illicit about it.

This formality over, Hugo re-seated himself, and without skipping a beat, resumed his conversation with Sylvia and Xander. Hugo regaled us with stories of his previous Cannes escapades, dropping names of industry heavy hitters who had always been beyond our reach.

"But honestly, I've been coming to Cannes for what, ten, twelve years now? And Xander, I haven't seen anything like your film. I mean, I was fairly gobsmacked by it. Your visuals, those camera movements. I'm sure you devised it on a fairly tight budget. . . . Ingenious."

Hugo shook his head in admiration, and Xander nodded beatifically, like a patron saint receiving devotions from a supplicant.

And so it began, this mutual stroking of male egos, this sort of strategic wankfest that would dominate our company dynamics for years to come. Xander was accustomed to praise from geeky fanboys and all sorts of women—giggling models and aspiring actresses and his agent and agent's assistants. But to hear it from this weathered, experienced man . . . somehow, to Xander, Hugo's compliments carried more weight.

At the same time, Xander was playing his own game too.

"Well, wait till you see what I have planned for the next film. Some really groundbreaking new ideas, so long as I can get the budget covered."

Hugo waved his hands breezily. "Let's get to budgets in a bit. First, I want you to take a moment and rest on your laurels. Realize how far you've come, and what an exciting position you're now in." He refilled his flute of bubbly and raised it towards us, looking around at each of us individually before continuing.

"Here you are, the talk of the town. This moment's been years in the making—relish it. Because it's not every day your first feature film premieres in Cannes."

And he was right. Sylvia and I had been so busy rushing around to meetings along the Croisette, focusing on impressing the next contact, that we hadn't paused to really savor the moment—the sense of victory we deserved to feel after all our hard work. Hearing Hugo's words, I allowed myself to relax, as the champagne worked its way through my body.

"Honestly, if you want to let loose tonight . . . well, I'm expert at showing people a good time." Hugo grinned. He poured some more Möet into each of our glasses. "But I want to give the three of you something to *really* celebrate. Are you ready to hear it?"

I was intrigued and sipped eagerly at the champagne. Besides, I liked how he kept referring to "the three of us." For so long, it had always been Xander and Sylvia in the limelight, me booking appointments for them, talking them up to industry contacts, making sure not to overstep my bounds. But now, I was actually included, considered an intrinsic part of the team.

Hugo reclined and gestured with one hand, a burnished signet ring on his little finger.

"I think filmmaking talent like yours, Xander, deserves to have the best resources, to truly bring your next vision to life. It's not fair that you have to scrimp and save just to get a film to happen."

Xander nodded and looked intently at Hugo.

"The three of you have put your all into an incredible picture that's wowed so many people here. And I really want to help you bring your work to the next level."

Sylvia stepped in. "The stage we're at now, Xander's film is pretty much ready to go, once we get the financing in place." She explained how much had been raised so far, through which sources.

"Sure, sure. And you don't want to waste another year raising money just to get the film made," Hugo agreed. "While there's all this buzz about Xander, you want to just—bam! Get in there and start rolling. In the best possible way. And that probably means in the best-*funded* way."

"Absolutely," Xander said. "I've paid my dues already; it's about fucking time." He glanced meaningfully at Sylvia, then back at Hugo.

This conversation was clearly above my pay grade, so I just listened with great interest. Even though I now had an associate producer credit, my function in the presence of Xander and Sylvia remained the same: when meeting new business contacts, don't speak until you're spoken to.

"So tell us a bit more what you're thinking," Sylvia said. "How would you like to help out?"

She noticed the bottle of champagne was nearly empty and signaled to me to order another. I looked around, trying to flag down one of the strutting waiters, while still keeping an ear on the conversation.

Hugo grinned. "Ah, I like you, Sylvia. You're direct, and that's so refreshing amidst all this . . . silly frippery on the Croisette." He gestured around at the terrace with its preening starlets and self-satisfied men, some of them still wearing sunglasses in the night air. "Well, I come from another industry. From what you in America would call real estate. So I'm used to buying a property and knowing for sure, one hundred percent, that its value will increase over the years. With film I know it's different."

"Quite different," Sylvia said dryly.

"I've invested in films and not received much of a return. I get it. And yet, at the same time, I'm still drawn back to Cannes every year, simply for the movies." Hugo closed his eyes momentarily. When he resumed speaking there was almost a quaver in his voice, which paired with the British accent, took on a theatrical resonance. "After all, it's *film*. There's nothing else like it. There's no other art form, no other entertainment that sweeps you away so fully. And a good film, the ability to tell a powerful story, and capture an audience just like that . . . it's just . . ."

He placed his hand over his heart and shook his head.

As melodramatic as Hugo sounded, the three of us all bought it. We had just devoted five years to making a movie which someone might see for ninety minutes and promptly forget. To us, that sort of madness was believable.

"So this is what I'd like to propose. Xander, you're a remarkable talent who has huge things ahead of him, and Sylvia, Sarah, you've both been instrumental as his producers. It's a team that works, clearly.

"I would love to, essentially, *contribute* towards your upcoming film, *Furious Her*. I admit I've only read the synopsis so far, but I loved it. So however much you need . . . within reason. Three million dollars? Five million? More?"

He looked between Sylvia and Xander, who were openmouthed, waiting for Hugo to continue. *Five million, just like that?* My eyes widened in shock.

"Consider it a long-term investment. I'm not just interested in this one film. It's *the company* that I see as having potential. All of you. Xander's next films. And the other projects you have lined up, with other directors, too."

There was an unusual gleam in Sylvia's eyes. Her standard shrewdness was there too, but I detected a singular new light, laser-focused.

"So what you're saying is you'd like to invest in the company?" Sylvia asked.

"Yes, give you an upgrade, if you will. I'm sure your five-year plan is sound. I want to make that a reality. If we shoot Xander's next film this year, and it comes out next year . . . Surely within five more years, there's room for another feature film or two, maybe a TV series. And that's just from Xander. From your other directors, who knows? Think of all the films you could be making with this kind of cash injection."

"And what would you want in return?" Sylvia asked, her eyes fixed on Hugo.

"Aha, down to brass tacks," he laughed. "Always the businesswoman, Sylvia . . . Well, it's an equity investment. So obviously, part-ownership of the company—"

"And how involved in the company would you want to be?"

This was the crux of the matter, the question that was haunting the entire meeting, as we sat amid the chatter and the tinkling piano, drinking this particular champagne on this particular evening with this particular man. I wondered if Sylvia would even consider partly handing the reins of a company she'd nurtured for years—to this stranger.

Hugo looked directly at her. "I'd want to be very involved. I may as well be honest. For years I've been looking for the right production company to invest in. One that can find top-notch talent, develop good projects, run itself efficiently . . . You'd be surprised how few and far between these are."

Sylvia smiled at me and Xander, a tacit nod to our success.

"Personally, I keep a low profile when I'm in Cannes," Hugo confided. "With my assets, do you know how many greedy filmmakers I'd get knocking on my door? But you three—Xander, Sylvia, Sarah—I want to invest in you. You lot are the real deal."

Xander didn't lose his focus. "If you were to do this, Hugo, what role would you want to play in the filmmaking process?" The last thing he'd want was this property mogul wading in cluelessly, muddying his creative vision.

But Hugo knew exactly what to say.

"You, Xander, are the creative genius behind each of your films, and I don't ever want to trespass on that. I hear Sarah is amazing on script, and Sylvia, of course, is the lady who makes it all happen." He nodded and looked at each of us in turn. "You have every right to be protective of what you've built. But really, just free yourself up for a moment. Think of what you could achieve with more financing."

In my mind, I recalled how tightly we had budgeted the last film, negotiating hard with the talent agents to hire actors at a lower fee, even angling for a deal on the catering.

"You can scale up: hire more staff, get a new office, maybe even relocate to LA—"

"Let's not get ahead of ourselves here," Sylvia said with a note of caution.

But already, my imagination had been set ablaze. To have an assistant I could delegate to. To earn a comfortable paycheck, dine out more often, no longer watch every price when I bought groceries . . .

"You want a big, fancy premiere at Cannes next year?" Hugo continued. "A splashy after-party that'll get everyone talking? You want to be on the front page of all the trades, touted for awards? Money can buy a lot in this industry. It can buy publicity and buzz. But it can't buy talent. *That's* what you bring to the table."

The three of us were quiet for a moment, perhaps each of us envisioning what worlds Hugo's funding could unlock. Quite likely dreams we'd nursed ever since working in film. Now for the first time, they seemed very possible.

"But money *can* nurture talent, take it to the next level. And that's what we're going to do with you." Hugo picked up the fresh bottle of Möet and refilled each of our glasses until they were brimming. "So I bring the money. You bring the art. Clean and simple."

Any doubts we might have had about Hugo during that first conversation were promptly drowned by the copious amounts of alcohol we consumed afterwards.

When we'd discussed the company long enough, Sylvia started to make noises about returning to her hotel room, so she could call her family in New York. But Hugo wouldn't allow it.

"Nonsense," he proclaimed. "They're six hours behind us, you've got plenty of time still. *I've* been invited to an exclusive party a few floors up, sort of an intimate gathering related to the latest Tarantino film, and it is my deeply held conviction that the three of you should accompany me as my guests."

What?! I thought. *A Tarantino party?!*

I knew better than to voice my excitement, though.

Sylvia hesitated. "Hugo, that's very kind of you, but . . . are you sure you can bring the three of us?"

At Cannes, there was a definite hierarchy of which parties could be crashed, and which parties were off-limits. And even though everyone wanted access to every party, you also didn't want to be seen as trespassing beyond your reach. No one likes an obvious status-seeker, especially at Cannes.

"Not a problem." He waved it off. "I've been told the more the merrier. Believe me, there will be so much champagne, I don't think three extra mouths will make much of a difference."

Xander was grinning. "I'm all for it, but there's some girls over there, some models I know, who I gotta say hi to. Give me five minutes."

He gestured to a flock of long-legged, glossy-haired sylphs across the room. By this point in the evening, they had attracted their fair share of men, who were orbiting them slowly, patiently.

Hugo raised his black eyebrows. "*Those* girls? Are they models you've worked with?" He eyed them, nodding. "Invite them along. I'm sure they'd be most welcome, where we're going."

So fifteen minutes later, I found myself crammed in a mirrored elevator with Hugo, Xander, Sylvia, and four towering supermodels, on our way up to a party on the seventh floor of the Carlton.

The coven consisted of a redhead, an olive-skinned brunette, a Russian blonde, and a regal Black beauty. They were also nearly a foot taller than me, so I couldn't quite read their facial expressions when Xander introduced us.

"Hi, I'm Sarah," I said to the redhead's clavicle. I didn't bother to add: "I read the scripts in the office." I doubted she'd care. Inside her stilettoed sandals, her impeccable toenails were pedicured a candy-colored pink; next to them, my chipped, self-polished toenails were clearly an amateur job.

"Now, I hope you girls realize," Hugo said, "that you are standing in the presence of one up-and-coming cinematic genius. Xander's film has just premiered here at Cannes, and he's the talk of the festival right now."

The models squealed, Xander nodded. "And Hugo here is the man to know. Looks like he'll be backing my next film."

"Oh wow," they chorused, as if they could sniff the wealth wafting from him.

Hugo said no further words, simply smiled at them. But their interest had been piqued.

Just then, the elevator *ping*ed and opened onto an elegant marbled hallway and the hotel's seventh-floor suites.

It was Hugo who strode purposefully towards the white-washed double doors of the Sophia Loren Suite, from which emanated the unmistakable throb of a party in full swing. It was Hugo who approached the hulking security guard, palming his hand and whispering in his ear. The guard glanced over at us, with our offering of four world-class supermodels, a sexed-up Benetton ad in the making. He muttered into his wrist, nodded, and then pushed open the door for us to enter.

It took a while for my eyes to adjust to the scene before me.

In front of us stretched a darkened, candlelit room. Nouvelle Vague lounge music floated in the air, as self-possessed men and women reclined on divans, posed against walls, lifted flutes of champagne from the passing trays of attentive waiters.

Apart from the occasional actor, the men in the crowd were fairly average-looking, though they'd all made an effort to dress more stylishly here at Cannes: linen trousers, partly unbuttoned shirts revealing chests of varying hairiness and pudge. But the women were jaw-droppingly gorgeous. Sprinkled throughout were a few women around Sylvia's age, and a few more normal-looking women like me, but by and large, glamazons similar to our supermodel companions stalked the room, their long legs slinking out from under billowing kaftans and sleek dresses. The men in the room were distracted every time one of these glistening beings walked past.

"Who *are* these people?" I wondered, wishing I'd at least taken the time to reapply my lipstick.

"Can I get you girls something to drink?" Hugo asked. At that moment, a waiter sidled up, proffering a tray with six champagne flutes. These promptly went to Hugo, Xander, and the four models.

Sylvia turned to me, a wry smile on her face. "Shall I get us some champagne?"

"Uh, sure," I mumbled, still taking in the scene around me. I thought I could make out Kevin Costner at the far end of the room. I wondered what films he'd been in since *The Postman*.

"This is quite the party Hugo's brought us to. I wonder who else is in the room," Sylvia mused, holding out a brimming champagne flute.

"No idea," I said, promptly downing the glass in one gulp. Heck, maybe even Quentin Tarantino was here. "Well, there's no point in waiting around to find out."

And, fairly confident no one would notice my chipped toenails, I pressed my way into the throng.

The next two hours passed in boozy conversation—and later, dancing—with a collection of film execs and sales agents and talent agents and the occasional actual filmmaker who milled about the Sophia Loren Suite. Many of them had heard of *A Hard Cold Blue*, some had even seen it. My face flushed when I heard the excitement in their voices, when they offered up their business card with a suggestion that we "have a chat sometime." Some of these contacts I'd been trying to reach via email for ages. Apparently, all it took was entrance into the right party.

Later, to escape the fetid press of the crowd, I ventured onto the terrace in search of fresh air. I leaned with relief against the carved balustrade. Lights bobbed in the harbor below, and the Marriott, the Majestic, the other waterfront buildings curved away towards the casino and the Palais. Their gargantuan film advertisements dwarfed the unnamed revelers who still whooped and laughed and consorted on other balconies, on the esplanade below, at unseen parties.

A breeze swept in from the Mediterranean, and I wondered if this was actually real: me in Cannes, seven stories above the French Riviera, at the same private party as Quentin Tarantino and Kevin Costner and a cast of supermodels, whom I'd probably recognize if I flipped open the current issue of *Vogue*. Somewhere in Flushing, local families were being seated for dinner at our restaurant, customers jabbering their orders, the cooks mopping their greasy brows as they paused over the sputtering grill . . .

I turned to see Sylvia next to me.

"How're you doing?" she asked, clinking champagne glasses with me.

"Pretty good." I downed the rest of my drink and set it on a low table, next to an overflowing ashtray.

Sylvia held something in her hand, and she tapped it into the ashes just then. It didn't smell like a normal cigarette.

"Sylvia, are you smoking a *joint*?" I cackled with a wicked glee.

She looked at me for a moment, then burst out laughing and nodded.

"I haven't had one of these in ages. Listen, I got it from someone over there." She waved towards the far side of the balcony. "From some French sales agent. Think his name was *Antoine*."

She spouted his name with a faux French vigor. We both dissolved into laughter.

"Want some?" she asked, and offered me the joint.

Surprised, I delicately took a drag or two, the harsh taste of the weed rasping the back of my throat. With my New York friends, I'd obviously encountered marijuana before, though my parents would flip if they ever knew my own boss was offering me drugs.

"A little bit of weed never hurt anyone," Sylvia mused into the night air. "*Don't* tell my seventeen-year-old son I ever said that," she added sharply.

I held my hands up in mock innocence. "My lips are sealed," I said, before we collapsed into giggles again. I could already feel the marijuana loosening my senses, and a calm hilarity started to bubble through me.

"So, who'd you meet so far?" Sylvia asked.

"*Other* than a bunch of supermodels?" I rattled off some of the industry people I'd come across—a *Variety* journalist, an acquisitions person at Fox Searchlight, junior agents from Endeavor and UTA. Sylvia was impressed at the business cards I'd collected.

"So you're still on the job," she commented.

"Of course." I looked at her archly and said with a sarcastic edge: "This *is* a work trip, after all."

Sylvia smirked, recognizing her mantra to me.

"Hey," she said. "I need to thank you, Sarah. For all you've done."

"Huh?" Already high on the party's buzz, I didn't expect to hear Sylvia's praise at two in the morning.

"I know you've worked really hard," she continued. "And I may not necessarily express it all the time, but really, thank you. You bring a lot to this company."

I paused. I basked for a moment in Sylvia's appreciation, a rare thing.

"Oh, well, hey . . . Thanks back. It's been fun so far."

The Chinese part of me was not very good at accepting compliments, and I cursed myself for my social ineptitude. *She's your boss! Show more enthusiasm!*

"But honestly, can you believe this?" I gushed. "We've done it! We're at this exclusive party in Cannes. Everyone loves *A Hard Cold Blue*. We got the funding for the rest of the film!"

Sylvia nodded. "It's pretty great." Despite the weed, she kept her usual reserve.

I was surprised she wasn't more ecstatic.

"Come on, Sylvia," I said. "I mean, Hugo sounded like he was going to foot the bill. Cover our overheads. Ease things up for us."

Finally, I wanted to say, *we don't have to hustle so much. We've made it.*

"Listen, I'm excited, of course I am," Sylvia said. "Who wouldn't be? But look around."

Sylvia nudged her chin in the direction of Hugo, who stood in the recesses of the party, deep in conversation with the willowy redhead from our group. I saw how she leaned towards him, her slender body bending around his staunch frame.

"Hugo's a businessman, pure and simple. He'll always expect something in return."

To me, it seemed pretty clear, based on our earlier conversation. Part-ownership in the company, an executive producer credit, a say in the casting . . .

"Look at the rest of this world, Sarah." Sylvia gestured to the entire party around us, the stunning models draped across the sofas and the shoulders of men, the men who reached their arms out casually to caress these women, rest their hands on the small of their gleaming, curved backs. "This is what it looks like sometimes. Are you sure you're ready?"

I wanted to shout: *Of course I'm ready, I've been waiting my whole life for this!* But part of me hesitated.

Behind us, our blond and brunette supermodel friends, staggering drunk, squealed against the threshold of the terrace doors. An older man lifted the brunette over his shoulder, and she laughed, kicking her stilettos back and forth.

The people nearby turned to make room for the commotion, gazing at them good-naturedly.

"These girls." Sylvia shook her head. "They've got everyone's attention now, but in ten years, they'll be married to some boring businessman and their modeling contracts will have dried up once they start popping out his offspring."

Shocked by Sylvia's acidic commentary, I bit my tongue and glanced sidelong at her. I wondered what she had been like a few decades ago.

"Do *you* want to be like them, Sarah?"

I balked. "Well, I couldn't. I'm way too short to be a model."

"*And* you have a brain," Sylvia added, with emphasis. "A really sharp one."

I smiled inwardly at the compliment.

"Listen, we all have our moment in the sun," Sylvia said. "It's what you do with that moment that counts."

In a reckless gesture, she flicked her joint and threw it over the balustrade. I watched as it glowed orange and disintegrated, disappearing into the air below.

"I mean it, Sarah." She turned to go. "Don't get too distracted by all the razzle-dazzle. You're far too good for all of that."

I nodded as Sylvia melted back into the crowd. After all, I was so accustomed to nodding at her orders. But as I looked out at the dark and shifting Mediterranean, her comment stayed with me, buried but not forgotten, anchoring me through the year that was to come.

9

AROUND FOUR IN the morning, I walked home from that party on the seventh floor of the Carlton. Xander and Hugo had stayed on, but Sylvia left to call her family in New York.

And me? I retired to the apartment I was sharing with six other twentysomethings at the far end of the Croisette. It was an arrangement I'd somehow discovered a few years ago, through a random contact. A three-bedroom apartment being shared by seven of us, with only one key to go around. We hid the key in the potted plant by the door. And even though there were only technically five sleeping spaces in the apartment, we somehow managed. Most of us hardly slept anyway, coming back at four or five in the morning after partying. There was one dour-faced, ponytailed male film student who arose early every day to brew coffee and attend the nine a.m. screenings, so there were only a brief few hours when we didn't have enough places to sleep.

Now, a decade later, I can't even remember the names of any of those people I shared the Cannes apartment with. Maybe they've since gone on to incredible careers, directing landmark films that won awards or screened on the Croisette. Maybe they've become respected film critics or festival programmers. But most likely, nothing ever came of their cinematic hopes. They strived for years, they offered up all their talent, their ideas, the core of their being, to an industry that didn't want or need them. And in the end, they faded away into nothing. Into normal, everyday people: copywriters, insurance brokers, account managers. Teachers.

But that possibility never crossed my mind that night, as I floated down the Croisette, beneath the Mediterranean night sky. I thought I was only on an upward trajectory from there on in. In two days there would be the second screening of our film, and that same day, the trade publications would announce the partnership between Firefly Films and Hugo North. It was the stuff filmmakers' dreams were made of.

I exulted, drunk and slightly stoned on my stroll back. I walked past the sparkling lights and the white million-dollar yachts, the sound of laughter and luxury from dealmakers and celebrities and all the accompanying riffraff who idolized them.

I walked past the end of the Croisette, where the outsize lights stopped, where the everyday, unspectacular residents of Cannes lived.

And I was only excited for the future.

I stop there now, because I see that expectant look in Thom Gallagher's eyes, like a puppy who's sniffed out a trail. With all this talk of Cannes, this reporter is too eager to hear a name he recognizes. A celebrity, the very currency the press trades in. The highly prized trump card I hold up my sleeve.

He didn't come here on a Saturday morning to learn about Sarah Lai's adventures in the world of film. He wanted to hear about Hugo North, but also, of course, about *her*. About Holly Randolph.

It has been years since she and I last acknowledged each other's existence. Even now, when I live my sad little life, shuttling back and forth from empty apartment to second-rate classroom, it does seem like a dream, a snatch of film reel, that I once lived that other life. That her name and number were programmed into my phone, along with Hugo North, along with Xander Schulz. Names which have since acquired such a glossy sheen, rising like stars into the night sky. While mine sank like a stone to the bottom of a forgotten pond. Does *anyone* recognize the name of Sarah Lai, other than sixty-odd college students who begrudgingly email me their middling attempts at screenwriting at 11:59 on a Sunday night?

If Holly's name emerges in this investigation, I know this story won't be going away. Her stardom will blow it wide open.

And I might be caught in the messy, inevitable fallout.

So I bide my time, pondering how I should play this next round.

I glance at my watch. It is early afternoon now, and my stomach growls, up on the twenty-fifth floor of the New York Times Building.

There is something about sitting in one room with one other person for a protracted period of time that makes it exceedingly intimate. Not quite erotic, but a certain level of communion that is a rare experience for me these days. When I have office hours with a student, I am in a room with them for twenty minutes, tops. Doctor and dentist visits run around the same length. And when I am catching up with a friend, there are other distractions: the meal we are eating, the flash of phone messages. Increasingly, the interruptions of their young children.

I am not accustomed to talking at length with one other person, in a guided, purposeful discussion like this. I find myself exposed, in a way I haven't allowed myself to be for years.

So I am on edge—and strangely pensive—when I stand up to stretch my legs. My eyes roam the cityscape beyond the window: the nameless lives scurrying about on the sidewalks below, the office workers in the finance building opposite, who are toiling in front of their computers on a Saturday afternoon. This is the city we all chose to live in, and this is the familiar refrain, echoed too many times in films and plays and books: the individual struggles we will never know about, the millions of existences churning through sorrow and joy and then fading into anonymity.

Still, the cliché has its impact even now, as I stand here in this fortress of the fourth estate, trying not to dwell on the situation I have voluntarily, foolishly entered into.

Behind me, I hear Thom's stomach rumble.

I turn back with a wry smile. "Hungry?"

He shrugs, almost sheepishly. "I'm starving."

"Me too."

We stand there, looking across at each other, and I wonder what the protocol is here. Is it too inappropriate to ask the journalist who's trying to unearth a hidden story from you if he wants to get a sandwich?

"Should we get some food?" Thom suggests.

I put out a hand. "Look, I don't want to keep you from your weekend plans. I've already been gabbing for a while."

"Sarah," he says, as if to correct me. "Not at all. I am really grateful for all you've told me so far . . ."

That well-practiced humility. I'm aware I haven't told him anything of real value so far. Just indulged my narcissistic need to tell my own story.

". . . and I—If you don't mind me saying, I think we're just getting started. I believe there's a lot more you could tell me. That maybe you *want* to tell me."

I look away and grimace.

Thom grins. "Well, this isn't an inquisition. I'm not gonna deprive you of food or sleep."

That you have done already, I think to myself. The past few nights, waking up suddenly, my stomach laced with cold from the anxiety.

"So how 'bout this? Let's run down, get some sandwiches, and bring them up here. There's a great deli around the corner. Obviously, the *Times* is paying."

I look down at the Dictaphone, now bereft of its red light. I won't say no to a free lunch, of course.

"I promise you I won't ask any questions about the investigation once we leave this room. Think of it as recess."

10

I LIKE EATING REUBENS, because they are so completely alien from anything my parents or grandparents would ever eat. In fact, I'm not sure how my mom even learned what a Reuben was, but one time when I was a kid, we were walking past a Jewish deli in Midtown—on one of those rare occasions when we'd ventured out of Queens—and my mom stopped and explained the Reuben.

There was an old white couple in a booth, hunched over their meals. I was hungry, and I dreaded my mom would make me wait till we got back to Flushing to eat.

"See that?" My mom pointed through the window at the white-haired man, his mouth wide open as he bit into his sandwich. "That's a Reuben. It was invented in New York."

Pastrami, melted Swiss cheese, Russian dressing, and sauerkraut on rye bread. Served with a pickle on the side.

They were all such exotic ingredients, so different from the rice and noodles and MSG-sprinkled stir-fry that I ate day in and day out. I didn't even know what Russian dressing tasted like. My parents hated cheese.

"Sauerkraut in a sandwich?" I asked. "Ick."

My face must have looked aghast, because at that moment, the man glanced up and saw me gawking at his food. He frowned and turned away. My mom burst into laughter.

My cheeks burned with embarrassment, but the old lady in the couple waved at me, which only made it worse. She motioned with her fingers, urging me to smile. My eyes only filled with tears. (I was a very shy kid.)

It's very good, she mouthed exaggeratedly, pointing at her husband's sandwich.

I tugged at my mom's hand, pulling her away from the deli window. Hoping I could sink into the ground, the dirtied sidewalk swallowing me up.

I didn't have a Reuben on that day, and for years I avoided them, reminded of my childhood humiliation. But as I grew older, I realized there was nothing hugely embarrassing about that moment. I just wasn't used to being around old white people. Or being caught as the person looking in.

And then, when I finally tasted a Reuben, I discovered what I'd been missing out on all those years. Maybe venturing into white culture was nothing to be scared of.

"I'll have a Reuben," I say now, leaning over the counter at Sam's Bagels & Deli on Forty-First Street. "And a . . ." My eyes frantically scan the board above and its intimidating selection of smoothies, every imaginable iteration of fruit and veggies blended together. "And an egg cream." Another one of those native New York concoctions that seemed so foreign to me in my childhood. Last time I'd had one was years ago.

"Nice choice," Thom says approvingly. "The avocado turkey for me, Mitch. And uh, is there that nice gluten-free bread you had earlier this week?"

"For you, Thom, anything." Mitch behind the counter spreads his hands out, exposing his white-aproned girth.

"Awesome." Thom nods for me to take a seat and wait.

Thom Gallagher eats a gluten-free diet, I register, and immediately file that away into my mental dossier of useless bits of knowledge.

"Avoiding wheat, huh?" I ask. Might as well aim small for small talk.

"Ah, it's this thing I'm trying. My mom suggested it to me." His mom, Petra Gallagher, whom I first heard about when she appeared on the cover of *Parade* magazine fifteen years ago. *Meet Petra: The New Matron of the Gallagher Clan. Classy, Sexy, Clever All in One.*

His mom had started modeling while a college student at Brown, then interned on Capitol Hill, where she met then-Senate-staffer Stephen Gallagher. The rest is history.

I don't need to ask Thom about his family background. We somehow all know it.

Then I ask another question, a riskier one, but I can't resist. "Does it ever get, um, stressful . . . all this work? Calling strangers up and trying to dig up their stories about some pretty personal stuff?"

Thom looks taken aback, surprised I asked that. Then the charming, self-deprecating grin breaks out. "Well, it's my job."

"Yes, I know it's your job." I gesture to a copy of the *Times* lying on the counter behind us. "But does it ever get stressful? I mean, how can it not? You're asking people to expose some really painful memories."

He nods. "Yeah, I know. It's . . . it's not easy."

"It's not easy for them to reveal these stories, but is it easy for *you* to listen to?"

"Oh god, no. I've had to hear—just, awful stories of manipulation, trauma. And yeah, people have cried on me in the middle of interviews."

"And how does that feel? That you made people cry?"

"Well, *I* didn't make them cry." A guarded note has crept into his voice. "It's the *memory* of the abuse that makes them cry. Or really, the abuser who originally made them cry."

Oh, Thom, you take such pride in your work. As I once did.

"Sure, but they wouldn't be crying in that interview if you hadn't asked them those questions."

He turns almost defensive. "You mean, do I think I'm re-traumatizing women by asking them to share these stories?"

I feign nonchalance. "I guess that's what I'm asking. Yeah."

He glances behind the counter at Mitch, who is still waiting for the cheese on my Reuben to melt. Thom Gallagher probably wishes Mitch could prepare our sandwiches a little faster.

"I think the trauma is there, no matter what. I think sometimes it helps women to be able to share their story, to be listened to. And if I can be of assistance in that way, then I'm happy to."

He scrutinizes me now, blue eyes unwavering. "I also think that kind of abuse of power needs to be called out. And some-times, trying to expose a certain injustice may require some tears and pain . . . speaking some difficult truths."

These words are measured, and he continues studying me. I eventually wrest my eyes elsewhere, unsettled. I wonder who else he's interviewing for this investigation, but I keep my face neutral. "Well said." I nod.

Damn, you're good, I think. *You really should follow your dad and run for public office.*

We are both still absorbing that moment, when two women in the deli come up to us. Or rather, to Thom.

"Sorry," one of them says. She has brown, curly hair pinned up in a cloud around her head, a hand holding a coffee cup peeks out from her merino wool poncho. "I hate to interrupt, but—aren't you Thom Gallagher?"

Her friend angles in, and they both have that adoring look in their eyes, when normal people approach celebrities in public.

"Uh, yeah. Yes, that's me." He assumes his usual humility.

Their starstruck gaze amps up a notch.

"Oh, we thought it might be you, what with the New York Times Building being right there."

"Wow, I mean, I just wanted to say thank you *so much* for the work you are doing." The woman reaches out her free hand and rests it on Thom's elbow. I notice he flinches ever so slightly. I don't think she notices.

"It is *so* important," the second woman chimes in.

"Honestly, like, every time one of your articles comes out, I know it will shed some light on another horror out there."

"And someone needs to speak up for these women! I am *so glad* you're the one doing it."

These women, I think. I sit there on the sidelines, watching the two of them gush. *Someone needs to speak up for these women?*

Thom puts his hands up, self-deprecating. "Listen, I'm just— I'm listening to the stories that need to be told. And helping to tell them."

"Well, you keep doing it. Because it's about time people start to call out the behavior of all those men."

"Disgusting, truly disgusting." The other woman is shaking her head.

"There are plenty more stories to tell," he says. And his eyes shift ever so slightly towards me.

"Oh, I bet," the first woman says. "I bet there's plenty more stories. And not just about Bill Cosby and what's his name— Weinstein—I'm sure so many other men, too."

"Heh heh, we're just getting started, right?" the other woman cackles, and slaps her friend on the shoulder.

Don't ask for a selfie, don't ask for a selfie, don't ask for a selfie, I telepathically chant to them.

"Listen, I don't want to keep you." The woman glances quickly at me, nods. "I know you're a busy reporter, so yeah, we just wanted to say: keep doing what you're doing, Thom Gallagher. We're cheering you on."

"Well, thank you, thank you. That means a lot to me." He clasps his hand to his chest in a show of gratitude, and nods good-bye.

The women beam and smile as they head out the door.

After they leave, there's a lull in the deli.

Mitch calls out from behind the counter, "Thom, look at you. Always attracting your fans. I want a photo of you on my wall one of these days."

He points to the obligatory collage of pictures showcasing the celebrities who have visited his deli over the years: Bill Clinton, Liza Minelli, Michael Bloomberg, Shakira.

"One of these days," Thom shouts back. "Speaking of, where's our sandwiches?"

"Right here, all wrapped up and ready to go. Waiting for Your Highness."

Mitch flourishes his thick hands in courtly deference, and Thom laughs. "Just hand them over."

On the way out of the deli, Thom turns to me. "Sorry about that."

"Don't worry," I say. "I was once pretty used to that, being around famous people."

We are at the corner waiting for the light to turn, edging forward the way New Yorkers do, impatient to cross the street before the next wave of traffic.

"I can imagine." He shoots me a conspiratorial look. "You'll have to tell me more."

Interview Transcript (excerpt):
Meeting with Sylvia Zimmerman, Private Residence,
Upper East Side, Sunday, Oct. 29, 2:07 p.m.

SZ: I understand how important your investigation is, Thom, but I'm not sure why you want to talk to me. Nothing happened on any of our film sets.

TG: I just wanted to get a sense of what the situation was like back in 2006. You do know whom I'm referring to, I imagine?

SZ: Well, yeah. I'm gonna guess one character in particular.

TG: Would you care to name that character? This is all entirely confidential, as you know.

SZ: I would imagine it's Hugo North you're inquiring about.

TG: And what led you to think it's him?

SZ: (scoffs) It would be fairly obvious. He's that kind of guy.

TG: Care to elaborate?

AM: Larger than life. Enjoyed his luxuries. Used to having things his way . . . You know the type. Don't say you haven't encountered people like him before, in your family's circles, Thom. We all have. Doesn't have to work for anything. Doors just open magically for him.

TG: How would you say he entered the film industry?

SZ: That way. Doors opening magically for him. Listen, I . . . I have no part in what he later did. I may have unwittingly played a part in him gaining a foothold in film, but . . . we can talk about that in a bit.

TG: Okay. What was your first impression of Hugo North, when you first met him?

SZ: I guess he seemed to be a man who could make things happen for us. It's funny, because I always used to say, a producer is someone who makes things happen. But the only thing that really makes things happen in this world is money.

TG: Is that the only thing?

SZ: I suppose there are other things. Drive. Family connections. Talent. "Passion," as they often say in this business.

TG: You sound cynical.

SZ: Of course I'm cynical. Thom, I worked for over twenty years in film. After that, who wouldn't be?

11

BACK UP ON the twenty-fifth floor, recess over, Thom and I attempt to resume the same decorum we had before. But there has been an indefinable shift after the deli downstairs.

"I'm just helping these women tell their stories," I mimic Thom, a mocking note in my voice. "Really? Do you think we need help?" There is a unique thrill, being this brash with him.

Thom lifts his hands up, innocent. "I get approached like that all the time. I'm not asking for the attention myself."

Yes you are, I think.

"It's just a fortunate by-product of the work you do," I quip, my sarcasm evident.

Thom attempts to laugh it off, with his megawatt smile. I can't help but laugh a bit too.

"So after that Cannes in . . . 2006." He checks his notes, trying to regain control. "What was it like, starting to work with Hugo North? What were your first impressions of him?"

"It was like Hugo North was from another planet. I mean, he was a British billionaire, that was the single identifying fact I knew about him. How many British billionaires had I encountered before in my life? I'm from Flushing."

At this, Thom chuckles out loud. There is a slight influx of endorphins when I see him laugh at my deadpan delivery. My cheeks start to flush, and I recognize this as a warning sign.

(*Don't even think that*, I warn myself. *Not this golden boy.*)

Hugo North was rich, and maybe he was famous in some circles, but not to me. An internet search uncovered his estimated net worth and photos of him and his socialite wife at various high-profile British weddings and gatherings. Then again, I didn't really know who was a big deal in the UK—apart from the royals, David Beckham, and the occasional film or music star who'd successfully crossed the Atlantic.

"Do you think that lack of knowledge about him somehow created a smoke screen for him? Because no one really knew what he'd been up to in other industries?"

Quite possibly, yes. Then again, that's how this industry works, right? Create an air of mystique around yourself, demonstrate your fabulous wealth, and suddenly everyone wants to work with you.

So Hugo knew what he was up to. And it unfolded in textbook fashion.

First, there was the buzz of the trade publications, right after Xander's film had premiered at Cannes. I have to admit it was exhilarating and surreal, seeing those articles in *Variety* and *Screen Daily*.

North to Buy Half of Firefly Films
Schulz Shingle in Deal with Brit Financier

Sure, Hugo featured in both headlines, with Sylvia nowhere to be seen, but that was understandable. If he came with the money, he'd get the fame. Sylvia and I were named later in the article.

North will join Sylvia Zimmerman in producing future work by Schulz, along with a growing roster of directorial talent. Sarah Lai will serve as head of development.

That last sentence I wanted to highlight, magnify, and frame for my parents. See, Mom and Dad? I made it. Head of Development. We made a film that played in the Cannes Film Festival! I got mentioned in an article in *Variety*! That career in film wasn't as foolish as you'd predicted!

My parents were indeed impressed. I snagged multiple copies of the trades from the Soho House tent and brought them home to Flushing. We had a family celebration with their special version of Peking duck and a new bottle of Courvoisier (which only my dad and I sipped from; my mom rarely drank, and my sister was now in her second trimester).

"So what does this mean?" Karen asked, perusing the *Variety* write-up. She kept stroking her rounded belly with her hand, a gesture that seemed so foreign to me.

"It means we're going places." I grinned. I wanted to add: *It means you guys can stop worrying about me.*

Ah, the foolishness of youth.

I know my dad saved the article, because a year and a half ago, when I went into his office to find one of his medicine prescriptions, I saw it tucked under the clear Perspex sheet that covered his desk surface. It wasn't hidden, but old coffee rings cast circles onto the text of the article. Spying it, being reminded of his unspoken fatherly pride, something in me twisted with regret. For the career I could have had. Or at least the career promised in that article. And for how mistaken I had been, thinking I could be part of that world.

Those same articles also mentioned Xander's next film, which was the main benefit of that publicity. *Schulz is finalizing development on his next feature film, and casting will begin shortly.*

And with that single printed sentence, our phone lines and in-boxes became flooded the very day the articles appeared. It was our next-to-last day at Cannes, and as I glanced at my BlackBerry, I was already getting requests to set up last-minute meetings.

Saw the great article in Variety! Would love to know more about your next project. Any chance you're still in Cannes to meet up for a chat?

When I returned to our New York office two days later, our voice mail was jammed with messages from casting directors, agents, and yes, the occasional foolhardy actor. (To any aspiring actors out there: Do NOT leave voice mail messages at production company offices. No one will even look at your headshot if you don't come through an agent.)

Distributors and sales agents were in touch, too—a sign that the tide was turning. Instead of us chasing them, trying to get them interested in *our* film (with *A Hard Cold Blue*, I had spent months crafting polite emails about Xander's promising credentials and "how excited" we were about completing the film)—now they were starting to take notice of us. And why? Because Xander's film had played at Cannes. Because we had publicity. Because we now had financial backing.

So talent, fame, and money. The holy trinity of this godforsaken industry. We're led to think that the last two don't happen without the first. But that's hardly the case.

Once we got over the initial flush of Cannes and the press attention, there were the usual boring logistical things to sort through. Hugo wanted to wire over the money, but his lawyers and our lawyers had to draw up the contracts. There were endless reams of paper being printed and initialed, signed and faxed back and forth. (Yes, this was back in the days of fax machines.)

I had to peruse the contract. For what, I don't know. But Sylvia couldn't be bothered to study legal documents, Xander even less so. So that dull legal grunt work fell to me, a twenty-seven-year-old with no one else looking over my shoulder. Nonetheless, I was meticulous. But it occurs to me now that if I was even half as meticulous or diligent, no one would have cared at the time.

As for me, I noticed my name was in the contracts, my position as head of development solidified on paper, and I was pleased with that. How slavish we are to our own fleeting sense of ego.

Our company also changed names. We went from Firefly Films (Sylvia's company name, ever since the early-'90s) to Conquest Films, which Hugo had decreed. Almost too obvious a name to even be ironic. Until then, our business cards had been graced by a whimsical, hand-drawn yellow firefly on a cream background. But now Hugo had a designer conjure a new logo for Conquest Films: gold against black. Tall, serifed letters that echoed a city skyline and recalled the gaunt, imposing typography of the 1920s. Yes, it conveyed class and sophistication and a refined, old-fashioned sense of power. Just like Hugo.

"And how did you feel about all these changes?" Thom asks.

Excited, obviously. Everything was a step up, and for five years, I'd been toiling away at the bottom of this pyramid, unacknowledged. So finally, I felt we were getting the recognition—and the transformation—we deserved.

Our company went through a total rebrand, with new stationery, new business cards, new email addresses, and a new website within weeks. All of them brandishing the new logo. Of course, I was the one tasked with implementing all this, liaising with printers, the website designer, ensuring invoices were paid, our new shiny identity announced to every industry contact.

All the quotidian operational activity that thrums behind running a business was left to me. Meanwhile Xander and Sylvia charged ahead with the final stages of development for *Furious Her*. Andrea was ecstatic over the buzz from Cannes, and like any top agency, the well-oiled machine of TMC clicked into gear. Phone conversations and emails led to meetings with a growing list of sales agents and distributors who had frequented our wish list for years. Xander's and Sylvia's diaries filled with appointments up and down the length of Manhattan. They flew out to LA once. They flew out to LA a second time.

"And Hugo North? Where was he this whole time?"

Hugo was busy relocating from the UK, but he would dip in for a day or two, before settling in New York for the summer. So for a while, Hugo remained this enigmatic celebrity in his own right, who might grace us with his presence whenever he deigned to cross the Atlantic and visit the teeming isle of Manhattan.

I didn't interact with him a great deal during this time. After all,

I was merely an employee of Conquest Films, not a stakeholder, so I wasn't deemed important enough to be in the early meetings. But there was one afternoon when Hugo sat in our office, discussing LA publicists with Sylvia and Xander—and he turned to me.

"And how about you, Sarah?"

"What about me, Hugo?" I joked back, my tone lightly sarcastic.

"Where do you fit into all of this? Or actually, wait a minute—" He checked his watch. "Fancy a drink right now? I'm meeting a friend at six, but I've got time to kill before then. I feel like you're always in the background, keeping things steady, but I'd love to know what you really think of us nutcases."

"A drink now?" I repeated. It was almost five o'clock; Sylvia preferred me to stay at the office until six. There was a certain frisson to it, a feeling of cutting school early. Plus, I'd never had a drink one-on-one before with a billionaire.

"Do you mind?" Hugo looked over at Sylvia. "Sarah's been working hard all day. Mind if I steal her from the office a little early for a quick cocktail?"

Sylvia peered at us, somewhat surprised. "I suppose I see no harm in that. Sarah, do you have anything else you need to take care of today?"

I shrugged. "Just a few emails that I can do tomorrow morning."

"Fine then, off you go for your cocktails." She raised a quizzical eyebrow at us. "But don't go making a habit of this, Hugo."

12

TWENTY MINUTES LATER, I sat across from Hugo North in a swish bar I'd often passed but never before entered. I'd assumed the menu was above my financial comfort zone, and I was right. But that afternoon, I sank into the soft velvet of a high-backed armchair and swilled a twenty-dollar martini (a drink I rarely ordered and figured I should when I didn't have to pay). I tried to hide my excitement and curiosity behind a pleasant professional demeanor. Hugo North was just another person, I reminded myself, albeit a billionaire.

Hugo smiled at me amiably. "So tell me, Sarah, how did you end up working with Sylvia and Xander?"

It's funny how people always say they "worked with" someone, not "worked for." Even though everyone knows who's calling the shots, and who's running around following orders.

"It just happened," I said, attempting a casual tone. "I saw an advertisement at Columbia that they were looking for an intern, and I got in touch. Guess I was lucky."

"I'm sure it was more than luck. You must have been very clever," he said. "There would be many young college kids out there desperate to work with those two."

In my mind I pictured that paper bulletin from years ago, folded into quarters and tucked away safely in my backpack, for no one else to see.

Hugo continued. "Well, I always make it a point to know who

I'm working with, especially the most valuable players in a company. And you certainly are that. I have a feeling you're the rock in the office, the one Sylvia and Xander always rely on."

I felt buoyed by the recognition: to actually be referred to as a "player," my role in the company hailed for once.

A bottle of Möet sat chilling in a coppered bucket of ice. He poured himself another glass from it.

"So, Sarah," Hugo continued. "You've been a loyal colleague to Sylvia and Xander for five years now. You clearly know how films are made. And you understand how the industry ticks."

I nodded and sipped at my martini, eager to hear more.

"In my line of work," Hugo pressed on, "I'm very used to acquiring businesses, finding their strengths. And there's nothing quite like young talent. So full of hope, so willing to work hard. Nurture it, and a company can really soar. Tamp it down, and the company suffers too."

He leaned forward now, his hands on his knees, and his green eyes sought mine. "Tell me, Sarah, with all your know-how, all your passion for films, what is it you *really* want to achieve?"

I was taken aback by his candid questioning. To be asked that blatantly about my heart's desire. Usually in this industry, I felt I should be masking my own professional ambitions behind a facade of teamwork. I hesitated.

"Come on, Sarah," Hugo said. "I'm not going to judge. I like to see ambition, and I like people to dream big. There's no point in hiding your goals when I'm only here to help you."

I wasn't sure how much to reveal, but it was refreshing to be given a chance like this, to be heard on my own terms by a superior.

"Well, I—I've enjoyed working closely with Sylvia, and being involved in producing," I began. "So I'd like to produce films of my own one day." I didn't say more, but the burden of always obeying Sylvia's commands was starting to weigh heavily on me. Maybe Hugo sensed that.

He smiled knowingly, regarding me with his thick-lashed eyes. "It must be a thrilling prospect, to see a film slowly come together. So you want to produce your own projects. To stop playing second fiddle. Well, I'm sure you'd be great at it."

"Really?" I asked. There had been an offhand, throwaway tone to his compliment.

Hugo seemed surprised to be challenged. His eyes gleamed with an unexpected delight. I wondered if I should push on, but I wanted him to know I wasn't a simple lackey.

"Well," I continued in a lighthearted tone. "You hardly know me. I mean, that all sounds very nice but . . . what evidence do you have that I'd make a good producer?"

Hugo squinted his eyes at me, then chuckled. "My, you are sharp, aren't you?"

He bent down and tapped my wrist. "First of all, this. Your willingness to call me out on what could be perceived as just a bullshit comment. You've been learning from Sylvia, I can see."

I nodded but privately grumbled. Sylvia again.

"Aside from the fact you're smart and you work hard—which are both plainly evident. And that you know what makes a good film . . . It's the fact that you aren't fooled by the exteriors. That's not why you're in this industry."

Pleased, I reclined back, cupping my martini glass. "What do you mean by that?"

"Believe me, so many hopeful young women, they're just in this because they want to be a star—or get as close to one as possible. Or even fuck one, pardon my language. But you're not interested in that, I can tell. You're in this for the films. Your love of movies. And that's why you'll make a great producer one day."

"You think?" I asked.

"No doubt about it. And I can help you get there, if that's what you really want."

His words hovered in the air, tempting, but still I hesitated.

"You tell me, how much does it cost to run the production company each month?"

I thought for a second, recalling the company accounts, then embellishing a bit. "Well, in its previous form, before you came on board, about fifteen thousand a month."

"That's what—under 200k a year?" Hugo raised his eyebrows, unperturbed. "That's a drop in the bucket for me. Not to be arrogant, but . . . I know my portfolio. I don't need to think twice about funding a venture like that. Especially if there's someone talented like you driving it. You want your own production company in the future? I can get you that."

I squinted at him, my heart beating a bit faster. "My own production company?"

"Come on, Sarah." Hugo smirked. "It's all very well to talk about 'the company,' but companies are made up of hard-working individuals. You put in your dues; you deserve to be rewarded. Someone as driven as you, I imagine you'd want to be your own boss someday."

"Well, sure," I said, thrown off by how openly Hugo was speaking. "But . . ."

I trailed off. There had to be a *but*.

"But what?" Hugo asked. "There's no *but*. It's a simple fact. When the time is right, when you really deserve it, I can get you your own production company. Just keep that in mind."

"I will." I raised my glass at him. An image flashed through my mind: me behind a desk, with my own assistant, reading my own pick of screenplays. No longer having to answer to Sylvia. I hadn't thought such freedom was possible, but now perhaps it could be. "Thanks."

"And you know what?" Hugo leaned in. "The beauty is that once you're in charge, once you reach a certain level, you can get other people to do your grunt work. No more scurrying around."

The thought appealed to me. I bit into the gin-soaked olive, and the last of the martini slid down my throat, cold and intoxicating. Its bitter taste masked the strength of the alcohol.

"Are you fucking joking?" Hugo said sharply into his phone, twenty minutes later.

I had helped him finish the bottle of Möet by now, and somewhat buzzed, I observed Hugo with a hazy detachment. Mild shock registered at his sudden switch in tone. I wondered who was the unlucky party on the other end of the line.

"I told you that already . . . no . . . it's not an option." Hugo's nostrils flared, his dark eyebrows hunched low. "Oh for fuck's sake, don't be a fool! Just sort it and don't call back again. I'm in the middle of something."

He hung up and slipped his BlackBerry into his inside jacket pocket.

"Sorry about that." He rolled his eyes. "When you work with idiots who won't listen . . . I'm sure I don't have to worry about that with you."

I swallowed, and silently hoped not.

"So," Hugo pivoted warmly. "Sylvia tells me your family is in the restaurant business. And you've already quite a lot of experience in that sector, at your young age."

Under the influence of the champagne, my usual embarrassment over the family business faded quickly. "Well, yeah, my family's been running a restaurant in Queens for nearly twenty years."

"That's an impressive track record. These days, there's so much turnover in that part of the hospitality sector. Cruel world out there. Do you know the chef Manson Wang? We've collaborated with him on some of my properties, especially our hotel in Hong Kong. Brilliant guy."

Manson Wang was a puffy-cheeked celebrity chef, often seen in cheesy photo ops with Hollywood stars. He'd gained his fame by gentrifying traditional Szechuan cuisine for Westerners, who happily paid a ridiculous price to eat "authentic" Chinese food in the comfort of their five-star hotel. Obviously, I knew of him.

"No, I haven't had a chance to meet Manson himself," I said nonchalantly, suppressing a giggle. It was ridiculous to even think that my family with our scrappy little dim sum outfit in Queens could circulate in the same orbit as Manson Wang. I added: "Though I think my uncle may have worked with him at one point."

A lie, but an inspired one.

"Ah, well, I must introduce you if I get a chance."

I wanted to laugh out loud. Then I realized, hey, if Hugo really meant it, and I got the chance to meet Manson, how impressed my parents would be.

Some stupid photo of me and Manson Wang, snapped during a passing five-minute meeting—that would surely resonate with them. And if I told them that I'd had a twenty-dollar martini with a British billionaire this evening—that, too, wouldn't fail to excite them. But for some reason, even after half a decade at Firefly, even after a premiere in Cannes, my parents were still skeptical that I belonged in the world of movies.

I looked up at Hugo, and a mischievous impulse ran through me. "Manson Wang, what's he really like?"

Hugo snorted. "Between you and me, he's a bit of a twat. But he sure as hell cooks a mean mapo tofu."

I cackled with delight. Hugo North knew what mapo tofu was. This guy was all right.

"Well," I said. "I'll have to try that someday."

Hugo smiled back. "I'll make sure you do."

With the new changes to the company, I thankfully got a slight raise. But I was most excited about hiring a full-time paid office assistant—someone more permanent I could delegate to, not this rotating door of college interns who stayed just long enough to list a production company internship on their résumé. More than anything, hiring another staff member promised an easing of my workload, a rise in status, even some camaraderie. A little less scurrying around. True to my roots, I advertised at Columbia, employing the same clichéd phrases we always see: hard worker, a fast learner, a self-starter. A love of cinema. I was hoping for someone bright and versatile, with a measure of real-world savviness. Someone, perhaps, not unlike me from five years ago.

But Sylvia and Hugo all had their own suggestions: nieces and nephews who wanted to work in film, children of various friends of theirs. They sent me a slew of résumés, and I leafed through them, unimpressed by the incorrect punctuation, the no-name colleges, the seasonal sales assistant work at Gap or their parents' offices.

"Do I have to interview *all* these people?" I asked Sylvia one day. "I have a lot on my plate, and we're only looking to fill one position."

"Well, at least humor Hugo," Sylvia said to me. "There's this one girl he really wanted us to consider. A family friend of his. Chelsea something or other."

Grumbling internally, I emailed twenty-two-year-old Chelsea Van Der Kraft and asked her to come in for a chat. When she arrived, she was a lithe blonde, with honey-colored hair that cascaded around her dewy face, her long, bronzed legs stretching out from under a summery dress.

Really? I thought. I gestured for her to sit.

She was pleasant enough to talk to, graced with the conversational ease that most affluent kids possessed, having grown up attending their parents' social functions. But beyond the small talk, I had trouble grasping what this girl could bring to the company.

"So what makes you so interested to work in film?" I asked her.

"Oh, I just think it could be really cool," she said, her blue eyes looking at me brightly.

I waited for her to say more, but no additional words came.

"Okay, well . . . it *is* really interesting," I continued. "So, um, what is your favorite film?"

She thought for a while about this. I was patient. Then she said: "Maybe, *Love, Actually*?"

I stared at her for a brief second, trying to mask my disbelief. *Let me guess, you watch it with your family every Christmas.*

Who am I to judge anyone on their taste in film, but inevitably

I do. Of course, there aren't really any right answers to the question "What is your favorite film?" However, I can tell you, when you're interviewing to work at a film production company, *Love, Actually* is probably a misguided choice.

Still, I gave her a chance to redeem herself.

"Believe it or not, I cried watching that one," I said. "The Emma Thompson scene, when she realizes her husband bought that necklace for his secretary . . ." That was true enough. I am a softie at heart, and often weep at the most ridiculous films. "What about it do you love so much?"

At this point, I was hoping (for her own sake) that she might say something vaguely insightful about casting, or intertwining storylines, or the culmination of the romantic comedy genre. But Chelsea Van Der Kraft just simpered and said: "It really makes me laugh. And I watch it every Christmas with my family, so it's a special film for me."

I forced a polite, close-lipped smile. I stared at her halo of golden hair.

Fuck this, I thought. *This girl doesn't have an original thought in her brain.*

I wanted to shout at her. *That's the best you can do? Love, Actually because I watch it every Christmas with my family? There is a metaphorical line a mile long of people begging for a full-time assistant position at a burgeoning production company, and I have to spend twenty minutes of my time talking to you?*

Instead, I asked Chelsea a few more bland questions, promptly forgetting her answers, and then thanked her for coming in.

"When do you think I'll hear about the position?" she asked innocently, as we both stood up from our seats.

"Um," I said. "We're still interviewing a few other people, so I . . . it'll be another week or so."

"Oh, okay," she said. "Because I have to start looking for a place here in the city."

I tried to hide my look of alarm and told her to maybe wait until I got back to her.

"Oh it's fine," Chelsea explained. "My parents were looking to buy another place here anyway, so now I can help them choose it. I've always wanted an apartment in Chelsea . . . same name as me." She giggled.

"Ah, of course . . ."

At that moment, Sylvia and Xander came in the door, fresh from a meeting, and I used this as an excuse to usher out Chelsea Van Der Kraft.

Upon my return, Xander raised his eyebrows at me.

"Who was that?" he asked.

"Some girl, Chelsea what's her name, who wanted the position. Totally inappropriate." I sat back down at my desk. "Dumb as rocks."

"Hire her." Xander shrugged. "She's hot."

"What?" I glared at him. "No way."

"I can think of quite a few positions to put her in." A leer spread over his face. "Body like that."

"Honestly, Xander." Sylvia smirked. "You're impossible."

He cackled. "I know, but you still love me."

Sylvia shook her head good-naturedly. Which was pretty much the same as saying yes.

This whole repartee assumed the standard joking tone of our back-and-forth with Xander, whenever he decided to exercise his inner pervert. We took it on the chin, as we were meant to, as women working in the industry. To call it out, to raise any disapproval might get you thrown out of the club.

"I have her phone number if you want it, Xander." I maintained my edge of dry sarcasm.

"Nah, my girlfriend would kill me." And this he meant seriously. For four months now, Xander had been dating Greta, an exotic new Calvin Klein model, half-Norwegian, half-Mexican. It was the longest relationship he'd had for a while.

Still, he kept at it. "I wouldn't mind seeing her around the office. Might actually make me show up here every day."

"Xander, we're weeks away from pre-production," Sylvia sniped. "If a hot young woman is the only reason you'd come to the office, find yourself another producer."

"Listen, I don't care what she looks like," I announced. "I'm the one who's going to have to manage her, and she's too dumb."

"I like 'em dumb," Xander said. "Takes the edge off having to work with you two."

"Her favorite film is *Love, Actually*," I added.

"Oh no, fuck that." He scowled. "She's out."

We all shared in a mutual laugh, and I thought the subject closed. But then Sylvia glanced over her glasses at me (she did this when she wanted to be taken seriously, as the oldest person in the room).

"Why'd you even interview her in the first place?"

"Oh, that's the girl Hugo suggested," I explained.

"I hope there's more where she came from." Xander grinned.

If only we knew then. Working with Hugo meant a veritable onslaught of slim, pretty, and often quite moronic twentysomething girls whom he was always sending over for internships or job openings. It became a running joke among the three of us. There were the people we were meant to genuinely consider. And then there were Hugo's Girls. And undoubtedly, it always fell to me to handle them, even if I had more important matters at hand. Humoring Hugo became the understood rule of my job, even if it was never spelled out.

But about those girls—of which Chelsea Van Der Kraft was the first—I admit I probably judged them more harshly than they deserved. Because they were beautiful and often wealthy and seemed to move with the sort of ease and immunity that pretty white girls seem blessed with. As if all the world—or the male world, at least—would surely orient itself to gaze at them, grant them a measure of attention that would never be mine, no matter how glamorous or slender or well-dressed I made myself out to be. Because by then, I was already riddled with too many resentments, too sharp a sense of my own inadequacy, even before I acquired the bitterness of my more recent years.

So maybe Chelsea Van Der Kraft wasn't actually dumb as rocks, but I never gave her the chance.

Maybe she was smarter than she projected herself to be. Or had some original ideas. But she was never expected to have them, and therefore I assumed she didn't.

So I apologize, Chelsea Van Der Kraft, for judging you. But then again, that's what we all do in the film industry. It's second nature to us.

13

I N THE END, we hired Ziggy Constantine, the twenty-two-year-old son of Sylvia's cousin, who also happened to be appropriately smart, witty, and energetic. Sylvia was pleased, I was pleased, and Xander didn't seem to mind, so long as there was another body in the office to fetch his coffees and shower him with compliments.

By then, the New York summer had started in all its glorious messiness, the teeming of a thousand fetid parties and arguments and muggings on this concrete grid of streets. It was my twenty-sixth summer in New York City. (I'd only ever spent one summer outside of it, living in Seattle with my aunt and uncle, who also ran a Chinese restaurant.) But this year, I hardly had a chance to enjoy New York's balmiest season. In the evenings, while my friends were drinking homemade kombucha cocktails on Brooklyn rooftops or picnicking under the green canopy of trees in Central Park, I was stuck in our office.

We were trying to finalize financing for *Furious Her*, plan distribution on *A Hard Cold Blue*, and at the same time, establish a working rhythm with Hugo. One pervasive fear—even though we never voiced it—was if we didn't make the most of this new status, get Xander's first film into theaters and his second film shooting this year . . . then surely the past five years would go down the drain. Xander was aware of this, and after Cannes, he became snappy and dismissive—as if he'd already ascended to the director's chair on a prestigious Hollywood picture, barking orders from on high. But this, I tried to ignore.

Sylvia, too, grew more demanding—but also more generous towards me, ordering lunches in for all of us, even gifting me with a new BlackBerry and a new fan (when my air-conditioning at home impulsively broke down). As if she knew instinctively that good conditions made for more productive workers.

And I had plenty to do, because a producer's job is endless: a constant stream of phone calls, emails, meetings. Producers are always thinking ahead to the next stage, continually paving the path for their film to secure a sales agent, a distributor in each territory, a film festival slot, then to get publicity, audience interest, to open with a bang.

We had already trod this tortured path with *A Hard Cold Blue*, but that was a small indie film, budget less than $3 million, with actors who weren't household names. To keep our budget down, Sylvia had waived half her producer fee—as well as half of my own associate producer fee (not that I was ever asked if this was okay). This wasn't a problem for Sylvia: her husband was CFO of a blue-chip company. But the fee I'd lost could have paid my rent for an entire year. Nevertheless, we saw this as a necessary sacrifice to make the production of the film achievable.

Xander, of course, was paid his full fee as writer and director of *A Hard Cold Blue*.

With *Furious Her*, it was a whole new ball game. Xander was now a hot director to work with, Conquest Films was seen as a promising new production company, and we had money. We scaled up our budget to $15 million: still peanuts for any Hollywood studio, but enough to help us secure bigger action scenes (possibly a small explosion or car crash), high-quality CGI, a recognizable director of photography, and some A-list actors. Because actors, remember, are the key to attracting your audiences.

Fans may rush in droves to see a particular star in a role she was "born to play," but at the casting stage, it's not too different from a Chinese restaurant menu for Westerners. Pick one actor from List A. And one actress from List B. List A is more expensive, but that star will hopefully bring in more financing, more publicity, more audiences. So it's a calculated gamble.

Perhaps that gamble is what drew Hugo to the business of filmmaking: the risk and the reward. For him, it wasn't art, and it wasn't a childhood passion. He understood the *business* of making movies was basically a process of assembling a product from a catalog of proven favorites, covering it with a sheen of popular taste, and finding the money to create it. Then marketing and promoting it until the public thought it was the best thing since fortune cookies. But he could afford to be that blasé about film. If it didn't work out, he had a $2.5 billion portfolio to fall back on. The rest of us didn't have that luxury.

Interview Transcript (continued):
Sylvia Zimmerman, 2:19 p.m.

SZ: I mean, what did Hugo North really know about filmmaking? (snorts) He didn't give a shit about the craft of movies. Hugo couldn't be bothered to really read a script, let alone know how to improve it. He couldn't pick a composer or an editor to save his life.

TG: How did it feel to be working with someone like that?

SZ: Well, in some ways, he left the creative side of things up to us. Me, Xander, and Sarah. Which was a relief. But it was also frustrating . . . maybe even demeaning, to have to *pretend* like Hugo knew what the fuck he was talking about. Flatter him and treat him like our savior. All for the sake of . . . (trails off)

TG: For the sake of?

SZ: For the sake of his money. We wanted to get Xander's next film made. And filmmaking is an expensive art. You can't make a film without a ton of money.

TG: So you felt it was a necessary—

SZ: A necessary sacrifice, I suppose. Sacrifice a bit of control—and self-respect—in exchange for Hugo's money. I'm hardly the first person in the creative industries to have made a decision like this.

TG: Aside from his money, what else did Hugo bring to the company?

SZ: For all his promises and all his partying, he did bring a certain ruthless practicality to the way we ran things. I mean, Xander was an artistic snob at the time. Him and his fancy film degree, his obsession with shot framing and homages. Xander saw himself as some kind of visionary, who thought he would one day transform the art of cinema. But Hugo knocked some sense into him.

TG: How did he do that?

SZ: I'm not sure. Because he was a man, and Xander was

more inclined to listen to him? (scoffs) But listen, as much
as I hate to admit it, it's people like Hugo who really
keep the machine of mass entertainment ticking over.
The ruthless operators. The ones with money. The ones
with nothing to lose. The men whom no one ever seems
to question.

14

BY MID-JUNE, HUGO had arrived "for good" in New York. He decided to celebrate the launch of our new venture by inviting us all for dinner at the private members' club that served as his temporary home. It was called the Spark Club, a discreet boutique outfit in SoHo, with a glass door and narrow, gleaming hallway that led into a surprisingly spacious lobby. Elegant flower arrangements, dim lighting, courteous and good-looking staff . . . you get the picture.

Hugo and Xander were already seated at our table, drinking an aperitif. Sylvia and I came in from the street, and I carried, as some sort of small welcome gift, two boxes of Hugo's new business cards: thick black card, with the Conquest Films logo and his name embossed in gold.

"Oh, now this is juuust perfect," Hugo gushed upon opening the first box.

He held up a single card in both hands reverently, like a sacred text. "Exactly what we need to kick off this fine dinner."

"Beautiful cards, Sarah." He placed a warm hand on mine, his green eyes lingering on me. "I can tell I'll be able to count on you for everything."

I smiled back, wondering if it would seem impolite to withdraw my hand from under his. I was slightly relieved when Hugo finally lifted his palm.

But mainly, I felt a distinct glow of pride hearing Hugo praise me. His affirmation that I was of value, that I had done a good job. Always the Chinese American student wanting to please the teacher, kowtow to the white man. I cringe now, realizing what self-validation I gleaned from a simple throwaway comment made by a man I hardly knew. A man who was my boss simply because he had power and money.

"A bottle of wine for the table? Or another round of cocktails?" our table hostess asked Hugo. He was seated at the head of the table, his broad shoulders dominating its width, and she—an elegant, ponytailed blonde with flawless foundation—naturally gravitated to him.

"Darling, remind me of your name again?" Hugo leaned in, his hand reaching for her svelte waist.

"It's Megan, Mr. North."

"Megan, you can call me Hugo." He smiled. "I'll be staying here for a few weeks at least, so I'm sure we'll be seeing lots of each other."

He shared a conspiratorial glance with her, and she simpered coyly.

After he'd dispatched Megan in search of a chilled bottle of Möet, Hugo turned to us with a flourish. "Now, here is some very exciting news . . . Xander and I have just been chatting about the film, and we thought: Why not shoot in LA?"

My skull seemed to tingle the moment I heard those words. *Shoot in LA?*

Sylvia had a strong reaction too.

"LA?" she nearly shouted in disbelief. Likely the first time she'd heard that suggestion. "You want to shoot in *LA*?"

"Yes, it's ideal," Hugo continued. "All the cast and crew we could choose from, shooting locations, studios, everything. And the perfect opportunity to grow our network there, invite financiers onto set, get to know all the agents and players."

Xander was nodding, not saying much. I was accustomed to Xander lording over people, occupying center stage, but here he seemed content to cede the limelight to Hugo.

Sylvia looked straight at Xander; I could tell she was peeved. "How long have you been talking to Hugo about this?"

There was an edge to her voice, and Xander seemed surprised by it. "Well, really, just now. In the past hour or so."

"You've been discussing it for an hour, without my involvement, and *already* it's decided?" Sylvia snapped.

"Well hang on, hang on, Sylvia. We're just chatting," Hugo interceded here, his large hand stretched towards her in a placating gesture. "Don't get your knickers in a twist."

Xander chuckled, then stopped promptly when Sylvia glared at him.

"We were only discussing *options*," Hugo explained. "I just think that if we really want the company to make a splash, and for this project to be the one everyone's buzzing about, what's the harm in bringing it to LA?"

"Because so many of our contacts are *here*," Sylvia said. "The post-production houses, the heads of department, the talent agents, the sales agents—"

"There's at least twice as many out in LA," Hugo reminded her. "More choice, more talent. We're on a new plateau now, we don't need to rely on our old networks. It's time we start expanding them."

"He's right," Xander said. "I've said this before. LA revolves around the industry. Not like here in New York, where filmmaking gets squeezed in and around everything else. Everyone's too busy, there's always more important things. But in LA, they worship it. It's the lifeblood of that city."

Sylvia nodded. "I get that, it's just—I think you should have involved me in the discussion from the beginning."

"We were merely having a casual drink," Hugo said, his voice calm and soothing. "And in this industry, all roads lead to LA, right?"

Everyone vaguely laughed around the table—me included, even though I had no real say in the matter. To me, it sounded so foreign, so exotic, this thought of shooting in Los Angeles, in the real, true place called Hollywood. I had never been anywhere close. The word "Hollywood" conjured visions of towering palm trees, and endlessly coursing freeways, broad cement culverts big enough for killer cyborgs to drive a truck down, and giant studio lots where you had to clear your name at a security booth before the colossal automated gates would welcome you onto that hallowed ground. I knew somewhere in Los Angeles were beaches, where permanently tanned women played volleyball in the sunshine, and permanently ripped men exhibited their gym-sculpted muscles. But somewhere in there were also Valley Girls and hookers with a heart of gold and aspiring models and actors who doubled as alarmingly photogenic waiters (though we had those in New York, too) and fast-talking studio execs who drove convertibles and faster-talking agents who drove faster convertibles and aspiring, troubled screenwriters (young, white, and male, obviously, all wearing glasses)—and of course, I was confusing everything with the images of LA I'd seen in the movies and on television. Somewhere in there too was South Central LA and the scene of the LA riots, so presumably there were Black people living there, and Latinos, and a huge number of Asians, but you would never know it if you were only going by the images you saw in the movies.

I had to admit that having never set foot in LA, the only things I knew about it were what I saw on-screen. And as a person working in the industry, I imagined—in fact, I *knew*—those images were very, very suspect.

Yet my body thrummed with excitement. Maybe Hugo was right: in order to take our careers to the next level, we should head west—to that fabled land of studio lots and casting couches and glittering red-carpet premieres at Mann's Chinese Theatre.

But Sylvia had other thoughts.

"Name one good reason why we shouldn't shoot our next film in LA," Xander said, trying to reason with her.

Sylvia looked at him in a state of semi-shock. "Because some of us have *lives* and *families* here?" she said, as if it were the most obvious answer in the world.

"Ah." A slight admission of shame from Xander.

"Xander, let me remind you, I have *three* kids," Sylvia spelled out. "My oldest, Nathan, is applying to colleges this year, so it's a really crucial time for him. Rachel is two years behind him and always has boyfriend trouble, and my youngest, Jacob, is dealing with asthma *and* a bar mitzvah in the next six months. So I can't just up and move to LA when I feel like it because 'that's where the industry is.' Some of us have other responsibilities, on top of making films, you know."

Xander nodded. There was an electric pause, a moment that hung in the air between the four of us. Then he shifted in his seat and asked another question: "How many kids do you have, Hugo?"

Sylvia threw up a hand in frustration.

"Oh, I have four, actually," Hugo said, his hands folded complacently in his lap.

"See?" Xander continued. "It's not a problem for Hugo."

"Well," Hugo scoffed. "I'm not much of a role model as a father. Runs in my family, actually."

I smothered a laugh.

"Xander, don't start this." Sylvia jabbed a finger at him. "I'm a *mother*. I gave birth to my kids, raised them every day for the past seventeen years. I'm not going to go leave them on another coast, just because I *feel* like being a film producer."

I wasn't sure if her last comment was a veiled swipe at Hugo, but at the same time, I realized I had never once heard Hugo mention his kids before. Did it surprise me he had four kids? Not really. It was expected that a man who had acquired so much wealth, so many business portfolios and international properties, would along with that, also acquire a wife and a few offspring.

I later learned that Hugo's massive wealth also paid for two live-in nannies, a family driver, several household staff, and a team of private tutors for his kids. Sylvia was well-off, but she was nowhere near Hugo's level of affluence. Which meant, really, just the private tutors, a cleaner, and a part-time housekeeper.

Xander may have been blind to Sylvia's duties as a mother, but

I, who'd spent my first three years at Firefly handling Sylvia's schedule, knew how much she devoted to her children. She still had in her electronic diary "Pick up Jacob" Monday to Friday at three p.m., even if half the time, it was her housekeeper who did that. I'd overheard her call her children's school, reschedule their music lessons, and book their summer camp.

But on that night in SoHo, I had to admit I, too, had difficulty understanding why the existence of those three kids would make it impossible for Sylvia to relocate her job. I was young, I was excited: to live and work and shoot a film in LA—maybe that long-held dream was now actually attainable. Maybe only Sylvia stood in the way.

"So just because your son has his bar mitzvah, we can't shoot in LA?" Xander sniped.

"Don't be like that," Sylvia muttered.

Hugo gave a pretense of calming the tension.

"Now now, no need to get all worked up about this. Nothing's decided yet, but I think at this stage, there's no harm in aiming as high as possible. Moviemaking wasn't exactly made for cowards, was it?"

We were interrupted at that moment by Megan, who had been lingering in the background for the past few minutes, most likely eavesdropping on our conversation with a furtive pleasure.

"So sorry to interrupt, but have you decided on your orders yet?"

"Ah, darling." Hugo pivoted effortlessly towards Megan. I could see the effect of his suave British accent on her, even though he must have been three decades her senior. "*I've* decided, at least I'll start with the seared scallops. And for my, ahem, 'entree,' as you call it here on this side of the Atlantic . . . the prime rib, please."

"The burger for me, bloody," Xander said, winking at Megan. She smiled back at him.

Sylvia followed suit with her order, and last, of course, was me.

A few hours later, the four of us lounged three floors up, in Hugo's private suite at the Spark Club. We were drinking generous tumblers of Lagavulin, and the bitter, medicinal taste of the single malt mixed queasily with the three glasses of champagne I'd consumed at dinner.

Needless to say, I was quite drunk by this point. I reclined on the blue velvet couch, closed my eyes, and felt the room and the conversation spin around me. It was a relief to no longer be seated at the table downstairs, in the straight-backed restaurant chairs, nodding to whatever my bosses were saying.

For much of the dinner, Hugo had entertained us with stories of private jets and fraught business deals, a luxury resort he once tried to build in the Maldives that never quite happened. I hadn't heard of the Maldives before, and spent a good portion of that conversation silently racking my brain, trying to imagine where on a globe those islands would sit. The three of them spoke about their preferred islands in the Caribbean (Hugo loved Mustique, for Xander it was St. Barts, and for Sylvia, Anguilla)—and again, I prayed they would never turn to me and ask for my opinion. The only vacations I'd ever had (aside from that summer in Seattle, which wasn't really a vacation) were a few visits to Hong Kong to see relatives, and one trip, at the age of seven, to Orlando.

And yet, as incongruous as I felt, I was flattered to even be at that table. These people from another realm had invited me, let me drink their champagne, order from their expensive menu. I had sat quietly, observing the dynamics between my three bosses, while enjoying an exquisite meal of slow-roasted lamb and summer vegetables, which I would never have tasted otherwise. As always, I was a secondary cast member, who would occasionally get a line here or there.

"Sarah."

I jerked my eyes open at the sound of my name. I was on the couch at our after-dinner drinks, and Hugo waved a hand at me. "Are you conscious?"

I flushed, embarrassed. The three of them wore amused looks. "Yeah, just . . . enjoying the atmosphere."

"Excellent. Tell me, I've heard you've got a good instinct for casting. Just out of curiosity, what would your strategy be for casting *Furious Her*?"

I jolted myself back into work mode. It was true: to save money on *A Hard Cold Blue*, I had handled the casting alone, writing the role breakdowns, approaching agencies, organizing auditions, and ultimately negotiating deals with the actors' agents. This time, with *Furious Her*, I knew we had the budget to hire a top casting director. Yet I sensed this question from Hugo was some form of a test. Despite my drunken haze, I managed to construct a cogent answer.

"Like you said, it's a plum role for a young actress," I started. "So someone really up-and-coming, who has Next Big Thing potential. Maybe a bigger name to play her father. That role really only needs a week of shooting, so we could find someone established— a name that'll help attract sales agents and distributors."

Hugo and Sylvia nodded, and Xander was listening in, an unimpressed look pasted on his face.

"We could also cast a recognizable name as the police detective, maybe a former action star. He might appeal to a type of audience who'd otherwise be put off by the young female lead."

Hugo clapped slowly. "You *are* as clever as they say you are. Well done, Sarah. Get this girl another drink!"

Though really, what I'd said was just common sense.

"Sarah," Sylvia spoke up. "You've already started compiling potential cast lists and headshots for the film, right?"

"Yeah, I've been putting some ideas together."

"Fabulous," Hugo said. "Let's talk about them tomorrow afternoon, in the office. Say, three o'clock? But for now, I say we kick back and celebrate a little harder."

As if on cue, the doorbell rang, and I saw our waitress Megan at the door. Her hair down, she was no longer wearing her black-and-white waitstaff attire. She also had with her two other women and a man—all four of them probably around my age, appealing, fashionably dressed, and white. I noticed the guy in particular was quite cute.

During dinner, I'd seen Hugo whisper something into Megan's ear, push something into her hand. Now, in his suite, she leaned close to Hugo as her slim hand, the nails lacquered a lustrous beige, deposited something unseen into his outstretched palm.

Drugs, I presumed. I felt a brief, sudden tingle of anticipation— I, who had hardly ever done drugs in my lifetime. The thrill of the illicit seemed to sharpen the angles in the room.

The energy in the group changed. Suddenly, Hugo's and Xander's attention was directed only at those three women, and Sylvia and I were forgotten, like the furnishings around us. I drifted to the window and gazed onto the street below, where pedestrians wandered in the spell of abandon promised by this steamy summer evening.

"There'll be more people on their way," Hugo said to me, offhand. "People you should really meet, Sarah." He shot a meaningful look at me. I didn't know what to make of it.

Before I could reply, Sylvia stood up with some finality, shouldering her substantial Mulberry handbag.

"Hugo." She interrupted his tête-à-tête with Megan. "It's late, and I should get back to my kids. You and Xander do whatever you want, but I'm taking Sarah with me." She glanced at me. It was a look I knew not to disobey.

"Oh no, don't ruin the party for her," Hugo implored, then turned to me. "Please stay if you'd like. We're just about to break out something special for all of us. What do you say?"

I was curious, wanting to know what would unfold in this room, but wary of opposing Sylvia so blatantly.

"Come on, Sarah," she urged. "We have an early meeting tomorrow. We should go."

"Really?" I tried to remember our schedule for the morning, nearly blurted that no such meeting existed. But Sylvia glared. I reluctantly moved towards the door. For once, I wished she'd ease up on me.

"Sorry, I probably should get back," I slurred an apology, to no one in particular.

"Don't worry," Hugo answered, as Sylvia ushered me out the door. "There'll be plenty more parties in the future."

And a peal of Megan's laughter, overly loud, rang out into the hallway as the door closed.

I didn't realize how drunk I was until Sylvia pushed me out the glass doors of the club, onto the street. Away from the air-conditioning, the humid night air hit me full in the face.

"I don't think I've ever seen you this wasted." There was the usual reprimand in Sylvia's voice, but also a warmth, as if speaking to an old friend.

"I'm not that bad." I tried to defend myself and turned my head, looking for a subway entrance. What line was I near? My thoughts swam in a thick murk. "Shit, the L is going to take forever."

"Sarah," Sylvia said sternly. "There is *no way* you are taking the subway home tonight."

"Do you *know* how much a taxi to Williamsburg costs?" It was a rhetorical question; of course Sylvia wouldn't know. She hardly ever left Manhattan.

"It's late." She gripped my right shoulder and stared straight into my eyes. "Take a taxi. You can expense it to the company."

"Really?" I was disproportionately joyful at this news, as Sylvia flagged down a yellow cab and deposited me into it. She crushed two twenty-dollar bills into my hand. "Remember to keep the receipt."

I nodded and muttered my address to the driver. The cab pulled away, leaving Sylvia on the darkened sidewalk. Still addled, I turned back, looking for that lighted window where Hugo and Xander and the others were, basking in a party I would no longer be part of. But I was too drunk to distinguish it from the grid of windows behind me, and I slumped into my seat in a blissful haze.

After all, it was the first time I'd ever taken a taxi all the way home to Brooklyn from Manhattan. It felt luxurious.

15

THE NEXT MORNING, I silently battled a hideous hangover, at a ten thirty meeting with Sylvia and Sammy Lefkowitz's team, the US distributors for *A Hard Cold Blue*. Sammy was a legend in the industry, known for acquiring small, independent gems and promoting them heavily to awards (and commercial) success. He himself wasn't at the meeting, which was a straightforward catch-up about the film's planned November release, in time to build word-of-mouth for awards season. Engulfed in a wave of nausea, I nodded throughout the conversation and downed copious amounts of water. I realized that while Sylvia and I were keeping the wheels greased with our distributor, Xander and Hugo were probably getting to sleep off the worst of last night's festivities.

When they stumbled into the office that afternoon, the damage showed. Dark bags bunched beneath Xander's eyes, and Hugo's face was shadowed with stubble. They slumped through the door and onto the couch, wordless.

"Good afternoon," I said with some sarcasm.

Hugo nodded at me. Xander grunted and looked away.

After a moment of silence, I attempted to advance this one-way conversation. "Did it go pretty late last night?"

"Oh yeah." Xander gloated. "Pretty late, and then some."

"We were up until four? Five?" Hugo asked Xander, who nodded absently.

"Wow," I said, deadpan. "Musta been fun."

They looked at each other conspiratorially and laughed.

"You bet it was," Xander sniggered. I was reminded of the jocks in my high school, trading smug, coded remarks about what had happened at their weekend parties. I decided I wasn't going to flatter them by asking about it. I went back to my emails.

Hugo was tapping away at his BlackBerry, and Xander was staring blankly into space, when Sylvia walked into the room.

"Oh, look who finally decided to enter the world of the living," she said dryly.

She stood in front of the two of them, shaking her head. "All right, I'm glad you guys had fun last night. Way to celebrate, but now we have a film to make."

Xander looked up at her and nodded obediently. Hugo was still occupied with his phone. Sylvia fumed.

"Are we ready to talk casting? Ziggy," she commanded. "Can you get these guys some coffee? And Sarah, do you want to bring out the headshots and suggestions from the agents?"

As Xander and Hugo sipped vacantly at their espressos, I talked through the possibilities for casting.

The lead in *Furious Her* was a female role, and a complex one at that. Katie Phillips, a single mother (age range twenty-five to thirty), grieving the recent death of her husband. Forced to defend her home and her daughter from dangerous intruders, while piecing together the conspiracy of criminals who had murdered her life partner. We knew this was a role that any aspiring actress would kill for. A "plum role," as the industry would call it.

Katie Phillips was a nice-girl name. Because Katie was, at heart, a nice girl, a good girl, forced to do increasingly desperate, daring things to protect herself and her six-year-old. She was feisty, she was brave, she was athletic, she was clever. She had a college degree, but was also already a mother in her mid-twenties. And of course, she had to be hot. Slim. Sexy. But not slutty. "A natural beauty," as Xander described her in the script.

The agencies all represented tons of female clients who could play twenty-five to thirty, all pretty, with varying levels of acting skill. When I sent Andrea's office the casting breakdown for Katie

Phillips, they emailed me the next day with the headshots and résumés of thirty women. And that was just one agency. I had over two hundred actors' headshots from calling just a few agencies.

Poring over those two-hundred-plus résumés, I scanned the experience of these women: their training, their previous productions, and sorted them into different piles of professional credibility. "Ideal" amount of experience, "Maybe," and "No."

Then I'd gone through the "Ideal" and "Maybe" pile and weeded out the women who just didn't look right, in my opinion. A little too plain. Too many freckles. Too horsey a face. In a word, not pretty enough.

I admit, there was a certain exhilaration for me in the process. To think that I, an unknown twenty-seven-year-old, could single-handedly determine whether an aspiring actress would be considered for a starring role, by a single flick of my wrist.

I may have been harried by my bosses, but in these moments, I felt a power rush, an exclusive sense of control over these strangers. Yes, I, a woman, was evaluating these other women on their looks. Actually, on the way they looked in a single black-and-white photograph. But what did I tell you earlier? All we ever do in the film industry is judge each other. That's sometimes our very job.

And I clearly wasn't as harsh a judge as Xander and Hugo.

Throughout our meeting, the two of them had been impatient to get through the male roles, encouraged by the prospect of looking at attractive young women who could play Katie Phillips. As I talked through the top suggestions from the agencies, Xander and Hugo held their hands out eagerly for the headshots, like kids trick-or-treating.

But they seemed disappointed, saying no to the majority of photographs.

Sylvia was more positive. "She could be good," she suggested, holding up the headshot of one earnest-looking blonde. "Jenny Oliver. She had a recurring role in a *Law and Order* series. Huge amount of stage experience. Nominated for a Tony."

"Nah." Xander shrugged. "Not with that nose."

"Or her?" Sylvia held up another headshot. "I remember seeing her in that TV drama about a small Midwestern town. She was impressive."

"Too old," Hugo scoffed. "Not hot enough."

"Here, give me the pile." Xander reached for the "Maybe" stack, and he and Hugo started flicking through it quickly, the way a bored magician might deal through a deck of cards. "Let's see if we got any hotties in here."

Hugo sniggered and gulped his coffee.

The two of them commented to each other as they worked their way through the pile.

"How 'bout her?"

"Oh, she's hot. I'd do her."

Flick flick. "Looks like a truck driver," Xander laughed, and tossed one headshot onto the floor.

"She looks inbred. Seriously, *she's* got an agent?"

More sniggering. Another headshot hit the floor.

"Oh wow, now this one. Hel-*lo* gorgeous."

Xander started a new pile of approval.

"Hey, look at this. Her 'Special Skills' include pole-dancing."

They both tittered.

Sylvia and I glanced at each other, a long-suffering look of mutual frustration.

"Guys," Sylvia said. "You need to be serious here. Don't waste your time on a complete unknown who'll scare off a sales agent."

"Her?" Xander said, holding up a headshot of a sultry blonde. "That's not scary. That's just lush. Look at those lips."

"Marie Playfair. Oh, I definitely *will*," Hugo said with approval. They continued. *Flick flick flick.*

Now that the meeting had degenerated into nonsense, I returned to my desk and started typing out some emails. Xander and Hugo continued muttering to each other and laughing.

Suddenly, Xander raised his voice.

"Sarah," he said, concerned. "What is this woman doing in this pile? She looks like a hooker from Harlem."

He held up the headshot of Theresa Josephs, a Black actress with high cheekbones and large, inviting eyes.

I wasn't sure what Xander meant, and hesitated.

"You mean . . . she's Black?"

"Well obviously she's Black. She also looks like a hooker."

Before I could ask Xander what exactly about her face suggested prostitution, Sylvia cut in, somewhat excited.

"How 'bout that, Xander? Katie could be Black. We could still cast a white actor as her dad, but we could have someone like . . . Halle Berry, maybe?"

"What?" Xander looked at Sylvia, aghast. "That wouldn't work."

"Why not?" she asked.

"'Cause I just don't see her as Black."

The way he spoke, it was a simple, irrefutable statement.

And just like that, an entire race was barred from the plum role of Katie Phillips.

Of course, it was likely more than just one race. Of all the headshots that had been sent over, I noticed there wasn't a single Asian actress whom the agencies had suggested. Latinas were few and far between.

And even though Xander had never been explicit, it was obvious that Katie Phillips was meant to be white. Hot and smart and sexy. And inevitably, unmistakably, white.

I returned to my emails, a small seed of disgust starting to germinate inside me. I would ignore it, pretend it didn't exist. I reminded myself this was just an unfortunate phase to get through. There were bigger things ahead: shooting the actual film, even a possible move to LA.

"She's not here," Xander pronounced glumly. "I don't see her here, not in this pile."

If you told two-hundred-plus actresses that they would be summarily judged just like that, declared en masse to be inappropriate for a lead role, their hearts would be crushed. But aspiring actors never suspect the cold reality of the business, they're too bewitched by the illusion that the industry peddles about itself: that if you're talented enough and passionate enough, you'll get your big break one day.

No one ever tells you that this is the most your career will ever amount to: your headshot glanced at for five seconds by a hungover director, before being dropped to the floor. And promptly forgotten.

I kept typing away, one ear still trained on the casting conversation on *Furious Her*, while I scanned a very boring list of technical elements that we had to provide our distributor for *A Hard Cold Blue*.

"You're seriously going to write off *all* these actresses?" Sylvia asked Xander in disbelief. She gestured to the litter of headshots on the floor, scattered like debris in the wake of a storm. "You don't even want to see any of their showreels?"

Xander shrugged. "There's some maybes in there, but no one who really stood out."

"Well," Hugo said. "It's only a preliminary search. There's plenty more actresses out there."

"Those are the *top four* agencies I reached out to," I reminded Xander.

"If he didn't see the right girl in there, he simply didn't," Hugo defended him. "You shouldn't have to settle for second-best. This is *your* picture."

"Let's have some conversations with casting directors," Sylvia said. "Sarah, can you find out who's available to meet early next week? Send them the script to read this weekend, if they haven't gotten it already."

She turned back to Xander. "How's that sound? A good casting director will have their finger on the pulse, be able to suggest someone we may have missed."

But Xander didn't show much interest. He stood up absently and put his sunglasses back on.

"Yeah, I guess." He shrugged. "What time is it?"

"It's ten to four," Ziggy said.

"God, I'm a disaster today," Xander said into the air. "I gotta go."

Hugo stood up too. "Let me buy you a drink."

"Wait, hold on—" Sylvia was shocked. "Xander, we're supposed to be meeting with the publicist for *A Hard Cold Blue*."

"I hate publicists," Xander muttered. "I'm in no mood to meet with one today. You and Sarah go to the meeting, fill me in on it later."

He was at the door by the time he said this, and Hugo followed him out before Sylvia could say anything else. We watched the door swing shut behind them.

Around the coffee table, beneath our feet, the discarded headshots lay scattered in a chaotic throng. The black-and-white faces of young women beamed up blankly from the floor, at no one in particular.

16

I CAN'T REMEMBER THE first time I heard the name of Holly Randolph. But somehow, as if by osmosis—in talks with casting directors, or on a trawl of the IMDb—her name filtered through to me. Until one day, I looked up her agent and asked for a show-reel, feeding it into the DVD player in our office. There were hundreds of these DVDs at the time that crisscrossed New York, borne by motorcycle courier in their plastic cases, with the agency logo printed on it. All these actors, hoping to be cast for another role, one that might be their "big break."

I was used to popping these DVDs out of their cases, into our machine, hearing the click of some unseen electronic mechanism, while I waited.

This time, like any other, the DVD whirred to life, and I sat back on the office floor, gazing up at our TV monitor with curiosity.

"Who's that?" Ziggy asked.

"Holly Randolph," I said, checking the name on the DVD case. I continued to watch, mesmerized. "Never heard of her, but she's good."

I pause here for a moment to consider what I know of Holly Randolph now, a decade on.

All this time, I have been following her career with great interest, and a hint of pride, almost parental. As if to say: *I* discovered her. Without me, none of you would know about the luminous acting talent that is Holly Randolph.

Of course, that is not the truth. Someone else may have gifted her a lead role in a decently budgeted film. She may have worked her way up through television to independent films to the big studio releases. The next year, she might have been cast as a sharp but charming girlfriend, or a clever college student, or the grown daughter of a man in a midlife crisis, played by a venerable Hollywood legend.

In the ten years that have passed, I've seen her take on all those roles—and more. Whereas a lesser actress would fill those parts with her obligatory pretty face and a flash of screen charisma, Holly Randolph brings an added depth, a concealed note of pain and rawness. Perhaps that rings with a particular authenticity. Because what was Holly braving this past decade? And all the while building her meteoric career, leapfrogging from Golden Globe nomination to the Oscars to the Tonys. Her face plastered on the front of *People* magazine, atop BuzzFeed quizzes—*Holly Randolph, Up Front and Personal* interviews. *Take this quiz on snack foods to see which Holly Randolph character you are.*

I now look at her career with an increased awe for her acting skill. To be wearing so many masks at once, simply in order to survive. The character she becomes on set. The version of Holly she must play, on talk shows or the red carpet. And then the real her, hiding the truth of what may have happened, keeping it safely tamped down, behind her celebrated facade.

I knew the real her once, before she became famous. At least, I like to think that was the real her. But what do we really know, after all?

Two weeks later, I finally met Holly Randolph in person. We had enlisted the services of Val Tartikoff, an expensive but reputable casting director, to work on *Furious Her*. On a Wednesday afternoon, at a hired casting suite in Herald Square, Val and her assistant Brian ran a casting session, where ten different actresses arrived at pre-appointed times to read for the role of Katie Phillips. In the preceding weeks, I'd touted Holly's showreel to Xander, who seemed to ignore my suggestion. So I was pleased to see Val had booked her for 3:15 in the casting suite that day.

Since Xander and Hugo were already attending, Sylvia saw it as a waste of company time for me to spend all day at the casting session. Still, I was curious and maneuvered my schedule to have one hour at the casting that afternoon, from three to four.

When Holly walked into the suite, she was a petite figure, like all the other similarly aged actresses who had been invited. But there was a certain assurance in the way she moved that made her slender frame seem more substantial. And the same could be said of her overall demeanor. Though at first glance, she was just another pretty, fair-haired twentysomething woman, once she decided to look at you and speak, you immediately took notice. And the camera magnified all of this, catching every little quirk of her features, every slight tremor of feeling that crossed those limpid blue irises, that sensitive mouth. When her face appeared on the screen in front of us, I saw Xander sit up. Hugo too.

"Hello," Val said, her thick New York accent warm to Holly. It was the seventh time that day she'd said "hello" warmly to a twentysomething actress hoping to land the part of Katie Phillips.

"Hi, I'm Holly," she extended a confident handshake.

"Everyone, this is Holly Randolph. This is Xander, our writer-director, and Hugo, our producer." Xander simply nodded at Holly, but Hugo stood up and did his European kiss-on-either-side-of-the-cheek routine. Holly accepted this courteously enough.

"Oh, and Sarah, one of our other producers," Val remembered to add.

"Hi," Holly said to me. I'd like to think she was relieved to see another young woman in the room.

"Have you had a chance to read the whole script, Holly?" Val's question had prompted other actresses to lavish the script with compliments, moaning their flattery of Xander's writing at almost orgasmic levels. I wondered if it ever got old for Xander, hearing women gush over him all the time.

Holly's response was well-mannered, positive, and smartly worded.

"I enjoyed reading it," she said. "So many different facets to Katie. She's a mother, a daughter, a grieving widow, an action hero. And in real life, most of us do play so many different roles at once."

"Maybe not the action-hero part," Xander quipped. General laughter all around.

"Well, you never know," Holly joked back. More polite amusement.

"Are you ready to read those scenes for us?" Val asked.

"Absolutely," she said brightly. "Can we start with the scene with her daughter?"

Even that, the decisiveness of her suggestion, marked her apart from other actresses, who were more content to be instructed. They would stand there, their willowy frames wavering, and nearly whisper: "Which scene do you want me to read first?"

The female desire to please has never frustrated me more than in the casting suite. Of course, all actors desperately want the part they're auditioning for. But it takes an extra skill to conceal that underlying desperation, and suspend the cynical disbelief of three or four people who have already seen a parade of performers read those same lines, attempt to inhabit that very same character.

Likewise, I'd observed that during the casting session, Xander and Hugo also assumed slightly different versions of their usual selves. Xander inhabited the role of Silent Artistic Genius, a role that no one questioned, since he was the writer-director. But Hugo was larger-than-life, exaggerating his Britishness with a hammy theatricality. Together, they had the combined impact of appearing even more unreachable to those auditioning. They knew the power they wielded in that casting suite, sitting in the dark, passing judgment on these young women who emoted and exhibited their very utmost, receiving little more than a nod or single comment in return.

But Holly Randolph seemed less intimidated, or at least she hid her nervousness better than the others. At Val's prompt, she repositioned herself within the lighted space, her body language instantly shifting from professional and friendly, to alert, motherly, concerned.

"Whenever you're ready," Val gave the go-ahead.

Val's assistant Brian was reading the part of the six-year-old daughter, and Holly gazed at him with a maternal worry.

"Mommy?" Brian pitched his voice high, like a child's. "Are there bad men outside our house?"

I was nervous for her. Already, in the space of a few weeks, I'd developed a personal investment in Holly Randolph, even though she hardly knew who I was. Perhaps it was my desire to make some lasting contribution to this project, to prove my worth as a producer. Or perhaps it was Holly's own star quality, drawing me in. She has always possessed the ability to make audiences and complete strangers root for her. Even though they mean nothing to her, in that moment, she means everything to them.

Holly hesitated, and a look of uncertainty clouded her face. Not the uncertainty of an actress auditioning for a part. But that of a mother in danger, unsure of how much to tell her young daughter.

"Yes, darling." She nodded. "There's bad men out there. And you have to promise me you will do *everything you can* to hide yourself from them."

"Like a game of hide-and-seek?" Brian asked innocently.

"That's my clever girl, yes." Holly smiled and her eyes lit up with pride at her fictional six-year-old. "Remember when we used to play with Daddy . . ."

Her voice broke slightly here, and tears started to well up in her eyes. We hung on Holly's every word, transfixed. She was both fierce and tender in the moment.

Almost instinctively, Holly knew to measure each beat of the dialogue, to allow the suspense to grow, along with our investment in her. Where other actresses reached for the sentimental, Holly kept the emotion to her eyes, her voice electric with tension.

After she delivered her final line, we sat in silence, in darkness, waiting for the moment to last. Not wanting to be reminded that this was just an audition, and now the scene was over, and Holly was going to walk out of that room, out of that building, down the street, and we would have to watch a train of new actresses attempt to play that same character again, when they would never live up to what we had just seen.

Holly held her stance, like any well-trained thespian, knowing not to break character until someone said "Cut." And maybe in that moment, she held us all in the palm of her hand. Or maybe in that moment, Xander and Hugo held her in theirs.

But Val broke that moment. "Nicely done."

Holly stepped back, out of character, and grinned, her face radiant. "Really? Thanks. I was pretty nervous."

"You shouldn't be," Val said, and I could sense the sincerity in her voice, usually so weathered and practical. "Really special reading."

When Holly left the casting suite eight minutes later, I felt like the enclosed shell of the world had cracked open and shown us the universe outside. This was what casting was about—and acting and filmmaking. The perfect union of character and talent. This was the alchemy that was possible.

Despite Xander's maudlin dialogue, the sentimentality of that young-mother-in-peril stretched to excess, Holly had somehow breathed spontaneous life into those lines. She had made us champion her, through the sheer pull of her own magnetism.

To be so natural, so assured, so effortlessly professional. All the qualities that men in this world expect women to be, though the appearance of such requires so much advance preparation.

Sitting on my own in the corner, I was quietly ecstatic at Holly's audition. Still, I watched three more auditions with other actors, to confirm if what I'd just seen was a complete fluke. But it hadn't been. The promise I had seen on that grainy showreel, that cheap, disposable DVD, was real.

There was no doubt about it. Holly Randolph was one in a million.

17

I KNOW THOM WANTS me to continue, but right now, I simply can't. There is some kind of corporeal refusal I've come up against at this point in the story. An interior roadblock.

I realize I am exhausted. Glancing at my watch, and then out the window, I see that the daylight has shifted. The sun casts longer shadows across Midtown Manhattan.

As for Thom Gallagher, I notice bags under his eyes, and I wonder how many hours he has spent in the past year, listening to stories from embittered, regretful women, surveying the psychological damage caused by the past.

There is a pause. Neither of us says anything.

"Do you want to continue?" I detect a note of solicitude in his voice; perhaps he does actually care.

I hesitate. "I don't know if I can. Right now."

Over the past few hours, a base level of nausea in my body has been inching up a notch, willing me to stop before I get any further.

I want to end things before we even reach LA. Stay here in New York, in this city that has always been my home, and none of those things will have ever happened. But I know that is a lie, because they had already started happening here on this bustling island, some forty blocks downtown from where he and I are now sitting.

"I can come back. I mean, the story's not over."

"Of course not," Thom agrees. "I've been working on this for months now, no immediate rush. If you want to continue at a later stage . . . Maybe some day next week, we can meet up."

Maybe, I think.

A cloud must have slid away from the sun, because now the light suddenly flashes out from the sky, blinding me. I hold my hand up to shield my eyes, as I squint at Thom.

"Listen," he says, not unkindly. "You tell me. What do you want to do?"

After I leave that august skyscraper, signing myself out at 4:21 p.m., returning that badge with a pixelated imitation of my face, I am not ready to go home.

What is there at home? An empty apartment. More student scripts to grade.

I rarely make it into Manhattan these days, so maybe I should treat myself. Catch the latest foreign film at the Quad, or sit on a bench in Central Park and watch old men play chess.

But whatever initial idea I entertain, I find myself walking downtown, away from the neon rush of Times Square, yearning for something more remote, more solitary.

Glancing at my phone, I see a text from my sister, but I ignore it. I no longer reply immediately to her messages, the way I once did.

A young Holly Randolph still rings in my mind, the thrill of seeing her in that audition. The hope I once felt at twenty-seven for what I could have been. What Holly has since turned out to be.

I get on the subway without thinking, resurface to the sidewalk at Canal Street.

I walk as if in a trance. My feet trace a familiar route on the pavement, but not one I would ever rationally choose. Somewhere deep down, my body must have remembered where it was, like some homing instinct for migrating birds, willing me closer and closer to that fated location. That address I had wound up in, too many times, on those summer nights before we moved to LA.

When I get there, I hardly recognize it. The private members' club has either shut down or relocated.

I don't recognize the businesses around it, either. The pizza place is now a luxury nail salon. A liquor store where I'd bought late-night supplies is now an organic coffeehouse offering turmeric lattes. But I recognize the entryway, where I'd often swished through the glass doors into that narrow, polished lobby.

I stand there on the sidewalk, gazing up, searching for the window on the fourth-floor suite. Where I would have stood, ten years ago, staring down at someone on the street very much like myself.

I would not have recognized my future self looking up at me.

Interview Transcript (continued):
Sylvia Zimmerman, 2:39 p.m.

SZ: Who else have you been speaking to? Sarah? Sarah Lai?

TG: I'm not in any position to identify my other sources, unfortunately.

SZ: Well, I imagine Sarah's worth talking to. She certainly came from a different place.

TG: What do you mean by that?

SZ: Sarah came from nowhere, Thom. Her family were immigrants from Hong Kong, they ran some restaurant out in Queens. She fairly stumbled onto the film scene and got to where she was through . . . all that stuff they say, passion and talent and hard work. (pause) I can't fault her for being ambitious. We all are, in this industry. But maybe Sarah was driven by where she came from. Maybe she wanted to prove herself, more so than any of the rest of us.

TG: When you say "prove herself," what does that mean?

SZ: Someone like Sarah, she'd only have one shot at making it in the business. There's no get-out-of-jail-free pass if you're someone like that, with no connections. So I was glad to have given her that opportunity.

TG: How would you describe your working relationship with her at the time?

SZ: She was good, always good. Always reliable. That's what you need in this industry: someone who always has your back. And that's who Sarah was. Until Hugo arrived.

TG: *Did* she prove reliable in the end?

SZ: There's no straightforward answer to that. (pause) In the beginning, she was. Almost a dream to work with: quick to pick up on things, not afraid to put in the long hours. But a part of her . . . seemed to always be wanting something more.

TG: What do you think she wanted?

SZ: Maybe she felt like she was above some of that early work?

That she should have been doing more than just stapling scripts together and making photocopies? But we all have to start somewhere. And a bit of humility never hurt anyone.

TG: How did *you* start in the industry?

SZ: Me? Same way. When I was younger, I was approached to do some modeling. Nothing big, but a friend of my father's got me noticed. I didn't love being in front of the camera. Always seemed too dehumanizing, too exposing. I wanted to be behind the scenes, seeing how things got made, how strings were pulled . . . (pause) So I worked my way from modeling into fashion publicity, then producing commercials and music videos. Sure, there was all the initial stupid work of making coffees and Xerox copies and answering phones, people treating you like you're just another idiotic pretty face. But eventually I got somewhere. And then I met Xander and realized that *here* was a talent worth latching on to. A director whose work I could nurture through the years, who I could promote and encourage, have that dream working relationship with. And eventually produce his feature films.

TG: So you forged your own way in the industry, then?

SZ: Sure, no one else is gonna do it for you. I saw my opportunities and I took them. (pause) I guess Sarah reminded me of a younger me. So someone like her, I wanted to give her a chance.

TG: Would you have called Sarah Lai naïve?

SZ: Yes, at first. But she must have wised up at some point in her time at Firefly. She was always a fast learner.

18

THE NEXT DAY is Sunday, and I have a family gathering to attend. So I take the subway to Queens, and there in the family restaurant, I'm reunited with my parents, my older sister, my younger brother, and their families. All good, dutiful Chinese American children, except for myself.

Karen has moved to DC, where she still works as an accountant for one of the big firms (all of them go by acronyms, some alphabet amalgamation of Anglo-Saxon surnames). Her husband's a lawyer, their two kids aged seven and ten. As the only son in a Chinese family, my brother Edison has always occupied his own privileged sphere—and never shown much interest in either of his sisters. Now a dentist in Boston, he is here with his fiancée, a Taiwanese American woman who does marketing for high-end luxury brands. All their stability, the steadily accruing IRAs and pension plans, the monthly mortgages, the new versions of smartphones—all this rankles me with a certain revulsion. And envy.

I know I bring shame upon my family, because my Columbia degree didn't result in a salary any higher than the meager one provided by my lecturer's position. I don't have children or a partner or even a boyfriend to show off. I am just Sarah, the one who moved out to LA to make movies, but that didn't work out, and now she's back in New York, teaching at a no-name community college. A cautionary tale for those who aspire too high.

On this Sunday in particular, I am in a more introspective

mood than usual. The previous evening was an unsettling one for me after I returned home from Manhattan. I could have read some student scripts, I could have watched some comedy skits on You-Tube, to try and rouse me from my stupor. But instead, I just sat in the dark, staring out the window, flicking the light on and off, like some creepy, lonely stalker in a formulaic thriller. If I'd started breathing heavily, that would have completed the picture.

I fell asleep in that position, woke up at two a.m., and dragged myself to bed.

This morning, I find the brightness of everything around me disorienting.

"Hey, sorry I didn't return your text," I mumble to Karen. "I was kinda busy with something yesterday."

"So how's it all going?" she asks.

She is looking at me sympathetically, the way big sisters are meant to, and I have a sense—not quite an out-of-body experience, but something similar—of specific, pre-determined roles and lines that we are expected to play. Roles and lines that we have been familiar with all our lives, fulfilling them as if by rote.

Karen is always the one who ticks all the boxes: the home-owner, the successful accountant, the mother of two, the dutiful daughter. I am always the one who demands pity: the single one, the poor one, the artsy one.

I am about to say the line I always say: *Yeah, it's going okay.*

I decide to improvise.

"Mmmm . . . things are a bit weird."

"Really?" Her curiosity is piqued. That wasn't my intention, I was merely trying to chip away at the truth.

I scrabble together more rice and braised eggplant with my chopsticks, shovel it into my mouth. Wash it down with some tea.

"What's going on?" Karen asks.

I don't really know what to say, since no one in my family knows about what happened ten years ago, or why my film career came crashing to a halt.

But maybe Karen suspects something. Not the actual truth,

just a hint of a thread linking me to larger stories, bigger names. She tries another tack.

"I saw that actress Holly Randolph was in the news, they were asking her about these latest accusations."

I try to hide my alarm. Did I miss a headline?

"What did she say?" Then, to cover up my concern, I add: "Since when do *you* watch *Entertainment Tonight*?"

"It's not me, it's Alice." Karen gestures to her ten-year-old a few seats over, who is waiting for the pan-fried turnip cake with wide eyes. "She's completely in love with the movies. Kinda like you were as a kid."

"Well, tell her to watch out," I joke.

"No, but seriously, these stories are all over the news." Karen rests her chopsticks and stares at me. "Didn't you used to work with Holly Randolph?"

"I did. But that was another lifetime ago. I doubt she'd remember me."

Karen can sense I am marking out boundaries with my words. Deflecting this way, closing down another avenue for conversation. A topic not to be discussed with our parents and her kids right there, all three generations of the Lai family staring at us.

She smiles and lightens the tone. "Do you know how psyched Alice would be if I told her you once knew Holly Randolph?"

I laugh. "Don't. She'll just be disappointed. I won't be able to get her an autograph or surprise visit to her school or anything."

And if I can't get one of those, does it even count that I once knew Holly Randolph? I doubt I even have any photos of us together to prove it.

"Hey you two," our mom shouts across the table. "What are you talking about? You better be telling your sister about some nice single man in your office you can set her up with."

Karen and I both balk.

"Mom, I work in an accounting firm. All the men there are too boring for Sarah."

Mom shakes a finger at me. "See, that's your problem. Always too caught up in movies your whole life. Only interested in having fun."

I quell my usual anger, bite downward and say nothing.

Mom laughs it off. "I'm just kidding. Stop hogging the Peking duck, you girls. Send it over here."

I give the lazy Susan a swift push and it circles towards my mom, bearing the requested dish to her. I feel like I have been doing this all my life, in this restaurant. Sitting at a turntable, wheeling it towards her so that it delivers exactly what she desires. Circular motion. The weight of parental expectations, wheeling round and round, getting us nowhere.

On Monday, during some downtime in my office, I sit in front of my computer and look up representation for Holly Randolph. As a producer, it once came as second nature for me, navigating my way through various websites and directories, or making a series of discreet phone calls, to find out who represented which actor, jotting down the phone number of that agent.

Today, Holly, like any A-list star, is represented by a squadron of professionals: agent, manager, publicist, lawyer, and their multiple assistants. I don't know any of them. None of them were working with her ten years ago, and when I visit their websites, they are glossy but opaque. Offering very little in the way of information or accessibility.

Hollywood, as always, remains such an insider's town.

I could draft an email to her publicist or manager, but what would I say? *Dear Holly, I don't know if you remember me —*

No, that would guarantee an immediate delete.

Dear Holly, it's Sarah Lai, one of the producers of your 2008 film Furious Her—

No, there would be that automatic association with Hugo North, and . . . I turn away, the nausea and guilt rising inside me.

I go onto social media, stumbling my way through Twitter. It seems bizarre, this instrumental platform where you can only ever type 140 characters in a statement. Yet somehow, these 140-character utterances have garnered stars, journalists, politicians, athletes, even chefs millions of followers hanging on their every tweet. These days, I read news articles and half of them seem to be summaries of tweets other people have sent out. Twitter has replaced the news, apparently. Twitter has *become* the news.

Holly Randolph, of course, has her own Twitter account, with the requisite blue check mark denoting her status as someone important. @HollyRandolph lists her location as Los Angeles, her title as "Actor. Lover of the World," her profile as "Storyteller. Vegetarian. Shows up on-screen from time to time." I find it so bizarre, this medium, where the words, the images, the retweets, even the very emojis are so curated, so much the polished, very public avatar of a supposedly real human being.

I scroll through her Twitter feed and see some ongoing conversations with other A-list actors, one or two tweets about a film of hers that will be released next month, and then some retweets from animal charities. She has 5.2 million followers.

I can see how Twitter must seem appealing to the average person—these direct utterances of a celebrity, coming straight from her phone to mine. But like everything else, it is all an illusion.

Holly must get thousands of tweets a day; most likely someone is paid to handle her Twitter account. The same can be said of Instagram, which seems even less intuitive to me, a disjointed stream of photographs. And yet, apparently the most popular social media platform in LA. Celebrities' Instagram posts are deciphered endlessly by fans and pundits: "What does this comment mean? Whose arm is her hand gripping in that photo?"

I am lost and amused, but mainly, I am just relieved that none of these channels existed when I was working in the industry. How much extra work to maintain an active Twitter or Instagram account, generating photos or witty commentary for your 5.2 million followers. To remind people you are still relevant.

I am free of that burden now. And for once, I am grateful.

I glimpse the clock in the upper-right corner of my screen.

Nearly forty minutes have passed, and I have another class to teach in twelve minutes. Forty minutes gone, just like that, trawling through a flood of virtual detritus.

And I'm no closer to establishing contact with Holly Randolph.

Thom had sent an email on Sunday, the day after I visited the *Times* offices, thanking me courteously for my time and my contribution.

> I look forward to speaking with you again, whenever is next convenient for you. To keep the momentum going, I'd like to suggest sometime this Wednesday or Thursday evening. But I am fairly flexible. I realize you may need some time between interviews.

I read his email Sunday evening, because I am a loser with no personal life, and I check my emails on a Sunday evening. I do not write back to him on Monday, because that is the day I am investigating Holly Randolph's social media accounts. Pondering the gap between the humble unknown actress she had been then, and the superstar she is now.

Tuesday morning, I wake up from a dream about Holly Randolph. We are sitting next to each other on a bench in Central Park, just talking, about nothing in particular. There is no moment of shocked recognition, no attempt to catch up over the past decade.

We are happily chatting away, like two old friends who meet up every week. She grips my hand in the dream, says something to me.

When I wake up, I still feel the squeeze of her hand on mine. But the words she spoke elude me.

Instead, I feel only an overwhelming sense of loss, a gaping void that encircles my solitary thirty-nine-year-old life.

I lie in bed, numb, and I cry.

Tuesday night, I am sitting in my living room, contemplating whether to scour Netflix for something decent to watch, when my phone lights up. A push notification from the *Hollywood Reporter.*

I have set my phone to receive these alerts from the trade publications. Perhaps to pretend that I still work in the industry, to keep my pulse on the latest developments—as if it has anything to do with my life now.

Bored, I pick up my phone—and freeze when I see the headline.

Xander Schulz: "I stand with all victims of sexual misconduct"

The headline alone is enough to inspire my vomit. The very thought of Xander grandstanding on these stories, as if he were the noble champion of all beleaguered women in entertainment.

I bring up the article, anxious to see the byline. Not Thom Gallagher in this instance, but someone named Carrie Seager. A temporary relief washes over me: this LA-based journalist has not tried to contact me. Not yet.

There's video footage of Xander speaking at an official press junket, and I cringe at him making such a show of this, raising a standard he never particularly bothered to wave before.

"Like many others in this industry, I am shocked and appalled at some of the stories that have come to light."

Xander is reading this out from behind a cluster of microphones, camera flashes smattering his face. It is still disconcerting for me to see Xander in the public eye. These days he churns out loud, albeit visually graceful superhero maelstroms, whereas the Xander I once knew saw himself as an auteur, striving towards an early Polanski. When I'm leaning back in the dark, buried in the padded comfort of an anonymous cinema seat, I will see his name break out across the screen—*directed by Xander Schulz*—always the last credit before a film is allowed to start in earnest—and I'll have to tamp down my emotions. But there is an undeniable glee in thinking, in knowing: *Xander Schulz, you fucking sellout.*

In this new video I watch on my phone, Xander is ten years older than when I knew him, and he has expanded outwardly, his hair thinning, his face thickened, his jawline less insistent. I am pleased to see him so visibly aged. A decade of Hollywood partying would have done this, and he only has himself to blame.

"While I have worked with some of the brave actresses who shared their experiences, I myself never personally witnessed any form of sexual assault taking place on the film sets where I worked. I only have the utmost respect and sympathy for these professionals and any other victims who have yet to come forward. I stand with all victims, and I sincerely hope we can find a way to hold these behaviors to account, so our filmmaking community can be one of trust and mutual respect."

I almost want to throw my phone across the room when I hear him say this. But I'm at the start of my Verizon contract and I can't afford a replacement. So I just sit there and grit my teeth.

So our filmmaking community can be one of trust and mutual respect . . .

Fuck you, Xander Schulz. What a hypocrite.

It's the standard "I'm a good guy" statement. Xander Schulz who regularly dated the models and actresses he worked with, who only ever cast beautiful women under the age of thirty, who often cracked puerile jokes about their physical attributes—*that* Xander Schulz is a good guy, in comparison to other men in the industry. And that is the sad truth of the matter.

I think for a moment about Xander—who now has a Golden Globe, a Toronto and Sundance win, five feature film directing credits, and a net worth I can't even estimate—and I know he will be fine. Because sure, his behavior was sexist and distasteful and immature. But it wasn't criminal.

Rewatching the footage, I notice how expertly worded his statement is.

"I myself never personally witnessed any form of sexual assault taking place on the film sets where I worked."

He said "sexual assault" here, not "sexual misconduct" or even "sexual harassment." And he specified "on the film sets" where he worked. He didn't mention the private parties, the hotel rooms behind closed doors.

Xander was careful not to name names, but his statement would have been painstakingly prepared by a publicist. (PR agencies in Hollywood must be making a killing right now.)

Carrie Seager does include some names in the last paragraph of her article.

In the past, Schulz has worked with actors such as Scarlett Johansson, Jennifer Lawrence, Reese Witherspoon, and Holly Randolph.

There is her name, plain for all to see: Holly Randolph.

But there is no mention of specific perpetrators, accused or rumored. I wonder how blind this journalist is, unable to ferret out the real charlatan who lurks behind the curtains. Or maybe she, like Thom Gallagher, suspects something, and is simply biding her time.

There is no mention of Sylvia Zimmerman, perhaps because Sylvia no longer works in the industry. Val Tartikoff, who continues to rank among the top casting directors, appears not to have been contacted either.

So the other women in this potential story have not been sought out for their opinions. At least to the public, we remain largely silent, our role in this drama forgotten.

And by that, I am not surprised.

Interview Transcript:
Phone call to Anna McGrath, Elite PR, Wednesday, Oct. 25,
12:15 p.m.

AM: This is Anna McGrath.

TG: Oh hi, Anna. My name's Thom Gallagher, I write for the *New York Times*.

AM: Oh wow. Thom Gallagher! Wouldn't have expected to hear from you.

TG: I'm interested in interviewing Holly Randolph about something. I know she must be very busy—

AM: Yes, it's manic for her. So many things going on. Is this about *Rainfall in Texas*?

TG: Oh, no . . . it's not specifically about one of her current films.

AM: I was gonna say. It's normally Sonal or Pete we hear from in your Culture section. You don't cover film. . . . You're investigative for the *Times*, right?

TG: Yes. I am. (pause) Listen, the story I wanted to interview her for . . . well, it's quite a sensitive subject matter, so I'm not sure—

AM: I know what you write about, Thom. I . . . (pause) I don't know. We'll have to speak to Holly and the team first, and I know she's got so much on her plate. I can't really see her taking something like this on.

TG: I noticed she's fronting the new L'Oréal campaign, the one about celebrating women's stories. So I would hope—

AM: Thom, what you're asking for is different from a makeup campaign. You know that.

TG: Well, yes, but I just thought—

AM: Send me an email. Outline the kinds of questions you want to ask, the kind of piece you hope to write, when you think it'll run, and we can take it from there. But if I were you, I wouldn't get your hopes up. She's just so busy right now.

TG: Sure, sure. I mean, we all are.

AM: Yes, but this is *Holly Randolph*. *She* gets to choose what stories she wants to tell. And I'm not sure I see her wanting to get involved in this one.

19

WE MEET ON Thursday night. Thom had offered to come to Brooklyn, but I like the idea of traveling into Manhattan after work on a weekday. It gives me the illusion I do still have some kind of life. Someone actually desires my company for a few hours, even if it's only for an investigative report he is researching.

This time, we do not meet at the *New York Times* offices. It would be too busy, too many people rushing around on a week-day evening. So Thom has arranged to meet in a small room at a private members' club on the Lower East Side.

The last time I set foot in a private Manhattan club, it was under Hugo's regime. Tonight, there is no bedroom suite. No table for cocaine-snorting, no bed. It is simply a small, luxuriantly furnished room, separate from the bar. Two armchairs, a table, lamp, and coat-stand. Hardly bigger than a walk-in closet.

"Is this okay?" Thom asks. "I know it may seem a bit weird, but I figured somewhere discreet was needed."

"It's fine." I look around, secretly delighted by the bizarreness of it all.

I wonder what nature of rendezvous normally takes place here. Clandestine arms deals. High-end escort bookings. Revelations of past transgressions.

It feels not unlike a confessional box (not that I have ever been inside one, but the Catholic imagination has produced enough films, I seem to have a vicarious understanding of confessionals).

A mere three-foot space separates me from the intensity of Thom's blue-eyed gaze. It has been a while since I have sat this close, in prolonged company, with one man, and no one else.

All clever investigative journalism is a seduction, is it not? He, the journalist, must win over my confidence, cultivate my trust, so that I will surrender my darkest secrets—to do with as he wishes, before he moves on to his next quarry.

I am both titillated and disturbed by the metaphor.

Once our drinks have arrived (a pot of peppermint tea for me, a fancy sparkling water for Thom—see how responsibly we are acting on a school night?), he sets the digital recorder on the burnished metal table between us.

"How's the rest of the investigation going?" I ask.

"It's going well." He is noticeably tight-lipped. I understand it is his journalistic obligation to be this way.

Still, it sits strangely with me. That I should be this open, this giving in what I reveal to Thom, and he himself so reticent.

"How are you feeling?" he asks solicitously. "I mean, after Saturday's interview. I know it can be troubling to bring up the past like that."

I nod, and my eyes well up with sudden, unwanted tears. What is happening? Crying in front of Thom Gallagher was not how I had planned to start this meeting. I look away abruptly, studying the intricate gilt pattern of the wallpaper, willing my tears to be reabsorbed.

I am here on my own terms, I tell myself.

Thom is respectably quiet. If he were to show any further demonstrations of concern, the tears would flood my face.

I am not used to people asking me how I am, in the context of the story I am about to tell.

Aware of how awkward this is, I focus on the distant chatter and music from the bar outside. Slowly, I am restored. My tears remain, but they do not fall.

"Um, yeah," I say, glancing back at Thom now. "It was unsettling. For sure."

He breathes out a warm sigh of acknowledgment. His gaze is reassuring.

"Whenever you're ready."

Despite her obvious brilliance at the casting session, neither Xander nor Hugo were as immediately convinced as I was about Holly Randolph. Xander insisted on seeing more actors. Hugo, for all his bravado about having a keen eye for talent, seemed less interested in the final artistic outcome than in the process of meeting so many attractive, eager young women.

But Sylvia saw the casting tape the next day and agreed with me.

"You were right about her," she said, nodding. "Holly Randolph completely nailed it."

I felt secretly reassured, knowing that Sylvia approved of my taste.

In the end, it took another two or three weeks for Xander to finally be convinced. To his credit, he did agonize over it, knowing the casting of the lead role would make or break his film.

Given the importance of this decision, you can imagine my surprise the week after the auditions, when I walked in on Hugo having drinks with another contender for the role of Katie Phillips. He'd asked me to bring him a few contracts and showreels to his club, meeting him at the bar. (Like most Brits, he felt his business dealings were somehow enhanced by alcohol.)

By then, Jermaine, the doorman at the club, recognized me.

"Hey, how are you?" I flashed a grin at him.

"My girl Sarah, great as always," Jermaine replied. "He's at the bar."

Hugo's usual spot. But once there, I was puzzled to see him sitting next to a slender, feminine figure in a short dress, her tanned legs crossed beneath her barstool. I wondered at first if this was his wife, Jacintha, whom I had yet to meet.

Then as I drew closer, I saw she was too young to be a mother of four. And I recognized something about the woman, in the curve of her cheekbone and the pitch of her eyes.

She must have sensed me studying her, because she looked up at me with a guarded expression on her face. I still couldn't place her.

"Ah, Sarah, great to see you're here." Hugo turned around brightly. "This is Sarah who works with me. Sarah, did you ever meet Jessica?"

Jessica shook her head at me. "I don't think we've met before."

And in that moment, I knew we had. Or at least, *I* had met her, when she auditioned for the role of Katie Phillips, two slots after Holly Randolph. But what was she doing here?

I was confused, and immediately, strangely protective of Holly. Surely, Hugo hadn't offered the part to someone else? But it wasn't my place to ask, especially in front of her.

"Pleased to meet you," I said. "I was there, actually, at the casting. I do remember you. Nice reading," I lied.

"Oh, thank you!"

Jessica had finely shaped lips and particularly large breasts, which were on abundant display in her tight dress. A germ of discomfort stirred inside me, standing there next to the two of them.

I noticed Hugo hadn't invited me to join them for a drink.

"Uh, I brought you these contracts and other things," I said to him brusquely, and handed over the stack of documents and showreels.

"Ooh, more showreels," Jessica remarked, her eyebrows lifting with curiosity. "Are you checking out my competition?" She teased Hugo.

The seed of discomfort quickly blossomed into disgust.

"Nuh-uh-uh." Hugo wagged a disciplinary finger at her. "That's top secret information. And besides, there's no competition with you in some departments."

He looked pointedly at her chest, and Jessica erupted in a peal of laughter.

"You naughty, naughty man," she reprimanded. "I'm going to tell my agent about you." Jessica pushed Hugo on the shoulder playfully, and he reached out a hand to hold her arm in place. He began drunkenly stroking it with his other hand.

I sensed that was my cue to leave.

"I'm gonna go," I announced to the two of them. "Anything else you need, Hugo?"

He shook his head and didn't even look at me; his eyes were trained on Jessica. "See you tomorrow, Sarah."

She didn't look at me either, or even say good-bye, and I backed away from them in a silent fury. To be rendered invisible just like that, because I didn't factor into their stupid game of flirtation.

I nodded to Jermaine and strode out onto the street, my mind churning.

I wasn't sure how Hugo had contacted Jessica—he'd probably had Ziggy or Brian contact her agent—but what was that bar interaction all about? Was he just trying to get laid? So it was the old game, the casting couch, which I'd never actually witnessed until now. Hugo sullying the artistic process of casting—one of the most crucial parts of filmmaking—with his sexual amusements. When in fact, he didn't have the final say in who got the part anyway. It was all so wrong, I couldn't fathom it.

The next day, I mentioned it to Sylvia in passing.

Sylvia rolled her eyes. "Maybe he's just lonely here without his wife."

She saw the look of disapproval on my face.

"I'll talk to him about it. He shouldn't be interfering with the casting process like this."

But I'm not sure if Sylvia ever did.

And you know what the worst part of it was? I can't remember Jessica's last name. In fact, I only remember her first name because Hugo introduced me to her. I never saw her again, in any TV shows or films or onstage. So I never knew what happened to her.

She remains a nobody. And her only claim to fame now is that Hugo North may have fucked her that night. That, or something worse.

=

After I've relayed the Jessica episode, Thom's Boy Scout–blue eyes spark to attention.

"Can you recall any other specific encounters between Hugo and female actors hoping to be cast?"

I strain my memory, as if forcing it through a sieve. That was the first time I'd noticed. "Undoubtedly, there would have been others."

"What do you mean by that?"

"Put yourself in their position. You're a young, aspiring actress. You audition for a role you desperately want, a 'plum role' that could launch your career. Then you get a phone call from the production, asking you to meet the producer. This could be when they tell you you've got the part. Or where you convince them of your talent and your passion. Any communication from a producer is a source of hope, of what might happen."

"Did Hugo ever ask you to get in contact with these actors?"

I hesitate. I have been losing sleep these past few weeks, trying to separate what I did from what I suspected, even that early on. These are fine gradations, painful reassessments for me.

"Most probably, he *did* ask me to set up meetings with these actresses, and I complied, just like Ziggy would have done. He was my boss, after all. It wasn't my role to question him, was it? I just thought, okay, this is how Hugo operates. He has money, he likes to meet attractive young women who want to work in the industry. He's certainly not the first powerful, wealthy man to act like that."

"What do you mean by that statement?"

I stare at Thom Gallagher and wonder how much easier this interview would be if he were a woman.

"Well, it's not just actresses who have to deal with this. In my experience as a young woman in the film industry, it is fairly standard that at some point, some guy you are working with will come on to you. It can be subtle: a middle-aged unit photographer to whom you have zero attraction, suggesting a pretty girl like you ought to have a drink. It can be more overt: an older actor you've worked with for months suggesting you stay in his hotel room that night. It can be shameless: a white-haired, sixtysomething male film critic planting a wet kiss on your lips as you leave a party, his hand cradling your buttock."

Such behavior was impossible to avoid. The rule seemed to be: if you're a young woman in this industry, you're fair game.

"How did you personally deal with that?"

I shrug. "You construct a stoic facade to fend off the unwanted attention. I mean, I didn't in any of those three instances sleep with the male in question. I came up with some witty but firm response, hoping it was clear enough I was uninterested, without having to be rude."

"Did it get tiring to deal with?"

"Absolutely. Of course it's irritating. Of course the naive you is thinking that maybe this older male film critic is inviting you to events because he's interested in your thoughts on genre and female directors—when really, he just wants to sleep with you. Eventually you stop being so naive.

"But the witty response, the ability to demonstrate a resourceful defense is key. Most importantly, you don't show weakness. Men are programmed to prey on weakness."

"Is that what you think?"

"Well, not all men, of course. But in film? There's always a power imbalance. The powerful prey on the weak. The weak become disposable, expendable, then vanish. So if you want to survive, don't show your weakness."

And for actresses, well, they probably have to deal with much worse.

"What do you think *did* happen that night, between Hugo and Jessica?"

"At the time, I thought Jessica seemed to enjoy his attention. She was clearly flirting with him."

"So you weren't surprised that she was flirting with Hugo. Why was that?"

You're a fucking Gallagher, and you're asking me that? That's what I want to say. But I don't.

"Listen, it's the film industry. You don't get anywhere without being social. If a powerful man offers you a drink at a bar, why would you say no? It would seem rude. And if this powerful man flirts with you . . . What is there to lose by flirting back a little? The odds are so stacked against you as an aspiring actor in this business, you use every trick in your arsenal to get what you want, to get cast."

"Do you really think that's true, or is it just a stereotype about female actors?"

"Because it's almost expected of them, some actresses end up behaving like that. As if it's a pre-written role. And with Jessica, a girl like that—"

"What do you mean, 'a girl like that'?"

Thom is looking at me, dismayed. Ah, the woke millennial male. You with your family pedigree, who has never had to scrape your way towards a faint glimmer of opportunity . . .

"A girl who wants to be an actress, who on some level wants the attention of other people, *may*—in some instances—be adept at using that attention to her advantage. And maybe that's what Jessica was hoping to do that night."

Thom stares at me, disapproving. "So what do you think happened that evening?"

I shrug my shoulders. "I don't know. I dropped off the contracts and showreels to Hugo, and that's all I can say. Maybe they went up to his room and slept together. Maybe she thought that would lead to her getting the part."

"So you assume something consensual would have happened between them?"

"Yes, at the time, I would have thought it was consensual. Because otherwise . . . well, it just didn't seem possible."

"Why not?"

"Because he was my boss. I worked with him every day, answered his phone calls, laughed at his jokes, drank his champagne. He was nice to me, he took my opinions seriously. I felt validated by Hugo. And I couldn't possibly contemplate the alternative."

20

I KNOW WHAT YOU'RE thinking. Here's me, passing judgment on poor Jessica what's her name, simply because she was an actress trying to make it in this industry.

But really, how much of this statement is fueled by my own envy? Because I will never be one of those women who know how to wear fake lashes, how to sit with their tits out, how to beguile the male ego. These women, so confident of their own sexual allure. Because actresses are capable of these skills, am I—a failed producer—secretly jealous?

But not all aspiring actresses are like that, I want to say. Holly Randolph was not like that.

As any quick Google search will now tell you, Holly came from modest beginnings, from a typical middle-class family in North Carolina. Her dad was a pharmacist, her mom a schoolteacher. The middle child of three kids, like me. She had no pretensions when I met her. And if her current-day talk show interviews are anything to go by, she still has no pretensions, even now that fame has found her.

I think that was what I liked so much about her, at the time. That such talent could reside in such a humble soul. That she was entirely dedicated to her craft. For her, it was about the acting, the immersion into a character. Not the glitz and the red-carpet parades and the free gift bags. Although we both enjoyed our fair share of the parties, they were not the point for us.

When I first met Holly, she had just changed her stage name to

Randolph. And her hair was a dirty blond, verging on light brown. Not the luxuriant red that has since become her trademark. (Ah see, white women get to change their hair color without being accused of hating their own race.) But her intelligence was already evident—as was the absolute commitment to her career.

Holly had a quietly assured magnetism that didn't demand your attention, but subtly drew it in. Until all eyes were looking at her, appraising the perfect symmetry of her face, the dimpled cheeks, the vast, emotive eyes—as if this face was where we were meant to be looking all along.

Of course, none of us could have anticipated Holly's future career when we offered her the part that summer.

The day we first welcomed her to our office, we were in the midst of a meeting with Val, discussing the riders in the contracts for the A-listers cast as the "Grizzled Detective" and the "Father." Ron Griffin, the Father, required a bottle of Johnnie Walker Black, a bowl of smoked almonds, and a Partagas Cuban cigar in his trailer every night after we wrapped. He only ate vegetarian. Jason Pulaski, the Detective, had a wool allergy and couldn't wear any fabric with a shred of wool in it.

"No wool, huh?" Hugo rolled his eyes. "That's a new one."

I heard the buzzer, and Ziggy rose to answer it. He waved to me through the glass wall of the conference room and mouthed, *It's her.*

I was strangely nervous, opening the door to greet Holly. As if I had matched with someone on a dating website and was finally meeting them in person for the first time. "Holly?" I shouted into the stairwell as I held the door open.

I saw her walking up, that light-brown hair still not dyed red yet. As she turned a corner, she looked up and smiled that radiant smile that would grace billboards and magazine covers in future years.

"Oh hi!" she said brightly.

"Hi, I'm Sarah. We met in the casting." I was keen to make it known I was someone of importance in the production.

"Of course I remember you." Holly climbed the last step, so we were now on the same level. I could tell she was genuine. We stood face-to-face, both smiling, as I extended a hand for her to shake.

"Well, it's great to have you here," I said. "I saw your showreel a while ago and was really impressed."

"Thanks." She beamed. "I still can't believe I got the part. It's like a dream come true."

She glanced down. "By the way, I really like your ring."

It was a slim jade loop I'd bought in Hong Kong when I was visiting my extended family. A simple ring, carved into an abstract rendering of a bird in flight.

For a lead actress, Holly was unexpectedly observant and kind like that. At least she was back then.

"So, as your agent confirmed, we will be shooting the film out in LA," Sylvia announced to Holly at the start of our meeting.

There was a slight edge of resentment in her voice. Xander, like so many men, wouldn't stop pushing until he got what he wanted. So Sylvia had finally relented on relocating the production to LA. I assumed she had figured out how to juggle the shoot with her three children in New York, the same way she always managed to handle everything.

"Have you been to LA before?" Val asked Holly.

"Only for meetings and castings," she answered. "So this'll be my first shoot out there."

"Well, we'll have accommodation arranged for you," Sylvia said. "A condo for you to stay in during the shoot. And obviously all ground transport, per diems, all that covered."

"Oh great!" Holly already knew these terms through her agent, who had handled the fraught and petty process of negotiating her deal. But to us, she exuded an appropriately fresh-faced excitement about the project.

"A good friend of mine owns several properties out in LA," Hugo added. "So you'll be staying in one of his condos."

All it took was a few phone calls from him, and the offices, studios, and accommodation for the production had been remarkably easy to organize. Well, I had ultimately done the legwork of arranging the details, but I'd marveled at Hugo's Rolodex, how expert he was at pulling the right strings from the right contacts, and how easily he got others (like myself) to do the work for him.

In that meeting, I remember Hugo looking at Holly with a marked fascination, the same way many a powerful man has viewed a beautiful young woman. "Do you have friends out in LA?" he asked her. "Otherwise, I could introduce you to some people out there."

"Yes, a few actor friends," Holly answered politely enough.

"So it won't be a problem for you to be out in LA for a few months?" Hugo continued to probe. "No boyfriend in New York or anything?"

There was an uncomfortable silence, and Val frowned.

"I'll be *fine* living out there for a few months," Holly said firmly. "It's what actors do, right? We shoot out on location if that's part of the job."

I silently awarded Holly an extra point.

"Look at you," Hugo said in a honeyed voice. "Total professional here. Well, I have no doubt you'll be amazing in our film. And we're clearly at the start of something incredible."

We all thought that, as we relayed other logistics to Holly. Travel details would go to her agent. We'd get the unit publicist out to her soon, to craft a good narrative about her humble upbringing, start connecting with possible media outlets. We lavished Holly with expressions of excitement as she stood up to leave.

And then Hugo asked her one last question.

"Holly, are you around tonight by any chance?"

A shadow of uncertainty crossed her face, but she quickly smoothed it away. "I need to call my agent first to see about a couple things. Why?"

"Oh, we're just having a few drinks at my club to celebrate having you on board our film. Would be lovely if you could make it."

Interview Transcript (excerpt):
Phone call to Val Tartikoff, Monday, Oct. 30, 3:32 p.m.

VT: Hugo? Oh yeah, we go way back. I cast his first film, the Xander Schulz one with Holly Randolph.

TG: *Furious Her?*

VT: Yes, that's the one. We discovered Holly Randolph at the time . . . Geez, that was a thrill for sure. You don't find stars like her too often.

TG: I guess my question is about how Hugo handled the casting process. On that film and possibly others. Did you ever hear of him using casting as a . . . means to develop certain types of relations with young actresses?

VT: Ac*tors*, Thom. They don't like to be called "actresses" these days. Though that's a bit trivial, if you ask me.

TG: All right, then . . . as a means of developing certain types of relations with young female actors?

VT: (sighs) Listen, Thom. I've been in this business practically forty years. Yeah, the casting couch exists. But not on my projects. (pause) I've got a good reputation for a reason. I find the best talent possible, no funny business. And I'm trusted because I'm a *female* casting director. I'm not interested at all in that other stuff.

TG: Oh, no, I'm not implying—

VT: When I cast a film, I know what I'm doing. All right? And from what I know, Hugo was completely upstanding as a professional. Women were probably attracted to him, sure. And quite possibly, he liked their company. But that's very different from him exploiting the casting process in a certain way.

(Pause)

TG: You worked with Hugo on several projects, right?

VT: Yeah, quite a few after the Holly Randolph one. And he was always a very good customer. Always very interested in casting, always respectful of my work.

TG: Okay. Do you think there's any chance—

VT: Listen, it's getting ridiculous, all these inquisitions happening right now. I know this business. There're a lot of girls who want to be stars, who'd do anything for attention. They might regret something they did in the past, want to twist it some other way. They might say anything just for a few minutes of fame.

TG: Do you really believe that?

VT: (sighs) I'm gonna have to go. I'm in the middle of casting four Netflix series and a James Cameron film, I really don't have time to answer all your questions right now.

TG: If I had some follow-up questions—

VT: Call my assistant, Henry. He can get back to you. But as far as I know? Hugo North is totally fine. I know a lot of assholes in this industry, and he's not one of them. There're so many girls out there, desperate to be seen. You never know what kind of gossip they'll start.

21

"SO DID HOLLY Randolph join you for drinks that evening at the club?"

Yes, she did. One drink. She was polite, she was professional. She met us in the Spark Club, where one corner of the bar had become Hugo's domain over the past few weeks. When Hugo entered the room, the service staff snapped to life.

"Megan darling, wonderful to see you." Hugo greeted her with a kiss on both cheeks.

The hostess nodded, and two other waitresses glowed as he headed towards us. AJ, the bartender, shouted out: "Mr. North, the usual?"

"Yes, a bottle of Möet . . . Make it a special vintage," he called back. By now Hugo had reached us, and he looked intently at Holly. "We have something extra special to celebrate tonight. Our production has *finally* found its leading lady."

That odd protectiveness flared up in me again, but just as Hugo stepped towards Holly, another club member—a broad-shouldered Texan—barreled into him.

"Hey Hugo, is that you? I wanna introduce you to my wife, she used to be an actress." An anorexic blond woman, twenty years younger than the Texan and wearing scarlet lipstick, beamed at him.

"Ah, Richard." Hugo was clearly annoyed by the interruption, but too debonair to ignore the man. He clapped him on the back, and then, somehow, the multitude descended. A swirl of people, some complete strangers, some vaguely familiar, trickled in and surrounded Hugo. The champagne was popped, flutes of golden Möet passed around. Over the din, he raised his glass, grinning warmly at Holly.

Sylvia seemed deep in conversation with Xander, and a clique of slender, quivering girls somehow materialized near Hugo. I took the opportunity to wrest Holly away from the hubbub.

"It gets to be a bit of a scene whenever Hugo shows up. I guess he knows a lot of people," I tried to apologize. "So, um, I hope you're excited about all this. Have you done many feature films before?" To be honest, I'd already seen her résumé. Two small parts and one significant role in three indie features over the past five years, none of which went into major release.

"Nothing on this level," Holly said. "I mean, I've never played an action role before. It's kind of terrifying." She shook her head and laughed. "Honestly, I never in a million years would have imagined this when I started acting in school plays."

"It's a bizarre industry we're in," I said, glancing at Hugo as he inveigled Xander away from Sylvia, towards his circle of sylphs. "I can imagine, especially for actors. One minute, you're struggling to get noticed. The next minute, you're in the middle of all . . . this."

"And how did *you* get started working in film?"

I looked at Holly in surprise; actors rarely asked me that.

"I guess I just loved film all my life, but never actually thought it was a possibility to *work* in it." I described all those unanswered cover letters I sent out, then the bulletin board at Columbia, meeting Sylvia for the first time. "And here we are . . . five years later."

"Here we are." She smiled at me and held out her glass to clink.

I sipped some more champagne. "Of course, I don't think my parents were exactly thrilled when they found out I wanted to work in film."

Holly laughed. "Me neither. Actually, they did everything they could to convince me to pursue more *stable* career paths. But when I got into Juilliard, they couldn't exactly say no."

"Well, my parents run a Chinese restaurant. It's about as mundane as you could imagine." I rarely ever shared this fact with people I met in the business. It was something to be ashamed of, the conversational equivalent of an oriental gong striking in the soundtrack of a bad 1980s comedy. But with Holly, somehow, it felt safe.

"Wow, a Chinese restaurant!" She seemed genuinely intrigued. I dreaded she might launch into a litany of her favorite Americanized dishes. But thankfully she didn't. "Where's the restaurant?"

"It's in Flushing."

"Oh, I've been to Flushing once, for Chinese food."

That didn't surprise me. Many a New York college student has ventured into Flushing on an intrepid excursion. I've seen them, curiously edging past the heaving crowds, staring fearfully into orange-tinged restaurant windows, at rows of roast duck hanging by their twisted necks.

"I'd ask you which restaurant, but honestly I can't remember."

"It's called Imperial Garden. Though I imagine they all blend together . . ." I trailed off.

"For an ignorant white person like me?" she joked.

"Well . . ." We both laughed.

"So," she asked, glancing out the window. It was the height of summer, and at eight p.m. it was hardly dark, the shops across the street caught in the amber rays of the lowering sun. "What's it like to work with these guys?"

I knew I was supposed to effuse about Xander's brilliant visual talent, his unerring cinematic eye, but for some reason, I said something else. "They, um, they definitely like to party. If you haven't noticed already."

By now, Hugo and Xander were passing out shots of Grey Goose vodka to the girls around them. Sylvia stood nearby, in conversation with the Texan and his wife.

"I've noticed." Holly bore a fleeting look of concern. "Is it going to be like this every day of the shoot?"

"I . . . don't think so. Xander didn't party very much during his first film; he's very focused when he's in production."

"And Hugo?"

"Hugo came on board after we shot *A Hard Cold Blue*. So . . . I couldn't tell you." I left it there.

"Yeah, my agent told me Hugo only joined the company a few months ago." Holly seemed to be digging for further nuggets of information.

"That's right. He . . ." I pondered how I could diplomatically say, *Hugo writes the checks, otherwise this film might not even be happening.*

"He has a vision for the production company," I finally said. "He's the kind of person who makes things happen." *Because of his money*, I wanted to add.

Part of me felt ill, spewing such PR drivel to a person I actually liked.

"Honestly," she said. "I am so grateful for getting this role. But I also *genuinely* have no idea what I'm getting into."

Holly Randolph peered at me with an unspoken question.

I smiled warmly and tried to laugh it off.

"Neither do I," I admitted, and then resorted to bland assurances. "It's a great script. We have a great team. It's gonna be an amazing shoot."

But I was lying, of course. I didn't know what to think, standing there in Hugo's vortex on that summer evening, as all the interlocking mechanisms of the film shoot were starting to click into gear. I was just saying what I thought I should say, the unrelenting surface optimism that glazed every conversation in this industry. If you tapped the surface, it was usually hollow inside.

22

S O. IT LOOKS like you and Holly are getting along pretty well,"
Sylvia remarked the next morning, her sculpted eyebrows
arched with approval. It was just the two of us in the office, a rare
moment of quiet in those final weeks before we left for LA.

I shrugged indifferently, but deep down, I was pleased that
Sylvia had noticed. "I guess. She's really nice for someone that
talented," I said.

Sylvia nodded. "It'll be a useful thing for the production if the
two of you are good friends. I mean, the best producers always
develop strong ties with talent."

I wondered if this might be my future: producing vehicles for
Holly to star in. Not just vehicles (that made it sound so cynical),
but genuine, worthwhile stories in their own right, ones that we
could shape together and bring to the screen.

"Meanwhile," Sylvia continued, deadpan, "I had to talk Xander
down from adding another car chase and explosion to the script."

"What?" I asked. "We've already budgeted and scheduled, we
can't just throw them in for the hell of it. Plus, the story doesn't
really need them."

"That's exactly what I told him." Sylvia's voice was full of vit-
riol. "Anyway, car chases and explosions are for insecure boy directors who need to prove they have big, swinging dicks."

We sniggered.

"Not to mention, our insurance would go through the roof,"
she added, ever practical. "Anyway, I told him if this film is a

success, he can have as many damn explosions and car chases as he wants in his next project."

I didn't envy Sylvia, having to wrangle with Xander's ego all these years and dissuade him from his last-minute whims.

"Listen, Sarah," Sylvia said. I stopped typing my email, recognizing the sincere turn in her voice. "I know I have a lot on my plate, between this production, the company merger, and my family. But what we're heading into now . . . this is big."

"Big?" I repeated, amused at her choice of vocabulary.

She smiled wryly. "All the craziness of production that we had for *A Hard Cold Blue*—it'll be like that, only ten times more intense. But in some ways, also easier, because we'll have more of a budget to play with."

"Yeah, I noticed." I'd seen the latest production budget, and some of the fees for the cast and crew were double what they'd been for our first film. My fee had gone up too—and this time, I hoped I'd be able to keep it.

Our office buzzer rang, and I moved to answer it.

"Hey, is that Sarah?" a teenage voice asked. "It's Rachel. I was just in the area. Is my mom in?"

"Sure, I'll buzz you in."

"Huh." Sylvia looked surprised. "Whaddya know, my own daughter acknowledges my existence. Maybe you can translate teenage girl talk for me. She's been unbearably moody the past few weeks."

"Happy to try," I said, thankful the insecurity of adolescence was behind me.

"Before she gets here, let me just finish," Sylvia insisted, her eyes seeking mine. "What happens with the film these next few months . . . It could make or break us. So just keep your eyes on the prize and don't get too distracted by the parties. It'll be worth it in the end, for all of us. Including you."

"I know." I nodded.

She grinned at me. "I know you can do it. Otherwise, I wouldn't have kept you on all these years. So, make us proud, Sarah Lai."

Before I could respond, the door opened, and Rachel poked her head in. She appeared alarmingly gaunt in her denim miniskirt, but I figured it was a new look.

"Hey Sarah," she joked. "Is my mom giving you a hard time? You and me both."

And so, that summer, my workload became near-impossible. I delegated as much as I could to Ziggy, but at the end of the day, he was too junior in the company to be speaking with our bigger contacts, or dealmaking.

I shoved myself onto the L train early in the morning, before the heat of the day had started to build. Once in our office, I switched on the AC, and generally sat there until seven or eight most days, ducking out for lunch or for meetings. I was starting to come in at least once on weekends, too, unlocking those steel warehouse doors, when it seemed all of New York was out enjoying the sunshine, slurping iced coffees. I didn't see much of my friends, or even my sister Karen, whose baby shower I should have been organizing. (I passed this responsibility on to her college roommate.) Each time I saw her, I was surprised how quickly her body was swelling. But I hardly had the time to ask her about it. There was always another email to answer.

"Did anyone ask you to come in on weekends?"

"No, but that was the only way I could get everything done. Chinese work ethic. I'm used to working weekends, right?"

I certainly wasn't being paid a huge salary in my position as head of development. Nor was anyone checking if I was doing the work. It was just assumed that Sarah would be able to handle her exponentially growing workload. And it was my personal sense of responsibility to the company that drove me.

That, and my desire to be a person of note in the industry. My ambition.

I automatically trekked to that office every day, checking my BlackBerry in the evenings, replying to Sylvia and Hugo at midnight. Think of all the people squirreled away in high-rise office buildings up and down this island, right now on a Thursday night at eight p.m. What ruse have we all fallen for? Believing this diligence will somehow be our salvation, grant us financial security, the esteem of our peers. As if that is somehow all that matters.

For me, that implicit drive of my twenties, combined with my culturally inherited work ethic, ensured that I never raised my head and questioned *why* I was working this hard. As an employee, I was a bargain for Sylvia and Xander and Hugo. I was smart and tireless and loyal—and I didn't demand much in return. I was completely willing to shape my life for the good of the company. A great deal for them, a poor one for me.

"What did your parents think of this?"

I don't think they really knew. They were so caught up in their own jobs, and in running the restaurant, attending to our large extended family, that I don't think they sought to interrogate my workplace. Besides, that's not really part of Chinese culture. You put your head down, obey your boss, flatter those above you. My parents were immigrants who came to the US; it wasn't their place to question these structures of power, or the white people who ran the systems around us.

I glance wryly at Thom Gallagher. He, whose family has become so emblematic of American leadership. What does it feel like to be spoken about like this?

But he gazes ahead, smoothly oblivious.

If anything, my parents were proud that I was such a diligent employee. That's how I was raised. Study hard, work hard, honor your bosses, and of course, your career will prosper. Such an innocent worldview my parents had.

If I slaved away unquestioningly that summer, I rewarded myself with the frequent, impromptu parties at Hugo's club. This, after all, was one of the perks of the job, right?

While my friends earned higher paychecks and pensions and

a decent healthcare plan, at least I had access to unending drinks in a private club every night. I could see highly anticipated films months before the public, rub shoulders with cinematic geniuses, or movie stars, or maybe just glamorous people who looked like they should be famous for something.

You could never really tell at Hugo's parties. Sometimes a man entering his suite might be a billionaire or a Grand Prix driver or a tech entrepreneur—but the women were often just aspiring actresses and models and dancers, PR women and art gallery assistants and random Brits who populated the space around him. (I think I even encountered Chelsea Van Der Kraft at these parties once.) I don't know where this constant stream of beautiful strangers came from, but they were often in their twenties or thirties, and lacking in any personality. As if Hugo always had to be the alpha in any given social situation: the richest, the most powerful, the most charismatic.

Sure, I never had any meaningful conversation with the people I met in Hugo's suite, but for me it was *fun*. It was a realm of unbridled, hedonistic pleasure that had opened up before me, unexpectedly. I could talk about films and down a few drinks with a clutch of friendly, gorgeous people who were impressed that I worked with Hugo, and then be on my merry way, the pressures of the production momentarily forgotten.

Gone was my previous life, wrangling waiters and voracious customers at my family's restaurant in Flushing. Here, I wanted to meet the crowd, not avoid them.

The last of these parties took place on the Friday before I left for LA. I'd been in the office late, finalizing some pre-production details and printing out important emails, so by the time I reached Hugo's suite, the party was in full swing. I desperately needed a drink.

I saw Sylvia talking to some of Andrea's colleagues, who represented writers and directors significantly more famous than Xander. As I started to head in her direction, Hugo intercepted me, his arm encircling my shoulders.

"Sarah, I was wondering when you'd show your lovely face. Surely you haven't been working until now?"

I smiled at Hugo, his hand still on my upper arm. "Well, I, um . . . yeah, I had some things to take care of in the office."

He shook his head and tsked, as you would a naughty schoolchild. "Always so diligent. You deserve to have some fun. Here, have a drink." He poured me a glass of the usual Möet and studied me. Then a thought occurred to him. "You're flying out on Sunday?"

"Yeah, Sunday morning. From JFK."

"What airline—Continental? Delta? Let's see if I can use my miles to upgrade you."

"Really?" I asked, secretly overjoyed. I knew we had budgeted for Xander to fly business class to LA, and Sylvia had used her husband's miles to upgrade herself. I'd never once in my life considered flying anything other than coach.

"At least to premium economy or something like that. It's the least I can do."

"Wow. Well, thanks so much—" I started to say, but Hugo waved me silent.

"Please, Sarah. No need. You fully deserve it."

Delighted by Hugo's favor, I downed my champagne. The release of the alcohol washed over me, and I welcomed it gladly. I looked around for the bottle, to pour myself more.

"It's a shame Holly couldn't make it," Hugo commented. "I'd really like her to enjoy these parties, feel comfortable with all of us. Do you think you could convince her to come to the next one?"

He leaned down closer to me, and I caught a whiff of his cologne, an appropriately moneyed scent, dark and weighty. "You see, Sarah, that's the trick to everything. Make sure everyone's having fun, and they won't even notice what you're asking of them."

Admittedly, that was probably easier to do if you were a billionaire and could afford limitless bottles of Möet. But I didn't say this to Hugo.

"I'm sure Holly will come along sometime."

"That's my girl. Go on now, enjoy the party." He filled up my champagne glass and sent me on my way.

A few hours later, the party had loosened to a scene of pleasurable messiness. I circulated through the suite, on a friendly basis with nearly everyone, although I couldn't remember most of their names. And then, the moment had arrived for Xander and Hugo to commence their signature version of spin the bottle.

I'd observed them perfecting this game at other parties over the past few weeks. Forget that awkward vision of nervous adolescents crouched in a basement, hoping to land their first kiss with a classroom crush (a scene repeated in countless coming-of-age comedy-dramas). Xander and Hugo had invented a more adult version, where the lucky individual designated by the spinning bottle got to either plant a racy kiss on Hugo's mouth (Xander sometimes substituted himself instead)—or, snort a line of coke off a half-naked woman.

I couldn't quite believe it, the first time I'd seen the game in person. But my embarrassment for the girls gave way to shock. You'd be surprised how many willing young women volunteered to strip and become a human cocaine-snorting surface. Or to kiss Hugo. I guess for some women, kissing a fiftysomething billionaire counts as a prize in its own way.

That Friday night, Xander stepped up on an armchair, steadying himself on a giggling girl's head, and announced: "I think it's about time we play spin the bottle. You know what that means!"

A collective shriek arose from the crowd in the room, who were already familiar with the game. I'd been chatting to Sylvia, who now looked at me, unimpressed.

"I think that's my cue to leave." She shouldered her bag. "I'm far too old to play these games. Come on." She glanced at me, expecting me to follow.

I hesitated. "Oh, I might . . . stay for a little longer." It was my last night to party in New York, and I was having too much fun to head home. "Friday night and all," I added.

Sylvia narrowed her eyes. She couldn't argue that there were any meetings tomorrow. All I really had to do was pack for LA.

"You sure, Sarah? You want to stay *here*?" She gestured to the swirl of strangers, laughing and reclining around the room, a mass of tanned legs and tousled hair and the occasional man soaking in the buzz of female energy.

"Sylvia, I'll be *fine*. You want me to text you when I get home?" I joked.

"Well, I guess I already have one daughter to worry about." She smiled. "Nah, enjoy it. But don't do anything I wouldn't."

We hugged good-bye. We'd see each other next in LA, to embark on our very first feature film shoot in Hollywood. It was still too surreal to believe.

And the moment Sylvia exited, the tenor of the party changed. It was as if Xander had been waiting for our adult chaperone to leave.

"Now. Let's get down to business," he announced. "Bottle." He planted an empty bottle of Möet in the room and motioned for everyone to crouch in a circle around it.

"And coke," Hugo declared.

He'd convinced a young woman named Christy to strip down to her panties, remove her bra, and stretch across the glass coffee table. She giggled as he poured a thin streak of cocaine onto her supple, heaving chest.

"Calm down, dear." Hugo laid a large palm on Christy's bare stomach. "This is A-grade, none of it to be wasted."

By now, I was accustomed to the spectacle of a nude woman stretched out on a table, as Hugo or Xander or someone else snorted coke off her breasts. At first, I'd thought this was only something people did in the movies. But as I watched everyone involved with a covert fascination, both the snorter and the naked woman devolved into laughter every time, as if it were a hilarious inside joke they'd been trading for years.

Some women chose instead to kiss Hugo, and would saunter up to him, entwining their arms around his tanned neck. Some enveloped him in an oceanic kiss, perhaps hoping to imbibe some of his renowned wealth through the witchery of their tongue and lips.

This night was no different. The bottle spun, as did the room around me. When it landed on one of the few men in the crowd, he might jokingly sashay up to Hugo (always provoking a roar of laughter), before snorting the line of coke instead. When the bottle pointed to a woman, she would often offer up a kiss, but might also beg to have the coke as well. Hugo usually let her have both.

Xander was the ringmaster of this circus, and he wielded his authority like some hyperactive game show host. The terse, silent Xander was banished in these moments. Here was the attention-seeking conjurer, the one who directed every movement and every body in this room.

"SPIN!" he shouted. And someone stepped forward to send the bottle into another whirl. It skittered over the carpet, and came to a stop, pointing to the girl beside me.

She put her face in her hands and began to giggle.

"Me?" she asked.

The crowd bayed in response, but Xander stepped into the circle.

"No no!" he declared sharply, holding his hands up. "Executive decision."

Everyone fell silent, wondering if this were some kind of joke.

Xander leaned down and nudged the bottle slightly, so it pointed to me. Then he flashed me a devilish grin and stepped back.

My heart jolted with outrage. *No fucking way, Xander.*

Every time I'd watched the game before, I'd felt exempt. As if the rules of inclusion could not possibly apply to me. But now the crowd watched me, expectant.

"Everyone, everyone," Xander explained. "This is Sarah, who works with me and Hugo on our films. I've known Sarah five years, and I have *yet* to see her snort a line of coke. Or kiss Hugo, for that matter. But one of those two things is happening *now*!"

He punched the air, and the horde cackled in approval. I felt my cheeks flush with fury and the five glasses of champagne I'd drunk. For a split second, I regretted not leaving earlier with Sylvia.

I looked to Hugo, who opened his arms up, beckoning me in a mock seduction. "Come on, Sarah," he crooned. "You know you want it."

Xander burst into laughter. I fumed.

"Xander, you can't just move the bottle like that," I tried to reason.

"No, no. I can," he shouted. "I'm the director, aren't I? *I* call the shots. Literally."

"Fuck you, Xander," I shot back, but the crowd only seemed to find this entertaining.

Xander snorted. "I love it when Sarah gets angry."

"It's about time we saw the naughty side of her," Hugo joked.

I glared at both of them, but realized there was no way out of this without being a killjoy. The evening's fun had suddenly pulled taut into this ridiculous, unnecessary choice. If I didn't agree to one or the other, I'd be branded a square by the entire room, my lowly status affirmed for all to see.

"Come on, Sarah. We don't have all night," Xander shouted. "What's it gonna be?"

My own personal consumption policy was alcohol-only and the occasional joint, no hard drugs. But kissing Hugo was out of the question. I wouldn't be able to look him in the eye or be taken seriously as a producer ever again. Especially not if it was all at Xander's decree.

Just snort the fucking line and get it over with.

"All right all right, *fine*," I said, and took a step towards the naked girl on the table.

Xander and Hugo both laughed.

"That's the spirit," Xander crowed.

I'd never really been confronted with another woman's naked body this close, and while I'd seen white women unclothed before, their pale pink nipples were always a weird reminder of their difference to me. I tried to avert my eyes.

"Go on, Sarah," Hugo wheedled.

I looked at Christy, and she eyed me from her supine position.

"Have you ever snorted coke?" she asked, her doe eyes smudged with blotchy mascara.

I didn't answer.

"Sa-rah, Sa-rah, Sa-rah," Xander started to chant, as if I were a contender at some raucous sports event. Hugo joined in. Somehow they got the rest of the room cheering, all of these unknown party people shouting, "Sa-rah! Sa-rah!"

Of course I'd never done cocaine before. Growing up, I'd heard so many lectures throughout elementary and junior high school about just saying no, bewildering TV commercials comparing your brain on drugs to a sizzling fried egg. Drugs were bad. Drugs would ruin your life. Message received.

But none of these school lessons ever warned you that at some point, working in the film industry, at three a.m. in a private members' club, your two male bosses would force you to snort a line of coke off a naked woman's breasts. That sometimes you couldn't just say no.

I pictured my mom and dad, railing at me in fury.

Pushing that image out of my mind, I leaned over Christy's naked body and picked up the rolled hundred-dollar bill that lay next to her. One end of the tube was moist.

That, more than anything, revolted me. That I would have to insert this very same bill, laced with coke, and stained with Hugo's and Xander's and everyone else's liquid snot, into my own nostril. I glared at the bill, then noticed Christy's eyes on me.

"Sorry," I muttered.

"It's okay," she giggled, then added: "You've got amazing hair."

"Uh, thanks," I said. Incredibly awkward.

Hugo leaned in and leered at us: "That's my girl. Go on."

I ignored him.

The mechanics of it were clumsy. I had to keep my hair back, pinch my left nostril closed, position the tube with my right hand. How did it look so effortless in the movies? But one long inhale and I vacuumed the line of coke into my right nostril.

I snorted some more, to ensure it all went inside. The frugal Chinese side of me instinctively felt that if cocaine was this expensive, no crumb of it should go wasted.

Then I wondered why the fuck I cared, because it was Hugo's money anyway.

Hugo and Xander cheered in victory. So did the rest of the room.

"YEESSSS, well done, Sarah!" Xander roared. "Enjoy the rush."

To my surprise, I felt a surge of triumph. There was momentary panic, brought on by those school health campaigns, but this was quickly swept away by an unexpected euphoria. I wasn't sure if it was the cocaine itself or the sense of trespass. But buoyed by the champagne and the drugs and the cheering, I somehow felt lifted onto a higher plane, amidst the gaze of this crowd, who now considered me one of them.

So this was how it felt.

To be in this unfettered world where rules didn't apply.

Hugo leaned in close to me and muttered: "Some other time, Sarah. Just you wait."

The cocaine having leached any anger out of me, I simply laughed in reply and glided onwards. I watched at a remove as Hugo leaned over Christy, who was now propped up on her elbows, flirting with him. Xander shouted again, the crowd cheered, and the bottle was sent spinning once more.

My head spun, too, whirling into its own liberated orbit. Perhaps all those warning tales about drugs were wrong.

If Hugo and Xander and so many others in the industry were always high on coke and managed to function, then I, Sarah Lai, could surely survive snorting a single line. There was nothing to fear. It was far too early to leave the party. The world was a wonderful place full of new possibilities, new sensations.

I would be fine. A single line of coke was nothing.

A few hours later, I rattled home in the painful light of a subway car, as the August dawn was starting to break. My brain synapses were still firing at a faster rate, and I decided not to tell Karen about the cocaine-snorting episode (she would never understand)—and definitely not Sylvia.

Sylvia would only say: "You know better than to do that, Sarah. You're not one of those girls."

And I wasn't. I was in control of my own narrative.

And so I rushed headlong through those last thirty-six hours in New York, moving out of my apartment and packing most of my adult life into boxes that I stored at my parents' place in Flushing.

I told them working in LA was temporary, just for the purposes of this film shoot. But secretly in my heart, I hoped I was moving to LA for good. That I was escaping the neurotic, demanding pulse of New York, the vertical confines of skyscrapers and dense city blocks and all my previous twenty-seven years of family expectations. This would be the start of the next stage of my life. The lure of Hollywood beckoned, gleaming on a distant horizon—and like many a fool before me, I crossed the continent, in thrall to that mirage.

Interview Transcript (continued):
Sylvia Zimmerman, 2:56 p.m.

SZ: Hugo seemed respectable enough to start with. The amount of money we needed to make Xander's second film . . . well, it was a drop in the bucket for him. And if his terms involved ownership of the company, it seemed fair enough. We'd had an agreement.

TG: So are you saying he didn't follow the terms of the agreement?

SZ: Legally? By all intents and purposes he did, the tricky bastard. (pause) But it was the *other* behavior, what went on *outside of* our professional realm of working together, which was the problem.

TG: What do you mean by this other behavior?

SZ: I suppose it started with the partying. The casual drink here or there, a line of coke offered . . . Of course, we're talking the film industry, in New York. Coke is omnipresent, but it was how these social encounters were used to foster professional bonds. Hugo was expert at that.

TG: Would you say this was unprofessional?

SZ: Again, it's the film industry. It's not about what's unprofessional or not. It's just that so much of what goes on . . . doesn't happen in the office, at meetings. (pause) With Xander, for example . . . I wasn't around to do all the late-night partying that they both loved so much. The drugs, the women. I mean, forgive me if that wasn't quite my scene. (snorts) So that undermined things. Here was a director I'd been working with for eight years, scrimping and begging just to get his first feature film made. And this billionaire simply swoops in with his open bar tabs and private hotel suites with fawning girls—and *that's* what his working relationship with my director is based on? I mean, it was all so juvenile.

TG: How do you think Sarah Lai took to it, all the partying?

SZ: She was young and impressionable. I'm sure she enjoyed it on some level. What twentysomething doesn't? I won't lie— that's one big draw to working in film, the parties. But I guess I was worried for her.

TG: Why was that?

SZ: A child of immigrants who went to Columbia? This was a whole different world for her. So much room for . . . corruption.

TG: What do you mean by corruption?

SZ: You hear stories of this all the time. Impressionable young girl or young man gets too caught up in parties, the drugs, the sex, the glamour. Gets used up, ruined.

TG: Do you think Sarah was susceptible to that?

(Pause)

SZ: No, I think she was smarter than that. But there was a side to her personality that could get carried away.

TG: Did you feel that you needed to protect her? From those kinds of corrupting influences? Or from anyone who could have corrupted her?

SZ: Hm. (pause) Listen, I'm not her mom, right? She's got her own parents, and God knows I was hardly present enough for my own kids. At the end of the day, she was a big girl, right? Twenty-seven? Twenty-eight? She knew how to make her own decisions, to deal with the consequences. And I guess you can say, as her employer, my responsibility to her only extended as far as the office and the film set. Everything behind closed doors, those were her choices. She should have been able to fend for herself.

(Silence)

TG: Is that really what you thought at the time?

SZ: Are you asking any male bosses these questions?

TG: I'm not at—

SZ: I get it, I get it. "You're not at liberty to say" who you're interviewing. (pause) Listen, it was a harsh world we worked in. When I was coming up, working in the eighties and nineties, there were even fewer women bosses around. And throwing yourself into the deep end, without any life vest, was the only way to learn. A lot of us drowned. But some of us floated to the top just fine.

23

"S O YOU FLEW to LA . . ."

After a bathroom break, I am back in our glorified confession booth, and Thom Gallagher nudges me on, eager to reach the buried treasure. "What were you expecting it to be like?"

God, what is any filmmaker expecting when they first get to LA? It is a city so saturated by the weight of anticipation, by previous screen incarnations, shot through with visions of golden sunsets and palm-lined avenues, that the reality of it becomes infused with the fantasy. You cannot separate the two.

How many films have been made about wide-eyed ingenues arriving in Los Angeles, hoping to break into a world that is hard-edged and cutthroat—but still has room for a singularly talented newcomer to reinvent the show business wheel? That is the delusional narrative Hollywood peddles about itself. But for every *Singin' in the Rain* or *La La Land*, there's a *Sunset Boulevard* or a *Mulholland Drive*. What talent and beauty and youth that City of Angels attracts. What hardened, money-hungry operators it churns out, casting the rest aside like unwanted detritus.

On Sunday, two days after that last party in Hugo's suite, I emerged from LAX International Airport onto the broad sidewalk and was struck by the balminess in the air, the bright sky, the cloud of exhaust fumes. My cab driver, Rico, helped me with my two suitcases, then rambled on about the wonders of LA. Gazing out the car window, I was surprised by the breadth of the six-lane highways, the volume of cars streaming past, the ridge of golden land that stretched on the horizon. In New York, every square inch of space had been built up and hemmed in, layered with four centuries of vertical architecture and human striving. In LA, wherever you looked, you saw broad skies and the hills—even beyond the sprawl of urbanization, there was always more space, more opportunity. I marveled at the individual homes, parceled out on their individual pieces of land, when New York households were stacked on top of each other, compressed and anonymous.

Rico was excited to learn I was a filmmaker in LA for the first time. He gave me a rundown of all the neighborhoods, stretching from Santa Monica, past the tony estates of Beverly Hills, the tackiness and tour groups of Hollywood, all the way past Downtown LA to the green lawns of Pasadena, and beyond.

I soon realized it would be impossible to get anywhere without a car.

As we drew up to the rented condos near Culver City, he cheerfully handed over his business card, should I ever need a driver again. I wondered how many eager young things he'd picked up from LAX, dreaming of a glittering career. Today, of course, I wonder how many he'd ferried back home, their hopes crushed, wishing to return to a normal life.

If this were a movie, Rico's card would come in handy. He would somehow rescue me at a crucial moment, revealing some hidden resource—martial arts or deadly marksmanship or a gang of Latino brothers—to fend off the villains I was sure to encounter in LA. Because when you arrive in a new place in the movies, the first person you meet always ends up being significant, someone destined to help you on your journey.

But since this wasn't the movies, Rico gave me his card—and I never called him again.

Sylvia, Hugo, and Xander all arrived later that week. Each of them organically adopted a style of residence and transportation that suited their individual personalities.

Sylvia stayed with a friend of hers in Malibu, occupying their house extension. They also lent her their spare BMW, which she drove over an hour each way, down the 1 and then the 10, to reach Culver City. Hugo already owned a house in Beverly Hills, but he seemed to frequent a suite in the Chateau Marmont for much of the time we were working on *Furious Her*. He had a personal driver, of course. And Xander took up residence in a bungalow at the Chateau Marmont for the duration of pre-production and the shoot. His car and driver were also included in the film's budget.

Through Hugo's contacts, I was staying in a modest rented condo complex a five-minute drive from our studio and production offices. I'd negotiated that the company would cover my accommodation until the end of the shoot. One other person from the production would be occupying a condo next to mine: Holly Randolph herself.

I was there for three weeks before Holly was scheduled to arrive. During that time, I mainly replicated the same work schedule I had in New York: moving from condo to office, spending ten hours on emails or on the phone or in meetings, ingesting dinner somewhere, and returning to the condo to sleep. I called up some of my college friends to meet on weekends, and hung out flirtatiously with Ted, the producer I'd met out in Cannes. Nothing significant happened, but for me, I was simply trying out another existence.

There was a strange, completely open sense of possibility: here I was in a city where I hardly knew anyone, and vice versa. I was no longer the diligent daughter of anxious Chinese restauranteurs. The weight of my family evaporated in the light and space and air of this new geography. I felt elated, liberated. I could be whoever I wanted, or write myself a different role.

Interview Transcript (continued):
Sylvia Zimmerman, 3:08 p.m.

SZ: Of course I resented having to move the shoot to LA. I'd
     made it very clear that I didn't want that to happen, and they
     bulldozed right over me. Xander didn't care one bit. All he
     ever wanted was to be a Hollywood director, and this was his
     big move.

TG: How did you feel about it at the time?

SZ: Angry. But I swallowed my pride and got on with the job. After
     all, if you're gonna have a clash of egos with someone like
     Xander, you're destined to lose.

TG: What do you mean by that?

SZ: Just . . . well, someone always has to back down. And as a
     producer for a director like Xander, I had to pick my battles.
     (pause) Funnily enough, it's not unlike being a mother.

TG: Really?

SZ: You have to cater to the needs of this demanding creature.
     Whether that's a film director or a five-year-old . . . well,
     sometimes there isn't a huge difference. (laughs) Producing
     and mothering. They're both never-ending jobs and they're
     both completely thankless.

TG: But you found it possible to do both?

SZ: Just barely. I don't know what I was thinking at the time. I
     wanted to be one of those successful working moms of the
     Upper East Side, and I guess I was. But I was also completely
     exhausted. And it didn't help that I felt other people were
     constantly encroaching on my territory, trying to steal away
     that little bit of space I had claimed for myself within the
     industry, after all those years of work.

TG: Other people, like who?

SZ: Oh god . . . Hugo, I suppose. And eventually Sarah, when
     she outgrew her assistant role. I mean, I tried to keep it all
     together. But once we moved to LA, everything got out of

control. Maybe it was in everyone's nature to act the way they eventually did. So maybe it was inevitable.

TG: Would you say *everything* that happened was inevitable?

SZ: No, that's a cop-out. People are responsible for the choices they make. Even me. (pause) Xander and Hugo were right. Moving the shoot to LA *did* open up a world of possibilities for the company. In ways I couldn't have anticipated. (pause) So looking back, what did the move to LA mean? I guess it meant I wasn't in power anymore. The tide had turned. But I didn't realize it at the time.

24

Hey! How's LA? Haven't heard from you in ages. I'm getting sooo big, it's crazy.

Karen texted me this a few weeks into my stay, and she was right, it'd been a while since I was last in touch. I sat at my desk in our production office, the buzz of six other phone conversations taking place around me.

Yeah sorry. Working lots, I typed back. That was true, but I'd also been out a lot, at various house parties and drinks with college friends and their friends-of-friends. If you're a producer about to shoot a feature film in LA, people are very interested in inviting you to social events.

For some reason, though, I felt I didn't need to pass this on to Karen. What do you say to a sister who is seven months pregnant? I wasn't sure.

I'm renting a car here in LA, it's nuts.

That much was true. My dad had insisted I get a driver's license a few years before, but in New York I'd hardly ever had a reason to use it. Here in LA's endless sprawl, I felt a terrifying unpredictability, driving my unspectacular Hyundai Accent around. I'd been too cheap to rent a GPS, so one wrong turn could lead to another, and I would inevitably be lost among thousands of streets. I also resented the lack of public transport or walkable distances here, the constant search for parking spaces. But I was getting used to it.

Have you driven to the Hollywood sign yet?

I frowned, somehow irritated by Karen's question. It seemed so silly, so unsophisticated.

I'm not a tourist, I typed back. And I don't really have the time.

Oh right. Well, try not to work so hard.

Karen had no idea.

But perhaps she had a point. I'd grown up worshipping the movies, after all, and the first time I drove the Sunset Strip, an undeniable electricity had jolted me. I turned off the impossibly steep slope of La Cienega, and towering above me were billboards ten stories tall, touting the latest television shows and blockbusters. I was here, and in one direction lay the studios with their gargantuan lots and bustling production offices. In another lay Century City, where the major agencies ruled from their high-rise complexes. All around me, in apartments and houses through all the neighborhoods—West Hollywood, Los Feliz, Silver Lake, Downtown LA, and beyond—people lived and strived and dreamed as aspiring actors, screenwriters, directors, designers, comedians, dancers, singers, producers. Each pursuing his or her own individual goal on an impassioned trajectory. And above all of this, set high on those not-so-distant hills, but apart and aloof from our mortal struggles, stood the unmistakable white letters of the Hollywood sign.

No, I never drove up to the Hollywood sign, not in the months I lived there. It seemed too desperate somehow. As if in making that pilgrimage to the holy site on the hill, I was giving myself too entirely to the myth. I was a professional; I wasn't going to worship at the populist altar of celebrity.

So all those months, I drove back and forth over roads and freeways, waiting at endless red lights, switching lanes, navigating my curious way around this temporary home that was Los Angeles. I wore sunglasses like everyone else. Because the sun was always too bright out there. All of us, too blinded by the glare of LA to really pay attention to where we were headed.

——

The doorbell rang, and Holly Randolph was standing on my doorstep.

She had just stepped off a six-hour flight, but she still glowed, looking casual in a striped T-shirt and jeans. There was a fizzing excitement at the pit of my stomach.

"Hey, welcome to LA!" I held my arms out for a hug. She hugged me back with equal enthusiasm.

In my calendar, I'd marked Holly's arrival date, partly because so much pre-production work would revolve around her (costume fittings, physical training, rehearsals). But also, after weeks of LA's estranged, car-dependent way of life, I was desperate for some close human company.

"I can't believe this is for real." She stepped into my apartment, which admittedly was nothing to write home about: the standard beige carpet and blandly furnished rooms of any American condo. "Okay, I can manage this," she mused, looking around. "Certainly beats my third-floor walk-up in Queens."

I uttered some positive comments about the production, how everyone was looking forward to working with her tomorrow.

"Anyway, I'm really glad we're living next to each other." She turned to me. "LA can be so big and alienating sometimes."

"Well, I've got a car," I said. "Should you care to risk your life, riding with a New Yorker who hardly ever drives."

Holly laughed. "Hey, I'd love to go for a joy ride sometime, get away from the shoot." And it seemed such a throwaway remark, that I told myself she was probably just trying to be diplomatic. But who knows, maybe she did actually want to be friends.

That day, Holly unpacked, took a nap, and the two of us went out to grab dinner at some buzzing Mexican place, all Latin pop music and fruity margaritas. Feeling like two kids at the start of the summer, we ordered cocktails: Holly a piña colada, and myself a strawberry margarita. As we clinked glasses, I looked around the restaurant and noticed so many of the other customers were young and perky like us: twentysomething, energetic, ambitious. This whole city of hopefuls, chasing our dreams to places we couldn't have predicted.

Holly's days were filled with training: fight choreography, specialized exercise regimes to achieve a physique that was muscular but still feminine. There were choreographers and trainers tasked with perfecting the way she would move on-screen. Clive, our hair and makeup designer, and Gina, our costume designer, were tasked with perfecting the way she would look. Holly was needed for fittings, tests, photographs.

The results of all this labor would be shown to Xander for approval, and sometimes, we the producers got to comment as well.

There was a significant dilemma over Holly's hair. Something about it just didn't work for Xander.

"I don't know what it is," he said to Clive in the production office one day. "It's just not right at the moment."

Clive was a lean, bearded man, a card-carrying member of the so-called "Velvet Mafia" of West Hollywood. He'd specialized in on-screen hair and makeup for nearly twenty years. Clive knew his hair. So far, he'd experimented with a ponytail and a messy bun on Holly, mocked up a long bob, a relaxed bob, a soft wave, but nothing too tight or polished-looking.

"The whole point is Katie's a natural beauty," a grumpy Xander insisted. "She's casual, she doesn't have the time to fuss over her hair too much. But we also want something about her hair to stand out."

Clive arched an eyebrow at him. "But what do you mean, 'stand out'?"

Xander was at a loss. Film directors are very good at declaring what doesn't work, but they're less good at identifying what does. So everyone else is left to guesswork, throwing forward suggestion after suggestion, on a quickly diminishing budget and time frame until something miraculously strikes gold.

"Maybe we can try a new color," he suggested to Xander. "If it's not about the style, maybe that'll make it *stand out*."

Clive directed a queeny eye roll at me, behind Xander's back.

Wordless, Xander just kept shuffling through the Polaroids of Holly in different hairstyles, as though they were a bad hand of cards, spelling out inevitable doom to him.

"Sooooo . . ." Clive continued grabbing at straws. "We could make her blonder—"

"No," Xander cut in immediately. "Not blonder. I don't want her looking cheap or anything."

"Sweetie," Clive crooned. "Not all blond is cheap. I didn't mean bottle-blond or platinum. Just a nice honey—"

"No, she's practically blond already! If you make her blonder, she'll end up looking like Marilyn Monroe."

"Number one: *no one* looks like Marilyn Monroe. Except Her Platinum Highness. Number two: there are many, many shades of blond out there. Ash, honey, strawberry, buttery, other things that I want to eat, except not ash. My job as hair designer is to demonstrate them to *you*, Oh Mighty Director Overlord." He said this with an exaggerated hand flourish, a courtier presenting to his liege.

Xander shook his head. "No blond. That's settled. What else?"

Clive widened his eyes in exasperation. "Okay . . . um, well, she is so fair-skinned, a darker shade wouldn't look natural. So we could always . . . try red?"

A moment's pause from Xander. "Red?"

"Yes. A good redhead. Always pops on-screen. You know, like Rita Hayworth or Ann-Margret from days of yore."

Xander tidied up the Polaroids into a neat deck and tapped them once against the tabletop.

"Or . . . drawing from more modern times, Julianne Moore?" Clive offered.

"Red," Xander muttered. "I wonder what that would look like . . ."

"Should I mock something up on a computer?"

"No, I need to see it real. Dye it red."

"Just like that? Just 'hey Holly, excuse me while I change your entire hair color—'"

"Just like that. Show me what you can do with red. But this other stuff—" He waved around the deck of Polaroids. "It's not working. Don't waste your time on it."

Xander flung the Polaroids onto the worktop, and they fanned across it in a stream of frozen Hollys, her hair different in each image. Then he turned on his heel and walked out.

One of the production coordinators had to re-jig Holly's schedule and bring her in to have her hair dyed ASAP. I happened to be in the studio when she sat there in front of the mirror, Clive breaking the news that her hair was going to dramatically change color that very day.

"You're dyeing it *red*?"

She gaped at Clive, aghast. But they were doing that disorienting hairdresser-client thing of addressing each other's mirror reflections, instead of directly looking at each other. I wasn't sure if I should be watching them or the mirror, as I followed their conversation.

"Yeah, I know, honey. It might be a bit of a shock."

"Well, I just . . . I mean, no one had mentioned anything before about my hair color."

"You know directors, they come up with all these things last minute."

In the mirror reflection, Holly's wide eyes stared into Clive's.

"Yeah, but it's *my hair* . . ."

"Are you upset about it? Do you want to call your agent? Do you want to have Sarah call your agent?"

Holly glanced at me briefly and shook her head. I was secretly relieved. Talking to agents is never fun if you're on the opposite side of a deal with them.

She sighed imperceptibly, her eyes growing pensive for a moment. Then that moment passed, and she turned to look directly at Clive. "You know what? It's fine. I'm a big girl, I can handle it."

Three hours later, Clive turned Holly's chair slowly, revealing the fruits of his labor to Xander, Hugo, Sylvia, and myself.

"Aaaaand . . . what do you think?"

She was still the same Holly (Clive had added more makeup for the viewing), but her hair tumbled about her face in richly vibrant tresses, the vivid red making her eyes bluer and more intense, the arc of her high cheekbones somehow classier and more assured.

"Wow," Hugo raved. "Simply *stunning*. I won't be able to get that image out of my head for a very long time."

He walked up to Holly and surveyed her, applauding in a slow, admiring clap.

Xander nodded. "You've nailed it. Amazing job." He said this to Clive, who performed a mock curtsy.

Sylvia was the only one who bothered to address Holly directly. "How do you feel about being a redhead? You look absolutely gorgeous."

Holly squinted at her mirror reflection, as if trying to recognize herself.

"Yeah, I think I like it. Let's go for it."

Of course, the rest is movie history. Holly Randolph became a redhead, and has stayed one ever since. Without her ginger locks, Holly might have remained just another hopeful blond starlet, one of thousands in Hollywood and New York. But red hair became her signature. It has come to define the essence of Holly Randolph, at least the version her fans want.

Ten years, fourteen movies, and two TV series on—even if she wanted to change her hair color now, I don't think she'd be able to. I think Holly Randolph is stuck with red hair for life.

Interview Transcript:
Meeting with Christy Pecharski, Cafe Julienne, Tuesday, Oct. 31,
11:41 a.m.

TG: Christy, you might be able to help. I wanted to ask about a
film producer you may have met at a party in New York back
in 2006.

CP: Geez. That's, like, really specific. I met a lot of people at parties.
Who's the guy?

TG: There's a British film producer named Hugo North who may
have thrown a party or two that you attended. It was at the
Spark Club in SoHo, which no longer exists.

CP: (pause) You have a picture of this guy? (shuffling) Ohhhh . . .
him. Yeah, I remember that guy. Kinda hard to forget.

TG: Really? Why is that?

CP: Well, for starters, I ended up in bed with him.

TG: You had—you slept with him?

CP: Yeah. It was just once from what I recall.

TG: Was it . . . what you'd call consensual?

CP: Yeah. (laughs) I mean, he didn't have to threaten me or
anything, if that's what you mean.

TG: So you slept with him willingly?

CP: Sure. Look, it was back in the day when I was out partying
practically every night. I went to a few of his parties, there
was a lot of coke around, so yeah, I was high. I'd sleep
with men—probably more than I should have. But I enjoyed
it for the most part. (pause) I don't do that anymore, by
the way.

TG: And if you hadn't been high?

CP: Would I have still slept with him? Hard to say . . . Probably?
He was kinda hot in his own way. I mean, he was older. But
he just seemed kinda refined and in charge, with that English
accent of his. And he had a lot of money. (pause) So if you're
a girl, there's kind of a thrill to it—can you snag the rich guy
in the room? You feel powerful for a moment, but . . . I guess

it doesn't last long. They sort of forget about you after that.
(pause) Anyway this—what was his full name again?

TG: Hugo. Hugo North.

CP: This Hugo North, he was throwing all these parties, tons of
champagne being sprayed around. I was a model at the time,
trying to be an actress. And here he was, this big-shot movie
producer saying he could cast me in a role. (pause) I mean,
this is a bit embarrassing. But he used to throw these parties
with spin the bottle, where part of the game was snorting coke
off a girl with no shirt on. And well . . . I was one of those girls
one night.

TG: How did that end up happening?

CP: I volunteered for it. I don't know what came over me. I guess
I was proud of my body back then and how I looked. I liked
it when guys were attracted to me. I guess in some way I
wanted the attention?

TG: So did he promise to cast you in a role if you slept with him?

CP: I can't remember exactly, but sure, he was saying stuff like
that. I suppose mainly just to get me into bed.

TG: And did he, in the end? Cast you in any film?

CP: (laughs) No. I mean, I was young and stupid back then. But
I didn't mind, really. I think the sex was fun, from what I
remember. He was a bit demanding, but as long as I went
along with what he wanted, it was fine.

(Pause)

TG: How old were you at the time?

CP: This was before I met Marcus, so I musta been . . . nineteen?
Maybe twenty.

TG: Did you feel coerced into sleeping with him?

CP: Not really. Looking back on it, a bit tricked, maybe? But it
worked out in the end. I mean, I didn't get cast in any parts,
but he introduced me to a better modeling agent—and I got
some good work out of them. A few covers, a lot of runway
gigs.

TG: Do you remember how that happened?

CP: I'm just thinking back now. In the morning, he said "Ring up my friend Steve at Apex, and tell him Hugo North recommended you." So I did and . . . It took some chutzpah, calling him, and I thought maybe it was a bit embarrassing, but I guess I had nothing to lose. So it paid off in its own way. But no, it wasn't assault or anything like that. At least not that time.

TG: Are you saying there were other instances where Hugo North—

CP: No, not with him. Like I said, it was only once with Hugo. But . . . heck, there's other stories I could tell you. Just— I don't know if you want to hear them right now.

25

HOLLY STOOD NEXT to me, her newly red hair gleaming in the streetlight, as we crowded on the sidewalk outside a West Hollywood bar. It was ten p.m. on a Friday—in fact, my twenty-eighth birthday—and Clive had promised he'd work his magic to get us into a legendary drag night.

"Mateo, how are you, darling? Don't make us wait too long, we're on Robert's list." Clive said this as we pushed ahead of the line that was building: middle-aged gays, twittering fag hags, gorgeous young men, and an army of preening, immaculate queens, all eager to witness the newest rising drag acts this evening.

Mateo the doorman had immense, sculpted biceps. He smiled in recognition of Clive and waved us through.

It wasn't just the three of us from our production. We'd also picked up Marisa (our makeup artist), Seth (our line producer), and Leila (our production accountant), who had been chatting in the production office as we wrapped work for the day.

"I can get us onto the guest list for my friend's drag night," Clive had bragged. "Menagerie at Dorothy's. It's an LA institution."

And so the six of us caught the tail end of happy hour at a Culver City bar, scarfed down Korean tacos from a food truck, and now found ourselves in West Hollywood waiting to watch a drag queen competition. My stomach was full of short rib tacos and rum and Cokes. I was fed and buzzed and very glad to be away from the office, celebrating my birthday with work colleagues. There had always been something unique about the camaraderie that was quickly forged from working on a production. Filming away from my home city, this was even more pronounced.

I had only known Clive, Marisa, Seth, and the others for a few weeks, yet they were friendlier and more welcoming than Sylvia and Xander had ever been in my first year at Firefly. Maybe, cynically, friendships born of film shoots were simply more temporary, and everyone knew it. So someone could act like a close confidante after only a few weeks of collaborating, but once the shoot came to an end, and the last call sheets recycled, people would drift apart, knowing the friendship had served its purpose.

But for the time being, I thrilled to the instant affection, the footloose hilarity of these nights out. There was so much more spontaneity to LA than in New York, where everyone (or at least the people I knew) had their weekend plans mapped out far in advance.

And this—Korean tacos, a West Hollywood drag show—was a very LA night out.

Holly and I clung to each other, like two wide-eyed seafarers washed onto this fantastical new shore. As we entered the dimly lit nightclub and passed through a beaded curtain, the thump of re-mixed disco classics pulsed louder through my body. I knew drag scenes like this existed in New York, too, but I'd never been to one. My life there had been so circumscribed by my family, the restaurant, later my Ivy League and work circles. In fact, it was only through Hugo that I'd ventured farther afield and discovered the debauched world of private Manhattan clubs.

"Can I get you guys a round?" I asked, as we pressed our way past the bar, lit up in hot-pink neon and a mirrored mosaic pattern. As the associate producer, I somehow felt obligated to offer a round. I think that was somehow expected of producers, whenever one was on the scene.

"No no." Clive swatted me away, towards the far end of the room. "We're in the VIP section. It's table service there. *Plus*, it's your goddamn birthday, and this place is like home for me. There's no way you're buying the first round here.

"Tarek, you stud, give me a kiss." Clive leaned over to the bartender, dark and muscled with a laser-cut beard. They exchanged smooches.

"*Love* your hair," Tarek shouted at Holly. "What a color."

"That's all me," Clive boasted. "This gorgeous girl is the lead in our current film, hair courtesy of me. Isn't she a doll?"

Tarek lavished attention on Holly and Clive, before we all pressed our way towards the VIP section. There, we had considerably more room to breathe, as we sat around a small circular table, waiting for two pitchers of sangria to be delivered.

"So tell me about Xander," Seth asked. "What's he like to work with?"

Ugh. Always the same question. As if Xander were some cinematic deity like Orson Welles. This was only his second feature film, for god's sake.

I said the usual formalities ("so sharp with visuals, knows exactly what he wants"), then asked some questions of Seth. "You tell me, you've been in this business for years. What makes for the best kind of shoot?"

"It's funny, it's this intangible thing you can't quite name." Seth leaned in, raising his voice above the din. "Some productions just run smoothly—on time, on budget, no big egos—everything's like clockwork. But they're just kinda . . . boring. Everyone gets along, but you don't come out of them thinking you're gonna be best friends with anyone."

"And then some shoots are complete train wrecks," Clive said, waving our waiter over. "Like, totally chaotic, nothing on time, everyone shouting at each other. But despite all that, you make some friends for life."

"*We* met on one of those shoots, right?" Marisa arched an eyebrow at Clive.

"Oh god, yes." Clive took a brimming pitcher and started doling out glasses of sangria. "Listen to this. Two weeks into a shoot, completely last minute, I had to replace a makeup artist. One of the stars, who shall not be named, fired our previous one for some mascara debacle . . . awful cow. And someone told me about Marisa. So I call her up, desperate, at ten o'clock the night before, asking if she could be in the trailer at four the next morning. And being the trooper she is, she said yes."

"How could I say no? Everyone knows Clive," Marisa added.

"Yes, that's true. Everyone does know me," Clive simpered. I was impressed. The guy had built his network. "And Marisa and I, well, we've been working together ever since."

"Ah see, you found each other in the end," Holly gushed. She had been quiet for some time, but we all turned to her, her blue eyes alight. "I know it's different for cast, we're not on set for the whole shoot, and sometimes—well, I get jealous—of how close-knit the crew seem. If I have a small part, I rock up for what, a week of filming? Sometimes just a day or two? And everyone else knows each other, but I only get to be a part of that community for a blink of an eye."

"Yeah, but it'll be different this time around," I said. "You *are* the lead. I think you're filming virtually every day of the shoot."

Everyone laughed.

"But that's it, it's all or nothing for actors. At least you guys get steady chunks of work. A few months at a time. I get a day or a week here or there, and then nothing for months on end, even years."

"Well, I don't think you have to worry about that from now on," Clive reassured her. "This is a great role for you, it's sure to get you noticed."

"God, I hope so," Holly pronounced. "Thanks again for having me on board." She looked at me with gratitude, and I shrugged.

"Holly, you were the obvious choice for the role. It wasn't even close." I smiled at her sincerely and raised my glass of sangria. "Here's to the shoot. May we all become great friends and may it *not* be a train wreck!"

"And may Holly never have to worry about working ever again," Clive said.

We downed our glasses and eagerly refilled them. The volume

of the music inched up a notch, in anticipation of the drag performance.

"How about you, Sarah?" Seth asked. "I mean, it must be so weird for you to hear about working a day here or there. You're a producer, you've been working on this project for *years*, right?"

"Three years, to be exact," I said, fishing an orange slice from my glass.

"Jesus, three years?!" Marisa was shocked.

"That's how long it takes to get the script drafted and redrafted, to get financing lined up, sales agents interested—" I stopped there. I was pretty sure they didn't want to hear about our struggle to get past 60 percent of the financing. It was probably quite boring to the crew.

And yet, none of them would be here working this particular job if we hadn't found that financing. Implicitly, I think everyone knew that and respected my role as producer. Maybe that's why they were being so nice to me.

"Fuck, I would never have that patience," Clive muttered. "In three years, I can probably work on what, forty productions? Easily more."

"So weird." Marisa shook her head. "The different time scales we all work on. Even though we're all making films."

But that's what I loved about being in LA at that particular moment. To live in an entire city full of people who knew the reality of the industry, who lived and breathed movies and TV, who could veer from talking about postwar noir to 1970s thrillers to *Twin Peaks* to the 1990s Disney Renaissance in the space of a minute. No one would scoff and say films were just a hobby or a diversion before you settled down to a real career. Film was a legitimate industry, paying for thousands of livelihoods out here, and everyone took it seriously. But also, everyone here knew how to have fun.

"Let's quit talking shop now." Clive took Marisa's half-empty glass and set it on the table. "The drag acts are about to begin. And the opening number . . . well, you won't want to be in your seat for this."

He ushered us from our chairs, motioning us towards the stage. As I drained my glass, I quickly checked my BlackBerry. Nothing from Sylvia or Xander or Hugo, thank god. A message from my sister.

Enjoying your birthday? Hope so! The doctor wanted another scan today. All good, though. This baby is kicking lots!

I paused for a moment, unsure of what to write. Then I pocketed my BlackBerry without sending anything. I'd message Karen later. For now, the music had started, the clientele squealed, and in the crowd, Holly looked towards me, wondering when I would catch up.

26

PRE-PRODUCTION RUSHED ON, barreling inevitably towards the juggernaut of production, the actual film shoot. I suspect Thom Gallagher must have some familiarity with show business, having interviewed so many sources. But I am a lecturer by profession, so let me expound.

Of the three basic stages of filmmaking, production is the one everyone knows about, because you see it in the movies. The cameras roll, the cast are ferried from trailers to set, the director commands from his chair, and behind it all, the producers manage and worry and extinguish whichever large or small fires crop up.

Production is also a giant logistical nightmare. Because shooting a film is expensive and money can't—or at least, shouldn't—be wasted. Every single person employed on set or behind the scenes is being paid a wage. If they go overtime, they're paid a higher wage. Renting a studio costs money. Dressing a studio to look like somebody's living room or a boxing ring or an alien landscape or whatever world the script demands costs money. Renting the camera equipment and the lights and everything needed to film the action costs money. Hair and makeup costs money. Costumes cost money. Hiring extras to populate a scene costs money. Shuttling the cast and crew to set and back to their trailers costs money. Feeding all these people costs money. Walkie-talkies and cell phone plans cost money. Printing out the daily call sheets and distributing them so cast and crew know what to do the next day costs money.

In essence, every single thing in a film costs money, and every single thing has its price.

And in that sense, working in the film industry was the most realistic education I could ever want.

But before the shoot can start, there's always the final script read-through. This is always a momentous occasion: the first time the entire speaking cast assembles, the first time you hear the actors voicing all your dialogue, when you realize this film—something you've envisioned hundreds of times in your head—is soon to become a reality.

For us, the read-through took place on a Monday afternoon, in the last week of pre-production. Xander, Sylvia, Hugo, myself, Seth, our unit publicist Jenna, and the main cast sat around a long table in the studio complex. Val was on speakerphone, listening from New York. A stack of twenty scripts awaited, neat and pristine, on either end of the table.

A palpable buzz charged the air.

Holly must have been nervous, but she presented herself with a polished calmness, a concentrated focus behind her comely face and lustrous red hair. Other cast had arrived early, like Amanda (the eight-year-old child actor playing Katie's daughter) and her insistent mom. We were still waiting for Ron Griffin and Jason Pulaski, the A-listers Val had cast as the Father and the Detective.

Ron and Jason did not have the extensive pre-production commitments that Holly faced. For one thing, established older actors like them couldn't have their time and schedule demanded in the same way as Holly's. And as middle-aged men, they weren't subjected to the endless fussing and tweaking that happened over Holly's appearance—over her hair, her makeup palette, her wardrobe, even the underwear she wore and how that would affect her silhouette.

Funny again, how easily the movies reflect real life.

Ron and Jason had worked together once before, on a gangster film five years ago. When Jason stepped into the room, they enveloped each other in a fraternal hug.

"How's it going, man?" Ron asked. They did that guy thing of gripping each other by the hand and slapping each other on the back.

"Good, good! So glad to be working with you again."

"Yeah, honestly, when my agent told me you were on board, I was like 'Sign me up, dude!'"

"Jason, Ron, this is our leading lady, Holly Randolph, who'll be playing Katie," Hugo cut in and gestured to Holly.

"Oh. Hey kid," Ron said. "Congrats, it's an awesome part. I'm looking forward to playing your dad. You look great."

"Yeah." Jason pointed a finger at her. "You're exactly how I imagined Katie. My girlfriend's a redhead. I love redheads."

Holly smiled. "Thanks. Glad to be in that group, then."

"Ginger, as they say in England, right?" Jason elbowed Hugo in the shoulder, and Hugo clapped him on the back.

"My favorite kind of woman," Hugo snickered in return. "Though *my* wife is a blonde."

At this, Sylvia stood up and clapped her hands twice, loudly, as if summoning a rowdy classroom full of schoolkids.

"All right, everybody," she announced. "It's really exciting to have all of you in the same room together. Xander and I—and Hugo—have been working really hard to pull this production together, and it's amazing it's happened this quickly."

Hugo cleared his throat to speak. "I'm so chuffed—as we say where I'm from—to be working with Xander, bringing his filmmaking genius to another level. Shockingly talented guy. You're all going to absolutely love working with him."

Sylvia nodded and continued. "We'll be having some drinks after this, and I hope you can all stay and get to know each other a bit more. And now, in case you haven't met him already, I'd like to introduce you all to Xander."

There was enthusiastic clapping as Xander stood up, his sunglasses propped on his baseball cap (which I noticed he had now started to wear backwards, as if he were channeling the early '90s). The day before, Xander had mumbled a few ideas to me, and asked me to craft them into a short speech.

"Fine," I'd grumbled, even though I had about ten emails and five phone calls I had to make in the next two hours. I was the best writer in the office, and it would only take me a few minutes to whip up something decent.

Now Xander (who had been sitting silently at one end of the table, observing everyone) snapped into charismatic mode. He looked around the table, grinned, and spoke the words I'd written.

"I wrote this script because I wanted to show a young woman— a young mother—who could be protective and fierce and vulnerable all at the same time. Katie Phillips is forced into a unique situation and has to rely on herself to defeat much more violent enemies. She has to protect her home and I guess, be both a mother and a father to her little girl."

He paused for emphasis here.

"But I don't think this is too different from what a lot of women have to do every day in real life. So I guess I wrote this film in recognition of all those real-life single mothers out there."

Everyone clapped again.

"Can I just say," the fiftysomething actress Marian Waters spoke out. She was playing Katie's estranged, unsympathetic mother, who was divorced and living a self-involved life. "It is a wonderful script, and so refreshing to hear a male director say that."

And how did I feel when I heard that? Proud, that I'd been able to create such effective lines for Xander to say, something he might never have managed otherwise. I was also the person who knew the script backwards and forwards, when each character was needed in which scene, how each narrative twist led to the next one. So I sat there quietly, soaking in this vicarious praise.

"Amazing script, can't wait to get started," Jason shouted. He turned to me in a lowered voice. "Hey, can you get me a glass of sparkling water before we start?"

It was the first time he'd addressed me. My feeling of pride shriveled. I opened my mouth, unsure of what to say.

Sylvia stepped in. "Jason, we're having a runner bring in San Pellegrino any minute now. By the way, this is Sarah, our associate producer."

"Oh shit." Jason looked at me, aghast. "Sorry."

But what did I expect? I was a young woman, and until then, no one had thought to introduce me.

A third of the way through the script, when Katie gets her second threatening phone call from the villains, I noticed Sylvia's phone light up on the table. She'd switched it to silent. Now she peered at it and wrinkled her brow.

"Hey little lady," Barry Wincock breathed. Barry was playing the villain, the main heavy who doesn't die until the final reel, and the one ultimately responsible for the death of Katie's husband.

Barry and Holly launched into a tense dialogue, each line of his filled with menace.

I saw Sylvia's BlackBerry glow again. Annoyed, she picked it up.

By the time we'd moved on to the next scene (a concerned Katie goes to visit her dad, her young daughter in tow), Sylvia had her BlackBerry below the table, scrolling surreptitiously through her messages. Other than me, no one noticed this. A troubled look crossed her face.

"Dad, can I ask you something?" Holly-as-Katie said. She turned to face Ron.

"Sure, sweet pea, whatever you want."

(Ron had been playing trustworthy fathers for the past twelve years of his career. He had the gravelly, paternal tone perfected to a tee.)

Under the table, Sylvia was quietly trying to tap out a message on her BlackBerry. I wondered what could be so urgent that she couldn't wait until the end of the script reading.

The read-through continued, every line falling into place

when it was brought to life by an actor. We were engrossed, sharing in this communal storytelling, our thoughts of the outside world momentarily suspended. But I saw Xander cast a frustrated glance at Sylvia once or twice, as she continued scrutinizing her phone.

And then, at a crucial point in the script—when Katie was turning to her daughter, telling her it was just the two of them, and she wouldn't let any bad men touch her—Sylvia stood up.

Holly and Amanda, the child actor, didn't notice; they were too gripped by their own reading. But everyone else around the table saw, and cast Sylvia a questioning glance.

So sorry, Sylvia mouthed, and quietly hurried out of the room.

The script reading carried on, uninterrupted. Hugo raised his eyebrows and exchanged a glance with Xander.

Puzzled, I took my own phone out, to see if Sylvia had messaged. Nothing.

"It's not going to be like that," Holly announced to Amanda, scared but insistent. "Even if Daddy's not with us anymore, I'll still be here to protect you."

Eight-year-old Amanda inched forward in her seat. "But with Daddy gone, who'll be left to protect *you*?"

27

SYLVIA DIDN'T COME back to the read-through until we had only ten pages left in the script. She looked flustered as she took her seat quietly. Only then did I notice the deep circles under her eyes, which her usual heavy makeup hadn't managed to hide.

The script reading ended with applause and more generic words of praise, including a pep talk delivered this time by Hugo. Afterwards, we filed out of the room chatting, heading towards the drinks.

Sylvia took my arm, drawing me to her.

"Listen," she said, a grave look on her face. "Something's come up."

I panicked, wondering if a financier had somehow fallen through, or the release plans for *A Hard Cold Blue*, or if Holly's agent had thrown up a last-minute obstacle. "What is it?"

"Um, it's Rachel. My daughter. She . . ."

Sylvia trailed off, debating how to phrase something. She lowered her voice. "So, she's been struggling with bulimia for a while. I knew it was an issue, I just didn't realize how serious it'd gotten."

I saw the concern on her face, a stain of guilt and regret.

Rachel? I had seen her just last month, and yes she'd looked skinny. But hadn't she always been?

"Is she okay?" I was genuinely horrified.

"She's . . . been hospitalized. She collapsed when she was out with friends the other night, and the doctors were shocked her weight had fallen that low. She's less than ninety pounds!"

"Wow," I breathed, unsure of what else to say, but also awe-struck someone could weigh that little. Here in Hollywood, where carbs were anathema, I was a chunky 125. I looked around the room at the actors, but Holly was the only young woman among them, and I was pretty sure she weighed over 100.

"I'm really sorry to hear that." Rachel had been so sweet to me when she was younger, and even as a teenager, she'd always shown a base level of politeness and common sense. But to deliberately starve herself for the sake of . . . I shook my head, uncomprehending.

"I'm a *terrible* mother," Sylvia pronounced.

"What? No you're not," I said.

"No, I really am," she continued. "I mean, how did I not notice my own daughter was that sick? And Nathan's got his college applications this fall . . . Listen, I can't be here. I have to fly back to New York tomorrow."

I was in shock. Sylvia had already been back to New York twice since pre-production started, but to leave a week away from the start of the shoot, it seemed extreme, almost irresponsible as a producer.

"I can't leave my kids like this. They need me right now."

The production needs you right now, I thought. I couldn't imagine how she would produce a film, three time zones away from the shoot.

"Well, you're coming back, right?" I asked.

Sylvia didn't answer right away. She just looked at me. "I mean, it really depends on Rachel and how she's doing."

I tried to digest this.

"Wait, you might not come back *at all*?"

She glared at me to keep my voice down. "It's a possibility. But don't go telling Xander and Hugo that, I'm having enough trouble with them already."

"Really?" I asked.

Sylvia didn't elaborate.

"And besides, there's still a lot I can get done from there. It's just—I can't call myself a mother and watch my daughter struggle with this alone. When you have a family of your own, you'll understand."

I nodded, but inwardly bristled. Sylvia with the condescending tone again.

"Plus, I have you." She smiled at me. "I'll have to hand over some of my responsibilities to you, Sarah. And I have no doubt you'll be able to manage it with flying colors."

I felt a surge of satisfaction at those words. And excitement. To finally step into the role of full producer, out here in LA, with an entire $15 million production beneath me.

"It's kind of what you've always wanted, isn't it?" Sylvia asked. I didn't answer, embarrassed. Was my ambition that nakedly obvious?

"Sarah, I'm going to rely on you to keep things running smoothly during the shoot. If any problems crop up, contain them. And with Xander and Hugo, stay on their backs a bit. You know how they can get."

An image flashed in my mind: me snorting coke off giggling Christy's breasts, while Hugo and Xander roared their approval to the crowd.

"Don't worry, Sylvia," I said. "I'm on it."

I offered what I hoped was a reassuring look. But deep down, there was a small creep of doubt, that maybe I was in over my head. I pushed that thought away. I could rise to the challenge. After all, didn't show business revolve around big breaks like this? The understudy finally stepping forward into the spotlight.

"Sylvia, Sarah, you haven't started drinking yet." I glanced up to see Hugo heading towards us, bearing two glasses of champagne. He shook his head admonishingly. "What is our cast going to think, that our producers don't know how to have fun?"

"I was just catching Sarah up on something," Sylvia explained, her voice a cool, polished surface.

"Come on." Hugo grinned at me. "You know that's not how we do things here. Drink first, talk later."

At the post-read-through drinks, Sylvia went individually to the key cast and crew, telling them about the emergency drawing her back to New York. After me, she went to Xander first, then Hugo, Seth, and the lead cast. I saw her apologizing to Holly, who shook her head, smiling.

From across the room, I read Holly's body language easily, then tried to conceal my curiosity by gulping my drink and grabbing a handful of vegetable chips. (There were never potato chips at a Hollywood event, since everyone watched their diet.)

"Sarah." Hugo edged up to me, conspiratorially. "How are you settling into LA?"

Hugo excelled at working a social gathering, so that every person in the room felt they'd had their own few minutes of private attention from this famed billionaire. Often it won him some kernel of trust or intimacy, a newfound familiarity. But shaken by Sylvia's news, I stuck to discussing mundane details about LA. I wondered what kind of trouble she was experiencing with him and Xander.

"It's, um, really different from New York," I answered. "Still adjusting to it, but I'm liking the weather."

That was a bit of a lie. Often I found Los Angeles to be a vast hellish concrete pit of parking lots and strip malls and freeways, which magnified the heat in cruel and unpredictable ways.

"I'm an Englishman. I'm predestined to love LA for its weather."

I gave an obligatory laugh.

"Listen." Hugo turned his green eyes on me. "I know Sylvia's news must be shocking, and the two of you have such a close working relationship. But, as terrible as it is about her daughter . . . you realize this could be a perfect opportunity for you, right?"

I peered at Hugo. "What do you mean?"

He smiled and took half a step closer to me. "Remember our conversation back in New York? I see how hard you work, Sarah.

And now, well, here's your chance. *You* get to make your own mark on the production, as the acting producer."

I nodded but didn't say anything. Spooked by how closely Hugo had read my mind. And all too aware of the strain I felt from Sylvia's constant, looming presence.

"I think with Sylvia away, you'll really get to stretch your wings, show us what Sarah Lai is capable of."

I thought of the freedom that promised, not having to run every decision past Sylvia, afraid that I might incur her wrath or disapproval.

"And we're out here in LA, with the entire industry dying to know about Xander's next film. It's the ideal opportunity for you to network, to be the ambassador for the company. *Our* company. Because *you'll* be the one here, running the production."

I took another sip of the champagne. Hugo's words stoked images of me striding into the offices of the big agencies and studios, chatting to *Variety* and *Hollywood Reporter* journalists at industry gatherings. To be here, in the living, beating heart of the film world, as the lead producer of a highly anticipated project. The horizons stretched broad and welcoming here, not tight and invisible like in New York.

"I'm hosting a dinner on Friday night with some industry people I know. Agents and managers, a studio exec or two. It'll be at the Marmont, where I'm staying. You should come."

I nodded, unsettled but intrigued. "Sure, sounds great. Thanks for the invite."

Hugo grinned. "Good girl. I'm glad you'll be there. I mean, I can tell you've got potential. And you're hungry for more."

I shrugged. "I don't know if I'd necessarily use the word 'hungry.'"

"No, that's the word." Hugo jerked his chin in the direction of Xander, who was chatting vigorously with Ron and Jason. "See Xander? He's hungry. That's why he's directing his second feature film by his age."

I admitted that was probably true. Plus he'd had Sylvia fighting in his corner for the past eight years.

"And you?" Hugo looked back at me. "Sarah, you've got a really promising career ahead of you, if you play your cards right. But what it really comes down to is this: How hungry *are* you?"

Interview Transcript (continued):
Sylvia Zimmerman, 3:38 p.m.

SZ: Did I feel responsible, leaving Sarah Lai in charge of the production? It's almost a moot point, isn't it? I mean, it already happened.

TG: But looking back on it, do you think it opened the door for later developments?

SZ: Are you asking me what would've happened if I'd stayed out in LA? You can't pin the blame on me, Thom, just because I was looking after my family.

TG: I wasn't—

SZ: Listen, certain people set out their intentions, and then they manipulate a given situation to reach them. If that situation doesn't work out, they move on and find another one. Ask any horny teenage boy at a party full of drunk girls. Sorry, crude metaphor, given the current climate we're in, but you get my point. (pause) So if me going back to New York inadvertently led to a situation that other people took advantage of . . . I'm not responsible for that outcome. There's no way I could have predicted what would have happened.

TG: Looking back, were there any warning signs—

SZ: You're asking me about warning signs? My own daughter had bulimia, and I didn't even notice. Do you know what it's like to be a mother? No, because you're like a twenty-six-year-old man and you're a Gallagher.

TG: I wasn't presuming to—

SZ: Being a mother of three with a full-time job . . . It's like an entire landscape of unending guilt. Your kids need you. Your company needs you. There's never enough of you to go around. So I thought I was giving Sarah this incredible opportunity, one which she probably deserved—and I knew she was gagging for. That girl, her ambition was so plainly obvious from the start.

TG: Was that a bad thing?

SZ: No, I don't suppose so. Ambition is often what gets us to where we want to go. But no one likes seeing ambition so visibly. Sarah was from that Chinese restaurant background of hers, so maybe there were some cultural ways of being that were lost to her. Or maybe we're just not used to seeing a young Asian woman in charge, so that kind of authority is harder to grant. Regardless of her competence.

TG: And what about Hugo?

SZ: (scoffs) Opposite end of the spectrum. I mean, someone with that much wealth, that much entitlement, you can't ever thwart their plans. Just slightly redirect them. Some people are accustomed to getting whatever they want.

TG: So you leaving Sarah in charge of the production—

SZ: I think it's unfair to call it a mistake. I was making the most of a difficult situation. Sarah was definitely capable of handling the logistics of the shoot. But the other stuff? What can I say . . . Power is the worst type of drug out there. Because it's so insidious. And so addictive.

28

SYLVIA FLEW TO New York the next morning, and when she texted from her gate at LAX, I felt a surge of relief, the way teenage children might feel when their parents leave for a weekend away. No curfews. And the whole production, the cast and crew, Holly, all to myself.

We rushed through the last week of pre-production. Holly's entire wardrobe was finalized. The sets were built. The studio space was ready. On Thursday, our line producer Seth and I had a brief meeting, as he ran through some final questions.

"Okay, Holly's driving scenes. Week Four. The hero car Xander wanted isn't available anymore, and the closest equivalent is about two thousand dollars more. Are you okay spending a bit more on that line item? I could look around for a cheaper version, if you really want."

Saving two thousand dollars would have meant the world to us when we were making Xander's first film. And in my own life, two thousand dollars was two months' rent. But in the context of a $15 million film . . .

"Do we have room for it in the budget?" I asked.

Seth nodded. "Yeah, I can move some things around. We haven't dipped into our contingency too much."

"Sure," I said. "Let's go for it." It felt electrifying, being able to authorize spending an extra two thousand dollars that easily, with no moral compunction.

"Do we need to run this past anyone else?"

I thought for a second. Xander wouldn't care about budget, nor would Hugo. And Sylvia was in New York tending to her bulimic daughter.

"No." I shook my head. "Let's just go with this." A new resolve solidified in me. I felt ten years older, in a good way.

Throughout these weeks, similar situations arose. Our publicist had secured interviews for Holly with *Premiere* and *Seventeen* magazines. Could she be free sometime during the second week of the shoot?

"I'm sure we can make it happen," I confirmed. "I'll ask her myself and let you know."

I mentioned it to Holly, who obviously had no problem, and then told Joe, our second AD, to schedule in the interviews for her.

It was as if suddenly, everything became easy: I simply had to tell other people what to do, and they would do it. I realized this was the kind of authority that Hugo exuded, getting others to scurry around, while he simply made phone calls, hosted dinners, and moved pieces around on the chessboard towards his ultimate goal.

Get other people to do your grunt work.

Hugo's words from earlier that summer rang through my head. So this was how the other half lived.

On Friday night, I crawled forward in typical Friday night traffic along Sunset Boulevard, heading towards the elegant, vaunted bastion of Old Hollywood which was the Chateau Marmont. I had dressed appropriately for Hugo's dinner: a flattering but casual white blouse, jeans, heels, and more makeup (natural, not conspicuous) than I was used to wearing. You didn't want to seem like you were trying too hard for a relaxed networking dinner, but it was LA and women were still expected to appear low-key glamorous, even if they worked off-screen.

Hugo offered his double-kiss when I appeared at the table. He commented on how lovely I was looking, and then introduced me to Simon, a fellow Brit, and head of acquisitions at a leading sales agency. The evening flowed easily enough. Anyone new and vaguely credible in town merited some attention, and as always, people wanted to know what it was like to work with Xander.

"He's fantastic to work with," I lied. "One of the finest visual minds I know."

"What other projects do you guys have lined up?" Simon asked.

"Aside from Xander's . . ." I described our quirky rom-com about fraudulent online dating profiles, our coming-of-age comedy about video games set in the early '80s, and the rest of our slate, which included some roles I secretly thought Holly would be perfect for. "You should keep an eye out for Holly Randolph," I added. "She's gonna be big one day."

"Well, your projects all sound great," Simon said. "I mean, we're always looking to meet new production companies. Do you want to come over to our office and have a chat sometime over the next few weeks?"

"Sure," I replied, amazed at how easy it all was. I gave him my card, and he said his PA would be in touch next week. An entire LA business meeting I could have on my own, without Sylvia.

I ran out of cards at that dinner, and later, I was not surprised when Hugo invited us back to his suite for "afters." Six out of the eight people decided to come along, myself included. I admit I was intrigued. Plus, I didn't mind the release that came with certain drugs. The cocaine appeared at a fairly early stage that evening, and this time, it was a mature, professional affair: no baying crowd, no nubile girl offering up her naked body to snort from. If anything, I noticed I was the youngest woman in the group.

"Sarah." Hugo tapped me on my bare shoulder. "Come help me cut these lines in the other room."

"Uh, sure." I followed him into an adjoining bedroom, where he handed me his hefty Platinum Elite Amex card and pointed to an ornate full-length mirror propped against the wall.

I'd never cut a line of coke before, but I'd seen it done enough times in the movies and in real life. As I bent over the mirror, arranging a small mound of white powder into neat lines, Hugo brushed up against me, monitoring my progress. By now, I was accustomed enough to him that these brief physical interactions no longer felt awkward; they were just his mode of operating.

"I saw you got a chance to speak to everyone at the table, that's good. Simon's a solid guy. We go way back." He deftly rolled up a crisp hundred-dollar bill and snorted the first line.

"And these agents, they're a slippery bunch. But the top ones hold the keys to the best on-screen talent. Do enough lines of coke with them, and they'll be a bit friendlier when it comes to negotiating."

"Plus," Hugo continued, "you have the added benefit of being an attractive young woman. An attractive young *Asian* woman, with a clever mind. You've got something unique to offer."

"What, that I'm Asian?" I quipped.

"Hah! No, I meant that you stand out. People will remember you."

"You have the added benefit of being a *billionaire*, Hugo," I reminded him dryly. Sober, I might not have said that aloud.

Hugo burst into surprised laughter and slapped his broad thigh. "God, I like you, Sarah. Such a quick tongue." He squeezed my shoulders. "I suppose that's true. But it's a pain, you know. Everyone just sees you as a walking vault of money."

He mimicked a series of high-pitched American voices. *"Ooh, Hugo North, fund my diabolically stupid action film. Ooh, Hugo North, cast me in your next movie and I'll open up my vagina for you, right now."* He snorted—this time, not for cocaine.

I was shocked by Hugo's crudeness, but said nothing. For the first time, I realized it probably did get tiresome for him, everyone angling to access his checkbook.

I'd finished cutting the lines of coke, and silently set his matte-black Amex card on the table. My eyes lingered on the sixteen-digit number, wondering what heights of luxury it could unlock.

"Yes, you do offer something else, Sarah. You're not just one of these brainless bimbos who spreads her legs at the slightest promise of reward." He pointed at me. "Believe me, a *smart woman* knows the right moment to give it up."

The moment hung in the air, and I said nothing.

It occurred to me then that if I wanted, I could probably sleep with Hugo that very night. There was no physical attraction in it for me, and judging by his female company, I didn't think I was his usual flavor. But the idea flickered out there, an unspoken dare. All I had to do was respond to one of his shoulder brushes, to place my hand on his elbow, look him in the eye—

Just then, we heard a knock at the door. Carrie, one of the agents, stuck her head in to admonish us. "I don't know what you two are getting up to in there, but don't snort it all!"

I edged away from Hugo, embarrassed by this hint of the erotic, but intrigued by his candor.

"Ah right, the cavalry has arrived," Hugo said, rolling his eyes. "Thus endeth the first lesson from Hugo." He offered me the rolled-up bill. "Go on, Sarah. Have your share before the others get to it."

I looked at him and quietly took the bill from his hand.

On Sunday afternoon, the day before our shoot began, Holly rapped on my ground-floor window.

"Hey," she said, her face unmade, her newly red hair up in a messy ponytail. "Do you mind running through my lines with me?"

"Sure." I opened my door for her.

By now, we regularly texted each other on weekend mornings, going on half-hour jogs in Griffith Park, before slurping organic smoothies at a West Hollywood juice bar. It felt reassuring to be with Holly when she wasn't wearing her makeup, her beauty flawless. Away from the peering eyes of others, when it was just the two of us, Holly was like any normal, down-to-earth human being.

"I'm so nervous," Holly continued, as we sat on my colorless beige couch. I wondered how many parties had taken place here, how much coke was snorted off the glass coffee table. Perhaps this very thought indicated I was spending too much time with Hugo.

Holly was still rambling.

"I mean, I've imagined having a lead role in a film for so long—it's every actor's dream. And yet, I'm so scared of fucking it up."

I brought out a pitcher of cold jasmine tea. It was a drink I'd chugged growing up in humid New York summers, and in hot weather, my mom always reliably kept a pitcher of it in our fridge back home.

"I mean, look at this, I think I'm developing eczema from all the stress." Holly held up her thin forearms. I could see a bumpy pink rash spreading across her alabaster skin, covering her wrists and hands.

I winced. Not a good look for a leading lady.

"Well, don't worry about that," I said. "Clive'll be able to cover it up with some kind of industrial-strength foundation for the shoot. And failing that, we can always deal with it in post-production."

Although the latter wasn't really an option. It would cost thousands of dollars per frame of computer-generated imaging to erase any skin blemishes. But I didn't mention that.

"Hey, how's your sister doing?" she asked, gulping down the jasmine tea. I saw from the look on her face that she was puzzled by the taste, but liked it. "Didn't you say she was about to give birth?"

"She's due in about a month. So yeah, it'll be right in the middle of our shoot." I set my empty glass on the table and shrugged. "But um, I'll probably have to wait until we return to New York before I can see her and my niece."

"That's a shame." Holly settled herself cross-legged on the floor, her back against the couch, and attempted some deep breaths in a yoga asana pose. "But aren't you in charge now? Or do you still have to get permission from someone to fly back? I'm sure Hugo will let you." She cast her voice low in imitation of his British accent and leaned back regally. "*Oh dear dear Sarah, please do use my million air miles to fly back to New York business class. Or better yet, I'll send my private jet . . . with its own special stash of cocaine. Just imagine: five hours flying through the air cross-country, high as a kite. Brilliant stuff."*

We both laughed. "Aaand, I'm sure my family will be thrilled if I show up to see my sister and newborn niece high on coke."

"They won't be able to tell." Holly shrugged. "The more I spend time in this town, the more I realize everyone's high. And just pretending to be sane and sober."

Forty minutes later, we were just barely maintaining a semblance of seriousness, as I ran through Holly's lines for the fifteenth time. We decided to finish with her lines for tomorrow's first scene, and they were a straightforward series of questions in a tense one-sided phone conversation ("Who is this? / Did you know my husband? / I think it's best you never call here again."). Sprawled next to Holly on the floor, I found it exhilarating being this close to her talent when it was this casual, this throwaway.

"Okay, one more time," I announced, then imitated a phone ringing. "BRRRING BRRRRING!"

Holly held an imaginary phone up to her ear. "Who is this?" she asked, intent and anxious.

"It's your great-aunt Sheila," I squawked in a thick Brooklyn accent. "Can you help me insert my enema?"

Holly broke character and laughed. "Stop!" she shouted.

She went back into character again. "Who is this?"

"It's Xander Schulz." I adopted his laconic way of speaking. "I was just thinking, we probably need to change your hair again—and you know, let's keep it red, but do sort of a mullet—"

"Aaaaghh, no!" Holly wailed. "NO MULLETS! IT'S MY HAIR! Honestly, Sarah, I have to rehearse." She put on her anxious face again. "Who is this?"

I paused, then spoke like a nasal Californian. "It's Steven Spielberg. I wanna offer you the lead in my next blockbuster."

Holly flopped back in exhaustion. "Oh god, if only."

"Sorry sorry sorry, I know, you need to practice . . ."

"No, that's fine. I'm done for now. If I'm not ready now, I'll never be." She lolled on the carpet, holding her arms up above her and examining the eczema again.

"Honestly," she mused. "What I would give for a phone call like that. Not that it ever happens that easily."

"Do you know anyone who's worked with Spielberg?"

"No, but my friend Jeff had a callback in front of his casting associate once. He didn't get the part." Holly reflected for a moment. "But that's just it. The things you hear . . . there's so much *uncertainty* in acting. Just because you're the lead in one film doesn't guarantee you'll get any roles in the future." Holly rolled over and stared at me, her blue eyes suddenly vulnerable and intent.

"Sarah, tell me. Why did I *ever* pick this profession?"

"You didn't pick it, Holly," I pronounced with an affected air. "It was a calling. It called out to yooooouuuuu . . ."

"Oh stop." She giggled and reached out for the pitcher of jasmine tea, draining it dry. "You remind me of my drama teacher in high school. Old Mr. McCormack. '*Holly, you have a gift. You've got to honor it.*'" She spoke gruffly here, with a Southern twang. "So much fucking pressure."

"Well, at least you had that. I dunno, maybe that's what it takes: someone who sees something in you and says, '*You got something, kid.*'" I cocked a finger at her, drawling like Humphrey Bogart.

"I bet you heard that a lot growing up," Holly said.

"Me?" I paused, contemplating. "Not really. I mean, I got good grades in school, so teachers liked me. But I think everyone expected me to be a doctor or an accountant or something like that. No one—and I mean, *no one*—ever said I should go into film. That was my decision."

"Well, I'm glad you did." Holly smiled. "Otherwise you wouldn't be out here in LA rehearsing lines with me."

I said nothing, silently absorbing the warmth of her last comment. But jealous of the encouragement she'd always had, the constant adoration.

I collected our glasses, bringing them to the nondescript gray sink in the nondescript kitchen. It occurred to me, how you could almost die from the wanting, all the striving with no reward.

"You never thought of being an actress yourself?" Holly shouted out, wanting to continue the conversation.

I snorted. "Me? God no, I'd hate to be in front of the camera. Plus, uh, you seen many casting calls out there for Asian women? I'd be limited to playing a lab technician, an anxious mom, or a courtesan."

Holly teased. "There's the occasional kick-ass female ninja warrior."

"Well, in that case, I'd be screwed. Never learned martial arts."

I returned to the living room and sat in the armchair, suddenly aware of the emails I still had to send before the shoot. Tomorrow would be an early start for all of us. "Anyway, I'd be a terrible *actor*." I said the final syllable with a Shakespearean flair. "'Cause I'm no good at being anyone other than myself."

"I guess," Holly said. "But that's not necessarily a bad thing. Especially in this town."

Later that night, Sylvia sent me a peevish BlackBerry message.

Hey, I haven't heard anything from you since Friday. Was expecting some updates. The shoot is tomorrow!! How is it all going?

Annoyed, I hammered out a response. What was there to say? If everything was going well, I didn't have much to update her on.

All good over here. Some last-minute changes (we had to get a new hero car for Week 4, but it's within budget) and everything inc publicity lined up for tomorrow. We are excited for the shoot.

Sylvia wrote back:

Good to hear. I knew I could count on you.

I didn't reply.

29

A ND THEN, JUST like that, it was Day 1 of the shoot.
Call sheets and movement orders had been distributed in advance, listing all the call times for the cast and crew, the studio location, relevant phone numbers for contacting everyone. I'd texted Xander the day before, asking how he was feeling, if he needed me to handle anything last-minute.

I'm fine. A bit nervous. But I think this is gonna be good. See you tomorrow.

I was almost touched by his admission. Even the reptilian can show their vulnerability. But who wouldn't be nervous? It was his second feature film, and a huge step up in budget and scale from our first scrappy outing. All of Hollywood, the studios, the programmers of Cannes and Sundance and every other festival were waiting with bated breath to see what would emerge next from the mind of Xander Schulz. We had come a long way from those early drafts of *A Hard Cold Blue* that no one wanted to read.

We're gonna rock this, I typed back, falling into the default peppiness that dominated out there in LA. See you tomorrow!

I drove to the studio early that morning, before the churn of commuter traffic could clog the streets of LA. Much of the cast and crew were up at the crack of dawn. A car had come to get Holly at five a.m., so she could go through three hours of hair, makeup, wardrobe. (The only way to achieve the "natural" look Xander demanded.)

As the acting producer, I had countless emails and phone calls to handle in the office, but no specific role for me on set, where every other crew member had their predetermined slot within the pecking order. But that day, I did have to deal with the publicity unit, who were arriving before lunchtime. A cameraman was there to shoot some B-roll, so they could poke around with their camera, asking inane questions like: "It's the first day of filming. How're you feeling?"

That's Hollywood for you. Of course you need a movie of a movie, in order to document the enchanting process of making said film. This B-roll footage, filmed on set, would get packaged into TV publicity, a few seconds of it squeezed into a piece for *Entertainment Tonight* or *Access Hollywood*; then later edited into an extra for the DVD. So I was there to make sure Xander was civil to the publicity unit, even though he likely hated them for distracting him from his more essential job: actually directing the film.

That morning when I entered the studio, it was the usual, incredibly boring atmosphere of a film set. Here's another myth about the movies: that being on set is actually fun and exciting. It isn't. Most of the time, it's as exciting as watching paint dry. Hours are spent setting up camera angles, adjusting lights, laying out dolly track for mere minutes, even seconds of filming. I often marvel at how those days and months of utter boredom can— through the magic of post-production—somehow become a piece of cinema that entrances millions around the world.

So when I stepped into the studio, I saw a bunch of men standing around the set: the lights, boom microphone, camera all trained on that illuminated patch of space where Holly stood in a mock-up of a suburban home. To be a screen actress means to have dozens of eyes watching your every move on set, and despite all that, to act "natural" in an artificial, specially constructed environment. It is perhaps the most contrived profession ever created for women.

Holly was the only actor we were filming that day, and the scenes were all in her suburban home, looking worried, saying those exact lines we'd rehearsed the day before. As I crept closer to the set, a runner handed me a cup of coffee.

"You're Sarah, the producer, right?" he asked. "Soy milk, one sugar. Just as you like it."

"That's me." I beamed with a distinct pride. The runner looked to be about fifteen, a pimply kid; I briefly wondered if there were labor laws against employing someone that young. "What's your name?" I asked.

"Cory," he answered enthusiastically.

"Thanks, Cory." I smiled.

But by then, my attention was on Holly. Her red hair was tied up in a faux-messy bun, as she stood in a turquoise terry-cloth robe, looking out a fake window.

"Let's check the lighting on that," Scott, our first assistant director was saying. It was his job to shout orders to the crew on set, so Xander could stare intently at the video monitor and sip his coffee.

They were just setting up this shot.

Holly saw me arrive at the edge of the set and flashed a smile at me. Some of the crew turned to see who she was looking at. I nodded to them, as if to announce: *"Yes, everyone, I am here, and I am the producer."* But like everyone else, I quickly turned back to look at Holly, rippling my fingers in a quick wave.

I scanned the rest of the studio, trying to place names to faces. Some of them I'd known for weeks, but other crew I was seeing for the first time. Stan, our director of photography, perched behind the camera on the dolly, awaiting confirmation from Scott and Xander, who conferred behind the video monitor. Xander wore his backwards baseball cap, and sat in his director's chair, which had "Xander" printed across the canvas back. Of course, our production team had budgeted for this, along with similar chairs printed for "Hugo" and "Sylvia." I climbed into the latter seat, trying to settle into the canvas bottom. Since childhood, director's chairs had always seemed alarmingly unstable to me; I never quite trusted them not to collapse on me.

Hugo was currently nowhere to be seen.

Xander and Scott had finished talking. Scott raised his voice. "All right, everyone. Picture is up. Quiet on the set!"

The random small conversations that had arisen among crew to kill time ("You worked with these guys before?" "What d'ya have lined up after this?") died down. An absolute silence settled around the illuminated arena of the fake living room, where Holly stared out of the fake window.

"Places!" Scott shouted.

Holly put the prop phone to her ear. Carlos, the boom operator, hoisted the microphone high above her.

"Aaaaaand . . . roll sound . . ." Scott said.

"Sound speed!" Carlos shouted, to indicate he was recording sound.

"Roll camera," Scott said.

"Rolling." Behind the camera, Stan started filming.

"Mark it," Scott instructed.

Chas, our clapper/loader, poked the clapper board in front of the camera. "Scene 15, A, Take 1," he said, then snapped the clapper board shut.

Everyone held their breath.

"Set. Aaaaand . . . action."

Stan and the camera dolly moved towards Holly in a smooth sweep. The camera shot followed, zooming in. She had already, in the moments before, assumed an expression of worry on her face. Her brows knit slightly, those large blue eyes projecting concern, as she fingered the curtains and peered out the window.

"Who is this?" she said on the phone.

On set, we only heard a one-sided conversation, as the villain's lines would be recorded and added in later, during post-production. With only Holly delivering her lines between pauses, it was hardly the suspenseful moment that you get in the actual film, where the music and sound design highlight the tension.

"Did you know my husband?" Holly's voice sharpened with curiosity.

The camera continued zooming in on her face, so the shot

finished with a close-up. She turned away from the window, towards the camera.

"I think it's best you never call here again."

That third line was filled with a precise finality, a young woman trying to sound brave and forceful. But she was quaking with fear underneath. Any viewer would know this phone call was only the start of the danger for Katie Phillips. (Mainly because it was just thirteen minutes into the film.)

"Aaaaand . . . cut," Scott said.

Everyone relaxed. Carlos pulled down the boom mic. Holly eased into a neutral expression.

"That was good, that was good," Scott said to everyone. "Let's just do a few more takes. Back to one."

Xander spoke up: "Holly, maybe with a bit more steel in your voice next time."

Fuck this, I thought. My patience was already at an end. It was shocking how an art as creative as filmmaking was reduced to such a technically precise and boring process on set.

I hopped off Sylvia's chair, nodding as I passed Xander. He acknowledged me with a slight lifting of his chin. Typical.

When I stepped out the studio door into the blinding daylight, the first thing I saw was Hugo walking towards me, the publicity unit by his side, glad-handing them with his usual British charm.

As he approached me, his grin widened.

"Sarah, Sarah, how lovely to see you," Hugo said. "Have you met our publicity team?"

Of course I'd met them. I'd hired them. I hid my annoyance and beamed. "Jenna, so good to see you again."

"We are *so* excited," Jenna started. Excitement seems to be the default state for any film publicist, but I shared in her enthusiasm as she introduced the B-roll crew.

"How's everything?" Hugo asked me genially, his green eyes smiling. "That was naughty. You left the party a bit early on Friday."

"Did I?" I asked. At three a.m., the remaining few of us in his suite at the Marmont had stumbled out the door. I recall Hugo suggesting I stay for one last drink, but I wasn't ready to face being in a bedroom late at night with him—and the inevitable conclusion that could be drawn from it.

"Yeah, it was a shame," Hugo continued.

I looked at him archly. So I would play the ingenue. "It's my first time in LA, Hugo. There's a whole world out there for me to discover."

"Hey, here's a thought!" Jenna piped up. "Let's get some footage of the two of you, talking to camera on the first day of filming."

"What?" I asked, horrified.

"Brilliant idea," Hugo said.

In another minute, their camera was rolling, and Hugo and I were standing next to each other, speaking in that heightened, sprightly demeanor necessary for filming.

"Hi, I'm Sarah," I said cheerfully, staring into the lens, a rictus grin pasted on my face.

"And I'm Hugo North."

"We're producing *Furious Her*, and it's an exciting first day on set," I enthused. "We're really looking forward to the next seven weeks of filming!"

Hugo reached an arm around me, a side-hug of camaraderie for the camera. I smiled.

"We've put together an amazing cast and crew," he asserted, his refined accent exuding an effortless gravitas. "And believe me, it'll be a film you won't forget."

Interview Transcript (continued):
Sylvia Zimmerman, 3:51 p.m.

SZ: You know what's the greatest con job men ever pulled? Their
supposed inability to multitask.

TG: That's interesting.

SZ: You tell me, Thom. You're probably juggling a bunch of different
leads on this article, different sources you're reaching out to,
different perspectives—I mean, that's multitasking. And then
some guy says, "Oh, I'm a man. I can't multitask. Save me."
That's just bullshit. That's just some excuse to not have to do
more work.

TG: I'm curious. What prompted you to—

SZ: Just . . . thinking about everything that went on in that film
shoot. All the moving parts we had to manage as producers.
Me and Sarah working like dogs. Aside from writing the checks
and connecting us with a few of his property contacts, I can't
think of a single constructive thing Hugo actually did as
executive producer. And yet, he's the one who walked off
and—(pause) Sorry, I'm just so angry. (muffled sob)

TG: Take your time.

SZ: And everywhere I look, it's the same. Who's raising the kids
most of the time? Who's trying to make sure that everyone's
happy? There's just so much emotional work that goes into
being a woman. (pause) I envy men sometimes. They get to
be single-syllable lumps who nod their heads, and everyone
listens to them. Barely lifting a finger because "oh, they can't
multitask," they have to focus on their artistic vision or their
financial vision or their vision to screw every single girl in
sight, so don't bother them. I mean, what the fuck is that?

TG: Do you honestly think every guy is like that?

SZ: No, of course not. I'm exaggerating. And a lot of that isn't
intentional on the part of the men, they just manage to get
away with it. But still, it's frustrating. If I was granted that

kind of freedom . . . just think how much easier my life would be. (pause) I'm sorry, I'm digressing.

TG: No, don't apologize. It's important to get all this subtext. Do you think a lot of that was in play during the shoot of *Furious Her*?

SZ: Absolutely. None of us ever stopped and identified it at the time. But it was there. It was there all along.

30

I meant to ask . . . do you think I might be able to fly back for a brief weekend, when my sister gives birth? It would be around Wk 4 of shoot.

I had this typed out in a BBM to Sylvia, but I hadn't hit Send. I was already going to miss my sister's baby shower this weekend. To be fair, I wasn't drawn to the prospect of sitting alongside a bunch of happily married women, watching them coo over onesies and stuffed animals. But to be there in person when Karen became a mother . . . She was being induced (whatever that meant) in late September, and I knew how important a moment this was for her, even though we hadn't spoken much lately.

I hesitated over my BlackBerry, pondering the optimal time of day to send this message to Sylvia. It was five p.m. on a Wednesday night, eight p.m. in New York. I didn't want to bother her at dinner.

Just then, another BBM from Sylvia popped up.

Rachel is driving me crazy. Never have a teenage daughter. Wish I were in LA for the shoot. How are things out there?

I deleted the BBM I'd just drafted. It could wait a few days.

Yeah, all good.

I paused. Earlier that week, Hugo had lashed out at me—a harsh, angry comment over something minor. I'd simply asked him if he could remind Xander about approving some publicity photos when they met for dinner that night.

"Why don't you ask Xander himself? You're the acting producer, after all."

It was an odd comment, steeped in a ready contempt. I chalked it up to stress; it was the first week of the shoot, after all.

I decided not to tell Sylvia, and continued typing.

We wrapped on time today. Cast and crew seem happy. Everything going smoothly.

And at the time—barring the Hugo episode—everything was.

31

S O WAS THAT unusual at the time, Hugo lashing out like that?"
Thom asks me this, and I wonder if he ever loses interest in
these stories of petty workplace dynamics from a previous decade.
Resentments and power struggles now long gone.

"At the time, it was." I nod. "Until then, Hugo had been civil
and charming. I thought he'd always respected me as a producer.
So I wasn't really sure how to handle what happened next."

"And what did happen next?"

I told my parents I had stepped into Sylvia's shoes as acting producer, and they were impressed.

"This means you have to work even harder. Do a good job,"
Mom reminded me over the phone.

As always, I could count on my parents for warmth and reassurance.

"I know that." I clenched my jaw in annoyance. "It's a lot of
responsibility."

More than I'd been anticipating. But I told myself it was just
seven weeks I had to get through.

Yet alongside this added responsibility, the bizarre shift in
Hugo's behavior continued. For all his words about spreading my
wings, he started to rely on me more and more to do small, petty
jobs for him. I didn't mind cutting the occasional line of coke for

Hugo at a party, but increasingly, these requests resembled the grunt work from my very first year at Firefly.

Print out five copies of this contract for me.

Get me a copy of this script.

Connect me with this agent.

If I didn't deliver these things for him right away, his brows would lower, and he might say something like: "How disappointing, Sarah. I thought you'd be on top of all this."

It didn't make sense, these conflicting signals. But between filling Sylvia's shoes as acting producer and Hugo's erratic, PA-level requests, it was becoming impossible to handle from a workload perspective.

The problem was, there was no one directly below me I could delegate to. The production coordinators and assistants were needed for the shoot itself. By Friday of that first week, I realized drastic action was needed if I was going to survive the next few months.

"Seth," I said to our line producer one afternoon in the office. "Do we have room in the budget for hiring a PA for Hugo?"

"A what?!" he asked, irritated. "You mean he doesn't already have one of his own?"

Seth was not pleased that I was springing this as a line item so late in the day, but I was adamant. And as acting producer, I pulled rank over him.

"We're not going to be able to pay them much," he said, punching some numbers into his calculator.

"That's fine," I said. I thought of that printout, pinned up on the bulletin board at Columbia so long ago. "It's LA. There's dozens of film school students who would kill to intern for someone like Hugo. Listen, just allocate something in the budget. I'll take care of actually finding the PA."

Buoyed by a sense of impending relief, I emailed USC and UCLA a job description to circulate that evening.

Feature film production in need of intern to work closely with British executive producer during six-week shoot. Director's previous film has played in Cannes. Exec producer has extensive ties in the international entertainment and property industries.

Candidates must be hardworking, enthusiastic, a self-starter. Must have your own laptop and car. We will provide a cell phone. Position starts immediately.

By the following afternoon, we'd received twelve emails and I'd set up in-person interviews with five of the candidates that weekend.

One candidate—Allan Nguyen—really stood out to me. He was sharp, he was funny, his BA was from Stanford. He'd already worked on ten shorts and had been selected for an Emerging Writers Program with Fox Studios. He was also Asian in a sea of white candidates.

But he wasn't what I was looking for.

Instead, I zeroed in on two girls, both of them fresh-faced in their twenties. They seemed equally capable and attentive, with comparable grades from their respective film schools. But one of them, Courtney Jennings, had the edge. The daughter of an entertainment finance manager, she wouldn't need the money, just the experience and the film credit. She had the requisite amount of knowledge about LA's hot spots and finest eateries. And most importantly, she was twenty-two, brunette, long-limbed, and fetching.

Perfect. She was just what I needed to keep Hugo happy.

Interview Transcript (continued):
Sylvia Zimmerman, 4:04 p.m.

SZ: Did I leave Sarah to her own devices too much? (pause) You know, it's funny. During the shoot, I sometimes worried about that.

TG: What exactly did you worry about?

SZ: Maybe on some level, I thought me being away might lead to Sarah forging this special bond with Hugo. I guess I was paranoid at the time. It was my company, after all, and my production. (pause) I mean, when you have someone working under you who's that smart and that ambitious . . . It's a cutthroat industry. Maybe I was afraid that Sarah would somehow use her youth and beauty to win Hugo over? Start to phase me out? (pause) God, it was all so petty, looking back on it.

TG: When you were away, did you ever give a thought to Hugo and how he might behave towards Sarah or the other women in the production?

SZ: I'm ashamed to say, no. I was thinking so much about Sarah being in charge, as acting producer, that it didn't occur to me. Her being on the receiving end of anything. (pause) Well, I'm glad in the end that she got her producer credit.

TG: Actually, if you look on the IMDb, she's credited as associate producer, not producer.

SZ: Oh really? I could have sworn she was credited as a full producer. Well, sometimes it happens. But at the end of the day, it's just a credit. There are more important things in life. Not that I'd expect Sarah to agree with me.

TG: Are you in touch with her these days?

SZ: No, I'm not. It's a shame . . . I would like to know how she's doing. I suppose she had a lot on her shoulders at the time, especially for someone so young. And she was only trying to do her best. Of all of us, Sarah was probably the most responsible about her job, isn't that crazy?

TG: What's crazy about it?

SZ: That the youngest of us was the most responsible. And probably in the end, got the least credit.

32

HUGO, I'D LIKE you to meet Courtney," I said the following Monday, when I'd managed to corral the two of them into a corner of our production office.

"So pleased to meet you," Courtney gushed. She held out a tanned, slim hand in that self-assured white-girl way of hers. A tennis bracelet dangled on her slender wrist. "I've heard so much about you."

Hugo's eyes lit up at the sight of her lithe figure and pretty face. "No, I believe the pleasure is all mine," he said, before launching into his European double-kiss.

"Courtney's here to look after you for the remainder of the shoot," I explained. "So any admin requests—research, errands, or other bookings you need her to do—Courtney's your girl."

I felt vaguely like a high-end pimp, practically gift-wrapping Courtney to use however he pleased. But I pushed that thought away. I was merely delegating, allocating the resources we had at hand to manage my workload while I handled Sylvia's job. Doing what all good producers do.

"I am so excited to be working on this production," Courtney asserted, confident and Californian. Yes, use that confidence on Hugo, I thought. "I'm completely at your disposal."

"Courtney, let's start by having a little coffee across the way," Hugo said. "What do you say to that?"

Courtney smiled and simpered, as I expected her to. "Sounds great."

I wanted to pat myself on the back for handling the Hugo situation so efficiently. But whatever relief I felt from deploying Courtney vanished the moment I stepped back to my desk. Ziggy had some questions about our deal with Sammy Lefkowitz. Andrea's office wanted an update on publicity interviews with Xander. Holly had texted, asking if she had any more press lined up this week. (*I don't know, Holly, but it'll be on your call sheet.*) Seth had emailed with the subject line: Production decision. APPROVAL NEEDED BY 3PM.

And then Sylvia sent a BBM.

How are things going? I'm thinking of flying in to visit the set later this week. Would be good to have a catch-up, too.

Something inside me caught and festered.

A blister waiting to break.

When Sylvia showed up on set later that week, I didn't think once of sitting in her director's chair next to Xander and Hugo. I let her chat pleasantly with Holly, Ron, Jason, and the important members of our crew. She dined one-on-one with Xander, while I slunk back to my emails and decisions, appeasing her sense of being a producer, as my workload mounted.

Shortly before she flew back east, Sylvia asked me to join her for a coffee. Though my to-do list was terrifying, I said sure, no problem. A childish part of me still feared getting scolded by Sylvia. So it was with some dread that I approached the Starbucks across from our production studio.

"Sarah," she said, once we'd settled down with our respective latte and cappuccino. "You seem to be getting on really well since the shoot started. Seth told me you're a natural."

"A natural?" I asked. "I mean, this part of producing is just about keeping to budget. And well, you know me, I've been frugal all my life . . ."

"That comes in handy for sure." She nodded. "Especially in production."

We paused and glanced out the window at the stream of traffic: cars and nameless passengers all on their way to somewhere urgent in the sprawl of Los Angeles. A ragged homeless man pushed an overloaded shopping cart past us on the sidewalk.

"Um, how's Rachel doing?" I asked.

"She's better than before," Sylvia said slowly. "At least she's not in the hospital anymore. But still, this whole body-image thing. I mean, I'm just worried it'll affect her performance at school, her grades and—what with college applications next year . . . Well, you know what it's like."

I did, but the anxiety of high school, the claustrophobic focus on getting into an Ivy League—that all seemed so long ago, so miniature now. Especially from where I was—a decade later, producing a film here on the West Coast.

"So I saw you hired that girl Courtney to work with Hugo," Sylvia ventured, stirring her latte. "You definitely know his type."

"Well," I said with a shrug, "there's no point in hiring a PA he won't like, is there? Plus . . . he's been acting a little weird lately."

"How so?" Sylvia knit her brows.

I edged my way around the question, uncomfortable. Even without Hugo there, something about him, the words he said to me, the things he had me do—these stained my conversation with Sylvia.

"He's been pretty demanding about small, menial stuff. Which is why I hired Courtney. But—the partying. He hasn't toned it down since the shoot began."

Sylvia narrowed her eyes at me. A bubble of guilt swelled in me; after all, I had snorted a fair amount of lines myself.

"Xander says you've been spending a lot of time with Hugo lately." This took me by surprise. What had Hugo told him?

"Well, just at social gatherings," I demurred. "Hugo knows so many people, and he invited me to a few things here and there. Wanted to introduce me to some people."

"Hm." Sylvia nodded. A single syllable. She stared at me, as if willing me to keep speaking.

I didn't. But the silence stretched out, suffocating, between us. I drained my cappuccino and focused on lapping the froth at the bottom of my mug.

"Sarah," Sylvia said—and this time, I heard the familiar remonstration in her voice. "Xander also said that you've been meeting with agents and other industry people out here, representing the company. Is that so?"

I said nothing for a moment, and slowly put down my mug, considering how to reply in the mildest way possible. Sylvia did not seem pleased.

"I've had one or two meetings. They sort of came up informally. I met this sales agent through Hugo, and he said I should come into their offices to chat about our slate. So I did."

"But you didn't tell me about it?"

"Well I—" I stopped and shrugged. "They were just informal chats. I wasn't doing a formal pitch or anything."

Sylvia kept her cool gaze on me. "Sarah, you know as well as I do that an 'informal chat' is the same thing as a meeting. Didn't you think you should tell me about these meetings first?"

When I tried to answer, I was surprised to feel something catch at the back of my throat. "Well, I am part of the company, too."

"Yeah, but you don't run it. You're not the one in charge."

"Only . . . you've left me in charge of the production," I reminded her. "And I'm head of development; I know our slate as well as anyone else in the company."

"But you can't go around making whatever decisions you want, especially when it comes to representing the company in front of potential partners."

The paradox of it all was a slap in the face. I'd been an intrinsic part of the company for five years, but I couldn't be trusted to take an initial meeting, despite running the entire feature film shoot? Yet somehow, I couldn't bring myself to say that out loud to Sylvia, who had hardly stepped onto set.

"Look," I said instead. "Hugo said it was fine for me to go ahead and have these meetings."

"Hugo can say whatever the fuck he wants," Sylvia snapped. "But he's not the one who built this production company from scratch."

But he is the one funding it now, I thought.

I silently bit back my anger. Words lodged in my throat, unuttered.

Sylvia shook her head at me. "I don't know what's come over you, Sarah. Maybe it's being in LA. Maybe it's . . . all this newfound authority. But you know, something in you has changed, Sarah. And not necessarily for the better."

"I'm not sure what you mean, Sylvia," I said. And I didn't. "Yeah, people change. But I've been working really hard for the company this entire time. I feel like I can represent it."

"That doesn't give you the right to have meetings behind my back."

I wondered briefly if unassailable, imperious Sylvia in her Upper East Side brownstone, was somehow threatened by me, this middle child of Chinese immigrants. If she felt insecure being away from the shoot, she needed some reassurance. I could reassure her, or I could say what I really wanted to say.

"I—I'm sorry," I muttered.

"I'm just disappointed, that's all. I really need to be able to count on you when I'm in New York." But what did she want: that I wouldn't have *any* meetings out here in LA? That I would happily work under her for the rest of my career?

I said nothing. Some element of pride prevented me from apologizing again.

Sylvia looked at her BlackBerry.

"Oh yeah," she added, almost offhand. "You mentioned your sister's having a baby in a few weeks."

My attention perked up, and suddenly I was worried.

"I don't think it's right to take it out of the production budget." Sylvia tapped absently at her phone. "So you'll have to pay for the flight yourself. But if everything goes smoothly until then . . . Sure, I don't see why you can't come back to New York for the week-end. I mean, just for a day or two. She's doing okay, your sister?"

I nodded, grateful and simultaneously irritated to feel grateful. "Yeah, I mean she's terrified. It's her first baby, but—"

"Shit, I gotta catch my flight," Sylvia cut me off, alarmed. "Is that driver here to take me to LAX?" The peeved tone in her voice was unmistakable.

"I'll, um . . . I'll call it," I said, looking up the driver's number. And still I hated myself, always following her orders.

33

FOR THE REMAINDER of the shoot, Sylvia flew to LA every two weeks. Yet after each of her cursory visits, our production soldiered on, unbothered by her absence. I felt vindicated by this, evidence that I was the real producer, not her. But also resentful of still being treated like an underling by Sylvia and Hugo. Only I had no time to dwell on this. The hours stretched on set and hummed in the office, as we hustled to stay on schedule, on budget, to stay lucid.

A film production is an organism in itself, a community of cast and crew that blooms for a few months or weeks and then shrivels into nothingness. During this time, deep friendships and intense rivalries form on set, secret affairs and private resentments smolder at production meetings, in greenrooms, at after-parties.

At the end of a shoot week—like many a more normal workplace—we would gather for drinks after we wrapped. But our weekly work drinks took place at the lobby bar at the Chateau Marmont, where Hugo and Xander were staying. Hugo particularly liked playing host here, acting as if all drinks were on his dime (though in reality, part of our tab was covered by the production).

Since introducing them to each other, I had noticed Courtney and Hugo were practically joined at the hip. She was often close by his side, nodding and making occasional notes in a purple Filofax. Her glossy hair in a pert ponytail, above a designer shoulder bag, she looked more polished and more native to Hollywood than I would ever be.

I couldn't help but feel a twinge of regret at seeing their shared intimacies, the playful laughs, the occasional comments Hugo would mutter into her ear. To be the right-hand of someone that powerful . . . had I just freely given that opportunity away? And yet, I knew it only looked glamorous on the outside. The job itself was simply to cater to his every demand: collating his documents, booking his social calendar, probably ordering drugs from his dealer.

Still, I comforted myself with my burgeoning friendship with Holly, who was the star of our production, both on and off set. At these Friday night drinks, I envied how the cast and crew alike gazed adoringly at her, following her every move, in much the same way that fans do now at the barriers of her every red-carpet appearance.

Holly, Clive, and I had developed our own set of inside jokes about the different personalities on set. Puppy-eyed Carlos, the boom operator, was clearly smitten with her, while we all agreed there was something creepy about Ralph the gaffer.

"The way he follows you around with his eyes, never speaking . . ." Clive said, then shuddered. "Never trust a gaffer."

We broke into peals of laughter, amplified no doubt by the generous gin and tonics we'd been drinking in a Los Feliz dive bar that night.

"And Hugo: what do you think of him?" Holly had asked me once.

"Now, he is a more complex character," I mused. "He likes his hot women, that's for sure." I told her about the young girls who were present at every New York party he threw, and his hedonistic version of spin the bottle.

"Literally snorted cocaine off a naked woman?" Holly was appalled.

I didn't mention that I had done it, too.

"Honey, that's kiddie stuff." Clive shrugged. "I've seen worse out here."

"I think they're almost like accessories for him," I said. "Some men accessorize with watches. Others with attractive young wo-men."

"Yeah, but is he creepy around them?" Holly asked.

"I dunno," I said. "I think they're kind of drawn to him any-way, because of his wealth."

"He's not bad-looking," Clive mentioned. "He must have been something back in his day. The British accent. The dark hair, the green eyes. Heck, I'd probably still do him, if I was drunk enough."

"I don't think you're his type," I muttered, and we all laughed at the obvious.

And that was my assumption throughout: of course women were easy around Hugo, because he was wealthy, he was powerful. The same way Jessica what's her name had flirted with him in the bar of the Spark Club, the same way those silly girls had willingly chosen to kiss him when the spinning bottle slowed and selected them.

But then one day during Week 3, I looked up from my desk in the production office to see Courtney approaching me . . .

I trail off here, suddenly wary, with a cautious smile at Thom Gal-lagher.

A thought crosses my mind, as the nausea swells inside me.

Thom seems puzzled. "Are you okay?"

"Uh, sure, it's just . . ."

Try that again. Take Two.

Then one day during Week 3, I looked up from my desk in the production office to see Courtney walking past.

Her high chestnut ponytail swung in concert with her slim

hips, as she perched her BlackBerry between her chin and shoulder and giggled into it.

Tara and Chip, two of our production coordinators sniggered once she'd left the room.

Seth coughed. "Shush now," he said mischievously.

"What?" I asked, puzzled, glancing from him to Tara and Chip, who avoided my gaze.

"Oh it's nothing," Seth said. But clearly it wasn't.

"Nothing that affects the production," Tara declared.

"Or does it?" Chip mused, and the two of them shared a conspiratorial look. I felt my patience wearing thin.

"Seth." I smiled pleasantly. "Do you know what this is about?

Seth turned away from the spreadsheet of Movie Magic Budgeting that glowed on his monitor. "It's just usual film shoot gossip." He rolled his eyes. "You know how Courtney and Hugo are attached at the hip? Well, someone saw her leaving the elevator at the Marmont and exit the hotel around one a.m. this morning."

"Who saw that?"

Apparently, Tara, Chip, and Joe, the 2nd AD, had stayed on late at the Marmont bar. Chip added: "She seemed like she was in a hurry to leave. Didn't want to be seen by any of us."

"Besides, is it that hard to believe?" Tara pronounced. "He's loaded. She's his assistant."

"You could almost say it was bound to happen, once you'd hired her," Seth added, with a meaningful glance at me.

"So you believe Hugo and Courtney had some sort of relations during the shoot?" Thom Gallagher asks me.

Always straight to it, staring down the lens of his microscope, with that unrelenting forensic eye.

I pause.

"I . . . I don't know," I say, uneasy. The bar outside has changed its music to something faster, and I can hear the beat through the walls of this room, insistent and throbbing. "There were definitely rumors. I didn't feel like it was my place to ask either Courtney or Hugo about what happened."

"What do you think happened?"

I sidestep his question. "You asked me this about that actress Jessica, too. Similar situation."

"In what sense?"

"Young, attractive woman who has much to gain from a close relationship with a powerful, wealthy man." I gesture beyond the walls of this room. "I mean, that dynamic, it's everywhere."

I am striving to shift the searchlight further afield, but Thom keeps probing.

"Would you say you fell into that dynamic too?"

"What?" I am offended. "Did I have anything to gain by . . . a close relationship with Hugo?" I hope the insult is evident in my voice. But I stop and contemplate, grateful we've moved away from the topic of Courtney. "The thing is, who *didn't* have anything to gain by having a close relationship with him? All that money? He drew us all in like flies to honey—and he knew it the entire time."

Thom nods and continues looking at me.

"I had a lot on my plate," I say defensively. "I was mainly concerned with the production, if we were staying on schedule, on budget."

"Do you think others knew about Courtney and Hugo as well?"

For a split second, I panic. I consider again who else he is speaking to in this investigation.

"I didn't tell Sylvia. I was afraid . . ." I trail off again, trying to walk a fine line between what I remember and what I wish to pass on to the world.

I was afraid of many things, it was true.

"I was afraid I might anger Sylvia more if she knew about these things happening when I was acting producer."

Thom knits his brows, and I pray he will leave it at that.

"Not that Hugo and Courtney having some sort of liaison had

anything to do with me," I add. "But I was afraid of it reflecting badly on me, somehow. I'm not . . . entirely sure why."

Maybe I wanted a sparkling track record, so I could fly back to New York for my niece's birth. Maybe I just wanted to appear like the perfect producer. Even today, I don't really know. But one thing is true, in its own way. It occurs to me how much my life ten years ago was ruled by that simple, vain, unconquerable fear: how I would look to others.

Interview Transcript (continued):
Sylvia Zimmerman, 4:20 p.m.

TG: Do you recall a woman named Courtney Jennings?

SZ: (pause) That name doesn't ring a bell.

TG: She's on the end roller credits for *Furious Her*.

SZ: Seriously, Thom? There are *hundreds* of people on the end
roller to a film. You can't expect me to remember every single
person who worked on the set of a feature film we shot over
a decade ago.

TG: There was a Courtney Jennings who was hired to work as
a personal assistant to Hugo North for the duration of the
Furious Her film shoot. Does that help at all?

SZ: (pause) Oh wait . . . A picture is coming to mind . . . Um, if I
think it's who you're talking about, a young girl, in her twenties.
Pretty, very put together. If that's the girl, then yes, I met her
one or two times.

TG: You don't remember anything specifically about her?

SZ: No. Not really. I mean, I wasn't on set that much in LA. Why
are you asking me about her?

TG: Is it possible anything happened between her and Hugo? Did
you hear of anything like that?

SZ: (laughs) Is it possible? Of course it's possible. Hugo and a
young, pretty woman? That's more than possible, it's highly
likely.

TG: What's highly likely?

SZ: That he would have slept with her.

TG: Well, in light of all the recent allegations that have emerged
about the industry, do you think it could have been something
other than a consensual sexual encounter?

SZ: You mean, do I think there was some kind of assault? Involving
this Courtney Jennings?

TG: Yes, some might call it assault.

SZ: Well, I certainly hope not. Listen, Thom, I barely remember
this poor girl.

TG: But did you ever suspect at the time?

SZ: Like I said, I hardly recall her. (pause) But did I ever suspect that Hugo's "dalliances" weren't quite consensual? I . . . Let me be honest, I never really thought much about it. That's how hardened you get to the whole scene. Wealthy, powerful older man. Young, pretty girl who wants to work in the industry, maybe appear on-screen. It's the oldest story in the book. Sure, in my day, when I was younger, I had plenty of lecherous men hanging around me, promising me this and that, if I just "had some fun with them." That's all part of the scenery. You put up with it because you have to. If you're strong enough, you learn to fend for yourself, you grow up. And then when you're a bit older, you no longer have to worry about it, because there's always younger, prettier, more susceptible girls out there.

TG: So you never felt any sense of responsibility . . . of needing to protect these younger women from Hugo?

SZ: Honestly? At the time, I think I was too busy. (pause) I know that makes me sound terrible, but if you're a good producer, you're busy all the time. There's no room for nurturing the young things out there. You don't have time to look around and make sure that all the socializing is above board. And a financier is . . . a financier. A means to an end.

TG: So you never felt like questioning Hugo about his interest in young women?

SZ: It's not like I invented the casting couch, Thom. Or led Hugo to a new form of debauchery. That guy had been alive for fifty-plus years, operating in these very moneyed circles, where I'm sure he had plenty of access to young, pretty girls. It's not just the film industry where these things happen—and it's certainly not just one single film shoot that's responsible for it all.

TG: But do you think anything like that took place during the production of *Furious Her*?

SZ: Well, clearly *you* think so—or you wouldn't be asking me this.

(sighs) I don't like to think that anything did. But I didn't have this all-seeing eye. I knew there were lots of parties taking place where I wasn't present. There's always an after-party to an after-party, right? Surely you can't expect me, an individual producer—one woman—to be responsible for the behavior of an entire film crew, both on set and off. As long as these people were showing up on time, doing their job, making the film, that's all I was supposed to care about.

(pause) And if the guy practically funding the entire thing can't behave himself, how do you expect me to control him? It's like an entire deck of cards built on very shaky ground. (pause)

So the way I see it, I wasn't in any position—not really— to do anything about Hugo's behavior.

TG: Was there any way Hugo could be held accountable for his actions towards other professionals employed on the film production?

SZ: (snorts) Can you call them professionals? A twenty-three-year-old fresh out of film school, who wants a film credit? Or a twenty-year-old aspiring model who happens to know the right people? These aren't professionals, they're just . . . fodder.

TG: Fodder?

SZ: Yeah, call me harsh. But that's probably the most accurate term. Fodder.

34

LATE ONE THURSDAY night, I locked up the production office at ten p.m. alone, and climbed into my rental car. The usual nighttime LA traffic streamed past me, and after the hectic rush of unending production issues, I reveled in the dark and the quiet, my BlackBerry tucked away unseen in my handbag.

I didn't feel like going straight home, even though I knew I needed my sleep. Holly was undoubtedly already in bed; her alarm went off around four thirty a.m. on most shoot days, and I generally only saw her on set or in her greenroom.

My stomach rumbled and I realized I hadn't eaten properly since late that afternoon, when I'd grabbed a piece of a Roquefort-and-chorizo wood-fired pizza that someone had naughtily brought into the office. (Carbs in LA? Now that was a true sin.) I turned the key in the ignition and wheeled the car onto Culver Boulevard, telling myself I'd just cruise down it aimlessly until I found some eatery that was still open.

I passed a lonesome looking taqueria. I passed a retro '50s-style burger joint, edged in hot-pink neon.

And then, looming up towards me, sandwiched between the other signs in a strip mall, I saw a yellow-and-red neon sign in typical orientalized lettering: Jade Mountain Chinese Restaurant.

The names of Chinese American restaurants are comfortingly familiar to me—and always a bit amusing, as if they're trying to evoke some Zen-like image of nature, even amidst the frenzied throng of an American city. Without a second thought, I turned into the strip mall parking lot, which was empty, save for one or two spaces occupied close to the building.

The restaurant was a modest affair, devoid of customers this late at night. One of the overhead lights flickered unsteadily, while underneath sat eight tables and familiar-looking chairs, simple metal frames and red vinyl padded cushions. Images of the Great Wall and Huangshan Mountain were framed in heightened Technicolor on the wall. A golden "Lucky Cat" sat on the counter, its mechanical paw bobbing away, just like the one in my family's restaurant, and all the other Chinese eateries in Flushing.

"Hi," I said, edging up to the counter. "Can I still order?"

The woman behind it glanced up from her phone. She looked to be in her forties or fifties, a tired face with an ill-fitting shade of pink lipstick as her one feeble attempt at makeup.

"We just about to close," she said warily. I detected a Hong Kong accent.

I paused, trying the words out silently first.

"You speak Cantonese?" I asked in Cantonese.

I was always self-conscious about speaking my parents' language outside of Flushing, but the woman brightened immediately at the change.

"Aha, Canto! Tell me what you want, little sister? Our cook hasn't gone home yet."

I glanced at the menu, with its dishes awkwardly phrased in English (Chef's Nest of Twelve Delights), then asked if they had a menu in Chinese. From a drawer, she handed me another sheet: Chinese characters marching down a page, encased in plastic.

I was never very good at reading Chinese, but recognized my favorite dishes.

"Turnip cake. One hot-and-sour soup. And one beef lo mein," I said. "Is that too much, this late at night?"

"I'll ask the cook," she answered.

"Hey, Fei-Zhai!" And she shouted my order. "Can you make these?"

"If you can't," I added in Cantonese, "don't worry. Just whatever is easy."

The chef grunted in affirmation from the kitchen, and an uncomfortable silence fell over us as I heard the hum of the extractor fan turned on, the sizzle of oil in a wok.

"Working late?" the woman asked.

I yawned and nodded. "Yeah. Too late. I still haven't had dinner."

"Ohhhh . . . you have your dinner now, then. Where do you work?"

"Um." I was hesitant to go into too much detail. "We're making a movie. Shooting at a studio not far from here."

"Oh, you're in the movie business! No way!" the woman exclaimed, and now appeared to size me up differently, almost as if she didn't believe me.

"What do you do? You an actress?" That must have been asked more out of politeness. I clearly wasn't thin enough, and I saw that in her eyes.

"No, no," I answered. "I'm a producer. I . . . produce the movie."

"Oh, waaaah! Imagine that." She nodded at me and raised her unplucked eyebrows. "Producer. So you in charge, then? You're the boss?"

"Yes. Well, not exactly." I thought of Hugo. And Sylvia in New York, firing me emails from her BlackBerry. "I'm in charge of a lot, but I still have a boss."

"Ah hah ha!" She laughed and slapped her knee. "I know what that's like. You run the show, do all the work, but still have a boss. For me, the owners of this restaurant. Pain in my ass."

"Exactly." I remembered that intense summer in college when my great-uncle was away from the restaurant. Sixteen-hour days in that pungent furnace, the smell of sesame oil and the jabber of customers inescapable.

"But still, so in charge, for someone so young as you . . . Tell me, how old are you?"

I could always trust Chinese women to be brutally direct towards younger Chinese women. I tried to hide my mild annoyance.

"I'm twenty-eight."

"Twenty-eight? I thought you're older. You seem older, at least. Well, you're young, then. You have a lot ahead of you still. No children, no worries. You enjoy your life."

I didn't say anything, just stared at the arm on the Lucky Cat, endlessly bobbing up and down. These cat figurines were meant to bring good fortune and prosperity; I only felt tired watching that plastic paw constantly bouncing.

"You know, my parents run a Chinese restaurant," I suddenly said. "Back in New York."

The woman perked up, intrigued. "Ohh no way, then you're really one of us!" We talked about the restaurant, how it was mainly local customers, none of these white people ordering abominations like lemon chicken, always adding soy sauce to their plain rice.

"Ah, look at you," she said. "Your parents must be proud. Now their daughter's out here, shooting a movie in Hollywood."

"You think?" I asked. "I dunno. I think they're probably worried about me and just wish I was back home."

"Ah, well, don't blame them. LA, this town is crazy. There's this movie shooting here, this movie premiere there." She gestured out the window, down Culver Boulevard one way, then in the opposite direction. "So many movie shoots. And us in the middle here, our little restaurant, just make dumplings day after day. Nothing change for us."

Something about that woman's last statement rankled me. The humility in her voice, but also the resignation. I felt the same tug of guilt that always accompanied thoughts of my family.

"Is the food ready yet?" I asked, signaling an end to the conversation.

"I'll get it for you now." She nodded. "By the way, my name is Debbie. Sister, you come back here anytime. End of a long day, buy dinner from us. We'll give you turnip cake on the house."

That last scene: I don't bother to relay it to Thom Gallagher, because I somehow know he wouldn't care. It has nothing to do with his investigation. There is no link to Hugo North or Holly Randolph. But still, it happened, me stumbling across that Chinese restaurant late that night. And somehow that humble, greasy menu, the uncomplicated chitchat with Debbie became a necessary refuge for me in LA, free from the emails, the demands of the film shoot, the need to appear bright and shiny. I would return there at least once a week on my own, shovel down the steaming turnip cake, and harbor no remorse about the carbs I had ingested.

I've since looked up Jade Mountain Chinese Restaurant on Google Earth, trawling that particular section of Culver Boulevard on my computer screen—and I can find no trace of it, as if it never existed. Turnover among LA eateries can be fast, and most likely it has gone out of business. For me, there is a peculiar sense of loss about this. As if without that island of familiarity, LA ten years later remains as anonymous and distant as ever.

35

THE PRODUCTION PLOWED onwards, and I didn't say anything about Courtney to anyone else on the shoot. Tara and Chip could gossip all they wanted, but I figured as producer, I should just rise above it all. Whatever happened behind closed doors, after a few too many drinks, wasn't my concern, so long as the shoot continued apace. Especially with Sylvia, the more she thought things were going smoothly, the less she'd be breathing down my neck.

But things were not going smoothly, at least not for me.

Xander shouted at me in Week 4, after a particularly grueling series of shots involving the murder of the Father character.

"I have a publicity interview tomorrow? WHY?" he fumed.

I tried explaining that his agent Andrea had already arranged it, it was important for the autumn festival premieres of *A Hard Cold Blue* — but Xander cut me off.

"I don't fucking care what Andrea says or anyone else. Do your job for once and get it changed." And he threw down his headphones and walked off.

I stood absorbing that last comment, livid. Maybe in my first year as an intern Xander could yell at me like that, but not now, when I was running the entire production. I *was* doing my job, and it didn't merit this kind of treatment.

Xander's outbursts were only intermittent, though. If anything, it was Hugo I wanted to avoid. Installing Courtney as his PA had been a temporary measure, a stopgap to deal with his most petty demands. Yet somehow, the unspoken nature of what had happened between him and Courtney—that unacknowledged grain of awareness—still soured our relationship. Perhaps it changed the way I acted towards him, and he was simply reacting. He became sullen, erratic, vindictive.

He could still slip so easily into the familiar affable Hugo—always offering a compliment, a glass of champagne, a snort of coke—but just as quickly, he could turn unpredictable, raging about something trivial. Gone were the exclusive social invitations. Instead, I might get an incensed phone call at midnight, his British accent slanted at me in harsh, spiteful curses—and then, the next day, find him perfectly cheerful and debonair.

"Sarah," he confronted me over the phone one day at six p.m. "Is it true you might be flying back to New York this weekend? That's not the most responsible decision now, is it?"

"I might," I answered. It had been a punishing day of filming. We'd just finished the final day of the car chase, with the $40,000 hero car dodging its way through choreographed traffic on an LA off-ramp. "I'm on top of things, Hugo. I'm not going to take off without warning."

"But what sort of producer abandons a shoot just like that?" I could hear him breathing into his BlackBerry, as a nasty edge sharpened his voice. "Are you trying to pull a Sylvia here? Don't tell me your sister's gone bulimic too."

I ignored Hugo's last remark. Earlier, I'd found an economy-class flight that would give me thirty-six hours in New York, enough time to go see my sister and hopefully my newborn niece, and spend time with my parents to reassure them I was still alive, before climbing back onto another five-hour flight. But I'd have to book it by that evening, otherwise the price might shoot up too much. Not all of us had a surplus of frequent-flier miles to cover last-minute flights across the continent.

Hugo, meanwhile, was still railing.

"What makes you think you can go? *This* is how you show yourself to be a real producer? I need you here, making decisions, and you drop it all because of some family issue?"

"It's the fucking weekend," I shot back, stepping into the corridor for some privacy. "Surely I can get thirty-six hours off. I mean, if I stayed in LA during that time, I wouldn't be working during all of it."

I camouflaged the ragged, tearful pitch in my voice. I was exhausted; the last thing I needed was an argument with Hugo at the end of a long day.

"Get over it: Your sister will have other kids. You'll have kids someday too. It's not that big a deal."

That argument didn't even make sense to me, but his tone was so aggressively nasty that I didn't try to counter back. Perhaps it wasn't worth aggravating him more for the sake of a thirty-six-hour trip.

"Listen," I said, "I'll think about it. I haven't decided yet."

"Well, you know what that decision should be. Your family's always going to be there, no matter what. But your career, Sarah? I just don't want you to fuck up this opportunity."

Oh, fuck off, Hugo, I thought, as I hung up the call. *What did he even know about my family?*

I paused for a moment in the corridor to regroup before reentering the office. Most of the production staff were still in there, glued to their computers, and I didn't want Seth and the others to see me upset. Eventually I returned to my desk, my face downturned, and angrily typed out some emails.

Undecided, I didn't book the flight that night.

Later on, at ten p.m., I made my way to Jade Mountain and chatted with Debbie again, while ordering my usual meal of beef lo mein and turnip cake. She gave me a free bag of chicken wings to take home. Perhaps it was the best I could do, in terms of assuaging my guilt over my family.

When I woke up in the morning, I saw a text from my sister.

I've gone into labor!!!! Wish me luck . . .

I gasped. Excitement for Karen coursed through me. But it was eclipsed immediately by regret. The airfare had shot up by four hundred dollars, more than I could justify spending. As always, my frugal side had won out.

I think my parents were secretly hoping I would show up in New York that weekend. But when I didn't, they seemed to understand. They told me work was important, and I should listen to my boss.

That Saturday afternoon, my sister sent me a photo of her newborn. A little pink thing, curled up into herself, so unaware of the world.

Her name is Alice, Karen wrote. She can't wait to meet you.

I trembled for a moment at the sight of my niece, imagining what it would be like to hold her small, fragile presence. Then I turned off my BlackBerry, trying to ignore the other five messages that had just arrived.

All that weekend, I was angry at myself for not booking that flight. On Sunday, I tried to take my mind off the production by sampling the wider film scene in LA. Holly and I had been invited to attend the premiere of an indie feature at the ArcLight Hollywood. Holly knew some of the cast, and I'd been invited by an agency I'd recently started talking to.

The film was billed as a heartwarming comedy-drama about a quirky, dysfunctional family of former hippies in the American Southwest. Without any recognizable stars, I didn't think it would do much box office, but the filmmaker showed promise. It was something the trades would later call: "A solid first effort."

I knew better than to actually voice any doubts at the premiere.

"That was great!" I enthused, as I pumped the writer-director's hand at the post-screening drinks.

"Yeah, Jeremy's performance was really impressive," Holly said. "He's so talented. We trained together at Juilliard."

"Oh, so you're an actor too?" the filmmaker asked. I could see him reassessing Holly, her red hair and photogenic face, with a newfound interest.

I explained that she was the lead in our production, and Holly introduced me as the producer. And so we circulated through that industry crowd, enjoying the wine and the attention that came with casually mentioning we were in production on a feature just then. Several people pitched me their scripts; several people wanted to know who represented Holly. This was standard Hollywood socializing, and in the right mood, with enough alcohol, we could revel in it.

And then—just as I took a cursory glance around the room—I spotted a familiar figure. Hugo, mired in an enthusiastic congress with a crowd I didn't recognize. And right next to him, self-contained in his usual reptilian way, Xander.

"Oh shit," I blurted.

"What?" Holly snapped her head in the direction of my gaze.

"Twelve o'clock," I said. "Hugo and Xander."

I wanted to hide, but it was too late: Hugo had already seen us. Now, the entire crowd of people around him surged towards us.

"I can't believe he was such an asshole, he wouldn't let you fly back to see your new niece," Holly muttered angrily. Then, a split second later, she reassembled her face into the pleasant expression which was her professional default. I attempted something similar.

"Hugo and Xander!" She grinned as they arrived.

"Well, well, isn't this a coincidence." Hugo smiled, bearing down upon us. "Fancy seeing the two of you here."

"Likewise," I said, offering up my wineglass to clink against his.

"It *is* a school night," Hugo pointed out. "And yet, look at us all: burning the candle on both ends."

Hugo introduced us to his circle: agents, managers, a product placement exec. Carrie, one of the agents I'd met before, over lines of coke in his hotel suite. On learning we were the star and the producer of Hugo's current production, his listeners immediately hummed their approval.

"You girls must be thrilled to be working with a hot new director like Xander." A short, intense man named Aaron said this. His aggressive, yappy behavior said agent to me.

We uttered the usual positive, noncommittal fluff. I added that I'd been working with Xander for five years.

"And to have Hugo on board," Aaron continued, elbowing him playfully. "I mean, this is *the man*. Who wouldn't *kill* to have your portfolio of assets! The amount of films you could be financing in this town."

"Shush now." Hugo wagged a finger at the shorter man. "Don't blow that trumpet too loudly, if you don't mind."

The circle broke into laughter.

Lisa, a helmet-haired exec, spoke up. "But honestly, Hugo. I'm so glad you finally did it. Came out here to LA, found a good filmmaker to back."

"Yeah," I suddenly cut in, driven by a rash, impetuous curiosity. "What drove you to it, Hugo? Wanting to invest in a film?"

Hugo glanced at me curiously, then launched into the standard spiel I'd heard twenty times over. "Well, as I said when we first met at Cannes, Sarah . . ." I let him ramble on about the joys of cinema, while I studied his rapt audience.

"Yes, but is it *really* the art itself," I interrupted him. "Or is it all of this?" I gestured at the crowd around us, raising up my glass of wine. "The partying, the glamor . . . the women?"

I thought of Jessica, simpering as she perched on her barstool in the New York club. And Courtney. I'd seen the way he looked at Holly.

His eyes glittered with a distinct displeasure at my question—and I found a perverse delight in that. I wanted to push him further.

"I'm not, of course, going to deny that those aren't added attractions to this industry. Certainly beats real estate." He looked around the group for agreement.

Aaron nodded. "I mean, when you're working your ass off day and night, it helps to be surrounded by hot women."

"And men," Lisa added. "It's not so one-sided these days."

More laughter.

Holly, the only actor present, had her brows knit. "Wait, hold on, hold on." Everyone turned to her. "I'm an actor, I know I'm expected to look a certain way. But give us some credit. We're talented, we work hard. We're more than just window dressing."

The circle was silent for a moment.

"Listen, honey," Aaron said. "I'm sure you've got talent. But until the rest of us get to see it, we're just gonna see your face, nothing more."

Holly nodded and smiled, but I could see her flinch at his patronizing tone.

Hugo spoke up. "I'm not so sure, Holly. *I'd* wager it's more than just your face that gets you noticed. It's your attitude."

"Oh, you saying I've got a bad attitude?" Holly joked, and the circle around us chuckled.

"*You* have a brilliant attitude, darling," Hugo oozed. "It's those who make themselves more accommodating, who know how to play the game, who end up succeeding. If you know how to push the right buttons . . . or *whose* buttons to push. Wouldn't you agree, Sarah?"

Surprised to be singled out by this, I hesitated.

"Well, sure," I said, prickly. I peered at Hugo, trying to figure what game he was playing here. "If all you want to do is uphold the status quo."

Hugo chuckled. "Do elaborate."

"If all we do is keep kissing up to those who are powerful . . ." I spelled my words out carefully, forming my argument as I spoke. "They just want the same formula over and over again, right? What if you want to create something new? Something more . . . revolutionary?"

"Sarah." Hugo smirked. "We're only making movies here, not

inciting a Marxist uprising. I mean, there's only room in history for *one* filmmaker like Tarkovsky, right?"

Everyone laughed, but Hugo's snide answer—as much as I expected it—only rankled me more. I scowled.

"Eisenstein," I finally blurted, with some severity.

"Excuse me?" Hugo asked, irritated.

"Eisenstein, not Tarkovsky." I knew this was petty, but I just wanted to score one point off Hugo. "If you mean the Soviet filmmaker who made *Battleship Potemkin*."

"Okay, whatever." Hugo waved his hands dismissively. "I apologize if my knowledge of Russian directors is lacking. I just finance the films, I don't live and breathe them, the way some of you geeks do."

Aaron and some of the others snickered, but Xander of all people spoke up.

"I mean, Eisenstein *did* practically invent the concept of montage," he pointed out. He seemed dead serious here. "You can't really confuse him with anyone else."

"Hugo." I wagged a finger back at him playfully. "In this crowd, if you're gonna make a film reference, it better be correct."

Xander laughed; so did Carrie and Holly.

Hugo's eyes went cold. "Oh for fuck's sake!" he suddenly snapped. "You lot are too much sometimes."

We were all taken aback, some of us suspecting Hugo might still be joking. But his anger seemed real.

"Like it's not enough for me to finance your fucking films, I also have to be an expert in cinema history if I want to get involved in producing? *You* people need my money, it's up to me whom I want to back. So I don't fucking think *any* of you are in any position to laugh in my face when I can't remember the difference between Eisenstein or Tarkovsky or Polanski or whatever bloody auteur you want to refer to. *None* of those guys would have made a film without any money, and the same goes to all of you. So show some fucking respect. And now, who wants more champagne?"

His eyes blazed, and he brandished the champagne bottle in a challenge.

There was silence for a moment, then Aaron raised his empty glass. "Me, more bubbly, for sure."

Holly and I shared a shocked, scandalized glance.

Then I saw Hugo staring at me.

"That's right, drink up, Sarah."

His green eyes burned both a playfulness and a warning.

Interview Transcript:
Phone call to Courtney Novak (née Jennings), Wednesday, Nov. 1, 6:12 p.m.

TG: Hi, yes, my name is Thom Gallagher. I'm a journalist for the *New York Times*—

CN: The *New York Times*? Oh. Yes . . . I know who you are. (pause) How did you get my number?

TG: Um, your boss Dan Gomez passed it on to me.

CN: Oh. Right. (pause) How can I help?

TG: It's for an article I'm writing . . . There're a number of people I'm reaching out to, and I think you might be able to shed light on something important.

CN: What's that?

TG: I might be mistaken, but back in 2006, did you work on a film shoot for *Furious Her*? It was a film starring Holly Randolph.

(long pause)

CN: I can't talk about this.

TG: But you did work on the film, right? You were Courtney Jennings at the time, and you're listed in the film credits.

CN: Yes . . . that was me. Before I got married.

TG: So you did work on the film in an assistant capacity, correct?

CN: Yes. I did.

(Pause)

TG: Would you be able to answer a few questions about the film shoot?

CN: No, I—I can't do that.

TG: You can't, or you won't?

CN: Both. Listen, it was a long time ago. I won't be able to remember much anyway. (pause) Why are you asking about this particular film?

TG: I'm . . . doing a little research into the producers. In particular, a man named Hugo North.

CN: (Pause) Um . . . I really can't talk about this. I'm legally bound not to—

TG: You're what?

CN: I'm not going to talk about this anymore. I really can't. Do me a favor. Don't call back.

TG: Can I at least ask—

CN: No. If you call back, you'll have to speak to my lawyer—

TG: But I really think—

CN: You know who you should talk to? There's an Asian woman who worked with him at the time—I can't remember her name. . . .

TG: Sarah Lai? She's on the film credits too.

CN: Yeah. Her. That's her name. Sarah Lee or Lai, something like that. (pause) Ask her. She's got a lot to answer for.

(CN hangs up.)

36

WHATEVER SMALL VICTORY I felt by humiliating Hugo that evening, it eventually wore off with the ongoing grind of the production. Week 5 was killer. We still had Amanda, the child actor on set, with her whole entourage of difficult parent, tutor, agent, manager, and a nosy health and safety officer. Ron and Jason were filming every day, and as A-list stars, their agents and managers haunted the set, requesting this and that. Our own publicity unit poked and prodded around with their cameras, eager to capture their celebrity presence.

My one balm was my friendship with Holly. Every lunch break, as the crew sat around shoveling their faces with catered salads and pastas, Holly would ask to see the latest photo of my newborn niece, which my sister sent unfailingly each morning from New York.

"She is just gorgeous," Holly would coo. "I bet you can't wait to hold her."

And then, for a few minutes in her greenroom, we would joke about the shoot, Xander, Hugo, the various personalities on set. Both of us hoping for some breath of fresh air on the weekend.

To celebrate the end of a tough work week—and with only two weeks left in the shoot—Hugo invited everyone to a production party at his Beverly Hills home that Saturday night.

"Sort of a fortnight-to-go party," Hugo said. "Because we've all been working so hard, we deserve to let off a little steam."

I'd grown warier of Hugo over the past few weeks, but as

acting producer, I couldn't risk not going. It was always easier to appease him than suffer another unexpected lashing of his anger. Plus, I was certainly curious to see his house in Beverly Hills. Was it as ostentatious as we expected it to be?

On Saturday afternoon, Holly and I drove to the party together. Though we never explicitly discussed why, we suggested maybe we just show up for an hour or so, and then leave. I steered my Hyundai through the broad, manicured streets of Beverly Hills, Holly dictating from the Thomas map that lay open on her lap.

"Okay, make a right here. And then . . . second left."

Already we'd passed houses that seemed to grow in size with each new street. Colonial mansions with mock Tudor facades. Mini-castles, complete with ivied stone turrets. Or austere contemporary cubes, all glass and reinforced steel. Wealthy LA neighborhoods are their own grotesque spectacle. A pastiche of every imaginable genre and style, writ large into the buildings themselves.

As we drove down Hugo's street, I noticed the road was at least twice as wide as the street Holly and I lived on. Porsches and shiny Priuses lined the sidewalk.

And then, we spotted the cluster of parked cars that surely announced a party.

"That must be it," I said, as we cruised closer to a palatial white mansion, tall palm trees towering before it, a semicircular driveway sweeping up to the front portico. I was surprised there wasn't a gate, but maybe Hugo was slumming it, since it wasn't a house he frequently lived in.

"Well, it's definitely bigger than my parents' house," Holly quipped, gazing up.

"Heck, at least your parents have a house," I shot back, and we both laughed.

In my mind's eye, I pictured our three-bedroom apartment in Flushing, the plastic-covered furniture and my parents' graduate degrees framed on the wall—and it seemed to belong to a character in a distant lifetime.

With Courtney unable to make the party, Hugo had asked me to print out some contracts at the office and bring them to his house. I had these in my handbag as we entered the high-ceilinged foyer. I gazed up at the soaring skylight, which floated above an airy central staircase. Impressive, but somehow the house just seemed empty, unlived-in. More than anything, it felt like an unused set, with furniture and tasteful decorations—a tall beige vase holding three slender stalks of some minimalist plant—but no magazines or books or photos of family members, indicating much of a regular human presence.

We had been welcomed in by event staff he'd hired for the party, and they milled about the house in short black dresses and ballet flats, all of them comely young women with flawless makeup, their hair in high blond ponytails. Weird.

"Are you looking for Hugo?" one of them chirped as she let us in. "He's just in the back by the pool."

The last thing I really wanted to see was Hugo in a pair of swimming trunks, his hairy upper half spilling over for everyone to view.

Holly and I left our bags in the designated room and exchanged amused glances. What kind of horrors lay further in the House of Hugo?

But by the poolside, it was really just a regular LA house party. Music spilled out from unseen speakers, and an abundant (but not outlandish) spread of catered food flanked the bar. A young man and a young woman in regulation black-and-white attire mixed cocktails with enthusiastic aplomb.

I spotted Xander, Seth, Clive, and most of our crew at the poolside, drinks in their hands. All of the less famous cast were around, hoping to network. Ron was the only other major cast member present, his hair swept back, aviator sunglasses on his face.

"And here are our real stars," Hugo crooned as he approached us, subjecting us to his standard double-kiss. "Where would we be without these two beauties?"

He draped his arms around us, and I was grateful his robe was securely tied around his girth.

"Sarah, who keeps us all sane. And Holly . . . gorgeous, one-in-a-million Holly who is destined for the stratosphere."

Hugo planted another kiss on Holly's cheek. She smiled accommodatingly, before extricating herself from his grasp.

"I'm just going to get myself a drink," she said.

"Oh no no no." Hugo held her arm. "I wouldn't dream of it. I'll get your drinks, both of you. What would you ladies like?"

Holly and I shrugged. She asked for a gin and slimline tonic.

"I'll just have a Corona," I said. I was driving, after all. And we were only going to stay for an hour.

Holly had already been sucked into a conversation with Ron, so I turned to the nearest group, our makeup artist Marisa and some of the lesser-known cast.

"Sarah the producer, right?" This was Brent, an actor I hadn't yet spoken individually with. He was playing one of the younger baddies, and like all actors, even ones playing villains, he was strikingly featured. Thick black hair and a lantern jawline.

"Yeah." I nodded. "I'm Sarah. Hope you've enjoyed the shoot so far?"

"It's a great project," he gushed. "It's such an amazing script. So taut and compact and intense."

I figured by now, I should voice my part in it all.

"Yeah, Xander and I worked really hard on paring the script down, really keeping it to Katie's story and her struggle for survival."

"Hey, so you work on scripts a lot?"

"That's what I like most about being a producer, developing the scripts." Three months in LA, and it felt natural to tout my own, undeniable status as a producer.

"Wow, that's such a valuable skill, a producer who likes script work." Brent leaned closer to me, his magnetic eyes seeking mine. "You know, I've been working on a script myself . . ."

I should have seen that one coming. The stealth script pitch, unavoidable at any LA party.

I nodded politely and listened as Brent described his gritty suspense story set in the cornfields of the Midwest. I tried to keep my eyes from glazing over, so I glanced around the pool, searching for Holly. She was now talking with Xander and Barry.

Just then, someone's hand teased my waist.

I turned to find Hugo right behind me, whiskey on his breath as usual. He inserted a cold bottle of Corona into my right hand.

"Best you start drinking now, Sarah." He smirked. "Need to catch up with the rest of us."

I nodded and smiled. "Thanks. But I'm driving."

He leaned in, his mouth right by my ear. "Oh, and you brought those contracts for me to sign, right?"

"Yeah, they're in my bag."

"Later on, I'm going to have to sign them for you, before you leave. Don't forget."

Then he rejoined the crowd with Holly's drink in his hand, making his way towards her.

At the time, I didn't think much of it.

An hour or so later, I had drunk two Coronas.

I'm not sure how it happened, when I'd only planned to have one. But after ingesting enough fish tacos and salads, I'd convinced myself my stomach was sufficiently lined to manage two beers without any impaired judgment.

The party had loosened, indie rock music amped up, the lowering sun gilded the poolside setting with that amber evening light of Southern California. Some of the male crew were splashing in the water, along with a number of bikinied young women whom I didn't recognize as either cast or crew. I clocked them as Hugo's Girls, all one shape and one size only.

Holly and I hadn't brought our bathing suits; neither of us relished the idea of baring our bodies to work colleagues. But we'd mingled easily enough with the crowd, and I buzzed with the excitement of another feature film shoot nearly completed, another community of talented, hardworking people coming together. Was it only a few months ago that we had first met Hugo in Cannes, discussing finance on that hotel terrace? And now here we were in LA with only two weeks to go before we finished filming.

I gazed in a sort of elated wonder at the party, marveling at how quickly life could take an opportune turn like that. I saw the crowd in front of me, all these actors and craftspeople and technicians gathered in this one place to create something I, Sarah Lai, had played a key role in forging.

A tap on my shoulder brought me out of my reverie, and before I knew it, Hugo had his hand around my wrist and was guiding me into his house.

"Come on, Sarah, before you get too drunk, we've got those contracts to sign."

"Huh?" I quickly glanced back at the poolside party, but Hugo was ushering me into his spacious, unused kitchen. One or two of the catering crew were picking at the leftovers in there, and regarded us absently as we passed through.

Then he was walking me into the hallway.

"Those contracts, where are they?"

"You want to sign them now?" I asked, baffled by the sudden change of scene, the shift in Hugo's behavior.

"Yes, Sarah. This is business. You gonna take this seriously or not? Filmmaking's not all fun and games, you know."

He gripped me by both shoulders, his florid face bearing down on mine, as we stood in the high-ceilinged entrance hall. There was an unhinged franticness about Hugo, and I knew better than to anger him in this state.

A quiet, unspoken panic started inside me. "Yeah, I'll just get them now. They're in my bag."

"Come back here right away so I can sign them," he snapped.

My mind swam with confusion. The contracts weren't that urgent, but was this some sort of test, even two weeks away from the end of the shoot? I crouched over my bag and fumbled through it for the copies of the contract, brought them out to Hugo.

He grabbed them off me and started to pull me up the stairs.

"Wait, what's going on?" I asked.

"Let's sign them upstairs."

I looked around and saw two of the high-ponytailed event staff, whispering to each other and stealing glances at us as we ascended the staircase. What did they think was going on?

But we were on the upper level now, and Hugo still had me by the wrist, pulling me down the corridor to a lighted room at the end. He pushed me through the door, and I was disoriented by my surroundings. I seemed to be in a bedroom, a monstrous bed looming large, with the covers thrown back and rumpled.

"Let's see this contract," he muttered, leafing through the printout.

My panic was starting to deepen into something more primal.

I watched him pacing back and forth, my heartbeat already racing. "Hugo, why'd you bring me up here to sign it?"

He glanced at me dismissively, then down at the papers. "I can't think with all that noise outside. I can only discuss business up here with you, Sarah. In private."

"Well . . . don't you think you should get back to the party?"

I was standing by the open door, frozen from taking any further steps into the room. But also frozen from leaving it.

He glared at me. "It's my party. I'm paying for all the food and drink they're having. I think they can bear a few minutes without me, don't you?"

He spat the question out, sharp and dismissive. Inwardly, I reeled in shock at the venom in his voice.

Hugo gestured for me to come closer. "Come here, tell me what this clause means."

I didn't move an inch.

"Sarah!" he hissed, impatient. "Do you need me to sign this contract or not?"

I crept forward, trying to stand a safe distance from Hugo as he bent over the papers on his bedside table. But he grabbed me and drew me close to him.

"Clause 22a. What does it mean?" he breathed. His arm was firmly wrapped around me. "Since evidently, I know nothing about film, you'll have to educate me."

The contract was to finalize our agreement with the audio post-production facilities in New York, where sound design, editing, and looping were to take place in a few months, along with the final mix. It was the driest imaginable aspect of post-production, but I tried to keep my voice calm as I explained it.

Inside, my stomach heaved with fear. I was in a strange bedroom. With Hugo. Everyone outside was having fun. My mind raced, as I thought back to Courtney, the rumors they'd muttered about her, the way she always avoided social situations now.

He nodded, apparently satisfied at my explanation. "Good, good," he mumbled. "Okay, I'm signing it."

With his free hand, he cast about for a Montblanc pen on his tabletop, then flipped through the pages, initialing the corners and finally scrawling on the signatory page. He did this for the addenda and the second copy as well.

The whole time, his other arm remained pinned around me, unyielding.

When he'd gathered the pages and handed back the folder, I thought he'd release me. But he didn't.

"Thanks for signing," I said, my voice flat, trying to hide my panic. "Now let's get back to the party."

Hugo laughed, a guttural sort of rumble. "No no, first a line of coke for us to share."

I shook my head. "Sorry, I can't, I'm driving."

"My driver can take you home."

"No, that's okay, I really should get back."

"Not so fast, Sarah." In a flash, Hugo had me against the wall, his wide girth pressing against mine, his sour breath in my face. I was still clutching the folder of contracts against me.

"Hugo." I squirmed, my heart hammering. His teeth, bright-white and crooked, gaped an inch from mine. "What the hell are you doing."

"I know exactly what I'm doing." His left hand was gripping my rib cage, pushing closer to my breast. My arm and the contracts folder were still pinned between us. His right hand trailed down the bare skin of my upper arm. I shrank against the wall.

"You know, I am fond of Asian girls like you. Skin like silk," he whispered. "From that first moment I saw you in Cannes . . ."

"What?!" I seethed, a single, stunned syllable.

"You know, you do owe me."

"Owe you for what?" I asked, furious.

"A girl your age wouldn't normally get this level of responsibility on a feature film this big. It's only because I allowed it."

In my horror, I was somehow reminded of Donald Sutherland's character in the final doomed minutes of *Don't Look Now*, piecing together an awful warning that should have been blindingly obvious. A line of coke on a mirror. Hugo's leer late one night. Courtney walking away quickly.

You knew this was coming all along.

"I think it's about time you gave me what I came here for," Hugo breathed. His left hand now pushed up against my breast, his thumb needling its way under the contracts folder, into my flesh.

Terror lashed through me. I was nauseous and disgusted, but my mind scrambled to figure a way out. The music outside was too loud for anyone to hear me scream. I could burst into laughter and pretend to acquiesce, before elbowing him in the face. But he was still my boss, and I'd never get away with that, long-term. There must be some bargaining chip I could use.

Xander.

"Hugo," I said, calm and deadly. "If you do a single thing to me, I will tell Xander."

He stopped and snorted. I saw his nostrils flaring, the way they did when there was too much stimulation, too many stupid girls and cocaine in his presence.

"And?" he asked, glaring down at me.

"Do you want to upset our rising star director? It'll ruin his respect for you if he finds out what you did to me."

He fumed, silent.

"Xander's a purist," I continued. "Demands the utmost collaboration among his team. Sure, we're almost done with the shoot, but we still have months to go before it hits the screens. You want to risk your $7 million investment—and your relationship with Xander—for a few minutes of fun?"

I hated myself for saying the word "fun" in this moment, but I pushed on, trying to talk my way out of it. What other argument could I press, what else sounded convincing?

"I've been working with Xander for more than five years," I said. "He depends on me to make his scripts work. How long has he known you?"

My eyes pierced into Hugo's, and I saw the anger mounting in them, feared what was coming next.

He leaned back slightly, then crushed against me, his mouth a hair's breadth from mine. "You think you're so smart, with your fucking Ivy League degree."

Hugo released me roughly, pushing me into the bedside table. I knocked into it, throwing a hand out to steady myself.

"You think Xander gives a fuck about you? There's hundreds of script doctors and producers who'd kill to work with him now. Who's the one paying for his film?"

I stood up and stared at him, as I clutched the contracts folder to me like some pathetic shield.

Hugo suddenly put his hand to my shoulder and shoved me back, towards the door.

"You get the fuck out of here. And don't breathe a word of this to anyone. Because nothing happened. I signed some contracts. No one'll believe anything else you say."

He stood gripping both sides of the threshold with his arms. His robe had fallen open, revealing the bare, hairy bulge beneath, his cock furiously erect.

I suppressed the urge to vomit and ran down the hall, tripping down the stairs. The two hired girls stared at me wide-eyed and stepped aside for me, saying nothing.

On the ground floor, I choked for a second, disoriented. I had to get out of there. But I had to get Holly, too. My mind churned.

Hugo was probably snorting cocaine for a few minutes; he wouldn't do anything in public to me.

I darted through the kitchen, bursting out onto the pool terrace, where the party was in full swing, as if nothing had happened.

Holly, where the fuck was Holly?

I found her in a circle with some of the cast and the wardrobe team, her radiant face crinkled in laughter.

"Holly," I said, aware how out-of-place my urgency sounded. "I'm leaving. Come on, we gotta go."

"Already?" she asked. She sounded so innocent. "Don't you want to stay for a little longer?"

"No," I nearly shouted, out of breath. "I gotta go. I gotta . . . I have a call with someone. You sure you want to stay?"

The rest of the circle was staring at me, surprised at my tone.

Holly looked around. "Um, I'd like to. Is that all right?"

I couldn't say anything else, not in front of everyone.

I turned to Clive in desperation. The bond between gay hairstylist and female star was always strong, and probably the most trustworthy safeguard. "Can you make sure she gets home okay? And don't let her out of your sight."

"Of course, honey. She's not eight, though." Clive peered at me curiously. "Are *you* okay?"

Something crumpled inside me, and I was on the verge of tears, but I forced them back. "Yeah, I just have to go. But you are personally responsible for getting her home." I pointed at Clive, deadly serious.

Then I backed away, and ran out of the house, stopping to snatch my bag from the front room. I imagined Hugo emerging any second from his bedroom and lumbering down the staircase, like the relentless villain in a slasher film.

But I escaped, my feet tripping over themselves to get out the double doors, down the semicircular driveway.

On the sidewalk, I panicked.

Where the fuck was my car?

The broad suburban street was eerily silent; I ran past luxurious houses towards my car, under an indifferent night sky. As I passed each house, its sidewalk sensor lights automatically switched on, and I could hear the distant chatter of other residents, streaming from lit windows in multimillion-dollar mansions.

I spied my car in a flood of relief and fumbled frantically to open the door. Once inside, I locked it and collapsed into tears, my heart thudding. My head and arms trembling on the steering wheel, I sobbed.

There was no one around. In a wide shot, it would have just been me, crying my eyes out, locked inside a rental car, parked on the side of an affluent residential street in Beverly Hills.

When I had regained myself a bit, I checked my BlackBerry, at a loss for what to do. I ignored a stream of messages about the production. I clicked on an email from my mom.

> Hey, how is everything out in LA? I know the shoot finishes soon, so you must be very busy, and very excited. I'm so proud of you. Keep working hard.

I was empty of tears by that point, entirely numb. I didn't think I could tell my mom anything. I didn't think I could tell anyone anything. I had been a fool this entire time, believing I was safe. I almost deserved my fate.

And on a Saturday night, with parties like this buzzing all over LA, I drove home alone. So I could climb into bed and cry.

37

M Y HEART IS still thumping, as I sit in close quarters with
Thom Gallagher. Aware that he is only three feet away, and
I have just now relived that moment from my twenty-eight-year-
old life, the one I always wanted to forget.

The press of male flesh against my body, unwanted. The fer-
vent wish I could shrink against the wall and merge with it, those
hardened molecules of wood and plaster, instead of me in my soft,
bruisable body, with all its vulnerabilities.

"Did you tell anyone else about it at the time?" Thom asks me,
his eyes empathetic.

I say nothing. It is too discordant to be here, this close to him,
when so freshly haunted by the memory of another, very different
male presence.

There is a long silence before he speaks again.

"It's . . . our standard policy when reporting a story like this.
We ask if you told anyone else about it at the time, a friend, or
anyone at all. So we can speak to them and verify that they'd heard
about it."

"What, because if I didn't tell anyone, that means it didn't happen?" I shoot this out in an accusatory tone.

"No, that's not what I'm saying."

There are tears in my eyes, and suddenly, I am so embarrassed
for crying in front of Thom Gallagher, with his reputation and his
world-famous family, his charmed, easy life.

"I'm just saying that . . . it helps if we can verify with another individual whom you confided in."

Confided in. Who was I going to tell? I was completely on my own in LA. My close friends and family were all here in New York. I had no resources, no safety net, and I was entirely responsible for a $15 million film shoot. I felt like a fool for walking blindly into that bedroom with Hugo.

"I guess I wasn't thinking far enough ahead," I say with bitter sarcasm. "I mean, surely I should have anticipated that sometime in the future, the *New York Times* would interview me about this. So unless I told someone about it in 2006, my story wouldn't count, right?"

He laughs ruefully, an attempt to make me feel better. "Well . . ."

"Sorry," I mutter. "I suppose I failed in that regard."

Another pause. "So you didn't tell anyone?"

I sigh. "Not right away. I had two weeks of the film shoot left, and all I could think about was how to get through that with Hugo around. And there wasn't really anyone I was close to out there."

Except for Holly.

There was no way I would tell my family. It would only confirm what they'd thought all along about me working in film: that I didn't belong in the first place. It was a den of iniquity, not a real workplace.

"There was . . . a friend or two I told, about a year later, when I was back in New York."

"A year later?" He seems disappointed with this information.

"Yeah, a year. Friends here wanted to know why I was no longer out there working in film."

"Why did you wait so long to tell someone?"

And why did I?

"I didn't think anyone would believe me. And I felt stupid. So stupid, because I should have known, especially after—"

I stop suddenly.

"Especially after what?"

I backtrack, seeking safer ground. "Well, all the rumors, everything I'd seen up until then with all those girls surrounding him. I should have suspected."

"But until then, as you've said, you thought it was women willing to sleep with him. Not—"

"Not assault?" I finish Thom's question.

He nods.

I sigh, trying to redirect the line of questioning. "In terms of my own . . . assault, as I guess I should call it." It's a foreign word that doesn't sit right in my mouth. A word I see emblazoned in news headlines, not one that should be woven into the fabric of my own past.

"In terms of what happened at that party, I just tried to minimize it. Even though everything changed for me after that night."

"In what way?"

"It wasn't until years later that I recognized the impact on me. I'd somehow lost confidence after it. I got dampened down, diminished. Kept thinking I could have avoided it, I should have seen it coming."

In that moment, an impossible gap opens up, between what I want to say and what I can. So I sit, strangely muzzled, my throat swollen. I study the elaborate pattern of the wallpaper, reluctant to look at Thom again, as tears stream silently down my cheeks.

"And it was the stuff he said to me that was the worst. How my working relationship with Xander didn't count for anything, how no one was going to believe me. I told myself it was just threats, but Hugo's words still got under my skin. And I loathed myself even more for being that . . . susceptible."

As requested, I provide the names and contact details of the New York friends I later told. I sit uneasily, watching Thom jot this information into his tidy little pocket-sized notebook. Aware of what I still haven't said.

I am reminded of that annoying existentialist conundrum: if a tree falls in a wood and no one hears it . . .

I wonder, how many trees need to fall, unheard, before we realize the entire forest is collapsing.

I feel hollowed out after the effort of telling that part of the story. Like the twenty-eight-year-old version of me on that awful Saturday night in LA, I just want to go home and climb into bed.

But Thom Gallagher gently pushes me to continue.

"Believe me, I've done enough of these interviews to know it's never good to end it on this note, right at the moment of trauma. Otherwise, you're going to go home miserable, and probably so will I."

It seems like an annoying attempt at gallantry on his part, but I can see the sense in what he's saying.

"That was an awful thing that happened to you," he continues, every word measured and considerate. "No one should experience anything like that. But you got past it somehow. Tell me what happened next."

You are good, Thom Gallagher, I admit to myself silently.

I close my eyes and take myself past that night.

I went to bed sobbing. The next day, I woke up, my eyes swollen, my brain muddled. And even though my world was falling apart, the sun was still shining. Like it always does every day in LA.

A particular brand of sunny amnesia that city specializes in.

At first, there was the blissful ignorance of the freshly woken. My mind registered only the bright sunlight, nothing else.

Then I remembered: the party, Hugo's hands on me, the terror. The self-loathing.

I should have known better.

After a few more hours of crying, I sent Holly a text.

Did you get home ok last night?

She wrote back forty minutes later. Yep, had a great time! Clive dropped me off.

A wave of relief washed over me. And envy, but I prodded that emotion away.

In the end, I didn't tell Holly what happened the night before. It was too humiliating: me, the acting producer, subject to an attack that base, that carnal, from Hugo himself. Reduced just like that, in the space of fifteen minutes, while the rest of the party carried on, unaware.

So I kept quiet. I started firing away emails, using work to obstruct the memory of Hugo pressed against me, his fingers gripping my skin. I dreaded even the thought of a text or email from him. Thankfully, my BlackBerry never lit up with his name.

But Sylvia called in the early afternoon.

Feeling numb, I answered her usual set of questions. I both dreaded and hoped that she might notice some slight change in the register of my voice—stop and ask, "Has something happened to you?"

Instead, it was her standard: "How's everything going? Are we on schedule?"

"How's Xander feeling?" she asked. As always, our director came first.

"He's good, I guess." I could care less about Xander at that moment, but I said something neutral. "He seemed to enjoy the party last night."

"Oh yeah, Hugo's party! How was it?"

A lump swelled in my throat, the nausea tightened inside me.

"It was, um . . . it was a Hugo party. Just with a pool, in a bigger place."

Sylvia scoffed, "As long as the cast and crew had a good time, that's what matters."

My heartbeat quickened, but I said nothing more. Silence seemed the best refuge.

——

"I'm sorry—I have to go." I say this abruptly to Thom Gallagher, with a certain finality.

This is what I'd wanted to avoid all along.

This is why I'd instinctively stayed quiet all these years. I knew the remorse would somehow paralyze me.

"Just like that? You're finished?"

"Rules of consent." I nod with a grim smile. "Not going any further tonight."

He looks disappointed, like he wants more.

Suddenly, I imagine myself as a washcloth, dripping and wet, which this golden-boy journalist is slowly wringing out, twisting me round and round to squeeze out every last drop.

"Listen, thanks for the tea," I manage to say, my voice low, barely audible. "But I have an early class to teach tomorrow."

Anxiety mounts in my head like thunderclouds massing. *Get out of there.*

I lean over and hit Stop on his digital recorder. The red light promptly blinks out.

I had thought tonight might seem like an unburdening, but instead, the strain has thickened into something darker, something heavier.

Because if I went back over everything I've said so far, I'd know there are a few frames missing. Something I'd conveniently cut out.

You see, Thom Gallagher, there's still so much I haven't told you.

Interview Transcript:
Meeting with Anonymous Source 1, Sal's Trattoria, Tuesday,
Nov. 7, 2:11 p.m.

AS1: Yes, it did happen. I didn't tell anyone at the time because . . .
It would have cost me too much.

TG: What would it have cost you?

AS1: Everything. My career. The way people perceive you. If they
ever want to work with you again. Are you the kind of girl
that's gonna make a fuss, or are you a team player? (pause)
On one hand, you have to put on this facade of being "fun,"
but you don't want to be known as easy to get into bed, or
someone who accuses a colleague. It's a tightrope walk. It
gets exhausting. (pause) So I figured it was just easier to
shut up, stay quiet, and pretend it never happened. There's
a certain strength in that, too, isn't there?

38

ON THE WAY home from Manhattan, I am tired as I climb up from the subway exit on Metropolitan Avenue, the smog thick in my nostrils, the train shuddering away underground. It is dark, and I hear my phone blip once I reach street level.

I look at my phone, curious. Hardly anyone ever calls me, and especially not at eleven p.m. on a Thursday night.

Two missed calls. No voice mail, though they would have heard my outgoing message.

The number is blocked.

I wonder if it's a coincidence.

Around me, there's no one on the street. Just the autumn night, with my breath puffing in the chilly air.

Somehow the next morning at nine thirty, I am in front of my undergraduates, regaling them about the three-act structure in screenplays.

Though I crawled into bed at midnight, utterly spent from the interview, I discovered a second wind upon waking. Perhaps I relish demonstrating my knowledge about something unrelated to Hugo North. In an arena where I'm in charge, for once.

"Who can tell me what happens in the third act?" I ask my students.

They stare back at me, bleary-eyed. I want to shout at them: *Do you know how lucky you are, getting to study this every day?*

In three years, when they're mired in office jobs, kowtowing to the ego of some middle-management boss just for a monthly paycheck—then they'll regret never bothering to read the fun stuff when they had all the time in the world.

"Come on," I say. "This is pretty basic. Classic three-act structure. Act One is the Set-up. Act Two is the Confrontation. And Act Three . . . ?"

"A big fight or something?" Avery suggests.

"The epic showdown!" Danny shouts.

"Yes!" I point to him, nodding. "The final battle. Rocky faces off against Apollo Creed. The Battle of Helm's Deep."

I think frantically for an example that isn't so violent.

"Dorothy and her friends take on the Wicked Witch."

Hm, still a death involved.

"Dumbo learns he can fly without the magic feather," I add, triumphant.

"So if Act Two is all about the conflict brewing, the growing confrontation, then Act Three is where that all comes to a head. What's the name for this high-point in the plot's structure?"

I tap the diagram that's projected onto the screen, an unlabeled plotline drawing itself to a peak.

"The climax?" Claudia pipes up.

There are one or two titters in the classroom, undoubtedly about the sexual meaning of the word, but I ignore them. Claudia shrivels.

"Exactly, the climax. Where everything will be decided once and for all. The resolution of the conflict."

"Like when King Kong falls off the Empire State Building?" someone asks.

"Another good example." I nod. "In a lot of films, it's where the hero or the good guy finally wins."

"But do they *always* win?" Danny, trying to be clever, arches a pierced eyebrow at me.

I narrow my eyes at him. "In movies, they usually do."

In real life, I want to add, *not so often.*

At 3:21 that afternoon, I am surprised to hear a timid tap on my door during office hours. On a Friday? I open my door to find Claudia, wide-eyed and shrinking. I am pleased to see her. I've always wanted to know what lies behind that curtain of dark hair, the defensive eyes.

"Hi, Claudia!" I enthuse. "Come in."

She shuffles in, parks herself on a plastic chair, and glances nervously at the open doorway.

Noticing her unease, I close my office door.

"How are you today?" I ask.

Claudia attempts a feeble smile. I wonder if there is any moment in her twenty-year-old life when she feels confident, proudly gazing out at the world instead of sweeping her eyes fearfully around, the way she is peering now at my office desk, the books and scripts ranged above it.

"Did you . . . want to talk to me about something in particular?"

I notice she has fingernails that are bitten to the quick, their edges jagged, like tortured husks. For a moment, I panic, thinking that she has not come to talk to me about schoolwork—but something else, some boy who pushed her down onto a bed at a party, some uncle whose visits are dreaded. I tell myself to stay quiet, give her space to speak.

Please just say something, I try to relay telepathically.

Finally she does. "I was—I was wondering if we could talk a little about my script?"

A silent flood of relief. I curse myself for leaping to such morbid conclusions.

I fish out her script from the pile in one of my drawers, and already in my mind, I know which one it is. Two Dominican American sisters, on the verge of adolescence, develop a fascination with the new, golden-haired teenage boy who's moved in next door.

Crafted differently, it could have been an unnerving suspense film or a trashy teen flick. But instead, it's a surprisingly poignant portrait of girlhood and outsiders, the gaps between children and immigrant parents.

"I thought it was great," I tell her honestly. "It felt really true to . . . being a girl at that age."

"Really?" Her face is alight, and it brings me such joy, seeing her emerge from her shell just this tiny bit.

I don't ask if it was based on something that really happened to her, because in some ways that's irrelevant. Nor do I mention that a script like this would struggle to get funded in real life. Instead, I simply talk about the screenplay itself, the stirring relationship between the two sisters, how the conflict with the parents can be strengthened.

Claudia seems elated and grateful. Perhaps this is the first time anyone's ever spoken one-on-one with her like this. Not about corrections, what should be avoided. But simply about what she's created.

I reference a few directors she might want to look at: early Catherine Hardwicke, Céline Sciamma, Alice Rohrwacher. For the first time in a long while, I feel the excitement of talking to another cinephile, even one who is half my age.

Oh, to have—still ahead of you—the joy of seeing *Wings of Desire* or *Killer of Sheep*. I envy the unwatched wonder of everything still to come to Claudia. To be that young, that easily delighted, that blind.

After Claudia has left, I check my inbox, half hoping to see something from Thom Gallagher, but also relieved when nothing's there. A quick flick onto the *LA Times* home page, and I pause on an interview with a revered, white-haired actor.

"We are undeserving victims of wild accusations," says the pulled quote. "The world has gone mad."

I shake my head and turn off my computer.

=

On my way through the department reception, I stop and say good-bye to our admin staff.

"Go home and rest up this weekend," Marnie, our office manager, says. "You look tired."

She has no idea.

"You too," I say. "Have a nice weekend."

"Ooh, nice champagne!" I add, admiring a magnum of Möet which sits atop her desk. It seems out of place, huge and gleaming, between a filing cabinet and a stack of overloaded paper trays. "You gonna crack that open at five o'clock?"

"Oh, I almost forgot!" Marnie gets up, alarmed. "That's for you. It arrived this afternoon. Classy admirer, hey?"

I stand still in my tracks, mute with fear. And stare at the outsized bottle, the gold-foiled bow wrapped tight round the sleek black neck. There's only one person I've known in my life who would send over a magnum of Möet, just like that.

The Möet comes with a card. Heavy cream stock, and printed on it, a brief message in Times New Roman:

Dear Sarah—
Just thought you might appreciate this, in remembrance of all our good times and cinematic successes together. Hope to be in touch soon.
H.N.

It takes every ounce of my will not to grab the bottle and smash it against the white cinderblock wall of our department office.

But then, I realize it's been ages since I've drunk the cool, crisp taste of Möet. It would be a shame to trash a perfectly good bottle of fine champagne.

So I lug the magnum home in a spare bag. The heavy, full bottle tugs at the cheap blue plastic, weighing me down.

Once home in Williamsburg, I store it under my kitchen sink, next to spray bottles of window cleaner and disinfectant. The card I tuck under the bottom of the bottle. Out of sight, out of mind, I tell myself.

But all I can think is that Hugo North knows how to find me. There's something he wants from me. And he hates taking no for an answer.

The next morning, Saturday, I wake up grateful for the October sunlight on my bed, the sounds of the street rumbling just below my window. All the night before, I'd been disturbed by the bottle of Möet under my kitchen sink. I ignored the temptation to uncork it and drink it in its entirety, simply for the momentary oblivion it could offer. Instead, I waited out the night in a state of semi-fear and fell asleep troubled.

Upon waking, I wish I could avoid the inevitable: the scrutinizing of my phone, the scrolling through apps and headlines. But I cannot resist. I am drawn unavoidably to the latest updates from the *Hollywood Reporter*. And there—boom! as I'd half dreaded, half imagined it—I see her name.

Holly Randolph on Her #MeToo Story

I sit straight up, the jolt of adrenaline and nausea agitating my gut this early on a Saturday morning.

I check my other messages, but no one has tried to reach me. A relief, for now.

I tap on the article link and scan through it once, then a second time more slowly.

At an interview for her upcoming film *Rainfall in Texas*, Holly Randolph made an enigmatic comment on the growing #MeToo movement. Asked if she had ever experienced any form of sexual misconduct or harassment on the job, she replied: "I'm not going to talk about any specifics right now," in a video interview with *IndieWire*. "I'm here to talk about my new film at the moment."

Good girl, I think.
Holly, ever the professional, always focused on the job.

Even when pressed further, Randolph stayed firm. "When I'm ready, I may choose to reveal my story in due course. What I want to get across right now is yes, of course I've had to deal with that. I think any young actress in Hollywood has had to. It's endemic in the industry."

This is repeated as a pulled quote on my screen, the letters in bold, framed for emphasis: "It's endemic in the industry."

"I'd like to retain my privacy on this for a little bit longer. So I ask that you respect that for now."

Randolph refused to acknowledge whether her past experiences involved any of the men currently accused of sexual misconduct.

Earlier this week, writer-director Xander Schulz issued a statement, confirming that he never witnessed any sexual assault on his film sets. Schulz directed Randolph in *Furious Her*, the film that is largely credited with launching her onto the A-list.

There has been growing speculation within the industry on which perpetrators remain unnamed, with the legacy of many stars and executives already tarnished.

So Holly has acknowledged it but hasn't told her full story. I wonder what the holdup could be. A legal threat? An NDA she may have been forced to sign later on, after I lost contact with her? A mysterious bottle of Möet sent, with its implicit threat? Or perhaps she is waiting for someone else to come forward, at least one other soul out there who can corroborate the truth she is holding back.

And I realize, even now, I don't exactly know the full story of what happened to Holly during our few months as friends and colleagues out there, in sun-drenched LA ten years ago.

So, like the rest of the world, I wait in thrall, hanging on to the next line to issue from her mouth.

Whenever you're ready, Holly Randolph.

I journey to Flushing on Sunday, as the dutiful daughter.

Dim sum at the restaurant, surrounded by the wailing babies and raucous multigenerational families gorging at circular tables, all around us. These lives that will go on, unbothered by the PR statements of celebrities they will never meet.

Later, my parents and I retire to their apartment, where we drink more tea and watch the latest videos of Karen's kids at their piano recital. I utter more assurances that my life as a thirty-nine-year-old single daughter is perfectly fine, that they should stop worrying about me, and no, they should not try to set me up with Dad's college classmate's son, who has recently separated from his blond Midwestern girlfriend.

"I'm fine. Seriously, I am," I tell them in my awkward Cantonese.

All I can think of is that outsize bottle of champagne sitting under my kitchen sink, like a ticking bomb, unseen.

When I step out of their apartment building, the sky has darkened, a cloud covering the October sunshine. Instead of heading straight to the subway, I decide to visit the Queens Library, my feet drawing me down that once-familiar route, to where it presides over a busy fork in the road, the crowds hurrying past as always.

I expect a rush of nostalgia when I push through the glass doors, but the place has been refurbished. It is disorienting, seeing these bright white walls, the high-tech touch screens replacing the humble card catalogs of my youth.

What hasn't changed is the demographics: the stacks still filled with Chinese people of all ages, old grandfathers and young kids and lonely teenagers with their backpacks. Everyone reading or tapping at iPads and computers, somehow individually striving their best to fulfill the stereotype of the studious, diligent Chinese.

I find this reassuring somehow, all the generations of learning and commitment taking place silently around me.

In the basement, I discover a few carts filled with secondhand materials being resold for $1–$3. Books, DVDs, CDs that the library doesn't need anymore. I am always drawn to shelves like these, curious to see what discarded treasures I might stumble upon. I flick through the DVD cases, my mind quickly moving past the action-movie sequels, the run-of-the-mill puerile comedies and romances which do nothing for me.

And there—on the middle shelf, tucked between a horror film remake and season 2 of a beloved '90s sitcom—I spot a familiar title: *Furious Her*.

Here? In the basement of the Queens Library?

I tell myself it's simply a coincidence: *Furious Her* was a popular film; the library probably owned multiple copies and decided to sell one off.

That minimalist font and color scheme I'd recognize anywhere. And when I turn the DVD case around, the close-up of Holly's face at a three-quarters angle, the hint of fear in her eyes, balanced by the gleam of heroic resolution.

The coincidence is jarring for me. Surprise, shadowed by the nausea which always accompanies the memory of that film.

But there is also a distinct pride.

I turn the case over, scan the credits block on the back. And there, if you squint closely enough, you can see my name sandwiched in among all the others. *Associate Producer: Sarah Lai.*

That's my name! I want to shout to the nearest person. *See, that's me! I made this film!*

I almost point this out to the librarian as I hand her the two dollars for the DVD. But I don't want to call attention to the irony of it all. She will ask me if I am still making films, and the disappointment will wash over her face when I tell her no, not anymore. So I shove the secondhand DVD into my bag, and walk out of the Queens Library, leaving behind that bright new interior, that space both familiar and new, thrumming with quiet minds that hope for better days.

I am just another person in a sea of black-haired individuals, trudging along the sidewalk, dipping underground to board the subway.

Back home, I pop the silver disc into my DVD player. It has some scratches—any library DVD would—but after a few stuttering attempts, the main menu glows on my TV screen.

You'd think I, as associate producer, would be more familiar with the DVD of *Furious Her*. But in the protracted timelines of film distribution, the DVD came out quite a while after we'd shot the movie—nearly two years after that autumn in LA. And by then, well . . . I'd stopped caring so much about the film, my feelings about it warped beyond recognition.

So I remember being sent a few copies of the DVD, but I felt little joy in owning them. I gave a copy to my parents, another to my brother and sister each, and the remaining copies sat gathering dust somewhere among my belongings, still inside their plastic wrapping.

In all these years, I've had little inclination to watch the film, despite its growing cult status as an exemplar of the indie thriller, despite my name compressed into its official credit block.

Now, a decade on, I sit on my couch staring at the DVD menu on the screen. The music that plays over it is tense but spare, a creeping pluck on the guitar that grows in a sinister crescendo, then repeats on an endless loop. It is unnerving to hear over and over again, and I eventually hit the mute button, as I contemplate what to select.

There is something diseased about the very thought of the film, a poison that has tainted my every association with it. I've done enough swimming in that toxic lake recently, ever since I started speaking to Thom.

So I ignore the Watch Film option and select the Extras instead. There are no deleted scenes, but I regard the original trailer for the film. The cheesy male voice sets the scene: *"She lost the man she loved, but she never knew the secret he was hiding . . . Or the people he was up against."*

I cringe. Well, that's certainly dated.

What else would lose its shine upon a repeat viewing, ten years later?

I notice Holly's audition is included as one of the DVD extras. The footage is grainy, the sound quality horrific. But it's fascinating to see Holly at twenty-three, before she achieved the superstar heights from which she now surveys the world. Her hair is dirty blond, and her makeup not nearly as polished as we're accustomed to seeing it these days. Yet it is still undoubtedly Holly Randolph, her face as expressive as always, the line delivery, the acting talent as palpable then as it is today.

This would have been the footage Brian, Val's assistant, had filmed from inside the casting suite we hired that summer day, where Xander and Hugo sat raining down their greetings upon the parade of actresses, while I observed silently from the shadows.

It is disconcerting to witness the exact same audition from another angle, a more official one. The camera zooms in to capture Holly in reverent close-up, the way countless other cameras would in subsequent years.

To think I was just there, off camera. My presence in that very room completely undetected by all the people who've watched this DVD extra since. Who will never know that someone named Sarah Lai was there, when Holly Randolph gave this exact reading of the script that would make her famous.

I probe further into the menu, my curiosity driven by a dark, inexplicable impulse.

And then, on the second screen of DVD extras, I see something called "Forged in a White Heat: The Making of *Furious Her*."

I'd somehow willfully forgotten that this feature existed, even though I'd been the one to hire the publicity unit to produce it. After everything that happened, I couldn't stomach another piece of PR gloss that testified to Xander's remarkable talent, our exciting team of cast and crew praising each other endlessly behind the scenes.

Ugh.

But this time, I hit Play.

The DVD whirrs towards my selection, the image fades in from black.

Holly, of course.

In close-up, speaking to a shaky handheld camera, Holly cracks a smile. "Hi, I'm Holly Randolph and this is Day One of filming *Furious Her*. And I'm really excited to be playing the role of Katie Phillips!"

Then a wide shot of Xander directing, saying something authoritative and serious. Another shot of Holly laughing with Carlos the boom operator, with Clive and Marisa. A few quick cuts of other cast looking convivial with the crew—and then, there onscreen, right in front of me: Hugo. A mid-shot of him grinning into the camera.

I am rocked with a jolt of queasiness, to be confronted with him like this, these moments on film captured so indelibly.

His supreme assurance, the twinkle in his eyes when he was being charming.

I don't want to keep watching, but I do.

His British accent slithers out at me.

"I'm Hugo North. I'm the executive producer of this incredible film, *Furious Her*. It's the first day of filming. Come join us as we take a closer look."

I even remember that take. They never ended up using the footage of me and Hugo talking to the camera, our smiling demonstration of camaraderie. That is hardly a surprise.

I hit Pause on the remote, and inspect the frozen image, the two white tracks suspended, jittering, across the screen.

Behind Hugo, I recognize the exterior of the studio we'd rented for months. I look at this background, and I can place myself instantaneously in that moment, on the first day of production.

And peering further, a few steps behind Hugo, I notice another figure: a young woman, her long black hair just inside the shot.

With a frisson of recognition, I realize that's me.

Haunting the background of this video, like something from a Japanese horror film.

I am there, virtually hidden in this very shot—unaware of what was coming to me, to so many of us.

But I am the only person who would think to look for these traces. No one else would even care.

Interview Transcript:
Phone call from Lily Winters, received Thursday, Nov. 9,
4:23 p.m.

LW: Oh hi, is this Thom Gallagher?

TG: Um, yes it is. Who's calling?

LW: I'm Lily Winters. I'm in communications, and I used to work with your uncle Paul on his senatorial campaigns back in the day.

TG: Oh right. Hello, how can I . . . how can I help? I'm not in touch with Paul so much at the moment.

LW: Well, it's not about that. I'm now calling from Conquest PR.

TG: *Conquest* PR?

LW: Yes, that's right. I work with the producer Hugo North on all his comms and media.

TG: Ah. How'd you get my number?

LW: I mean, you're a journalist, I'm in PR. It's not that difficult.

TG: What's this about, Lily?

LW: (pause) We've heard that you might be working on a piece about Hugo, his start in the film industry and maybe his journey since then. Is that correct?

TG: I'm speaking to a lot of people about various stories, so . . . it's too early to say what's gonna shape up into an actual publishable piece or not.

LW: Of course. But we were a bit concerned that you might not be speaking to the right people. In regards to Hugo.

TG: What do you mean by that? The "right people"?

LW: Well, Hugo's a very successful producer and businessman. You can imagine there's always people who want to take down someone with his profile. We'd hate to think the *Times* would engage in something like a smear campaign.

TG: A smear campaign? No, that's not the kind of journalism I write.

LW: I'm sure it's not. But still, you should be careful and make sure you're only speaking to reputable sources.

TG: And what determines if a source is reputable or not?

LW: I think we all know what kinds of women are credible and who isn't. There's probably a lot of very bitter people out there. (pause) We'd be happy to work with you on the piece. If you tell us a little more about it.

39

TWO WEEKS LATER Thom Gallagher is in my apartment in Brooklyn, on the seedier edges of Williamsburg.

I have invited him to my place for our final interview. I tell myself there are no ulterior motives here—only to give myself the home turf advantage.

I have been reading enough recent exposés to know that many of the sources have invited the journalists into their homes, where they unspool their tale from the past. Some stars have even recounted their stories to reporters in the intimacy of a hotel room—a morbid irony I somehow find amusing.

My own home is hardly impressive, a humble abode that my lecturer salary can barely afford. It has been some time since I have let a man of any age into my apartment. But looking around this morning, I realize there is very little that could be embarrassing.

My apartment is plainly furnished, posters of art and nature fixed to the walls with SticTac, as if I were still in college. A cursory glance would offer little hint that I once worked in the film industry. There is a large Japanese poster for *King Kong vs. Godzilla* (1962) in my hallway, but no photos of me on set or on the red carpet, no souvenir clapper boards, certainly no Oscars or Golden Globes on display.

But if Thom were to look closer, he would see the stacks of student film scripts, the books on screenwriting and film criticism, the size and unusual breadth of my DVD collection, piled on the floor, my tables, the windowsill.

I've left the DVD of *Furious Her* on the coffee table, an obviously planted MacGuffin. Sure to elicit some commentary from an eagle-eyed investigator like him.

But I am nervous as I wait for our tea to brew, watch Thom politely perusing the titles of my books, the art I've chosen for my walls. Why should I care what this twenty-seven-year-old thinks of my choice of reading material?

He is just a journalist, here to do his job. To extract the rest of a story from me.

And I am just a source, relieving myself of the past. Still pondering how much to reveal to him.

It is a transaction, a pragmatic exchange, and nothing more.

As if on cue, Thom nods at the *Furious Her* DVD lying on my coffee table. "Have you watched it again?"

We are both sitting down on opposite ends of my couch, a cushion and a half between us. The digital recorder is nearby on the coffee table, but not turned on.

"Funnily enough, I came across that in a secondhand sale at the Queens Library. Just the other week."

I describe the incident in more detail, playing up my shock.

He responds with a reflexive enthusiasm, his blue eyes alight. "What did the librarian say? About you working on the film?"

"I didn't tell her. I just . . . I mean, what would be the point?"

There is a silence, and I look down at the steam lifting off my Moroccan Mint tea, feeling the weight of the past ten years pressing on me. During this moment, he places his finger on the Record button of his Dictaphone.

"Do you mind?" he asks.

The red light blinks alive, and he leans back, the distance between us safely restored.

"How do you feel about the film now?" he asks.

"I know I should be proud," I say. "I mean, it's a good film. It won awards, it's a cult classic in some circles. But . . . that was another version of me who was involved in making it. A younger, more gullible me."

The Sarah who cared only about appearing in the credit block, my name squashed beyond recognition.

"I'm ashamed for being that gullible. For working that hard for . . . nothing in the end."

"Would you really say nothing?"

"Yes," I snap back, irritated. "Nothing. I mean, honestly . . . Where has it gotten me?"

I gesture around to my tiny apartment, the piles of unread student scripts, which will never get made.

"How do you feel now when you think about the film? And the production and everything that happened?"

"I feel ashamed. For being that stupid . . . And I feel guilt." I look away, at the blank TV screen. Our two figures are silhouetted vaguely on its dull black surface.

In my mind, I see the figures of two young women stepping into the gilded elevator of a Los Angeles hotel ten years ago, their backs to me.

"Guilt?" The inquisitive note in Thom's voice rings like a bell.

"Yeah, guilt." I fix my eyes back on his. "Ready for the rest of my story?"

After that party at Hugo's house, I was a zombie for the rest of the shoot.

"What do you mean, 'a zombie'?"

I could crack a joke here about George Romero, *Production of the Dead* or something, but there is nothing funny about it.

I guess the numbness I felt from the morning after that party . . . well, that numbness lasted for the rest of production, probably for months after. Unable to tell anyone what happened that night, I retreated into a solitary, joyless cocoon—and all I focused on was finishing the shoot, plodding through the logistics of my job, the never-ending to-do list, externally playing the role of the friendly, competent producer.

But that was all I could manage. I lost all other drive, all real sense of delight or camaraderie.

Inside, I'd crumbled.

Hanging over all of this was the shapeless dread of seeing Hugo again. Something raw had been ripped open inside me, even though I told myself he'd done little more that night than pin me against a wall, stroke my arm. But I know he would have done more, given the chance.

An underlying terror throbbed just out of my range of hearing—like a low, thumping bass—insistent, unnerving, every time I found myself in the same room as Hugo. Yet he was impossible to avoid. He was everywhere, louder and more spirited and more celebratory as we drew closer to the end of the production.

Towards me, Hugo acted as if nothing unusual had happened the night of his party. I'd simply gone up to his room to get those contracts signed and then gone home.

And perhaps, for him, it wasn't strange. Perhaps that was how he acted towards all young women in his orbit.

During the penultimate week of the shoot, I was haunting the Chateau Marmont bar uneasily, chatting to some of the cast and crew, while puzzling over Hugo's whereabouts. Courtney had gone home already. She left me with two scripts Hugo had asked her to print out and hand to him that night.

I took them unwillingly, as if they were infected.

But I glanced at the scripts out of curiosity. *The Dead Can't Speak. Invisible Fires.* The titles suggested thrillers, possibly in the horror genre, but I didn't recognize the names of the screenwriters. The scripts didn't have an agency logo on them, which meant they'd somehow come to Hugo independently. Was he talking to Xander about new projects, without my knowledge or Sylvia's?

This was potentially something to worry about, but I didn't have time to dwell on it, with the production marching on. "I think Hugo wants to read them this weekend," Courtney had said to me obliquely, before she got into her electric blue RAV4 and drove off.

And sure enough, within an hour, I'd gotten a BBM from Hugo. I need those 2 scripts from Courtney tonight. Bring them up to my room 72. I'm here now.

I felt sick at the thought.

No way was I going up to his room alone.

Another message flashed through, as if he'd read my mind: Bring them in person. Don't you dare have concierge do it. We have lots to talk about.

I pondered if there was some way I could literally just stand at the threshold of the room, chuck in the scripts when he opened the door, and sprint away.

But then I remembered how he'd pushed me up the stairs and into that bedroom. He was physically stronger than me. All he had to do was drag me in, slam the door shut, lock the bolt . . . The feel of his meaty hands gripping my forearm like a vise, his finger tracing its way down my bare shoulder, those words he'd said. I shuddered, sickened.

I stood by the hotel elevators, furious that this was my evening: trying to figure out how to avoid being molested by my boss again.

I must have been engrossed in my thoughts, because I nearly missed Xander walking by quickly, in his standard black T-shirt and jeans. He stopped when he saw me.

"Sarah, didn't expect to see you here."

I glanced up. Away from the shoot, Xander seemed more relaxed, none of the self-serious presence he carried on set. He looked ready to go out: his hair was gelled, the baseball cap gone. As much as I'd resented his surly attitude these recent weeks, a strange relief washed over me at the sight of him.

"Oh hey," I said. "Where you headed?"

He shrugged. "Meeting someone at the Mondrian. What are you up to?"

"I, um . . ." I paused. An idea flashed through my head. "Hey, can you spare five minutes?"

Xander looked displeased, glanced at his watch. "Not really."

I ignored him. "Listen, I really really really need you to do me a favor. Hugo's asked me to hand him these scripts, and I don't want to go up to his room. Can you run up and give them to him?"

"What?" A single sharp syllable that he spat out. It was the sort of thing you'd ask a PA or an intern to do, not the writer-director himself when that film was in production.

I'd have to hint at the truth. There was no other way I could convince him.

My eyes looked pleadingly at him, my breath became ragged, and I hated myself in that moment for having to play the damsel-in-distress with Xander Schulz, a role I loathed, and a person I loathed to ask for help.

"You know what Hugo's like when he's drunk or high," I said. "I just—I just don't want to go up there. As a woman. On my own."

Xander paused and looked at me. Perhaps this might work.

Every single feminist molecule of my body seethed in revolt, but I pressed on.

"You know what he's like. With women."

And maybe Xander knew exactly, and maybe he didn't. But he was still standing there, considering what I'd said.

"It's literally only going to take you five minutes," I added. "Room 72. Please. If I were a guy, I wouldn't be asking you."

Xander stared at me, as if assessing the truth of my statement. He gave a single nod, with a knowing gleam in his eyes—or maybe I imagined it. "Okay," he said. "I'll do it."

My body flooded with relief. "Thank you thank you thank you," I said, and handed the scripts to him. "I totally owe you."

Xander furrowed his brow. "How are you holding up, by the way?"

This was unheralded. Xander asking how *I* was, showing some rare sign of concern for a fellow human being?

"Um . . ." I caught a wobble in my throat, surprised that I should tremble this easily, at this slightest show of compassion. I shouted at myself not to cry. Not in front of Xander. I could think of nothing more humiliating.

"Um, yeah, I'm fine. Just tired after so many weeks of shooting." I looked away, feeling my eyes start to water.

"Yeah, you seem tired. Well, we're almost there. Come on, where's that kick-ass Sarah I've always known? Where'd she go?"

I don't know, I wanted to tell him. *Something happened to her. And she's gone into hiding.*

40

THAT MOMENT WAS the closest I ever got to revealing the truth about Hugo to Xander. Maybe he already knew but simply didn't care, because Hugo's behavior never adversely affected him, the director who benefited from his largesse.

If I'd said something then . . .

I shake my head. What's the point in asking that question?

So I moved in a haze through those last weeks of the shoot. Exhaustion stretched me thin, as I flitted from the production office to set to drinks or dinner scarfed down somewhere in the grid of LA's streets. But the location that rings most palpably in my memory—the one I keep returning to—was the lobby of the Chateau Marmont.

Walk through the entrance, and there are the relaxed art deco armchairs, the shadows of palm trees cast on the walls. Ahead looms the bar, where our cast and crew spent many an evening, quaffing a drink or two before heading home. And around the corner, the elevators, discreetly whisking visitors to the luxe private rooms and suites above.

One week before the end of our shoot, I was headed there as usual—and I realized I'd hardly seen or spoken to Holly all week. After six weeks of filming, Holly was likely worn down by the grueling workload, the weight of expectation that this role would be her big break, if only she nailed every single scene, every take, every waking moment that she existed in front of the camera.

As for me, I'd retreated into my wretched cocoon, paralyzed by the shame that flooded me after Hugo's house party.

I was also secretly envious of Holly. Despite our friendship, a wall had slowly risen between us during the production. How could it not have? As our star, Holly had every single desire catered to when she was on set. Someone to hand her a coat if she was cold. Someone to re-touch her makeup at a second's notice. Someone to drive her wherever she needed. Actors exist like these immortal beings who grace a film set with their presence, the lights literally arranged to illuminate their unearthly beauty, directors and wardrobe and hair and makeup crew continually reminding them that they look amazing, they're fantastic, they're perfect (so long as they comply).

Meanwhile, I labored away under a nonstop flood of emails and phone calls, the demands of Sylvia and Hugo pressing heavily on me.

So yes, I had started to begrudge the ease with which Holly existed, the pampering she received. Who wouldn't?

That Friday evening, one week before the end of shooting, I finished up late at the office, long after everyone else had left. Due to the traffic, I arrived at the Chateau Marmont for our weekly Friday drinks on the late side. I briefly contemplated using the valet parking, but the cost was astronomical. Instead, I wove my car around the neighboring blocks, before finally managing a grievous parallel parking job, followed by a ten-minute walk up the hill to the hotel.

I was out of breath when I arrived in the lobby, the doorman less than impressed by the obvious fact I'd parked elsewhere and walked in. At the lobby bar, I saw only a handful of lighting and sound guys, a fraction of the usual crowd.

"Where's everyone?" I asked.

"Went home early," Chas, the clapper/loader mumbled. "Or left already to get dinner."

"Ah okay." I cursed myself for staying at the office so late. "Where's Holly?"

"Oh, she had to go do something." Chas swigged from his craft beer. "She might still be in the hotel somewhere."

Disquieted, I drifted out into the foyer, checking my Black-Berry. Maybe Holly had to use the bathroom. The bathrooms at the Chateau Marmont were always worth a visit anyway, for their period decor and the chance to glimpse a celebrity in some state of intoxication.

As I looked up from my phone, though, I spied Courtney and Holly just around the corner, about to enter the open door of an elevator.

I shouted their names. They turned.

"Hey!" I said. "You guys leaving?"

Courtney nodded decisively. She was in her efficient mode, her hand on Holly's arm, as if guiding her to some unspoken fate.

"Hey!" Holly shouted back, her luminous smile flashing at me.

"We're not totally going," Courtney explained. "It's just, Hugo said he wanted to talk to Holly about something now."

"Wait—" Alarm bells clamored in my head. "You're going up to his room?"

I looked at Courtney in dismay, wanting to—*(Deep breath. Start again.)*—wanting to make some connection, but the expression on her face was blank and gave me nothing.

"It'll just take five minutes," Holly assured me.

"Did he say what it was about?" I asked, trying to stall them.

"No." Courtney shrugged. "Only, he said it was pretty urgent, so I should take her up there right away."

By now, I was only a few feet from them, but they'd stepped into the elevator and looked out at me, unsuspecting. Courtney pressed the button for the seventh floor.

A knot of tension lodged inside me. "And you'll be with her the whole time?" I spoke directly to Courtney, seeking confirmation.

"Maybe," she said. Her face was inscrutable.

"Just—" I wanted to say something else, anything. I glanced at Holly, who gazed back at me, curious.

"Sarah, is there something wrong?" she asked.

I hesitated, openmouthed.

And in that moment, the elevator door slid shut, cutting them off.

"Oh no," I whispered, to no one around me.

I stood rooted to the spot in that gleaming lobby, willing the elevator not to operate, the cables not to move, for the door never to open on the seventh floor, bringing the two of them closer to room 72.

It was just a moment, really. Suspended like a quivering of dewdrops at the end of a leaf. A globe of water gathers and gathers until you can stare into it, imagining an alternate future, a thousand possible ways things could have gone differently.

But another breath, and the previous world inside that trembling moment is gone, fallen to the dirt, never to exist again.

"So what have you since thought about the events of that evening?"

Thom Gallagher waits for my answer.

There is an uncomfortable prickling in my throat, my mouth, as if the numbness from ten years ago has returned, paralyzing me from saying more.

"I think . . ." I croak, then clear my throat. "I think it's impossible to know, unless there had been a camera on the scene. But if you were to ask either Holly or Hugo what happened that night . . ."

The accounts of their evening would be very different indeed.

I still can't bring myself to say something, so I attempt a more roundabout approach.

"You know, as the years have gone by, I've always felt a strange gap, a sort of guilty rift between me and the women who've experienced it."

The girls in college I heard rumors about. What happened to them that night they came home in tears, leaning on the arm of a friend. Or the acquaintance who posts something on Facebook, commenting on an "incident," a "bad date" that took place years ago. What do you say in those instances? How do you bridge this awkward division? This simple, unequal equation: that one of you has been raped, and the other has not?

There is no logic, no explainable arithmetic that justifies why the cards fall as they do. It is pure happenstance. A random game of luck. That much I know now. Or at least I tell myself that, to ease the guilt.

"You say the word 'guilt' a lot," Thom points out, like an overpaid therapist.

I don't respond, but the word "guilt" has been threaded through this entire conversation, the past ten years of my life.

So yes, when I consider that moment in the lobby of the Chateau Marmont—me standing in front of the elevator door, just before it closed and sealed Holly's doom—I wonder what I could have done to avoid that outcome. Because it was inevitable, wasn't it? Sure, on that given night, I could have paid the twenty dollars to valet my car, arrived in time to have a drink and, maybe, somehow prevented Holly from going up to Hugo's. Or standing in front of the elevator doors, I could have not hesitated, and barged in there, telling Holly the truth about Hugo: what I knew, what had happened to me.

But in the end, Hugo would have won somehow.

He was so accustomed to getting what he wanted, that one night's proceedings would never have deterred the outcome he desired. Whether it was through charm or wealth, power or intoxication: these made no difference to him. These were merely various, equally justifiable methods to achieving his aims.

I'm not, of course, just talking about sex. Most things he could buy. Because of his money, most people he could convince. He finagled his way into the film industry, and the three of us—Sylvia, Xander, and I—were stupid enough to throw the door wide open for him. And once he was bankrolling the production, he felt that everything was ultimately his. Including Holly.

"Do you believe Hugo raped Holly that night?" Thom asks outright.

"I believe so, yes," I finally say, my voice hoarse. "Now I do."

"But at the time, you said nothing?"

I nod.

I didn't want to envision it then, though I surely feared it. I stood in front of the elevator long after it closed, frozen in thought. Until the gilded dial at the top turned back down to one, and the door opened again, releasing only a squat waiter pushing a cart with an upended platter and an empty pair of wineglasses.

I considered telling concierge to call up to Hugo's room, saying there was an urgent visitor, but the Marmont prided itself on leaving its guests undisturbed. And surely that would only incur his wrath further.

Besides, how could I be sure what Hugo had planned for Holly? I reminded myself he would never treat Holly the way he'd treated me the night of his house party. Holly had an agent, she was our star, she was protected in some way. An enchanted aura seemed to surround her every time she stepped on set. Surely it would protect her now, when we were still a week from wrapping the shoot.

So I turned on my heel and walked out of the lobby, across the neon stream of Sunset Boulevard, and back down the hill to my humble rental car. Whatever happened between Hugo and Holly was between the executive producer of the film and the star. She was an adult, she could fend for herself.

Somehow, I slept solidly that Friday night. Perhaps I was so worn down from the shoot, that sleep became a welcome escape for my body.

But the next morning, with a sinking feeling, I recalled that abortive moment in front of the elevator of the Chateau Marmont, the brass panel sliding shut to cut me off from Holly and Courtney.

The numbness in my body deepened, as it does now.

On my nightstand, my BlackBerry blinked. I didn't want to face the onslaught of emails, Sylvia asking me for an update—or worse yet, any message from Hugo. But when I checked, there was nothing significant. The usual automated emails, a peppy message from production, wishing us a restful final weekend.

And one missed call from Holly at two a.m.

I paused, wondering if I should call her back. Perhaps I shouldn't bother our star on a Saturday morning.

In the end, I sent her a brief text.

Hey, sorry I missed your call. You ok?

I never heard back.

I pause, the silence thudding and monstrous around me. I realize I have been digging my fingernails into the worn upholstery of my couch, as if I could claw myself back into hiding.

I stand up, dizzy. Apologizing to Thom, I stumble into my cramped kitchen and draw myself a glass of cold water from the tap. I lean against the counter, my forehead pressed into my hands, my eyes closed, trying to shut out the unsaid.

You still haven't told him everything.

The words ring, singsong and taunting in my ears.

Those frames that were conveniently edited out, a few scenes ago. An opportune cut, here and there, that elides the truth.

What do they ask for in court? The truth, the whole truth, and nothing but the truth . . .

The whole truth.

"Are you all right?" Thom calls out from my lounge, the Dicta-phone paused and waiting.

"I just need a moment," I say weakly.

You fucking idiot, I tell myself. *Where did you think this would get you?*

I am aware of how suspicious I must seem to Thom. The textbook guilty confessor in any crime film, fidgeting in the interrogation suite.

You tell him now, or you lose all credibility.

Beneath this kitchen counter, that gleaming magnum of Möet still sits, unopened. And tucked beneath its heavy glass, the inconspicuous note from Hugo.

In remembrance of all our good times and cinematic successes together.

I take my phone out of my pocket and dial voice mail again. Listen to the message that was left there a week ago.

"Hi, Sarah. It's Hugo—looks like I've just missed you again. Listen, I know it's been years, but sometimes . . . you need those years to appreciate the people who truly deserve recognition. You're too talented and too committed not to be working with us again. You know how to reach me."

There was a time, years ago, maybe even two months ago, when I might have responded immediately, pathetically to such a message. To be invited back into the fold just like that. My sins erased, my place in the industry reinstated.

But I didn't. And a few days later, I received another message, darker in tone, his voice lowered.

"Sarah, it's Hugo. One other thing I wanted to say. If you are talking to anyone, any journalists, I'd be very wary. The press can twist anything you say. And well . . . you know what you knew back then. Don't act like you were completely innocent. After all, you need to protect yourself."

The suave British accent, the voice I never wanted to hear again. A decade later, it still triggers a cold revulsion in me.

But even after hearing this second message, I've chosen to speak to Thom Gallagher. Why?

The trash can icon on my phone screen beckons. I'm tempted to delete the messages, yet stop.

They, too, can serve a purpose.

And then I realize, if Hugo North, the man responsible for a raft of successful films, a chain of luxury business properties, and a portfolio now worth $3.8 billion—could be bothered to reach out multiple times to me, Sarah Lai, lowly lecturer at a little-known community college, then he must be very scared indeed. Perhaps there is some power in the truth I hold.

I know him too well to be tricked by the exteriors.

Pondering this, still unsure what to do, my eye falls on the windowsill. There's a framed photo of myself and three-year-old Alice, her face crinkled in delight at me—and next to it, a jade plant that my mother gave me when I moved into this apartment two years ago. The rounded, rubbery leaves gleam in the weak late-afternoon light.

"This brings you good luck and prosperity," she had said, positioning it carefully to face north, towards a dingy air shaft in my apartment building.

I snort at the irony. A whole lot of good that's done me.

With another deep breath, I refill my glass with water and pour it into the soil of the potted plant.

Fuck it.

I'm done hiding. You win, Thom Gallagher. You get to hear it all.

Interview Transcript (continued):
Sylvia Zimmerman, 4:45 p.m.

TG: Would you have called Holly Randolph "fodder" at the time?

SZ: Listen, I don't care if you're recording this, but you do *not* publicly quote me on any of this. (pause) Holly Randolph *could* have been, if she was a different kind of girl. A lesser girl would have just crumpled beneath Hugo's demands, become his plaything or something. But Holly was tough. That's why we picked her for the role. (pause) I heard no such rumor, that she was sleeping with Hugo, or that there was anything at all between them. Or if she did, she was very discreet.

TG: What do you think *did* happen to Holly, during the making of *Furious Her*?

SZ: I have no reason to suspect anything untoward happened. I mean, that film was huge for her, in terms of her profile. I doubt she'd have anything to complain about.

TG: Do you think there's a chance some incident may have gotten covered up, and you wouldn't have heard about it?

SZ: *I* wouldn't have heard about it? I was producer of that film, after all. (pause) But, like I said, it's film, it's Hugo. Anything's possible. And I wasn't there in LA for much of the film shoot. So yes, I guess there is that slim possibility.

TG: Why do you say slim?

SZ: Well, because . . . Holly seemed fine. She was acting too normal for any of us to suspect something bad had happened.

TG: She is . . . very good at acting, of course. You might say that was her job.

SZ: Still, I'd have been surprised.

TG: Do you think anyone else on that film production might have known about something happening to Holly?

SZ: Well, if she'd told her agent, I would have certainly heard. (pause) I suppose . . . I suppose Sarah was quite close to her at the time. They lived next to each other in these rental apartments for the shoot. They were—they seemed to be friends.

TG: But Sarah never said anything to you?

SZ: No. And I'm positive that Sarah would have told me, if she'd suspected anything.

TG: Why is that?

SZ: Because she'd always been reliable, ever since I first hired her. We were a team. I mean, what would she gain by hiding something like that from me?

41

OF COURSE, I didn't tell Sylvia a word of this. Because there was almost nothing to say. That I'd seen two people step into the elevator, on their way to Hugo's room? Told one way, that wouldn't even be news. Women get invited to hotel rooms all the time.

But my silence was my punishment. I lived the remainder of the shoot in a fearful paralysis. Days passed before I saw or heard from Holly, even though she lived right next door to me. The entire weekend she never responded to my text, which left me feeling alternately worried (Does she still want to be friends?) and relieved (If something were wrong, she surely would have told me).

I did send another subdued text: If you need anything from me or want to chat, just let me know.

But again, nothing.

It seemed almost absurd that we still had one week of production left. On Monday, I had to spend most of the day in the office and only glimpsed her leaving the set when I arrived. Tuesday was like that too. But Wednesday was a big day, because it involved the re-shoot of a climactic scene which we'd attempted to film in Week 2. The final struggle between Katie Phillips and the main villain Max takes place on the roof of her isolated summer house, after everyone else has been eliminated from the fight. It's nighttime, Katie has just survived a cat-and-mouse hunt throughout her house, and now—in the midst of a thunderstorm—she gains the upper hand in a desperate fight. Max, in the tradition of all great movie villains, plunges to his death.

It was a complicated shoot, involving rain, wind, occasional flashes of lightning (all artificial, of course), and a choreographed fight between Holly and Barry, while on a set that had been built at a height and a slant (to re-create the sloping rooftop). The camera was on a rig that moved across and over the roof, to shoot the fight at different angles, an added thrill for the audience.

We'd scheduled that scene in the second week, but the machine that was meant to replicate lightning wasn't working properly: it didn't produce the lightning effect on cue, at the exact moment Xander wanted it. (Seth had then argued with the lighting company to have the lightning machine replaced and to give us a discount.) Hugo, Sylvia, and I tried to convince Xander to manage with the footage we already had, but he was adamant.

"No, the lightning has to illuminate Katie's face at the *exact moment* she's saying that line. We didn't get it right last time, and we can't fudge it in post-production," he insisted. "We have to re-shoot."

Directors are demanding perfectionists and must always be obeyed, so the only time we could reschedule this re-shoot was in the final week of production, when everyone was thoroughly exhausted. Most of all, Holly.

On the day of the re-shoot, I and many others stood around the edge of the set, our eyes gazing up at the lightning unit as if it were some kind of Trojan Horse, imbued with the power to either grant us victory or defeat on this day.

I saw Holly enter the studio, with Joe, the 2nd AD, attended by Clive and Marisa. Her character Katie wore the same costume for the entire second half of the film: jeans, a form-fitting zip-up hoodie, and underneath, a flattering gray tank top. But by this point in the story, the hoodie had been cast aside, and her upper torso was clad only in the gray tank top, which was appropriately ripped. Clive had also added, through makeup, the scars, bruises, and dirt that Katie gradually acquired on her arms and face, through her struggles. There was a particularly becoming graze on her clavicle, which graced her porcelain skin, just above her breasts. That would have been dictated by Xander.

In reality, these scars were a nightmare for Clive, who had to photograph and painstakingly re-create them every day, in the exact same positions on Holly's body. Similarly, there were at least ten versions of the gray tank top, in various stages of distress and ripping, according to when in the story the scenes were taking place.

For all the artificial grime and scars, Holly still glowed with her effortless magnetism. Even when she preferred to go unnoticed.

I wondered about my unanswered texts.

On the far side of the set, Hugo acknowledged Holly's arrival with a grin. The grin seemed forced, but he waved at her. She turned away. I could sense a distinct stiffening of her shoulders, a definite placing of her slight, tank-top-clad back in Hugo's direct line of sight. Hugo returned to his conversation, raising his voice just a decibel too loud.

Pushing away the doubts in my mind, I stepped a few feet towards Holly, who was nodding to Marisa about something.

I placed a gentle hand on her upper arm—Holly flinched. She spun around, a wild, startled look in her eyes.

"Hey, it's just me," I whispered, smiling at her. "How you doing this last week of shoot?"

"Oh," Holly spoke with a note of surprise. And distance. For a second, I felt like we were in high school, she the popular cheerleader, and me the awkward, forgotten geek, desperate to be recognized. "Hiya," she said. And then added: "Sorry, I just needed a quiet weekend to myself. Gearing up for the final week, you know."

"You okay?" I asked, still anxious.

She didn't answer. Instead, she grimaced, a genuine expression. "I'm tired. I just want to get this over with."

"I hear you." I nodded. "This scene has been a nightmare—"

"Not just this scene. The whole fucking production," she muttered, with uncharacteristic spite.

I didn't have time to react, because Joe was now ushering her onto set, and Clive followed along, hastily trying to touch up the waterproof powder on her face.

I stepped back, wondering if I'd imagined what I'd heard. The bitterness and the anger in her voice, so different from her usual sunny nature.

She climbed up onto the sloped rooftop (which in reality was only five feet above the padded floor).

Holly was always the consummate professional, even then. It was her preternatural ability to mask everything, pretend the world was already perfect, which allowed her to rise above it. But perched on that rooftop, I saw her glance around the room, her eyes searching the edges of the set, the surrounding darkness, for one particular figure. When her eyes found him, a momentary fear clouded her face—and promptly vanished.

I think I was the only one who noticed it. Everyone else was still fixated on that damn lightning unit.

"Are you ready, Holly?" Scott, the 1st AD, was shouting this to where she stood on the artificial rooftop.

It was two hours later, and we were finally ready for Holly's close-up. The one where the lightning had to strike at the exact same moment she delivered her climactic, triumphant lines to the villain.

Barry, the actor playing her enemy, had gone back to his greenroom and was taking a break. The next few set-ups were just Holly, the camera in her face, her hair and body drenched by the fake rain we'd been splattering at her.

In this shot, Katie was meant to be resolute, all-powerful, a young mother fighting to protect what's left of her life. She had a few lines of dialogue, as the camera inched slowly towards her face—until the lightning struck on her final line, illuminating her victorious close-up.

So Holly assumed the appropriate stance, as Carlos, the boom operator, lifted the mic just above her.

The camera began its slow push in.

"Have you ever felt what it means to be truly alone?" she said, looking down.

Then, the air from the wind machine gusted, and a wet lock of hair slapped Holly across the eyes.

"Cut," Xander growled.

"Cut!" Scott shouted. "Clive, is there any way we can prevent that from happening again with her hair?"

"Not really." Clive shrugged dryly. "Not unless you want me to pin it back, but I don't think that's the natural look you're going for. With a wind and a rain machine, it's always a risk."

"Okay, just thought we'd ask," Scott said grumbling. "Everyone, back to one."

The camera eased back to its position at the start of the shot.

Holly began again. "Have you ever felt what it means to be truly alone?"

The camera kept pushing in, while wind and rain swirled around her face. She glowed with a knowing sense of victory, despite the storm and the dark and the scrapes on her skin.

She began her next line. "I mean, really alone. As if all the world has left you, and you're the only person alive who exists in *your* version of the world . . . And soon you, too, will be forgotten."

I had silently read these lines countless times in my incessant editing of the script. But Holly gave a different reading of these words every time, illuminating some new meaning with a simple shift in her timbre.

Now, her voice shrank small, nestled in a quiet strength.

"Well, guess what, Max," she said. "You *will* be forgotten."

The camera pushed in closer, the lightning flickering in the background.

Her voice grew even smaller.

"Because in my world, it's not just me."

On cue, the lightning struck: Holly's face was magnified in a flash of brilliant white light.

"It's me and my daughter."

The last line came out practically a whisper. There was something chilling about the quietness of her voice, but I heard Xander grunt with dissatisfaction. After a moment or two, he mumbled "cut."

"Cut!" Scott shouted.

Everyone on set eased down, the tension gone. Behind me, Hugo chuckled.

Xander was now speaking sharply into Scott's ear, with a visible displeasure. I sat next to him in Sylvia's chair, right in front of the monitor, which still showed a close-up of Holly, even though we weren't recording.

If I looked at Holly directly, she was a small, frail figure sitting alone in the dark, her thin legs dangling off the roof-ledge.

But if I looked at the monitor, her face filled the entire screen, timeless and immaculate, even when she was trying not to be seen.

I peered closer. Holly's face was wet from the fake rain, and someone had handed her a cloth to dry herself between takes. But I could glimpse some other moisture glistening on her skin, trickling down her face. Tears.

Suddenly, her eyes darted off-screen and she wiped her cheek, flashing a smile at someone. Clive blocked the camera as he crept into shot to fix her makeup.

I stood back and considered. Holly crying on set.

It was a taxing scene for sure, but I had never once seen her cry before, unless it was for acting. Only at this point in the script, Holly's character was meant to be triumphant, almost gloating. Not terrified or sad.

Concern for Holly suddenly welled in me, yet I was cut off from reaching her. She seemed so inaccessible on that roof, even though I could see her close-up on the TV monitor.

"Okay, Holly," Scott was saying. "That was a good first take, just to start with. Can we try that again, but can you speak up on the final line? Your voice almost faded away at the end, and this is supposed to be a moment of victory for Katie."

Holly nodded. "Okay," she said flatly.

I saw her face compose itself, the professional mask reassembled, while she waited for the shot to begin.

"Going again!" Scott shouted.

"Aaaaand . . . action."

Holly did fifteen more takes, each time investing a slightly different intonation in her reading. But the emotion was always there, just below the surface of her voice, threatening to spill over.

After every take, Xander grunted, annoyed.

"That one was great," I said after the fifteenth attempt.

Xander glared at me, as if I shouldn't even be offering an opinion in his presence.

On Take 16, Holly changed the rhythm of her delivery, consciously or not. "Because in my world, it's not just me."

The camera pushed in, and I saw her draw a breath, and pause, as if caught by something—some measure of unexpressed pain. And then finally: "It's me and my daughter."

But Holly's pause had thrown everything off. So the lightning had struck first and didn't coincide with her words, though it was perhaps her most effective line reading so far.

Xander quietly fumed and threw off his headphones. Scott looked at him with muted alarm.

"What the *fuck*, Holly," Xander muttered under his breath.

Janice, the script supervisor, looked up from her binder.

"She seems tired," Janice suggested. "Maybe a break?"

"We've got sixteen takes of this already," Scott reminded him.

"No no." Xander shook his head adamantly. "She can do this; she's being difficult. Let's just get this shot in the can."

Scott was about to raise his voice, but Xander stood up and stormed his way over to the fake rooftop.

Everyone watched. Xander hardly ever left his chair on set.

He stood below Holly now, jabbing a finger at her. We could all hear his voice. It wasn't overly loud, but it was full of concentrated anger.

"Goddammit Holly, why'd you pause? You missed the cue on the lightning."

Holly snapped back, uncharacteristically.

"Xander, I'm trying to *act*. If I want to pause before that line, I should get to pause. I can't be dictated all the time by your fucking lightning unit."

Xander seethed, smacking his fist inside his palm. "It's timed to the specific second! That's the whole fucking point of this scene. The lightning!"

We gathered around the monitor now, watching Holly's face during the argument. She shook her head, incredulous.

"The lightning is the whole point of the scene? The *lightning*, Xander? How about *my acting*?"

Xander's eyes flashed with fury. "Stop being such a fucking diva, Holly. Not everything's about your acting. Get it right for once."

All around set, the rest of us cringed.

Holly spoke slowly now, her words invested with a palpable venom.

"I have gotten it right every single time. I haven't flubbed a line *once* today. I am putting *everything I have* into this scene, and you keep rejecting it."

"I don't care. It's still not good enough," Xander snapped back.

"What do you mean, not good enough?" she seethed.

"Honestly, what is your fucking problem, Holly?" Xander shouted. "Can't you follow directions? Just get it right!"

He marched back to his director's chair. None of us dared to look at him or at Holly.

Janice and I raised eyebrows at each other and glanced at the monitor. I could see Holly crying openly now, the silent sobs racking her thin frame, while Clive alternately tried to comfort her and fretted about retouching her makeup.

Everyone pretended not to notice that Holly was crying, even though we all knew she was. The boom operator turned his back, the camera operator switched off the camera and glanced at his phone. Clive was the only one who stood by, handing her tissues one by one.

I walked over to her, about to ask if she was okay, but she waved me away.

Back at the video monitor, Xander scowled at me and shook his head in disbelief. "What a crybaby."

Behind us, Hugo stifled a laugh and quietly walked out of the studio. His footsteps echoed to the sound of Holly's sobs.

I shivered.

Ultimately, Holly was right. In the final cut of the film, the version that got released into theaters and grossed $100+ million domestic, it's not the lightning that audiences remember from that climactic scene. It's Holly's acting. Her face, so beautiful and crumpled in the rain, somehow finds a new composure as that final line is delivered, like a knife finding its true mark.

Critics raved about Holly's performance, which earned her multiple awards, including a Golden Globe win and an Oscar nomination. Many viewers shed tears, watching her brittle, thoroughly realistic combination of fear and bravery. It was as if some genuine pain shone through Holly's acting in that scene.

But the lightning did make a difference. It enhanced Holly's performance, much like the rooftop scene in *Blade Runner*, when Rutger Hauer's terrifying replicant dies a sudden, peaceful death, right there in a rainstorm. Acting and atmosphere create the complete package. Without the lightning, Holly's performance would not have seemed as indelible.

The take that was ultimately used in the final cut was only filmed after Hugo left the set. As if his absence somehow allowed Holly to achieve her true potential, knowing Hugo was no longer there in person, watching her.

Interview Transcript (continued):
Sylvia Zimmerman, 4:56 p.m.

SZ: It would be silly if Sarah felt that she was somehow responsible for Hugo's behavior. I didn't expect her to control an exec producer.

TG: But you did expect her to be responsible for the film production, especially since you weren't there a lot?

SZ: Yes, for sure, but that's a professional responsibility, overseeing the shoot. Everything else, how people were behaving at parties at night—well, none of that matters, so long as the film is thriving on set.

TG: That's where a producer's responsibility ends, you would say?

SZ: Yes, otherwise it's an endless job. You have to draw the line somewhere, for your own sanity.

TG: What would you say about Xander? Did he always act professionally on set?

SZ: Xander knows how to make a good film. That's all that matters, if you're a director.

TG: Nothing else matters?

SZ: As far as the industry is concerned, no. (pause) Did I think he was guilty of abusing or assaulting actresses? No. He had models fawning all over him, he didn't need to use any force.

TG: Do you think he turned a blind eye to what may have happened with Hugo?

SZ: Thom, what would they call this in court—hearsay? Speculation? I can't say what I thought Xander knew. Or what I thought Sarah knew. All I can say is what I knew or suspected—and that was very little, at the time.

TG: And yet, you say you "wouldn't have put it past Hugo." "He was that kind of guy." "Always expects to have things made easy for him, including women." How could you say that, and also not suspect him?

SZ: Because *everything* came easy for him. He didn't have to try, girls would just fall all over him. He didn't even have to work at being a producer and—poof! Like that—he just became one. Us women, we have to graft for years. If you're a guy like Hugo, with money like that—you waltz right in with your checkbook, and things always go your way.

TG: So is that why he may have gotten away with certain behaviors for years?

SZ: "Certain behaviors." Thom, you're so diplomatic. (laughs) Just tell it like it is. What do you mean, like fucking barely legal young girls? Snorting cocaine regularly off a teenager's breasts? You don't need to "get away with" that behavior, if everyone's doing it. That stuff has been going on in Hollywood ever since the place was founded. As a woman, you learn to just live with it, turn a blind eye to it, and stay on your own path. (pause) Call out Hugo, and there's fifty other guys like him. It's disgusting, but it's not really that out of the ordinary, what he's been doing.

TG: Why do you tolerate it? If it's that disgusting?

SZ: Because what option is there? There's no one you can report that behavior to, if he's the one writing the checks. (pause) Who's gonna call it out? Who's gonna put their neck on the line for something so commonplace it's almost not worth pointing out? I'm not. (pause) I mean, maybe I should have, if I'd known anything. But there's a lot of things *we should have done* when we were younger. Few of us actually do them.

42

I N RETROSPECT, I have no idea how Holly did it. If what we all suspect happened on the previous Friday night did in fact happen, then . . . I can't begin to imagine her state of mind the day we reshot the rooftop scene.

"What do you mean by that?" Thom asks.

I try to reason this aloud. "I hear that kind of violence, it leaves you in a certain state. Really traumatized. Holly somehow managed to fool us all into thinking she was okay."

"Why do you think she would have done that?"

"Because that's what being professional means. You don't postpone the shoot. You show up, you do your job. And that's what Holly did. She's an actor, after all. She acted her way out of it."

That's what we all did, I want to add. Acting, in our own way.

Thom's next question is the least delicate. "What makes you so sure she was raped?"

"And not just groped?" I shiver, remembering Hugo's fingers on my skin. "Because Holly seemed like a totally different person afterward. Maybe not on the surface. But I'd gotten to know her fairly well over those months—at least I thought I had. And she completely closed herself off after that night. Wouldn't allow anyone to reach her."

Perhaps this was the most painful truth of all. That she wouldn't let me in. "If he'd tried to grope her or kiss her, she would have been angry and disgusted. She would have told me, and we might have laughed about it. But rape . . . was just too terrible to name."

I reimagine that eager Holly, ten years ago.

"To be the star of a film and accuse the executive producer of something like rape . . . that could jeopardize an entire production. And this project, this role was important for Holly's career. She knew that." Thom nods, taking this in. "So I guess it was about survival in the end. She was playing the long game. And she turned out to be right. Look where she is now."

I sit for a moment and marvel at Holly's nerves of steel. To make a decision like that, just after you've gone through something so horrific . . . Here again, my *attempt* to imagine is the work of the ignorant in these scenarios. The fortunate, the un-raped.

Because that is ultimately what all of this is about, right?

The same lurid fascination. Those of us who stand on the out-side, horrified by what can happen between two human beings. This unmentionable act.

"I mean, you really just want me to speculate grossly about what others went through, right?" I ask with a note of distaste.

I am suddenly tired of it all. All these hours sitting in close proximity with Thom Gallagher, being duped by his blue eyes and his chivalrous attitude and his celebrity pedigree. I don't see what has been gained by spilling my guts to him. Only pain and shame and self-hatred. And envy.

But, let's be honest, the envy was always there. Even from the first moment I stepped into the Firefly offices and met Sylvia. Or even before that, when I turned on the television and watched the Oscars or *90210* or *Dawson's Creek* or any goddamn show fea-turing glossy-haired white teenagers, living impossibly privileged lives in manicured suburbs.

Envy is built into the immigrant experience. It is what drives the American dream, after all.

Thom Gallagher has been watching me carefully and seems disturbed by my last comment. "It's not *speculation*. Certainly not from the victims themselves. It's evidence. It's *fact*. You yourself were a victim, Sarah."

pmid
</br>

I wasn't expecting that last remark. I stare at Thom in a state of suspended shock.

"What do you mean?" I ask.

There's a look of incomprehension on his face, as if we're suddenly speaking different languages, unintelligible to each other.

"Sarah, what happened to you at Hugo's party . . . at his house in Beverly Hills," he says slowly. "You were a victim. What he did to you didn't result in rape, but it was still an assault."

"Yeah but—I could have prevented that," I say. "If I hadn't gone up to his room. That was me being stupid."

"It was still an assault," Thom continues. "And no, you weren't being stupid. You were doing what your boss asked. He's the one who decided to assault you. He's the one who committed the crime."

It is the first time I hear it spelled out like that, plain as the letters of the alphabet.

"You did nothing wrong," Thom says.

"But I did, Thom," I insist.

I look at him, and the moment has arrived, unavoidable since I first typed my reply to his email. The silence bears down on me, as I clear my throat, my heart hammering an agitated rhythm. Freedom, if I can just tell him the whole truth.

"You see . . . I haven't been entirely forthcoming with you."

The words drop slowly, like stones into a still pond. But he shows no admonishment, only patience.

"Can we backtrack a few weeks? Halfway through the shoot."

Let's see the original take of that scene. The unedited version.

Then one day during Week 3, I looked up from my desk in the production office to see Courtney approaching me with some trepidation. Her usual relaxed California demeanor seemed askew.

"Courtney," I said. "How's it going?" It was unusual to see her here, in the production office, and not at Hugo's side.

"Hey, are you busy? Can I . . . talk to you about something?" she ventured.

I was actually in the midst of reviewing the publicity materials that Andrea's office needed within the hour, but I didn't want to be rude. And something about Courtney seemed off, subdued.

"Uh, sure. You wanna talk here?"

Wordless, Courtney shook her head and gestured for us to go into the hallway. I noticed her lip trembling.

A dark unease stirred inside me as I followed her out of the room, down to the very end of the corridor. Here, no production staff were rushing around.

We stood and faced each other in the relative quiet, a bright square of sunlight slashing the air between us.

"Are you okay?" I asked.

She shook her head again. I noticed her eyes were brimming with tears and she crushed her hand to her mouth. Still, she didn't speak.

"Courtney, what is it?"

Now she started to sob quietly, her willowy body shaking. I placed a tentative arm on her shoulder, realizing it would be awkward if I didn't try to offer some comfort.

"What happened?" I asked again, though I was afraid to actually hear.

Finally, Courtney managed some words.

"It's . . . I don't know . . . Hugo," she stuttered, her voice shaking. "I don't know—I'm not sure what happened."

"What do you mean?" I was bewildered. She seemed so confident and pleased to be around him, all the times I'd glimpsed them together.

"Last night," she sobbed, then broke off. "Oh god, I don't know. I don't understand how it all happened. . . ."

My worry started to curdle into dread. I glanced around, thankful no one was nearby, and pushed open the door to a small, anodyne conference room. A square table and bland padded seats offered some quiet respite here.

"Take your time," I told her once we were seated. "But please, if it's important . . . tell me."

"Well, that's the thing. I don't know if it's important, or if I'm just . . ." She trailed off, unsure of herself. "Last night, he—he asked if I wanted to have a few drinks after work. I was happy to, of course. We'd done this before. *You've* seen us drinking before."

I nodded. Everyone had.

"But then, well . . . I don't know . . . He started . . . He asked if I wanted to come up to his room. Which I'd done before too . . ." She stopped.

"Did he . . . offer you coke?" I asked, trying to fill in her words.

"Well, obviously, there was that." Her dismissive tone told me drugs were commonplace. "It's more . . . well . . . he started kissing me, and I didn't want to be rude because he's my boss and, sure he's attractive, but . . . still, I didn't really want—"

The silence took over again, and I hesitated, struggling to piece together what she was trying to say. I imagined what *could* have happened. It was like staring into a shapeless mist, trying to envision the outline of some behemoth rearing up, just out of sight.

"Did he . . ." I started. "Did you . . . ?"

Courtney suddenly nodded and burst into a fresh round of tears. "Yeah . . . I did," she gasped. "I don't know how it happened so quickly, and then it was over, and then . . . it was like he was acting like it was no big deal. He just wanted me out of the room."

I knit my brows, but still no clear, definitive shape to their evening emerged for me. In leaving that gap open, Courtney allowed me to fill it with the most acceptable version of the story. It could have been anything, just a casual one-night stand. But here was Courtney in front of me, clearly upset, and that was the immediate problem.

A good producer contains the problem, I reminded myself.

"How has he acted towards you since?" I asked.

She shrugged. "Like nothing ever happened. So I don't know if I'm imagining what it really was, or . . . But then, why am I crying?"

She stared at me, the tears streaming down her sculpted face. Courtney's words were still so vague, but if the worst of what she implied was true—and I couldn't imagine it, I couldn't fathom Hugo overstepping the bounds like that—and if word got out . . . This could affect the rest of the production.

I shook my head sympathetically. "I can see how you're upset. There's a lot going on with this film shoot, everyone's stressed, and sometimes Hugo relies a little too heavily on partying to blow off steam." I felt sick at my lame excuse.

She cracked a wry smile. "You can say that again."

I wrapped Courtney in an embrace and stroked her back, a gesture that seemed alien to me, something Chinese people would never do to a virtual stranger. I let her sob into me, and in the meantime, my mind raced, trying to sort through the possibilities, wondering how to handle the situation. Coming on to the shoot a week late, Courtney didn't know much of the crew or production staff. She was isolated, and worked entirely with Hugo. I might be the only person she would tell.

"I feel so stupid for letting this happen. They always warn you about this," Courtney sobbed. She looked at me, her face crumpled in self-loathing. "What do I do?"

I hesitated, knowing what I said next could throw a muffling layer of soil over the whole situation.

"Listen," I said, and looked her in the eye. "You do nothing. Don't beat yourself up about it. We all have too much to drink sometimes, and well . . . I've certainly done drunk things I regret. I'm sure most of us have."

She put her face in her hands.

"You're a smart girl with an exciting future ahead of you," I continued, taking a page out of Hugo's own playbook. "Don't let this one incident ruin the film for you."

Courtney sniffled. "It's just—how can I face him again?"

"Act like he's acting. Pretend it never happened. And it's perfectly within your rights not to have to drink with Hugo ever again, if you don't feel comfortable."

"It's so humiliating," she mumbled, eyes downcast. "You won't tell anyone, will you?"

"No, of course not." I felt sorry for her then, for her youth and naivete, her helplessness. "I wouldn't dream of it. I don't think it would help anyone involved."

I believed I was speaking the truth there. The deeper we buried this, whatever had happened, the better. I patted Courtney on the back, and made my decision.

I finish, the regret subsuming me like a vast, silent tide, and look out the window, where the November sunset is bleeding into evening.

"So . . . what are you saying?" Thom asks me, digesting all of this. "At the time, you actually *knew* something had happened to Courtney Jennings?"

"I . . . suspected," I answered. "But I didn't know for sure. And without that certainty—if it was a one-night stand or something worse—I did nothing about it. I looked the other way. I guess I had the whole production to manage, and felt overwhelmed."

"And at the time, you weren't sure because . . ."

"Because she'd never stated it outright. What Hugo had done to her. I guess she left the door open for interpretation . . . and I took the easy way out."

I closed my eyes, and saw again Courtney and Holly, their two slim figures, retreating into a gilded elevator.

Thom nods. "And now . . . with hindsight, what do *you* think happened between Hugo and Courtney?"

A long moment stretches between us, wordless.

"I think he raped her," I finally say, my voice low. "The way he tried to . . . assault me. The way he probably did to Holly."

Thom nods.

"I think he did that," I repeat. I allow the guilt to surge inside me and block out all else. "And everything that came after—what happened to me, and Holly, and any girls since then—it was all my fault. Because I said nothing."

Interview Transcript (continued):
Sylvia Zimmerman, 5:03 p.m.

TG: Do you think Hugo North was capable of something like rape or sexual assault?

SZ: Hugo North was capable of a lot of things. You don't attain his level of power and wealth without crushing a few people along the way.

TG: Didn't he inherit his wealth?

SZ: Sure, he inherited his wealth. Along with a sociopathic dose of entitlement. Which meant that he didn't really give a fuck about anyone else, as long as he got what he wanted.

TG: What do you think drives a person like Hugo to act the way he does?

SZ: Power? Ego? I'd be lying if I said those things didn't drive me, too, in my own way. We all like being listened to and respected. But there's a fine line between being in charge and abusing that power in a way that damages other people. Some of us take care not to cross that line—and clearly, others don't.

TG: In retrospect, ten years on, how do you make sense of Hugo North?

SZ: Plain and simple: he's an asshole. An entitled asshole who grew up listening to everyone saying yes to him. Who learned that he could just take whatever he wanted, without any consequences. (pause) But if that's the kind of person he wants to be, go right ahead. People like that may be rich and famous, but who actually likes them? Take away his wealth, and Hugo's nothing. His own children don't even want to speak to him.

TG: So there *is* a sense of justice, in the end?

SZ: Well, barely. It's about time some real justice was administered. So yes, I'm very glad that all these accusations are coming to light now. These guys . . . they've always been able to escape the consequences. (pause) But you know what? I'm sick of talking about Hugo. It's always about the men. Never about the women who raised them or worked in the background or found themselves ignored or passed over somehow. Or even the women who were in charge.

TG: When you were in charge, do *you* think you may have damaged other people, unknowingly?

SZ: Clever, Thom, clever. (sighs) It's possible. It was never my intention. But I admit it's possible. (pause) When you're in the thick of it—trying to get a film made, grappling for power in your own company—you're not always aware of the impact of your actions. So yeah, maybe, I hurt some people along the way. But I tried my best not to. And that's more than Hugo North can say.

43

FOR THE WRAP party, we'd rented out a 1950s-themed bar in Venice Beach, everyone making their way there by cab or personal driver or—the brave few—by their own driving. Sylvia flew back (of course) for the wrap party, but there was so little I felt I could tell her. She, who had managed to avoid the nitty-gritty of the production, who hadn't witnessed Holly and Xander's on-set spat. She, who remained oblivious to all of this, while for me, everything had now become a labored PR job, requiring me to exude false enthusiasm to the cast and crew about how wonderfully the shoot had gone, how amazing this film was going to be.

Holly only made a brief, perfunctory showing at the wrap party.

I'd texted her in advance, asking when she was planning to go. Hours passed before I finally got a single, factual text from her: I'm pretty busy packing. Moved my flight up to tomorrow. So just going for an hour on my own. See you there.

The message was clear. We weren't going together.

I thought of how we'd explored the dive bars and restaurants of LA the past few months, and even on the night of Hugo's house party, how we'd driven there together, gaping wide-eyed at the mansions of Beverly Hills.

Now, our energy at the wrap party was stilted, an unacknowledged wall between us.

Whereas everyone else seemed to have grown closer over the past seven weeks, Holly and I were just polite colleagues now.

Maybe our friendship was no more. Maybe it had served its purpose.

"So, see you in New York sometime," Holly said, after she'd finished saying her good-byes to everyone else. It seemed she was just trying to be polite.

We looked at each other. It was still early in the evening, and in the background, someone selected a completely inappropriate track on the jukebox—Vanilla Ice or something like that. Half the party groaned, while the other half threw up a nostalgic cheer. Across the room, I saw Sylvia eyeing us, and the discomfort rose in me.

"Yeah, I'll be back there in a few weeks," I said cheerily. "Just got to tie up some loose ends here. Most of our post-production is happening back in New York anyway."

Holly smiled, the close-lipped one. "Well, good luck with it all."

"Good luck to you. With everything," I said. "I mean, I'm sure there'll be lots more exciting roles coming up for you after this."

I cringed at my hollow words. It was like I was taking lessons from Hugo in condescension.

Holly didn't respond, and I tried to save myself by talking more. "Oh hey, Xander's first film is coming out in the next few weeks. So you should come to the New York premiere!"

She nodded diplomatically. "Well, be sure to send the invite to my agent Paul, and he'll get it to me."

Her agent. She pulled the agent card on me. I instinctively knew it was over then, but in a final, desperate bid for friendship, I went for the sincere expression. The truth.

I leaned in and peered into Holly's eyes.

"Hey, I know the shoot's been manic and awful at times. But personally, it's been . . . incredible to work with you." I paused, unsure. "I just wanted to apologize for—"

But she held out her hand, put it on my arm, as if to ward off the rest of my sentence.

"You don't have to apologize for anything, Sarah."

She squeezed my arm lightly before releasing it. "You were great," she added. "I don't know how you put up with it all. With them. But I'm glad you were out here. You . . . made things a lot easier for me."

And then, just like that, Holly was gone, her now trademark red hair bouncing as she walked out of the bar. I was the last person she spoke to at that wrap party, before she flew back to New York.

I felt relief—maybe what I'd feared, hadn't happened. Maybe there was nothing to apologize for after all.

But somehow, I didn't believe that.

You made things a lot easier for me.

I didn't, I wanted to tell her. *I fucked it all up.*

44

I DON'T KNOW WHAT else to tell Thom. I mean, that's the end of the shoot, but everything that came after . . . it wasn't a neat and tidy ending, not by a long shot.

"Tell me about finishing up the film, post-production, all that."

Usually, nobody ever asks about post-production because it's deathly boring to your average person. A bunch of experts toil away in their studios and edit suites, and then show various versions of the film—ungraded, rough cut, no VFX, etc.—to other people, before going back and making more changes. The stars are nowhere to be found, no parties, no on-set publicity in post-production.

Back in New York, I was still functioning like a zombie, simultaneously juggling post-production on *Furious Her*, as well as the imminent theatrical release of *A Hard Cold Blue*. I had left New York at the height of summer, but when I returned, we were already into the second half of October, when the drop in temperatures became crisp and the turn towards winter inevitable.

I finally got to meet my niece Alice, when she was five weeks old. There was just something so . . . pure and untainted about holding a tiny newborn girl. As if gazing at her sleeping face, I could forget temporarily about Hugo, the films, everything that happened in LA—and only dwell on all the good things due to Alice in the life ahead of her.

But it was bittersweet for me. My sister's husband had recently accepted a job offer down in DC, so they would move in the new year. I wasn't going to have many times to hold Alice before they left the city. And it seemed inevitable that the gap between my life and Karen's would continue to widen.

Otherwise, I slotted back easily into my New York existence, found a new place to stay with a college friend, and relished my commutes on the subway, when I could read a book or people-watch, instead of nervously checking my side-view mirror for a chance to switch lanes. After months of having to wrangle with Hugo's erratic behavior and the constant logistical onslaught of production, it was a relief to be back in our old office, with Ziggy's wry comments and the familiar view of the Meatpacking District.

But my interaction with Sylvia was strained, uncomfortable. Out in LA, I had made important day-to-day decisions as acting producer, yet Sylvia seemed unwilling to acknowledge that. She still snapped when I replied to a group email to our sales agent; she was the top producer, after all, I should have let her respond first.

Meanwhile, Sammy Lefkowitz was grooming *A Hard Cold Blue* as an independent longshot for awards that year. When the New York premiere approached, I sent Holly an invite, via her agent, but she politely declined. I never really saw her again, even though we said we'd get in touch. Her number stayed in my phone, and for months after that wrap party, I thought occasionally about sending her a text. *How are things? The edit is coming along nicely. Do you have any other roles coming up?* The same noncommittal things you might say to anyone else in the industry, to keep tabs on them, cataloging them as a useful contact for the future—even though the potential for friendship was always there, if either of you weren't so busy.

A Hard Cold Blue opened to mainly positive reviews, as it had in Cannes. Two thumbs up from the usual culprits, spots in most of the TV review shows. Your fine publication, the *New York Times*, even gave us four stars, calling the film "taut, sharp, and chilling, with an underlying humanity that belies its genre stylings." In the office, we were ecstatic.

And then, we got nominated for a Golden Globe.

Twice, in fact: for Best Editing and Best Original Screenplay. Xander himself was the nominee for the screenplay award.

The day the nominations were announced, our office phone rang nonstop. Congratulatory emails flooded our inboxes, and Ziggy and I had to send a peppy, grateful reply to each of them. Flower bouquets, magnums of champagne, and other unnecessary gifts kept arriving at our office from industry contacts we hadn't seen in months. After half a year investing so much energy in Holly and *Furious Her*, I found it jarring to switch focus to our previous film. But producers juggle projects, we follow the spotlight. And the spotlight now was most firmly on *A Hard Cold Blue*.

With this film, we were going to the Golden Globes ceremony the following month. We would actually sit there in that fabled awards banquet, at those round tables, dining and quaffing wine with the Hollywood elite. There would be a red carpet with cameras and TV presenters along the way, A-list stars ascending to present onstage, and I would be in the same room as them. Maybe even sitting one table away.

Later that week, Sammy Lefkowitz took us out to dinner, when Hugo had flown in from London. It was a lavish, self-congratulatory affair at some austere place in Midtown. Even Sylvia threw back shots of tequila, as if her underlying competitive streak wanted to prove that she, too, could be as fun and hard-partying as Hugo.

I kept a wide berth from him, and at some point late in the evening, I made my way closer to the front door, to get some air, or at least to get away from the press of the others. The initial buzz of being nominated for a Golden Globe was starting to wear off. The nomination just meant more work for me, more conversations with our publicist, more screenings and travel itineraries to organize, alongside the ongoing post-production of *Furious Her*.

Part of me just wanted a break from it all. My head spun, and I closed my eyes.

Then I felt a hand at my waist.

My eyes snapped open. Hugo was right in front of me, an unreadable smirk on his face. He said his usual things, meaningless pleasantries and candied compliments about how much we all deserved to enjoy the nominations. I stood mute, agitated.

"And have you thought of what you'll wear to the ceremony?"

It was such an unexpected question, a look of surprise must have crossed my face.

"Does Cinderella think she'll not make it to the ball?"

Hugo didn't wait for me to respond. He pressed closer, his expression intent.

"You know there's only so many seats at a table for the Globes, right? I hardly think Sammy Lefkowitz gives a fuck about inviting the twentysomething associate producer."

A sudden fear coursed through me. I'd assumed that, since I'd worked on the film from the very beginning, I'd surely be invited to the ceremony.

I finally found my voice, laced with indignation.

"Hugo, the first time you even *saw* the film was in May. Some of us have been working on it for years."

He shrugged. "That's not really how these things work, is it?" There was a look of mock pity on his face. And perhaps he did really pity me for my naivete in that moment.

Then, in another instance, he relaxed into a grin, all the menace gone.

"Don't worry, darling." He reached out and traced a finger along my cheek. I flinched and drew back. "I'll do my best to see to it that you get invited to the Globes. I know for others, it's certainly not a priority."

As much as I hated to admit it, Hugo was right.

A week later, I sat through a painful lunch with Sylvia, just the two of us and a crisp white tablecloth, a waiter dutifully pouring us glasses of pinot at twenty-minute intervals. Sylvia thanked me for everything I'd done for the shoot in LA, and then apologetically explained that she wasn't 100 percent sure I'd be going to the Globes in January.

"I'm so sorry. I know this must be a huge disappointment for you." Sylvia shook her head.

She explained that Sammy, one of the most influential distributors in the industry, was paying for our film's table, so ultimately it was his decision whether to bring me or some more of the cast. Herself, Xander, Pete (our editor, who was nominated), and Hugo were of course going. "Look, I can see how it might seem to you. I know how hard you've worked on this. But Hugo's the main investor in our company now. It's really important for him to be at the Globes."

My voice felt strained, my throat taut, and I could feel the tears threatening to garble my words.

"Sylvia," I began. I stopped short of saying: *I deserve to be there. I was the one who fixed the script for Xander.*

Instead, I said: "I've put everything I have into this job."

I wanted to add: *I don't have anything else. The rest of you all have families and nice homes you own, and if this filmmaking career doesn't work out for you, then it's not the end of the day. Because you have other things. I don't.*

This is all I have. Me and my career in film.

But Sylvia didn't see that—and I don't think she ever has.

Interview Transcript (continued):
Sylvia Zimmerman, 5:10 p.m.

TG: But Sylvia, there *are* high-powered women in the industry. You yourself were able to achieve quite a lot being in charge.

SZ: Sure, we've accomplished things. But look at what it's cost us. So many of those top female agents, they don't have a family of their own. We pour our everything into our careers, and where does it get us? The men are always one step ahead.

TG: And you would say Hugo North was a prime example of that?

SZ: Of course. He just showed up out of nowhere, with no filmmaking experience of his own, and completely changed my company. We went from a lean and dedicated team, focused on making the best possible film on a modest budget, to this sort of bloated, decadent circus. It became the Hugo North Show, and we were relegated to the background. *I* was relegated to the background. And so was Sarah. (pause) I should have seen it coming. But at the end of the day, I couldn't compete with his checkbook. This stupid frat-boy culture took over, and once that happened, I couldn't fight it.

TG: How do you feel—about how everything ended?

SZ: Of course I'm bitter. How could I not be? Listen, I get it. Men have more money, they run the world because of it. I wouldn't be where I am without my husband's more-than-comfortable salary. I admit that. But that doesn't mean they should get to run *everything.* We had a good setup before Hugo came. Sarah Lai, she had a lot of promise. And we could have worked well together, made lots of films together, who knows. (pause) I keep thinking what a different industry we'd be in if it was just women working with women. No men involved. No one trying to compete for some guy's checkbook, or a chance at his checkbook by sucking him off. I mean, how little do we value ourselves? Starving and primping ourselves and stabbing each other in the back—for what?

(Pause)

We're mice being toyed with by cats. We keep thinking we'll get to be cats one day too. But the world doesn't work like that. The cats keep to themselves. We're just the entertainment. And later, the food.

45

I TRIED TO BANISH my disappointment over the Globes by immersing myself in the hectic familiarity of the restaurant. In fact, Christmas Day was one of our busiest days, as several Jewish community groups had made it their annual tradition to dine at Imperial Garden. After closing for the evening, we gathered in my parents' place, still feeling festive, despite our hair smelling of stir-fry.

My sister cradled baby Alice, who, at three months, was starting to laugh and smile more. My brother had come down from Boston for a few days. At least they were more impressed with the Golden Globe nomination than my parents (who were mainly besotted with my niece). I explained to my family I wouldn't necessarily be going to the awards ceremony.

"That's bullshit," Karen said. "You spent five years of your life on that film."

"Yeah but Sammy Lefkowitz doesn't care about that," I muttered as we both sat in our parents' living room, surrounded by framed photos of us when we were younger. "That's par for the course in the film industry."

"I guess it's like being a first-year associate in a law firm," she reasoned. "Only you're getting paid a lot less."

"*And* I've been doing this for five years!" I reminded her. We laughed at my lamentable situation. "Oh god, *why* did I ever start working for these people?"

"Because you love it," Karen said. "Honestly, I've never seen you happier than when you're talking about film. And you know more about movies than anyone I've ever met."

My family is not very demonstrative with praise, so coming from my sister, this was a compliment.

"I mean, you *do* enjoy it, don't you?" Karen looked at me a bit closer. "Working for these people?"

I didn't answer right away. It certainly wasn't an unequivocal yes. There were lots of times recently when I'd been overworked and miserable. But there were also the highlights: flying to LA, sitting through casting sessions, discussing script notes and knowing they were valued, seeing everything come together in a finished film. And of course, the chance to connect with other film lovers: the screenings, the parties—and what I presumed were the big moments, like the Golden Globes.

"I guess," I sighed. "I mean, these people are ridiculous. And sometimes, kind of awful."

The thought occurred to me then to tell my sister what had happened with Hugo, at his house in Beverly Hills. But I knew her accountant-like brain would only look at the facts, see if everything added up. Why did I go up to that bedroom in the first place? Why didn't I tell anyone else about it? If nothing happened in the end, was it even worth getting worked up about?

I didn't want to deal with her questions, and the lame, unsatisfying answers I would have to provide, so I just stayed silent.

"Well," Karen said. "I hope you get to go. But like your boss said, I'm sure there'll be other chances in the future."

I wasn't so sure. Nothing in this industry was ever a given.

But then, the next day, my BlackBerry beeped with a message.

A BBM from Hugo, who was currently in England.

Hey, I managed to get you into the Globes. Book your flight. Happy Christmas.

I sat up in shock. Was I thrilled to be going? Yes. But did I resent the fact it was Hugo's handiwork? Even more so.

Sylvia emailed me the same news five minutes later.

Suddenly, I was going to LA again. To the Golden Globes. And I had no idea what to wear.

46

THE GOLDEN GLOBES are Hollywood's glitzy, booze-soaked way of kicking off the new year's awards season—with a hedonistic bang.

Awards season is an industry in and of itself. Hollywood is at its most frenetic and self-congratulatory, when those well-worn cogs of sycophantic media coverage and behind-the-scenes hobnobbing creak into oily gear. In my five years of working in the film industry, it was unlike anything I'd seen before, as I stood there on the red carpet of the Golden Globes, having swapped the wintry chill of New York for this balmy golden California evening.

There on the red carpet, my rib cage was squashed inside the beaded bodice of a shimmering, emerald-green gown that I'd borrowed for the occasion. Borrowed makes it sounds like I knocked on the door of my next-door neighbor, who graciously lent me a $15,000 dress out of the goodness of her own heart. But in Hollywood, there's a complex sub-industry where designers lend out gowns, jewelry, shoes, and handbags to stars, just so their products can be seen on the red carpet.

Of course, the bigger labels would have no interest in lending their products to a no-name associate producer like me. But lesser-known designers would still see this as an opportunity, so long as they could secure a photo of their product worn by an appealing young woman on the Golden Globes red carpet. Always the smaller fish circling around, looking to swim their way into that murky pond.

In the end, it was Clive who managed to pull some significant strings for me. Once I'd heard the news from Hugo and Sylvia, I texted Clive in LA. After the initial freak-out—*You're going to the Globes?! OMG, incredible!*—he insisted I could stay with him when in town. He also very calmly assured me he'd take care of my look for the evening.

I didn't have hundreds of dollars to spend on a gown, certainly not one I'd wear only once in my life. And why buy a dress, when I could get one for free?

So Clive asked me what I wanted—*no ruffles, no bows, no pink*—and made some calls around to publicists representing designers. "Listen, she's a sample size and a stunning Asian woman. Most things will look good on her."

A week before the Globes, Clive sent me images and asked me to pick three dresses out of all of them, which I promptly did. One of these dresses was already in New York, so I wandered over to the Garment District to try on their sample.

And that's how I ended up wearing this viridian dream to the Golden Globes, green beads on an emerald-green bodice, held by a halter neck, a sleek skirt that flowed downwards, leading to the smallest of trains.

I did have to buy a pair of shoes for the evening, which I found on a trip to Century 21: $300 stiletto sandals, knocked down to $70. It was still more than I'd normally pay for shoes, but I figured this was a special occasion.

I hadn't thought much about jewelry until I landed in LA three days before the Globes—and panicked. Again, I called Clive. Again, he made a few phone calls.

"After I do your hair and makeup, make your way over to the Chateau Marmont. My friend Diego in room 37 has some pieces you can try on."

Ah, the fucking Marmont again.

It felt like some high-end scavenger hunt, and hours before the Golden Globes were to start, I entered a room where a thin, lacquered man sat, his heavily-gelled hair combed into a ferocious quiff, an earring dangling from his left ear. He reposed behind a small table, where an array of jewelry—necklaces, cuffs, earrings, rings—glinted from a dark-gray velvet display.

"Hi, I'm Sarah, Clive's friend. Are you . . . Diego?" I asked.

He smiled at me. "Any friend of Clive's can be my honey." He gestured to his wares. "Okay, chica, what do you want?"

"I can borrow any of these?" The jewelry gleamed, more luxurious than anything I'd ever worn.

Diego shrugged, unbothered. "Yep, that's what they're here for. They'll look better on the red carpet than squirreled away in my case. Anything you want, it's yours for tonight."

I wondered if there were some catch involved, but surely Clive would have mentioned it to me already. In awe, I fingered a few of the necklaces and tried them on in the mirror. In the end, I selected a graceful collar-necklace and a ring, both of them sleek, diamond-encrusted, impossible.

"Now let me just value them and get you to sign for it."

Unsure of what was going on, I watched what seemed like a fairly routine process for him. Diego whisked out a pad of paper, glanced again at the jewelry I'd borrowed, and scribbled a few lines on it.

"Okay, hon, can you sign here?"

He'd valued the necklace and ring I borrowed—$15,000 for the necklace, $7,000 for the ring.

"What does this mean?" I asked, internally reeling at the figures. That was a very significant chunk of my annual salary.

"Oh, it just means you're liable, in case they go missing."

"Ah. Sure," I said. Riddled with nausea, I picked up the ballpoint and signed on the dotted line: $22,000. No problem. My stomach felt like it was going to fall through.

"What film are you with again?" Diego asked casually.

"*A Hard Cold Blue*," I said, summoning up a shred of pride. His blank face stared back at me.

"Um, it's an indie," I explained. "Sammy Lefkowitz is distributor."

"Ah okay, good old Sammy," Diego snorted. "Well, at least he'll be good for the money. I hope. Otherwise, my Mexican ass is cooked."

I was instructed to leave the jewelry at the hotel concierge the next morning, and that was it.

"I just 'leave it'?" I asked in shock. "Do I have to sign it back in or anything?"

"No need. You *are* staying at the hotel, right?" Diego asked.

"Well, yeah," I fibbed. "A bunch of us are. Our producer is Hugo North, and he'll have a suite under his name here. Besides, you know Clive, and he knows how to get ahold of me."

Reassured with this, Diego waved me off to the Globes: "Remember to get totally shit-faced and tell Meryl I miss her and love her till the end of time."

Still agape, I headed down the hallway. Was it literally that easy to walk off with thousands of dollars' worth of jewelry in this town? Like everything else here, it was all for show, and it was all borrowed.

Genuine ownership was such a slippery concept in LA.

So gown, shoes, jewelry—I was now ready and equipped to go to the Globes.

The eight of us—Xander, Sylvia, Hugo, Pete, me, Gary (one of the stars of *A Hard Cold Blue*), Xander's girlfriend Greta, and our publicist Cindy—met up in Hugo's suite in the Marmont. This time, it wasn't room 72, and the usual tension with my bosses had momentarily eased in the excitement of the evening. None of us had been to an awards ceremony as starry as this before. We downed a few celebratory bottles of Möet and climbed into our rented black limo, inching along the stagnant traffic of Santa Monica Boulevard on this sunny Sunday afternoon.

On the red carpet, I was like a deer in the headlights—we all were. We had no idea what to do. The red carpet, it turns out, is really only for the stars. Anyone who's not an actor or a director,

a rock star or celebrity has no business on that crimson thorough-
fare, in the glare of the public eye. Because what is *Entertainment
Tonight* going to ask a balding, middle-aged film editor? The
American public is only interested in the same stars they've seen
on-screen, in the tabloids, on the posters.

So Cindy, ever the no-nonsense pro, split us up. Herself, Xander, his supermodel girlfriend Greta, and Gary would go down
one side of the red carpet, hobnobbing with the cameras and journalists. Somehow, Hugo also ended up going down that side, and
Sylvia too.

But myself and Pete, the editor, were shunted to the other side
of the velvet-lined rope, the nobody side: the film professionals
without a shred of celebrity, whom the media have no interest in.
We drifted past, glancing across occasionally, where Xander and
Greta bathed in the glow of the cameras. Greta was hardly of significance in Hollywood, but she was sure as hell eye-catching in
her gold gown. And Xander knew that as a first-time director,
he'd immediately draw more attention if his date was—well, if not
an actual A-lister, then at least someone who looked the part.

Pete scoffed good-naturedly as we ambled down the red carpet.

"I think we're lucky, being able to avoid all that," he remarked.
"Though my daughter would certainly be jealous."

I didn't answer.

There was a sense of being very visible, with all the cameras
around us, broadcasting to media outlets and TV channels around
the world. But also being very invisible: forgettable human col-
lateral in the presence of these luminaries.

I was about to say something, when a security guard—broad-
shouldered, tuxedoed—leaned in towards us.

"Keep moving," he said sternly. "Don't linger on the red carpet."

For a brief moment, I thought I might glimpse Holly on the
other side. That somehow her agent had snagged her a ticket to
the Globes, and I would see her turning effortlessly, in the glare of
the flashbulbs, braving her very first awards season procession. At
any moment, we'd catch each other's eye.

But I didn't see her there, even though I kept searching for her throughout the evening.

Pete and I reached the end of the red carpet and the entrance to the Beverly Hilton. I fumbled inside my sequined clutch for my digital camera. I remembered I had to get a clear, well-lit photo of me in front of the Golden Globes sign, the red carpet beneath my feet. That was my price for borrowing the designer's gown that evening. That was my cost of entry.

At first, we were all too starstruck to know how to act at the Globes.

Actors whom we'd admired on-screen, their faces projected twenty times life-size, were at the tables next to us, drifting by and joking gaily, making a show of their chumminess, their complete comfort in this scenario. On my way into the ballroom, I nearly stepped on Helen Mirren's gown, and passed within two feet of George Clooney, then Tim Burton. Steven Spielberg edged against our table, his arms outstretched to hug Tom Cruise. I mean, how was I even supposed to function within arm's reach of celebrities like this?

Only Hugo seemed to warm to the situation immediately. He stood up, grinned, and hauled Xander out of his chair.

"Come on, let's go say hi to Sammy. He's bound to know some people to introduce us to."

I watched, intrigued, as Hugo and Xander crossed the room to Sammy's table. Sylvia followed suit, although she moved slower in her heels; she wasn't about to be left out of this very public welcome, surrounded by all of Hollywood. When the three of them reached Sammy, I saw the smiles, the hugs, the congratulatory pats on the back—and underneath, I could see the performance of it all, the unspoken parlaying for Sammy's attention.

Vaguely amused, I turned back to our table.

"That's Sammy. Everyone wants to speak to him on a night like tonight." Eric Brower said this, Sammy's VP of acquisitions, who was also included in our table seating. He was around my age, and I'd interacted with him fairly regularly over the theatrical release of *A Hard Cold Blue*.

"I can imagine," I said.

Speaking to Sammy Lefkowitz was above my pay grade, but as an associate producer, speaking to one of his VPs seemed more appropriate.

"You've been to the Globes before?" I asked.

Eric nodded. "Once before. Only at the last minute, when someone above me wasn't able to go."

So I wasn't alone then, this feeling of inferiority, being at the bottom of the pile, having to scrape our way to the top. Were we just meant to be patient, or were we expected to be constantly ambitious, constantly ruthless? I wondered about the paths other people took.

"How long you been working for Sammy?"

"Three years now. I moved around a bit. Before that, I was with TMC for four years, and Caliber for two."

"Ah okay." Working at a top agency, you could survey the entire fraught landscape of our industry. I dug further. "You prefer working for a distributor to agency work?"

"Absolutely." Eric nudged his seat closer to me. "You're working on finished films, ready to be pushed out to audiences. None of this packaging talent for hypothetical projects that never get made."

I thought of all those scripts stacked on the shelves of our office, fever-dreams of writers who'd spent months crafting something which would never make it off the page, onto film.

"Plus," Eric added. "At an agency, my boss would've been livid if I tried to make a move on any of our clients. Working for Sammy, it's way easier to get close to the ladies."

He winked at me, as he said this last part. My interest in the conversation suddenly wilted.

Oh, it was going to be that again. Even at the Golden Globes. Disappointment mixed with disgust for me. I forgot: it was the film industry, and any man might make a pass. I just had to stomach it.

I could see it already, how the night was going to be. Eric pestering me, flirtatiously doling out nuggets of industry wisdom, determined to lure me into his bed later that night. But I couldn't just get up and leave Eric right now. That would be rude, it might reflect badly on our company. So I stuck it out with the conversation.

"And you?" he asked. His eyes wandered down and lingered at the gap in my gown, where the curve of the bodice hugged my breasts. "How long have you been working with Xander?"

"Nearly six years," I said confidently. "I joined them right after I graduated, when it was just me, Sylvia, and Xander."

"Oh wow, that's a long time." Eric seemed surprised. I wondered if I was supposed to be changing jobs in the industry more often, angling for better employers, better titles. Expanding my network.

"Well, yeah," I said. "I like seeing a film through from start to finish. I worked with Xander a lot on the script of *A Hard Cold Blue*, so to be here at the Globes is . . . huge for us."

"Oh, so you're a D-girl, then?" Eric joked, invoking the Hollywood term for female development executives. "And if Xander wins tonight, you're gonna get a shout-out?"

"Well, I'm a bit more than that. Working in a small company, you have to cover a lot of jobs. But yeah, my favorite part is the scripts. And it's probably what I'm best at."

"Xander must be really lucky to have you working on his scripts, then."

I had never really thought about it that way, because I'd enjoyed the script work so much. But Eric was right. I was good at scripts.

"I guess so," I said.

I looked around, at the whole room of us, primped and styled to the nines, all of us speaking in a similar tone of voice, humble-bragging or outright bragging about our latest accomplishments, our exciting new projects. All of us stroking each other's egos, angling for some connection, some subtle promotion of our individual interests in this silly moneyed charade.

I wasn't any different from the rest of them. Or was I?

"Ladies and gentlemen, the Hollywood Foreign Press Association kindly asks that you take your seats," a suave, disembodied male voice boomed over the crowd. *"This year's presentation of the Golden Globe Awards is about to begin!"*

In fact, this same suave disembodied voice had been announcing the imminent start of the Golden Globes ceremony for the past thirty minutes, giving everyone plenty of warning to wind down their networking. Now, with the final announcement, the lights dimmed, the cameras near the stage swiveled forward, and everyone in the room fell silent.

If there's one thing a room full of screen professionals knows how to do, it's how to shut up for a rolling camera.

Two large screens on either side of the stage flickered to life, relaying the camera feed to gargantuan size.

A drumroll prefaced the announcement of our host. And despite the cynical thoughts I'd just been contemplating, there was something deep in my stomach that throbbed with a childlike glee, an excitement I could only match with being a kid on Christmas morning. A flush of perfect anticipation that could never be adequately fulfilled—and made you sick with hoping.

Our host was introduced, self-effacing jokes were cracked, and the awards ceremony forged its way through the television prizes first. Back then—in the first decade of the new millennium—TV was still seen as the poor younger sibling of film. So the film professionals among us sat politely through the TV awards. We drank champagne continuously. By the time the film awards were given out, everyone was tanked. The buzz inside the auditorium flared up. Speeches grew messier, less lucid. I had been watching awards shows like these on television since I was a kid, but here in the auditorium, everything felt more real. Awards for costume design, visual effects, score—each of these was a genuine recognition of someone's shining artistic achievement. I heard the gratitude of the winners as they thanked their crew and colleagues, their family, their partners—and it all seemed so beautiful. For the first time, I belonged here: I understood the passion and the struggle. I, too, was part of this filmmaking community.

The Best Editing award was up next, the first one we were nominated for. We all knew it was a long shot. (*A Hard Cold Blue* was the only nominee in this category not to have also garnered a nod for Best Motion Picture.)

But still, we could hope. It was a wild chance, but we staked our claim to it emotionally. Sylvia insisted that we all hold hands around the table, as if we were some embattled team of heroes in an action film, praying to survive the next onslaught of murderous aliens. But the excitement and trepidation were real. We all looked warmly at Pete when his name was announced as one of the nominees; he grinned back sheepishly. Xander flashed him a thumbs-up. And as the presenters opened the envelope onstage, I'm sure each one of us at that table inwardly chanted the name of our film—*A Hard Cold Blue*—hoping that it would be announced by the presenters.

The next moment, it was not.

None of us were surprised, least of all Pete.

He shrugged his shoulders—and each of us mouthed *sorry* to him. We released our hands around the table, chastened.

It was still a victory for the film and for Pete, even to be nominated. He would be considered for weightier projects, offered a higher rate of pay. Awards are not superficial tokens of recognition; they have tangible effects on a film professional's working life ever afterward. Everything, as always, translates back into money.

So we were happy for Pete either way.

And now, Xander was up for the Best Screenplay award.

Sammy had said repeatedly in the past few days that things were looking good for us, according to insider talk. *Variety* had listed us as a dark horse in this race. Our film was a "sleek, unexpected, and elegantly tense portrait in suspense and alienation." The *LA Times* predicted the prize would go to a historical epic, which was also the frontrunner for Best Motion Picture (Drama). But online, IndieWire had predicted Best Screenplay votes might be split between that film and the glossy, feel-good musical which was favored for Best Motion Picture (Musical or Comedy). They wrote: "the ever-unpredictable HFPA may end up falling for the genre thrills of Xander Schulz's surprising, gritty *A Hard Cold Blue*."

Perhaps if there hadn't been that anticipation already, I might have reacted to things differently.

But as the presenter took to the stage—a likeable young actor, who has since been paired with Holly Randolph twice on-screen—I felt my heart in my throat. Perhaps we all did around the table. We joined hands again, Pete's dry, papery one in my left hand, Gary's massive, leathery one in my right. I was grateful I didn't have to hold either Hugo's or Eric's hand. Across the table, Sylvia caught my eye and smiled. I saw Xander look across the room, to where Sammy half stood up, flicking his index finger at Xander like a gun, as if to say: "You got this."

We heard the presenter say a few lines about the importance of a good story, how no film could get far without a gripping narrative, etc. etc. Then he announced the nominees.

"Xander Schulz for *A Hard Cold Blue*."

When he said this, we all squeezed hands—and kept the squeeze. As if the collective pressure of our palms could somehow affect the outcome that had already been printed and sealed inside that envelope onstage.

We sat patiently as he announced the other nominees.

Sylvia had her eyes closed. Xander's were staring straight ahead, nearly emotionless, boring into his uneaten dessert on the table. Hugo merely looked down and grinned.

Onstage, the presenter opened the envelope. He cleared his throat and spoke: "And the award goes to . . ."

This young, charming actor looked up and smirked at the camera. "I shoulda bet on this guy," he remarked, before announcing in a raised voice: "Xander Schulz. *A Hard Cold Blue*."

Around the table, we collectively exploded. Disbelief shot through me. And joy.

"Oh my god!" Sylvia shouted, enveloping Xander in a hug.

Hugo slapped him on the back, then hugged him, muttering, "We did it!"

Greta smothered him in a ravenous kiss and whispered in his ear.

On our side of the table, I hugged Pete, then Gary. Eric had somehow found his way to me and gave me a too-friendly embrace, sneaking in a kiss on my neck. I pulled away, and went to congratulate Xander, but he was already making his way to the stage, threading his way among tables of well-wishers, who didn't know him but surely made mental notes that they should, later on in the evening, befriend this promising new writer/director, a definite star on the rise.

Sylvia had come over to hug me, the strain between us gone, and I saw she had tears in her eyes. I did too.

Everyone at our table was still standing out of pure excitement, but we were back in our seats by the time Xander reached the podium.

Onstage, Xander looked surprisingly comfortable. I knew he didn't particularly like being on camera, but he didn't have that awkwardness that some craftspeople—usually sound or VFX technicians, composers or makeup designers—have when thrust in the spotlight. In fact, directors know all about manipulating a spotlight.

He was as always cool, calm, and collected. And a little too cold.

There was no "wow" or staged gasp of disbelief, which often

behooves award-winners into seeming humble or likeable. Xander strode up there and accepted his trophy as if he'd deserved it from the very beginning.

He leaned into the microphone to speak. Watching him, elation and shock and adrenaline all coursed through my veins—and an impossible flood of pride.

"The first people I have to thank are my mom and my dad. They gave me a Canon AE-1 when I was ten years old, and ever since then, I've been looking at the world from behind a camera lens, trying to tell stories through pictures."

An appreciative murmur swept the room.

"So thank you for always encouraging me, Mom and Dad. For always believing that I could be a photographer, then a filmmaker. That nothing was too out of reach for me."

I quivered with anticipation, for the moment when Xander would finally mention my name—and just for a brief instant, the world would know someone like Sarah Lai existed and had contributed to this film.

"It's a big leap for a visual guy like me to switch to writing words on a page. I was never much of a writer, so this award—a screenplay award from the Hollywood Foreign Press Association—means a lot to me. It proves that you can do anything you want to do, if you set your mind to it."

For a second, I thought here, he might mention my name as his script editor, but surely it was too early on in the speech.

"I'd also like to thank my brother and sister, David and Emmy. For giving me something to aspire to. For being my first models and subjects when we were kids."

A chuckle from the audience.

"As far as agents go, Andrea Paris and the team at TMC, I can't imagine having a more solid squad behind me. Sammy Lefkowitz, when I found out you'd picked up our film, I thought I was dreaming. But this is real, you've made it possible."

He hefted the award in Sammy's direction, and Sammy grinned, the entire room staring at him.

"Sylvia Zimmerman, my producer, this film owes a great deal to you, so thank you for all your hard work through the years, from the days when we were still making commercials together. Pete Jorgenson, I'm so glad you cut this film for us, you deserve every recognition. Al McKendrick, you were an amazing DoP. Who else, who else . . ."

Xander looked at our table, and we all gazed at him like he was the Messiah returned to earth, even the Jews and nonbelievers among us. He could do no wrong in that moment.

"Sam—and Bob, and Joseph, and—and Chauder, and Kyle, the entire cast and crew. It's every director's dream to work with people like you on his debut. Annie for the costumes, John for the music, Danielle for the hair and makeup . . ."

Xander paused. I waited, along with everyone else in that room.

"Greta, you're with me tonight. Thanks so much, babe. Schlomo Summers, who made me his photography assistant when I was only sixteen, who gave me my first break, showed me what light and a simple frame can do for a story. Thank you, thank you. Insurgent Media, who gave me my first music video, thank you, I learned so much on that job."

"And yeah. Finally . . . one person who's really expanded my horizons, even though I've only had the chance to know him recently: Hugo North. It's so incredible what we've managed to build over the past few months and will keep on building. This is just the beginning. Look out for our next film, everyone. It's gonna be something. Thanks to my producers, Hugo, Sylvia. I can't wait to keep making more films and doing what I love. This means so much to me. Thank you, and good night."

In retrospect, it would go down as an earnest, gracious speech. A first-time filmmaker paying respect to all those in his life who'd made it possible for him to claim this trophy. The room erupted into considerable applause, and at our table, everyone but me was on their feet, cheering and whooping and clapping ecstatically.

I sat for a moment longer, wondering if I'd missed something. If my ears had stopped working for a millisecond, and somehow omitted the sound of Xander mentioning my name in the whole litany of names he'd reeled off.

But I hadn't missed it. I'd heard Xander's entire acceptance speech—and I wasn't in it.

I might as well have been invisible, sitting at that table at the Golden Globes in my borrowed designer gown, my rib cage being slowly crushed. Inside, I felt empty.

Meanwhile, Hugo and Sylvia and Greta were hugging and crying uncontrollably, gesturing for me to join them. I slowly rose to my feet, applauding, pasting on a grateful smile to match theirs.

Sylvia looked at me and grinned. Maybe she hadn't even noticed the omission.

I felt tears prick my eyes, but they weren't tears of joy. At least everyone else could think they were.

Scanning the table, my glance caught Eric's.

"Congrats," he said, clapping. But in his knowing look, I detected a trace of pity.

47

IT SEEMS JARRING, now, to switch from that evening ten years ago, the buzz and excitement of the Golden Globes, the cheers and the adulation all around us, to my quiet apartment here in Brooklyn. Thom Gallagher watches me from my couch, neither of us speaking.

Outside the window, the sun has set. We sit here in the deepening twilight, and to draw us away from that scene, I switch on my lamp. We both squint at the sudden flare of artificial light.

I notice there are tears in my eyes, and I wipe them away, looking down.

Shame is still the dominant emotion I feel right now. Shame that—in the end—so much of it was about my own ego.

If Xander had named me in that Golden Globes speech, would I have felt validated? Would I have continued working for him and Hugo, lying for them and their increasingly awful behavior, tolerating it all for my own chance in the spotlight, my own name immortalized on-screen or on another movie poster or in another *Variety* article?

I wonder what type of person I would be now, thirty-nine-year-old Sarah Lai, living in LA, driving to work every day from a house she owns in the Hills, a respectable list of producer credits on her IMDb profile, invites to screenings and parties every night of the week, possibly married to someone in the industry . . . And probably, somehow, still unhappy. Hollow inside.

"Do you feel that . . . because you weren't thanked in Xander's acceptance speech, that somehow you were excluded?"

"I'd always been excluded, even from the beginning," I say with a certain resentfulness. "I mean, there is nothing in my DNA that could ever make me part of that club."

Thom nods, and scrawls something in his notebook.

"Listen, I know it sounds so petty. It *is* so petty. I mean, I doubt very much that anyone else in this world is bothering to analyze Xander Schulz's Golden Globes speech from a decade ago."

"But it didn't *feel* petty to you at the time," Thom says.

"No, it felt like I'd been stabbed in the heart. Like everything I'd done for Xander and that script, for the company—like all my contributions had been totally erased, overlooked. That was the worst part of all."

Not objectively worse than what Hugo tried to do to me at his party. But unlike Hugo, I'd worked with Xander *for years*. That film may never even have been made if I hadn't improved his script. And he couldn't even think to slip my name—three god-damn syllables—into his whole list of people to thank, up there on that stage, with all of Hollywood staring at him.

He'd even thanked Greta, the model he was fucking at the time, whom he'd only dated for eight months prior to that, and would promptly dump a week after the Globes.

"Actually, no—" I correct myself. "The worst part wasn't that. The worst part was that it mattered so much to me, whether I was mentioned in his speech or not. A better person would have just been able to . . . rise above it all, right?"

I look straight at Thom as I ask, and suddenly there is something liberating about this. I have nothing left to hide.

"I'm just as bad as they are, aren't I?"

I phrase this as if I'm asking for some confirmation, but Thom shakes his head slowly. "Well, we all have our egos. But that's being overly harsh on yourself."

I absorb this in silence, allow myself to believe it.

"So after the Globes, you walked away from Conquest?"

"After everything I'd done for him and Hugo and Sylvia . . . that was the last straw for me. But I didn't run off willingly," I admit.

I muddled through the rest of the Golden Globes, pretended to be overjoyed, drank a lot more, fended off the attentions of Eric, who eventually discovered someone more pliant to take home. And somehow at around six a.m., as the sky was starting to lighten, I found myself wasted, pathetic, coming down from some kind of high, at the house party of someone I'd never even met. I was shivering by their pool outside on my own—and I realized in horror that I was wearing $22,000 worth of borrowed jewelry around my neck and fingers.

"So what happened next?"

"Did you think I ran away with the jewels?" I ask, deadpan. "What is this, some kind of heist movie?"

We both chuckle. "I probably should have. The borrowed jewelry was linked to Hugo's room number, and I would have loved to get him in trouble."

But my life is hardly that exciting, and I'm nowhere near that brave.

Miraculously, the designer gown I wore was still intact, as I sat there by the abandoned pool at the end of that January night. No sequins had fallen off, no one had stepped on the emerald-green silk or spilled anything on it.

But I felt this sudden, visceral need to rid myself of the gown and the jewels as soon as possible, get them off me, return them to their rightful owners, and slink back to the normal, humble radius of existence I never should have left. So I called a cab. I didn't even know where in LA I was, and only discovered the address by rummaging through a pile of mail stashed in the laundry room of the house I was in. Eventually I let myself into Clive's apartment with the key he'd lent me.

And hours later, in the glaring light of a hungover Monday, I wore my sunglasses as I handed the jewelry to the concierge of the Chateau Marmont. It was the last time I ever set foot in that hotel.

With Xander's Golden Globe win, our fortunes actually sky-rocketed. Back in New York, Sammy's company handled the publicity around *A Hard Cold Blue*, but there was even more interest in us as a production company, and in *Furious Her*. This eventually led to another premiere at Cannes, a first-look deal with Sammy's company, in Xander being flooded with opportunities which, played cleverly, could have minted our futures for the next few years.

But neither Sylvia nor Hugo nor Xander noticed that my heart wasn't in it anymore. And quite possibly, none of them cared. I stopped working so hard, my enthusiasm plummeted. I grew to resent every instruction Xander gave me, I no longer showered him with compliments, at a time when that had become standard for him.

And then, a few weeks later, Hugo and Xander would play their final trump card. There was something in the contracts we had drawn up so hurriedly a year before, after our fateful meeting with Hugo in Cannes. Remember, Sylvia and Xander hadn't bothered to look at the fine print in the legal documents? They'd palmed the paperwork onto me, but what did I know about company mergers at twenty-seven? Of course, Sylvia had her lawyer handling the contract, but lawyers at the end of the day aren't responsible for their clients taking up a pen and deciding to sign a piece of paper.

There was a particular clause in the contract which became Hugo's final weapon. The clause claimed that if two out of three of the company's co-owners (Sylvia, Xander, and Hugo) chose to no longer work with the third, they could decide to liquidate the company and return everyone's proportionate ownership to themselves. Originally, that clause may have been included to protect Sylvia and Xander from Hugo. But Sylvia likely never predicted that it would result in her own expulsion from Conquest, the rapid undoing of a production company she'd spent nearly a decade growing.

She called me up one day in April, furious. Despite having experienced many shades of Sylvia's anger in the past, I'd never heard her voice this livid.

"Sarah, *you* were the one handling the contracts when Hugo invested in the company last spring, right?"

"Yes . . ." I answered slowly. Already, by the tone of her voice, I knew this was a conversation I'd rather avoid.

She railed at me for fifteen minutes straight. Did I even realize what I'd done? Hugo was pushing her out of her own company, and I was responsible. Unbeknownst to either of us, while I was busy overseeing the production in LA and Sylvia was in New York, he and Xander had been acquiring scripts for the past eight months, building up a slate for what would be their own separate production outfit. I'd made this possible after the careless way I'd handled the paperwork last spring. I was irresponsible and ungrateful. After all the opportunities she'd given me over the years, *this* was how I'd treated her?

I didn't know how to react. I cried, for sure. (I am sometimes shocked when I think about how much I cried on the job in my twenties, but I was sensitive and passionate. And working with people who were given to nasty outbursts.) I tried to defend myself, but against what kind of reasoning?

"I'm not a legal expert, Sylvia, I don't know anything about company mergers—"

"Then you should have said something to me!" she shouted back.

But I knew Sylvia and Xander didn't want to be bored with the legalities back then. All they cared about was moving ahead with the film. And did she really expect me, a twenty-seven-year-old, to have the expertise to supervise all the documentation?

There was no point in trying to convince Sylvia, because her mind was already set. Everything was my fault, of course.

"You don't get it, Sarah," she said towards the end, her voice trembling, the anger finally dissipated into despair. "You've ruined it all. I'm going to lose the company I've worked so hard to build.

I'm going to lose Xander to Hugo. Maybe you're too young to understand what that means."

She hung up shortly afterwards, her fury spent.

I did understand, in fact. What it felt like to have all your efforts negated, all your accomplishments ripped out from under you. But she'd never given me the chance to say any of that.

Sylvia didn't leave the company without a fight, and a few weeks later, Hugo called me into a one-on-one meeting with him. In my gut, I knew what this was about.

There is a moment, just before a man assaults you, when you as a woman realize, way too late: *So that's what this is going to be.*

A brief, terrible instant of clarity before the storm closes in.

Eventually you start to develop a sixth sense for it. To almost anticipate it, to always be on the alert.

It was like this with Hugo, every time I was alone with him, after that night at his party. So when I stepped into the glass-walled conference room in our office and faced him, sitting on his own at the far end of the long table, it seemed like a predestined showdown, the necessary conclusion to what had begun in his empty mansion in Beverly Hills.

I was grateful for the transparent wall of the room, for Ziggy tapping away at his keyboard outside (I'd asked him not to leave the office for the duration of my meeting with Hugo). But for all this, I was still on high alert, my reflexes primed, my mind racing to anticipate from which direction he'd attack.

"Morning, Sarah," Hugo murmured, and gestured to the chair diagonally next to him. I took a seat two chairs away. "It's been so long since we've seen you properly. As you know we've been quite busy."

Hugo pattered through the usual formalities: how exciting things were, hammering out the deal with Sammy Lefkowitz, buying a new town house here in Manhattan so his family could visit from England. I nodded and tried to be civil.

"Now, it was most unfortunate that we had to come to that arrangement with Sylvia," he then said, making the inevitable pivot. "But you know, Xander, he'd worked with Sylvia for so long. He just felt the relationship was getting stale. As a creative, he wanted a new lease on life, new inspirations."

I glared at Hugo, wishing he could cycle quickly through this meaningless monologue and arrive at his point.

"Which brings us to you, Sarah." Hugo fixed his gaze on me, the way an eagle might leer at a lone rabbit on a hill. I stared back. He shifted his eyes slightly.

"Sarah, we are so grateful for everything you've done for the latest film, for your notes on Xander's scripts over the years."

My notes? I wanted to seethe. *How about the way I single-handedly got him to rescue what was just another mediocre screenplay?*

"As I've said before, you have a very exciting career ahead of you. But we feel that, maybe you're just . . . not the right fit for us moving ahead. So along the lines of starting afresh, we'd like to try out a new team at our production company. New team, new slate, new ideas, new everything. I hope you can understand."

It wasn't a surprise, of course. I'd been expecting this for some time. So I simply said, "Okay," in a tone that made it clear I needed to hear more.

"We do want to honor all the work you've put into Xander's projects thus far, and we do know you'll be without a salary as you look for somewhere new. So we wanted to offer you ten thousand dollars as a parting gift, just to help you towards what I know will be a promising future."

Ten thousand dollars? I would have been better off running away with the jewelry.

Ten thousand dollars was less than what Stan our cinematographer made in a week on *Furious Her*. It was probably less than the total of Hugo's two-week bill at the Spark Club. Xander could easily make that amount in a day of still photography shoots for a fashion label.

And *that* was what they were offering me after six years of hard work furthering Xander's career? True, in my youthful eagerness, I hadn't signed a contract with Sylvia when I first started working for her. And last year's agreements with Hugo had named me as head of development but hadn't specified what would happen to me in the case of the company's liquidation. So everything was up for negotiation.

I still hadn't said anything.

"How does that sound, Sarah?"

I cleared my throat, trying to calm my heartbeat, to own the moment.

"I appreciate the offer, Hugo, I honestly do. But I don't *quite* think that's adequate compensation, in terms of everything I've given to the company over the years."

I said that last sentence slowly, as if measuring out a poison drop by drop into a pool of water. When I finished, I looked at Hugo. I was still terrified, but I'd said it. I told myself I had nothing to lose. I remembered Sylvia's words from years ago. *When the time is right, know your worth.*

Just look in him in the eye—and negotiate.

Interview Transcript (continued):
Sylvia Zimmerman, 5:28 p.m.

TG: Do you miss it? Working in film?

SZ: Of course I do. I was a damn good producer. I knew how
to make films. I'd built up the company, but also my whole
network. So after what happened with Hugo, I could have
started a new production company, found new directors,
nurtured their careers. But part of me was like, I'd done that
for Xander, and where had it gotten me? (pause) So why
waste my time and effort on someone who's just gonna walk
away when they get offered a bigger paycheck? Directors can
so easily fuck off and forget their producers. At least with
motherhood, your children are stuck with you for life. And
somewhere down the line, they'll learn to be grateful. It may
take a while, but they don't forget their mothers.

TG: So would you say motherhood is more rewarding than work,
then?

SZ: (laughs) Only because certain workplaces can be that
fucked up. But really, this whole career versus motherhood
question . . . there shouldn't *have* to be a choice for women.
I mean, there isn't for men. (pause) Look at Hugo, for god's
sake. Four kids—and I don't think I ever heard him talk
about a single one of them. His wife off doing her own thing,
happy with her credit card collection, and him fucking every
girl in sight.

(Pause)

If something bad *did* happen to any of those girls on our
film shoot, then I am truly sorry. I just . . . got distracted,
I guess. We all did. I didn't see Hugo North for what he
really was.

TG: Are you still in touch with Xander?

SZ: Nominally. (snorts) We send each other holiday cards each
year. So I know what his kids look like, at least. But no, not
really. Considering I used to talk to him a few times a day when

we worked together, I haven't actually had a real face-to-face conversation with him in years. I mean, how could I, after what he did to me and the company?

TG: How do you feel about his success now?

SZ: Maybe Xander was always going to be successful. Because he had that type of personality. So maybe, sooner or later, he was always going to ditch me as his producer.

TG: So do you regret what you did in that year?

SZ: Of course. If I hadn't brought Hugo on board, things would have gone very differently. (pause) And yes, it was amazing going to the Golden Globes. But Hugo shouldn't have been there. He didn't even work on that first film. Only, of course, everyone was interested in him because of his money. And Sarah, poor Sarah Lai. The way they treated her—well, she deserved more.

TG: Do you feel responsible for the way they treated her?

SZ: Like I should have stood up for her better? (pause) I did . . . I tried. (pause) I suppose I was a bit harsh on her, too. But in the end, I was angry at myself for letting that happen to me. To us. It was my own goddamn company. And I didn't even notice what was happening. (pause) You see, Hugo knew exactly how to push Sarah's buttons. The way he did virtually everyone else's. For all I know, he probably got her into bed, too, and she never told me.

TG: Is that what you think?

SZ: I dunno . . . I certainly hope not. I think Sarah didn't trust me in the end. Something happened. Somehow, she got it into her head that she could be a cat—when she was only ever going to be a mouse. As smart as she was and as hard as she worked, that girl never had a chance, so long as she played it straight.

TG: Is that really how it will always be—the cats and the mice?

SZ: No. No, I think it will change. I look at my daughter and her friends, and I'm hoping it will. Don't ask me how, but it's got to.

48

I N THE END, Hugo agreed to $45,000. I knew that was still peanuts to him, and if I'd brought in a lawyer, I could surely have gotten more. But it was a lot to me, an entire year's salary.

I also wanted a full producer's credit on the film, but Sylvia had made it clear, in no uncertain terms, that she alone would get a producer credit. (At least, this is what Hugo said. Sylvia and I were no longer on speaking terms by then.) Associate producer was the only credit I would receive.

It was a torturous negotiation; the only way I could gain significant ground was by raising the issue of what had happened to me, to Courtney, to Holly.

"But I thought you weren't sure what happened to them?" Thom asks.

"I didn't know the *details* of what happened," I explained. "But I'd heard enough and experienced enough to know it was bad. It was something he'd want to hide."

"And did he make you sign a nondisclosure agreement?"

"There was something *like* an NDA, but not exactly. I guess it was the start of Hugo's career as an exec producer, so he hadn't quite perfected the legal art of covering his tracks."

We both know we shouldn't laugh at this joke, but we do.

"It was all wrapped up in an agreement about me leaving the company, so there was a more general clause saying I was 'not to disclose publicly about the details of my employment at the company, etc. etc., for a period of ten years.' Something like that."

"Ten years, huh?" Thom arches his eyebrows at me. "Ten years is up now, isn't it?"

"That it is." I nod. There is a mischievous gleam in my eyes. "Ten years is definitely up."

"What'd you do with the money?"

"Lived off it for a bit. After working that hard for six years straight, it was so surreal, so liberating to have no professional obligations. No office to commute to, no boss to answer to."

My parents . . . well, it was awkward, having to explain why I was no longer working at Conquest.

"They're . . . restructuring the company, they want new people in," I mumbled to my uncomprehending mom and dad, as I sat across from them in their airless living room. The smell of stir-fry was especially strong coming from the restaurant's extractor fans below.

"But you worked for them for five, six years?" Dad frowned. "I thought they liked you."

"Well, Sylvia's not there anymore," I explained. At least that much was true. "Anyway, it's probably for the better, I don't really like this new boss."

"The British billionaire? You piss him off somehow?" Mom asked, aghast.

"I'm not . . . sure, really." I pushed away a wave of queasiness.

"Well, you must have done something wrong for this to happen," Mom pronounced.

I gritted my teeth. "Maybe I'm just not the right fit," I breathed.

"How you going to earn money now?" I saw the two lines of worry appear between my mom's eyebrows.

"I sort of don't have to for a while," I said with a shrug. I told them about my payout, without mentioning the other conditions attached to it.

"Huh." My dad was puzzled. "That guy must be loaded. Just like that—they cut you a check that big?"

I wanted to tell him it wasn't that big a check—and it hadn't happened just like that.

I didn't explain much to Karen, either. She wouldn't get it, with her stable accounting career and her new life as a suburban mom. I'd just bury the whole business and try to move on with my life.

So, like any responsible child of immigrants, I put the money in a high-earning bank account and didn't touch most of it. When the recession happened soon after, I didn't bother to look for another job in film. I supposed I could have networked and scratched my way towards one, but something about that entire industry seemed so . . . tainted.

Instead, I traveled around the world for a year, on a shoestring budget. It was my first significant chunk of time outside New York, and it helped clear my head. I visited countries and places I'd only ever seen before in film: the sweeping Highlands of Scotland, the elegant streets of Paris, even the dense, humid rain forests of Thailand, quivering with the hum of insects.

My world expanded, but wherever I went, people still connected through movies. Villages of locals would gather in a dusty square to watch an unsubtitled DVD of *Star Wars*, projected onto a sheet. In market after market, I saw knockoff DVDs of domestic hits and Hollywood blockbusters, arrayed on a blanket on the ground by some street-seller desperate to make a profit of less than a dollar. Earlier, I might have been horrified by such flagrant flouting of copyright. But now I secretly cheered them on. Everyone needed to make a living somehow—better yet through a love of film.

When I returned, I applied for a few scholarships at various universities, securing one for a master's in film studies. And then, somehow, I ended up in this teaching job.

"And what is it like, teaching screenwriting?" Thom gestures to the pile of student scripts on my windowsill. "Do you enjoy reading the students' work?"

"I mean, they're not at the level of the scripts I worked with at Firefly," I start, not wanting to sound bitter. "But every once in a while, I'll read a promising draft. And I'll think . . . that student's got something."

"So it's not all doom and gloom, then?" He smiles.

"Not entirely. And the people I work with are a lot nicer."

"Have you ever thought about writing your own screenplay one day?"

"Me? Oh god, I don't know." I imagine sitting down to a blank page on my computer screen, the cursor waiting patiently. There is some new, hidden thrill in that: my own anticipation for what is to come, and the complete lack of expectation from anyone else.

Then I think about the whole business of finding an agent, my script being printed and bound and ignored on the shelf by someone's stressed PA, and my heart crumples.

"I don't know," I admit. "You know, they always say those who can't do, end up teaching."

But I can do more than just teach, can't I?

I don't ask this last question out loud.

In his journalistic diligence, Thom has asked to see the termination of employment contract that I signed with Hugo a decade ago. So I root around for those pages I'd resentfully signed years ago. They are tucked away in a file called FIREFLY/CONQUEST, pushed to the back of my filing cabinet.

Once the money reached my bank account, I'd never bothered to look at the contract again.

But while Thom is examining it, carefully photographing it on his phone, I am still contemplating everything I've related. The whole pitiful arc of my journey in that world, the unspoken journeys of others I never really got to know.

A sadness weighs inside me, an awareness of my own callous

ignorance at the time. I look up, exhausted, as he asks his final few questions.

"If there's something you could say to Holly or Courtney now, ten years later, what would it be?"

"Are you in touch with them?" I ask, hopeful. A question that's been lingering inside me, ever since we first sat down in the *Times* offices.

"I can't disclose that," he says apologetically. "That kind of goes against my journalistic ethics."

Ah, of course.

We sit in silence. And then, suddenly, I can't hold it in any longer.

"I would say I'm sorry." I nod. "Really sorry."

Too quick, my eyes fill up with tears, and my voice becomes strained.

"I mean, I'm not the person who did those things to them. But I guess I enabled it. I didn't warn them, I didn't believe them enough. And I should have. Given what *I* went through . . . Given how I treated Courtney."

I squeeze my eyes shut, the tears streaming thick down my cheeks. "I was just so fucking stupid . . . just thinking about the good of the film, about my career. And where did that get me in the end?"

"But you were abused too. Hugo was an abusive boss. So you were operating under his threat the entire time."

I sniff. "I know. I see that now. And it's not like Xander or Sylvia were particularly looking out for me. But still, I feel really guilty. Like I should have done something else."

"You did what you *felt* you could at the time. Under the circumstances."

I know Thom has probably been trained in the art of comforting platitudes, given the number of traumatized sources he's interviewed over the past months. Yet still it feels good to have another person grant me this small absolution, offer this kind of balm.

We both remain quiet for a moment.

I wonder if people I once worked with—Ziggy and Seth and Carlos and Clive and everyone else on that set, and on all the subsequent sets and productions—had any inkling of what Hugo North was really up to, behind all the suave comments and the British accent and the champagne toasts and open bar tabs. What he was capable of.

"If there's something you could say to Hugo now, what would you say?"

"The printable version?" I joke.

"Well, as printable as possible." Thom smiles.

"You know, he almost sounds like your stock British villain from a movie, but he was real. I even heard from him recently." I throw this out, knowing it will spark a reaction. "Can you believe that? It can't be a coincidence."

I show him the messages Hugo sent, haul the expensive bottle of Möet from under the kitchen sink. Thom raises his eyebrows.

When I play him the voice mail, I am no longer frightened to hear Hugo's voice this time. I even detect a note of desperation lurking beneath the polished accent.

"Funnily enough, some of my other sources have reported similar things, getting messages from Hugo out of the blue. Attempts at bribery, that sort of thing."

"Has it scared them off?" I ask.

"Not entirely. Most are still going ahead with the interviews."

That horde of the undead, closing in on their quarry. No longer silent.

"I'd say it's about fucking time," I announce to Thom, my hand shaping itself slowly into a fist. "I want him to be confronted with all the careers and lives he disrupted. All the movies we could have made, if we'd stayed in that industry. If we hadn't been . . . touched."

My mug of jasmine tea is empty now, and I wait for the sound of a siren in the neighborhood to die down. There is something else I want to say.

"You know what about sexual assault makes it so dehumanizing?" I ask, defiant.

"What?" Thom replies. "Tell me."

Because it reduces you, a woman, down to simply that: sexual meat for the desires of someone else. Everything that comprises you as an individual—your intelligence, your talent, your education, your years of experience, or an entire lifetime spent idolizing movies—all that is obliterated the moment you are unwillingly pushed up against a wall, grabbed, manhandled, or worse. It is a simple elimination of yourself as an actual person, with anything worthwhile to say.

Then again, look at how we're portrayed on-screen, our bodies on display, our ages slashed, our roles diminished. Maybe it's no surprise: the image and the reality.

"I have this pipe dream," I say. "That if only we were able to work together in a different way . . . no bullying, no ridiculous parties, no casting couch. Just people brought together by a love of the craft. Think of the films we could make."

"Well," Thom offers, "things are changing. And it starts with stories like yours being heard."

I nod. "I'm pretty sure there've been other women since then. So there's no good in hiding the truth anymore. What happened happened, after all."

"You've come out of it better than others," Thom adds. "Some women . . . There have been suicide attempts, thousands spent on therapy bills. You've come out the other side okay."

I consider this, a new stone unearthed.

Thom's blue eyes peer into mine, then break away suddenly. "Well, I think that's about it. You have my email if anything else comes up. I'll be in touch, for sure. I'll keep you posted as the piece develops."

I sit up straighter, and a veil of loneliness falls over me.

"One last thing." Thom perks up. "Really important. You don't have to tell me right now, but start thinking about it. Are you okay to be named in my article when it comes out?"

He tosses that last question out so casually, when it is the biggest one of the day. I stare at him, openmouthed, trying to picture my name in print in the *New York Times*, maybe even in the same article as Holly Randolph.

"You want me to answer that *now*?"

"No, of course not. Think it over. Take your time."

49

T IS JUST like Thom Gallagher to leave me with one last question that simmers at the back of my mind, when I was hoping to be done with everything on that final interview.

We stood up at the end of that talk, on that Sunday evening.

He thanked me, I thanked him.

Now that I'd expelled the last of my thoughts, I felt cleaner, somehow. Absolved.

He asked me if I was going to be all right, and I said yes, even though I wasn't really sure. I toyed with the idea of suggesting we have a drink, some way to ease off the gravity of it all.

He paused for a moment, and then said: "Why not?"

Just a normal conversation between two New Yorkers getting to know each other. No hidden agendas, no blinking red lights, no release forms necessary.

At one point, giddy and loose from the beer, I asked him: "Why do you do it, Thom? I know we'd all love a Pulitzer, but why this topic?"

He hesitated, splayed his patrician hands on the scuffed wood of the bar countertop. "It's a chain. You keep on pulling and there's more and more. It's like there's no end to the stories."

I nodded. "I can only imagine."

And an hour later, after I'd learned just a little bit more about the enigma that is Thom Gallagher, after we'd finished one bottle each of Brooklyn Lager at the bar around the corner, we said our actual good-bye. I thought perhaps it might be safest to just shake hands, and he did as well, but somehow, with the release brought on by alcohol and our exhaustion, that became a gentle hug, a pressing in of our shoulders, nothing beyond that.

"You take care of yourself, okay?"

And I echoed a similar sentiment. It can't be easy for him, hearing so many damaged women expose their private injuries, collapse into tears, as part of his day-to-day job. And yet, he presses on.

We parted ways and there was a startling lightness in my body, my face flushed from the beer and perhaps something more. Even though I suspected that might be the last time I would see him.

So this is still on my mind, this rare buoyancy, when I am sitting at my office hours, later that week. There's a timid tap at my door. Looking up, I see Claudia.

New rules now require faculty to keep our office doors open during one-on-one student consultations. I apologize and explain this to Claudia, but she doesn't seem to mind.

She revised her script following my suggestions and wrote a few more scenes, actually finished it. Would I mind looking at it sometime?

"Sure," I tell her, surprised by her enthusiasm. "Email it to me and I'll read it by the end of the month."

"I also saw all those films you told me about," she adds. "I really liked them. Can you suggest some more?"

I'm impressed—they're slow, subtitled films, very different from the movies most of my students adore. We talk about what she found unique: the pacing, the tone, the introspection. I remember again the joy that happens when one cinephile meets another. I tell myself things are different now than when I was starting out. There are summer institutes and labs and initiatives to encourage young people from different backgrounds to become filmmakers. "Diverse voices" are something to be nurtured now, so what harm can a little encouragement do?

"Hey Sarah," Claudia says, nudging me out of my reverie. "Did you used to write screenplays?"

I shake my head. Her comment reminds me of someone else I've heard recently. "I've never actually tried. I used to work with directors and screenwriters to make theirs better."

"Wow, cool," she says, wide-eyed. "You should try writing one sometime. I bet it'd be good."

"Well, it'd probably be decent," I admit. "I'd have to find a story first."

Something catches a spark in the back of my mind, and I remind myself to let in a little air, nurse it and fuel it, until it's ready to burst into flame.

Claudia has stood up to leave, but I can tell by the way she's lingering, she has one more thing to say.

"Hey, so, we were wondering . . . the student filmmaking society is having a screening of our short films next Thursday. Do you want to come? They're just little short films, probably kinda embarrassing. And I bet you're busy anyway."

If only she knew. My social calendar is hardly jammed, and my life of ambitious twelve-hour workdays is long past. And it's been a while since I've seen a short film anyway.

"Well, actually, I could easily be free," I say.

Claudia looks surprised and delighted at once. "Really?"

"What time are the screenings?"

"Six p.m. in Quad B, next Thursday." She grins. "Wow, everyone will be so excited if you can make it."

"Do *you* have a film that's screening?" I ask her.

She shakes her head. "No. Not yet . . . I'm still working on mine."

"Well, I look forward to seeing it one day."

Claudia smiles and sets off down the hall. Her dark hair rustles over her backpack, and I watch her thin frame passing through a patch of sunlight beneath a row of windows, then into shadow, then into sunlight again.

I think for a moment, turn back to my computer. I scroll

through my inbox, searching for a particular name, a particular email I've been meaning to reply to.

Not much later, it is Thanksgiving, and my sister and her family are back in town. For the first time, my parents have decided not to work the restaurant on Thanksgiving, so we have all descended upon their apartment: my siblings and their partners, my niece and nephew, and of course, me. Various cousins, uncles, and aunts are also here, and we alternate between gazing out at the frigid streets of Flushing below, and catching up with each other.

On Thanksgiving Day, there are fewer street hawkers trying to sell their bargain deals of bok choy and bitter melon. The streets are quieter, gray, the crowds in the city withdrawn to its lighted, warm interiors.

My parents haven't hosted this much family in years, and I see their visible excitement: my mom rushing around, offering bowls of watermelon seeds and peanut candy to the guests, my dad pouring out small libations of Courvoisier XO for those over twenty-one. He is particularly impressed by the magnum of Möet I've brought to share.

"High roller, eh?" Dad laughs at me.

"Ooh," Mom gapes, as she reaches for the bottle. "Save this for later, for extra special occasion."

"No, Mom." I grab the bottle back to open it. "Why wait? Let's drink it now."

Perhaps in preparation for this gathering, my parents have set out new framed photographs of us, their children, as grown adults. Atop the bookshelves and cabinets march the usual parade of our successive high school and college graduations: unfortunate haircuts, gawky grins lined with braces, academic robes and mortarboards.

But then, there are the new framed photos. Karen with her husband and two children in one of those awkward, posed family shots taken at a photographer's studio. Edison and Julia, their arms around each other, in their official engagement photo (Julia had insisted on getting one). And to my surprise, there is the photo of me in that emerald-green dress, on the red carpet of the Golden Globes, ten years ago. I look thinner and younger (but not noticeably so), and that borrowed $15,000 necklace still glints as bright as day, around my neck.

I peer at the image, as if reacquainting myself with someone I once knew from my early childhood. It is disquieting, to be confronted with visual evidence of that era I have tried to forget for so long. And yet seeing it, a long-missing puzzle piece slides into place.

"Whoa, I remember that photo!" Karen sidles next to me to gape at it.

"I can't believe that was ten years ago." I shake my head. "All *your* photos are from last year. Mom!" I shout across the room, "That's the best you could do for me? A photo from ten years ago?"

"Don't worry," my mom shouts back, giggling. "You look the prettiest in that photo! You should be proud."

"Oh god," I mutter to Karen. "That's probably the photo they use when they try to set me up with someone's son or nephew."

My sister stifles a laugh. "Because sure, you dress like that every day."

"It's a good photo, no?" my dad asks. He has come by to offer us more Courvoisier for the third time. "I found the image you sent me and managed to blow it up to a bigger size. See, I'm learning how to do all this young people's stuff."

"We're very impressed, Dad," I say. Karen nudges me in the ribs.

"So Sarah, how are the kids doing at that place where you teach? How's your job?" Dad asks.

I realize my parents must have heard me complain about my job so many times over the years. No wonder they've come to think that Brooklyn Community College is a catch basin for the deadbeat and unmotivated.

"Well, actually," I say. "The job isn't that bad. I even read a

good script by a student the other week. I've been pleasantly surprised."

"That's good, that's great!" my dad cheers. "See, I told you it
would get better. You were just too stubborn to believe me."

"Was I stubborn?" I ask, more as a musing to myself.

Karen widens her eyes and nods. *Oh yeah*, she mouths.

At that moment, my mom starts trying to herd everyone to the
front door, so we can begin making our way down to the restaurant for our private Thanksgiving dinner. Snatches of conversation
continue, as we shuffle to get our coats on.

"Auntie Sarah?" I look down to see my niece Alice tugging at
my hand. She gazes up at me in awe. "Did you really work with
Holly Randolph? Before she became a star?"

I nod. "Yes, I did. She was very nice. But that was a while ago,
almost before you were born."

"Do you think she's still nice?"

"I think she still could be. Some famous people stay nice, you
know."

"Wow, I wish I could meet Holly Randolph."

I raise my eyebrows at Karen, who grins sheepishly.

"Sweetie, let's get you down to Grandma and Granddad's restaurant. I know there's a huge turkey waiting to be sliced up!"

As we filter out into the hall, Karen says to me: "You know, I
started reading some of those #MeToo stories from Hollywood.
They're kinda crazy, aren't they?"

"That whole world is crazy. But what, you don't believe them?"

"No, I believe them. I'm just shocked, is all."

"Well," I say, as the last of us leave the apartment. "Shocking
things do happen. I could tell you some stories."

Karen looks at me, puzzled. I shut the door behind us, deep in
thought.

I realize I can't leave my own sister in the dark like this. Surely,
she must know before the rest of the world does. So I make a note
to myself to find some time this Thanksgiving weekend and tell
her a little of what happened, a decade ago in LA.

50

I AM ON THE subway, alone as usual, when I first see the headline.

A copy of a morning tabloid is folded over on the seat next to me, and I fish it up, turning it over to see the front page: photos of a Hollywood leading lady on the red carpet, and juxtaposed next to that, the latest studio exec to be accused, his head down, handcuffed behind his back.

But in today's ever-churning news cycle, what was laid out last night and printed this morning is now old. There have since been further developments.

My phone lights up with the latest push notification from the *New York Times*. One glimpse at my screen, and I know what it is: *Holly Randolph and 9 Others Accuse Billionaire Hugo North of Sexual Assault.*

Nine others. I know if I click on that article, written by one Thom Gallagher, Holly's story will be first. Because she is, of course, the biggest draw. And somewhere later in that scroll of text, I will find my own name. And discover a summarized version of what I relayed to Thom in the course of our three interviews. All those fraught months of my life, the subsequent years of doubt, compressed into a few paragraphs for strangers to read.

I am curious to know who those other eight women are, to learn their stories. But there is no rush for me this time.

Unlike the other headlines that have come streaming through these past few months, me greedily clicking to read the latest tale of infamy, this one can wait.

Instead, I check my messages. If the *Times* article has only just come out, none of my friends or acquaintances or colleagues or people who claimed to know me in the distant past will be reaching out right away. The story will need time to pollinate, to percolate.

But in my email inbox, I see a familiar name.

My mouth creases into a small smile when I open Thom's message.

> Hi Sarah,
> Well, it's out. If you haven't seen it yet, here's the link.
> I hope you are feeling okay about everything, but in case you need some reassurance, it's a strong contribution. I cannot express how grateful I am to you for sharing your story and experience, and I know a great many others out there will be too. So be proud of yourself. This is a huge and important thing you've done.
> By the way. I apologize if this is a little unorthodox. But are you free this Saturday morning in Midtown? There is someone who really wants to see you in person—I felt it was an invitation I had to extend. Someone you might like to see, too.

And one week from now, I will step into the relative quiet of an elegant, but understated brasserie with the city rumbling outside. I will search through the preoccupied crowd for Thom Gallagher and one other person seated inconspicuously at a table in the corner, her back to the outside world. A shuffling of her chair, a glimmer of red hair, and she will be there: Holly Randolph, flashing her familiar smile at me—as if all these years that have passed were nothing. As if there is nothing to forgive, nothing to feel guilty about, only a future that lies ahead, unwritten.

Perhaps that is the momentous meeting, or perhaps it has already happened. When I recently stood outside that Upper East Side brownstone, climbing the stoop to ring the bell. A minute's wait, and then the door opened. And there was Sylvia, her hair more frosted, a few more wrinkles around her eyes. But still the assured stance, the calm voice.

The knowing look, which broke into a smile.

"Sarah," she said. "It's about time."

And she opened her arms wide for a hug.

I had googled her daughter, Rachel, who is now twenty-six and works as an assistant editor at a publishing house. We all find our way forward somehow. And the years behind us, they are only emerging from their camouflage. There is much Sylvia probably never suspected, which I decided to tell her. But all that is in the past.

What matters now is this very moment. I sit in the shuddering subway car, and I gaze serenely at the headline on my phone. It is done.

It is no longer just my story to bear. I've passed it on—to you, Thom Gallagher. And to everyone else who comes into contact with it, who will leaf open the page to his article or click on that link, seeking the salacious details. It is no longer just my burden.

I turn my phone off, zip it away, to give myself the space to contemplate it. Something glows within me, a measure of quiet satisfaction.

It is not fame I have been chasing. It never has been. But to be seen, to be heard, to be remembered. That is all we really need in our lives.

I wonder where Holly is this very moment, three hours behind me in LA. In her airy house in Malibu, gazing out at the Pacific, when she gets a text from her publicist or spies the very same push notification on her phone, or maybe reads a similar email from Thom Gallagher of the *New York Times*.

How will she react, with her very different side of the story, her very different existence?

Later on, there will be video interviews with her on *Entertainment Tonight* or *Good Morning America*, endless questions on red carpets. That will be her extra burden to bear, being who she is, Holly Randolph.

So I am satisfied to be one of the masses, the everyday, the unrecognized.

The F train lifts out of its subterranean tunnel now. I squint in the November sun, and I am thankful for where I am.

You know the shot, the final one in so many films. This is me, looking out the window of the train as it arches aboveground, rattling over the rooftops of Brooklyn. This is the camera, pulling wide into a helicopter's view: all of Brooklyn, then Manhattan in the background, the skyscrapers gleaming in the sun, the East River glittering beneath a vast bright sky.

The sun flares out at us, the train rushes on.

This is me. This is the city. This is all of us.

Acknowledgments

FIRST CONSIDERED WRITING this book in the wake of the Weinstein allegations in autumn 2017. Thank you first and foremost to all those involved in the invaluable reporting of his crimes: the journalists and media platforms, but especially the victims and survivors themselves—for bearing their truths to the world. Of course, many abusers remain at large, so I'd like to recognize those who continue to uncover these experiences, to hold perpetrators to account, and to champion the voices of the women and men whose lives and careers were so unfairly impacted.

Writing and promoting my first novel, *Dark Chapter*, took a lot out of me. Even though *that* was the book about my real-life rape, *Complicit* presented me with a new challenge, and I would not have been able to complete my "difficult second novel" without the support of many friends and advocates.

In the book business, fiction writers can't get very far without an agent, so a huge thank you to my agent, Robert Caskie, for his unwavering belief in *Complicit*—and his patience over two years, as I dealt with an overactive schedule, pregnancy, birth, early motherhood, and a pandemic. After long years of toiling unpaid on a manuscript, I cannot fully describe the financial relief that an excellent book deal can bring to an author.

Thanks of course to my UK editor, Francesca Pathak, for backing *Complicit* so quickly and overseeing its journey with her expert eye for storytelling, as well as a canny sense of the marketplace and for her constant encouragement and enthusiasm. Likewise, thank you to my US editor, Emily Bestler, for championing this book and its themes so passionately and ensuring that it reaches as many North American readers as possible.

At Orion, I must thank Francesca Pearce, Brittany Sankey, Jessica Purdue, Lucy Brem, and many others for bringing their specific skill sets to *Complicit*. At Atria, Lara Jones, Liz Byer, and the rest of the team deserve a big thanks. Credit goes to Tomás Almeida and Kelli McAdams for designing such striking book covers for the UK and US editions respectively.

Arts Council England supported the writing of this book with a National Lottery Project Grant. I was also helped in the early stages by a free partial manuscript read by the Literary Consultancy, as part of my SI Leeds Literary Prize win in 2018. So thank you to those organizations for continuing to support diverse writers, emerging and otherwise. I'd also like to recognize Writing on the Wall in Liverpool and Spread the Word in London for fostering the wider literary community.

Much gratitude to Gray Tan and his team at the Grayhawk Agency for finding a home for my books in Asia. And to Emily Hayward-Whitlock at the Artists Partnership for enabling another life for my books on-screen.

Thank you to my former agents Maria Cardona and Anna Soler-Pont for suggesting I would be the right person to tackle this kind of story, and to Alia Hanna-Habib for her earlier encouragement on the manuscript.

I worked in film for a number of years in my twenties, and I almost want to thank my former boss Lene Bausager for being a decent person and *not* being an abusive manipulator . . . but perhaps that goes to show how low our expectations can be in certain industries. Nevertheless, thank you, Lene, for that proverbial foot in the door and your generosity. Thanks to Mary-Lyn Chambers, Ryan Shrime, and Greg Marcel, for their authentic perspectives on living in LA and working in the industry. And to Ray Liu and Saukok Chu Tiampo for their New Yorker insights.

Writers thrive among other writers, so thank you to my fellow

Goldsmiths alums for their encouragement in our informal weekly workshops (since 2014 and still going!). Thanks to early readers of my manuscript for their invaluable feedback: Anna Kovacs, Chandra Ruegg, Bonnie Lee, Jessica Montalvo, Heather Menze, Hazel Nolan, Annie Bayley, Charlotte Reid, Laura Martz, Jo Bedingfield, Ghislaine Peart, Annie Gowanloch, and Trina Vargo.

I still dream of one day having a dedicated writing room with a desktop computer, but until then, I'll tap away on my laptop wherever I can. Thank you to those who offered up space in their homes, enabling me to focus on this book: Nicola and Bob Grove, Clare Shaw, Wiebke Pekrull and Andreas Schaefer, Tijana Stolic and Ile Kaartinen, Charlotte Reid, and Allan Tulloch and Alison Plessman. And Paul Maddern's River Mill Retreat in Northern Ireland is a blessed space for any writer wanting peace and quiet.

I wrote this book over the course of different phases in my life, starting it as a longtime singleton and finishing it as a partnered mother of a young child. Navigating this many life changes in a short period of time (also during a global pandemic) can threaten to derail any creative project. I owe a great deal to my family and close friends for their unequivocal support through all this: to my parents, Alice and Chauder; to my sister, Emmeline; to my in-laws, Nicola and Bob, for welcoming me into their countryside home—and especially to my partner, Sam, whose love, insight, and commitment as a father to our son has made this current phase of my life possible.

And thank you finally to my Timo for even existing. I started writing this book when you weren't even a glimmer of a possibility in my mind. I finished the second draft the day I learned I was pregnant with you. You were born between drafts three and four. And you'll be over two years old when this book reaches the outside world. Thank you for teaching me the joy of small moments, the wonder of new possibilities, and the value of a long-gestating hope—in creativity and in life.

COMPLICIT

WINNIE M LI

This reading group guide for *Complicit* contains discussion questions that are intended to help your reading group find new and interesting angles and topics for your discussion. We hope that these ideas will enrich your conversation and increase your enjoyment of the book.

Topics and Questions for Discussion

1. *Complicit* tells a story that we think we already know through real-life headlines, but from a lesser-known perspective. How did the book make you feel about this topic in the end? Did it make you feel angry? Sad? Empowered? Hopeful for change? Did any part of the story come as a surprise to you? And what does this say about our expectations around so-called #MeToo stories?

2. Can you understand why Sarah Lai made the choices she did at the time, when she was working with Hugo North? Do you believe she was complicit in a system that abused and mistreated women, or was she a victim in her own way? What could she have done differently, and how would this have affected her

subsequent life and career? Does the book help you understand why some real-life perpetrators were able to get away with their behavior for so long?

3. At first glance, some of the characters in the book may seem like stereotypes: the wide-eyed starlet, the visionary film director, the hard-working Chinese American woman, the gay hairdresser, the wealthy Brit, etc. But did these characters go beyond the shallow outlines of these stereotypes? In what ways? What do you think the book is ultimately saying about stereotypes and the ways individuals are judged externally?

4. Did you like the character of Sylvia Zimmerman? How would you describe her relationship with Sarah? Was she a protective mentor toward a younger woman in the industry, or did she exploit Sarah and expose her to other dangers? What about Sarah's relationships with Holly and Courtney? Do you think women can do more to support each other in the workplace? And is it their responsibility to support each other, or should the professional world be designed to be more gender equal?

5. Sylvia's career suffers because of her dedication as a mother, and Holly undergoes rigorous scrutiny over her appearance. What are some other examples in the book of how women are disadvantaged and held to a different standard from men? How does the book depict female ambition in a male-dominated workplace?

6. *Complicit* portrays an "old boys' network" where men retain most of the power in the film industry. They socialize with each other after hours and give each other opportunities, while treating female colleagues in a very different way. Did you find this realistic? Have you encountered scenarios like this in your own working life? And how does one speak up about sexual harassment and other gendered injustices in the workplace?

7. We also see a workplace where young talent is exploited, under-paid, often unrecognized, and exposed to other dangers like sexual abuse. Could you relate to this at all? Do you think this is particularly pronounced in industries like film, which are heavily glamorized?

8. Did you enjoy the film industry setting and the many references to films? Did you learn anything surprising or eye-opening about how films are made? The book makes use of "familiar" settings we associate with Hollywood, like the Cannes Film Festival and the Golden Globes. How did it make you feel about the glamor and spectacle of movies versus the reality of making them?

9. How does the book portray fame and celebrity? We get to know Holly Randolph before she becomes famous, and yet Sarah refers to that fame as a "burden." What are other examples where the book uses motifs of surfaces, illusion, and artifice in depicting the entertainment industry?

10. Why do you think the author inserted the transcripts from other interviews Thom Gallagher was conducting in his investigation? What does this say about the different perspectives that people can have regarding instances of sexual harassment and assault?

11. In exploring the media world, the book considers the question of who is allowed to tell the story. What did you think of the Thom Gallagher character? How did his gender and class privilege help him in uncovering a story and in enabling his own professional success? How does this notion of privilege and success play out in other characters in the story?

12. *Complicit* interrogates the concept of the American dream: that in America, anyone can work hard to achieve individual

success in their career. Does the book agree with this idea? At one point, the book claims: "Envy is built into the immigrant experience. It is what drives the American dream, after all." How did envy affect Sarah's own ambition—and her attitude towards other women like Holly and Courtney?

13. How does race play a part in Sarah's professional life? Do you think she was perceived and treated differently because she was Chinese American? Do you think her parents' cultural attitudes toward career affected her own choices and behavior at work? Could you relate at all to this aspect of Sarah's experience?

14. Sarah is embarrassed by her family's Chinese restaurant in Flushing, and yet it is also undeniably her roots, and a place where she developed many of her own skills. What does this seem to be saying about immigrant communities in the US? And when she stumbles upon the Chinese restaurant in Los Angeles, what is the importance of this scene?

15. Sarah claims that in the film industry, money ultimately decides everything. Do you think this is true in other contexts? Do you think that every character in the book was swayed by money? And what does the book say about the ethical and artistic choices we can make in a world dominated by money?

16. Storytelling and silence are important themes in *Complicit*. The book opens with a bitter, cynical thirty-nine-year-old Sarah, who has kept silent about what happened to her when she was young and eager. Over the course of the novel, what do you think the process of sharing her story does for Sarah? And what does the end seem to be saying about the collective value of sharing so many individual stories?

Keep reading for an exclusive look
at the next gripping novel
from Winnie M Li

Prologue

Somewhere in Arizona
1991

WHAT ALEX MAINLY remembers is the dust. Or maybe, it is somehow easier and safer to ignore the memory itself, shrouded in the haze of her childhood, and to think only of the inescapable dust that day. Getting up her nostrils, under her fingernails. Sifting in through the car window, when she rolled it down a crack to peer at the blue sky beyond.

She was eight years old, and they had stopped the car at some gas station in the middle of the wide, flat desert. Back then, her family drove a beige station wagon. The kind of color they don't make cars in anymore, nor the kind of shape, either. It wasn't a car that inspired great love or adoration in any member of their family — although she hesitates now, wondering if her thirtysomething mom and dad had swelled with joy when they'd handed a check over to the car dealership salesman sometime in the 1980s and received a set of keys. At the time, it would been their brand-new family car. At one point, it would have shone, undented. An object of pride.

Like everything in their family now, the car was functional. It got them from A to B, from home to school, to the supermarket, to piano lessons, to soccer practice. And on rare occasions, on longer trips like this, to places like the Grand Canyon.

That day when she was eight, the car had jolted and rolled over miles of interstate, green signs whipping past, and she sat through it all, wide-eyed and then, later, sleepy-eyed. But always soaking in the miles and miles of emptiness that bordered the highway. Dry, dusty scrubland with nothing to see, except for the exit ramps leading to towns she would never actually visit, but occasionally glimpse: a cluster of buildings in the distance, housing subdivisions starting to speckle the land.

Watching all of this, what struck her most was a sense of wonder: that there could be so much land. This was America: miles of it rolling in every direction, and however far their car traveled, there would always be more. Sea to shining sea, as they sang in school. If they kept driving on the interstate, how far would it take them? All the way to the Atlantic Ocean? If they picked any one of these exit ramps, what would they discover? There were probably hundreds of them, branching off this highway alone. It boggled the mind, to be confronted with the vastness of this landscape.

Somewhere in Arizona, they rolled off one of these exit ramps, and left the interstate. Their beige station wagon joined a stream of other cars on a smaller highway north, and there were signs here and there mentioning the Grand Canyon.

"Not too far now!" Her dad glanced back at them, speaking in that embarrassing singsong voice he used when trying to get them excited.

"Aiya, look!" Her mom tapped the gasoline dial in frustration. She muttered something in Taiwanese, and Alex knew it was a reminder to fill up the gas. The arrow was at less than half a tank.

Then followed an irritable exchange between their parents in Taiwanese. She didn't need to understand the language to know what they were saying. Mom always wanted Dad to fill up the gas once it reached halfway. Dad always said that was too soon.

The car trundled along in the desert heat; the sun climbed higher in the sky.

They passed a few gas stations, eyeing the price of gas.

"A dollar twenty-two! So expensive!"

"No, we can find cheaper," Mom had said.

Finally, they saw one where gas was remarkably cheap. $1.14 a gallon. Alex didn't recognize the brand—it wasn't one of those familiar colorful logos like Mobil with the winged red horse or Shell with the yellow clamshell. Just a dusty, no-name gas station, a hand-painted sign out front faded in the desert sun.

Dad turned off the highway, the car jolting over ruts and holes in the macadam.

Two men sat out front, and they stared at them, unsmiling.

Otherwise, the place was empty.

"Um . . . do they work here?" Kevin asked, watching the two men warily. They were white and what you might call grizzled: cowboy hats pulled low, blue-jeaned legs splayed out, their boots in the dust. Very unlike anyone Alex had seen in Orange County.

Dad parked the car in front of a gas pump and turned off the ignition. The car keys dangled and swung from behind the steering wheel.

"Well, we fill up the gas anyway."

He shrugged and started to get out of the car.

The two men continued to stare at him.

Alex watched as Dad motioned to the gas pump and their car.

"I just fill up here, okay?" He shouted this to the two men, who looked back in silence. Alex was very conscious of her Dad's accent, his willingness to please. She saw how the two men grinned, slowly, as if there were an unspoken joke.

"That's what it's there for," one of the men shouted back. "Just make sure you pay for it." Not mean, not serious. One of those unfunny jokes men sometimes make to fill up the space.

"Oh, ha ha, of course I pay for it." Dad attempted to laugh back. The sun glinted off his wire-framed glasses.

But Alex felt the fear coursing beneath the glare of the sun.

"We got our eyes on you," the man said. Again, posed lightly as if it were a joke. Suddenly, she was ashamed. She no longer wanted to be there, in that hot and strange gas station, staring through the dusty windshield at the two men.

Dad started to fill up the car. Alex heard the whir and the chug as gasoline poured into their tank. The men kept staring.

"I have—I have to go to the bathroom," Kevin said, nudging Mom.

"You wait until your Dad finish, then you go with him together." There was a protective note in Mom's voice, as if she too sensed a danger in the air.

"I have to go, too," Bonnie said. "Do you think the bathroom will be gross?"

"Aiya, can't you wait?" Mom asked.

"No, Mom, it's my . . ." Bonnie looked around, then her voice quieted. "I think it might come any day."

"What? What are you talking about?" Alex asked. Why did Bonnie have to be so secretive about things sometimes? Bonnie looked at her, but didn't say anything.

Mom let out an exasperated sigh. "Okay okay," she relented.

Alex still had no idea what Bonnie was talking about. She hated being left out, when everyone older than her spoke in this mysterious kind of code.

Mom instructed Bonnie. "You and me, we go together. Kevin, your Dad finish filling the gas, so you and him go to men's room. Alex, you need to go bathroom, too?"

Alex saw her dad hanging the nozzle back on the gas pump, then taking a used tissue from his pocket to wipe the rim around the fuel tank, before snapping the little door shut. He seemed to hesitate, uncertain about crossing over to the building to pay.

"Yeah, you coming, or you just gonna staaaaaayyyy?" Kevin taunted her, as he slid towards the open back door.

"No, I—I'll stay," Alex said, looking at them.

"You sure?" Mom asked as she got out of the car. She leaned down towards Alex, her face in shadow, her body blocking the sun. "We not stopping again till we get to the Grand Canyon."

"Yeah, I'll stay." Alex nodded. Something in her told her to stay clear of those men. She'd rather be here, in the car on her own. As far from them as possible.

"Okay." Mom nodded. "Stay right here. Don't get out of the car."

She wanted to tell them not to go, too. But the gas had to be paid for, and they needed to use the bathroom.

Alex watched as the rest of her family crossed the broken macadam towards the gas station building. They were four slight figures, and the desert heat rose from the ground, distorting them so they looked wavy.

She pushed down the locks on all four of the car doors. And waited.

Near Boston
Present day
Bonnie

At 5 p.m. Eastern Standard Time, Bonnie is sitting in her home office, leaning forward in the luxury ergonomic chair that she bought to get her through all those endless Zoom meetings of the pandemic.

Her family members flicker to life one by one, until they are all there stacked in a neat four-square—centimeters apart on screen, thousands of miles apart in real life. This is a rare occurrence, all five of them on the same screen at once.

Her parents peer into their camera, always slightly mistrusting of any pixelated form of communication. They must be sitting in bed together, because she can see their pale blue padded headboard, unchanged for forty years. The iPad on their lap catches their faces at a low, unnatural angle.

Mom in particular looks thinner, paler, a wizened ghost of the tenacious mother she's known all her life—and Bonnie registers this with a shock. But she tamps down the gnawing worry and greets her parents with her usual cheeriness.

"How was the hospital, Mom?"

Her mom sniffs and shrugs, revealing her familiar defeatist attitude. "It was okay. The food was lousy. I'm glad to be back."

This is a grumpier version of Mom, shorn of all softness or pleasantness.

"Are you . . . is there a procedure happening?" Kevin ventures.

"I'm sick of procedures." Mom shakes her head. "They are doing something else to me in about a month."

They all nod in silence.

Bonnie notes this is the first time Kevin and Alex have shared the same space (virtual or otherwise) in five years. But with Zoom, they don't have to acknowledge each other's presence. They can just exist, side by side on-screen, never making direct eye contact. Which is impossible anyway with Zoom, Bonnie realizes. You can look at your sister's eyes on-screen, but you'll never know if she's actually looking at you.

Each of them contemplates the unspoken, nodding silently around the fact of Mom's medical condition.

In the meantime, they cycle through some more pleasantries of catching up: how is Alex's job, how are Jess and the kids, Chris and the boys. Bonnie is distinctly aware that the news Alex confided in her just yesterday remains a secret to the rest of the family—and that it is not her place to hint at any of it.

"So, Mom, why did you want to have a Zoom with all of us?" Bonnie finally asks, trying to be as gentle as possible.

"Can't I see my children all at once?" Mom jokes, a righteous note rising in her voice.

"No, of course you can." Bonnie imagines that in ten years, she may be asking the same thing of her sons.

"I never get to see all you," Mom continues. "I mean, one by one, yes. But when was the last time we were all together?"

"I think that might have been Christmas sometime," Bonnie offers vaguely. She shoots a look at Alex, then Kevin, but they're staring straight ahead, offering no assistance. *Thanks, guys.*

"So long ago." Mom shakes her head sadly. "What happened?"

Does Mom really have no idea? Something did happen, they were all there to witness it at the dinner table. She remembers Kevin's taunting voice, Alex storming off. Her parents, as always, pretending like nothing ugly had happened.

"We just sort of . . . got really busy," Kevin finally says lamely. "Raising two young kids in lockdown, that was nuts."

"I know," Mom says. "I raised three of you. All while your Dad was working to support us. I know what it's like." Again, the defensive note.

Whatever Mom says, it always lodges a shard of guilt deep inside Bonnie.

"I'm sorry," Alex finally speaks up. "I've been really terrible at keeping in touch. . . ." She trails off, takes a breath, and Bonnie wonders if this is the moment when Alex will share her news, as startling and revelatory as it is.

But before Alex can continue, Mom launches into a deep, hacking cough, the phlegm gurgling in her throat, and Bonnie shudders. *How long has she had that cough for?*

"Mom, you okay?" Alex asks.

Mom shakes her head, clears her throat again, reaches for a cup of water.

After she's sipped and recovered, she continues.

"So I think it's time. I want to see all of you again."

It's time? There is a terrible finality to the phrase, which alarms Bonnie.

"What, like, now?" Kevin asks. He sounds just like Bonnie's fourteen-year-old son. The teenage indignation.

Mom nods. "Now. This month."

"This month?" Kevin repeats. (Does he ever say anything of substance?)

Bonnie panics. "Is it that serious?"

Mom shrugs. "What is serious, Bonnie? A mother wants to see her children after years apart. Isn't that normal?"

Years. Bonnie absorbs this fact. What it would be like to go years without seeing Max and Henry and Milo? Impossible to even contemplate. She wonders if the ache of motherhood subsides with age.

"My procedure is on the twenty-sixth. I want to see you all before then. Together."

Kevin sighs audibly, and Alex is still quiet—her video frozen for a split second.

"Okay," Kevin says, ever the obedient son. He glances down, presumably at his phone. "What weekend?"

"It doesn't matter what weekend," Dad speaks up. "We're retired. It's all the same to us. You three work it out."

"But," Alex says, then pauses. "I'll—I'll have to look at flights."

Mom shakes her head, then explodes into another violent fit of coughing.

"No. Don't just fly here." Mom finally says. Then she gestures at the screen with her hand, as if to admonish them. "I want you to *drive* together. The three of you."

Bonnie lurches in shock. "Drive?! Mom, you live in California, I'm near *Boston*. . . ." She does a quick calculation. It would probably take five, six days to drive all the way to the East Coast. Can she be away from her family for that long?

Kevin's eyes are wide in disbelief, and Alex still appears frozen. Or maybe just in shock, too.

"You don't have to drive the whole way," Mom argues. "I just want you to drive *together*. A road trip, like the old days."

What old days? Bonnie thinks. But then she grasps a memory of sitting in the back seat of their old beige station wagon, the three of them watching the backs of their parents' heads, as miles of highway slid past. There had been road trips, on occasion.

"I want you to drive here to California. And I want you to . . ." Mom stops and coughs, then resumes. "I want you to see the Grand Canyon together."

A strained, unfamiliar feeling of regret blossoms within Bonnie. The Grand Canyon. She lingers on an image: flat, dusty desert rolling endlessly past their car windows.

They had once tried to drive to the Grand Canyon, as a family. When she was fourteen. Why they never made it, Bonnie still can't quite understand.

She notices everyone on the Zoom has gone quiet.

"The Grand Canyon?" Alex finally repeats, her voice low.

"Yes." Their mom nods, uncompromising. "Have any of you been there?"

"Uh . . . no." Kevin shakes his head.

"No. It's a little far," Alex says.

Bonnie admits that she, too, has never stood on the edge of that great natural wonder, this geological marvel that all Americans instinctively know about, even if they grow up thousands of miles away in New England.

"No, I haven't."

Mom nods, her argument complete. "So then, go. Drive there,

and then here to California." She pauses before looking straight at the camera, straight at them. "You owe it to me."

Near Chicago
Kevin

They owed it to Mom? They *owed* it? Like it was a debt that could be repaid after all these decades.

A peculiar feeling of anger slices through Kevin when he thinks of the Grand Canyon. How could she claim they owed it to her, when they had only been children for god's sake.

But Kevin tamps down this resentment, the way he always does with his parents.

"That's a long way, Mom. . . ." He starts to say.

"I know it's a long way. That's why we never got to go when you were little."

Well, we could have. If you hadn't decided to turn around.

"I just want you all to spend time together, now that you're all grown up. You never see each other. You never see your Dad and me."

"I'm sure there's another way we can all see each other," Bonnie offers, characteristically practical. "I mean, we just need more time to plan ahead. . . . Like six months or something like that."

She trails off. Because they all somehow know that the three of them wouldn't ever get together without their Mom's insistence. That's how far apart they've drifted.

The guilt trickles in again, pooling into a dark, secret puddle inside of him.

Mom snorts. "Maybe I don't want to wait six months."

Maybe she doesn't have six months. That's what goes unsaid.

"Okay, then this month. Before the twenty-sixth." Kevin finally acquiesces. Always the first to appease his parents, because his sisters have always been too set on having things their own way.

Bonnie sighs and he can imagine her rearranging her family's overpriced social schedule mentally. Oh, what a shame if it affects their Club Med this year, or their stay at Martha's Vineyard.

Out of nowhere Alex speaks up, with unexpected enthusiasm. "*I* think that's a cool idea."

Alex? She's the one who has to travel the farthest.

Mom's face brightens up on-screen. "See, I can always count on you, Alex."

Kevin seethes in silence.

"No, let's do it!" Alex exclaims. He is reminded of the zeal his younger sister always had in childhood: her harebrained ideas for family plays at Christmastime, or an art project for Mother's Day, or an elaborately devised Easter egg hunt. "Come on, it'll be fun!"

Fun? And that is so Alex, only thinking of what's fun, never what's responsible or sensible. And can you even say the word "fun" when Mom's upcoming operation is the real reason for this trip?

"You really want to do this?" Bonnie is asking Alex, as if Mom weren't right there on the call.

"You heard what Mom said. It's been ages since we've all been together. Even longer since we've done a road trip."

And we all know why, Kevin thinks. *Or maybe you forgot, Alex.*

"Yes, Alex, that's it." Mom grins. Kevin has to admit, it's the first time he's seen Mom smile on this call. "Don't be so serious, like the others."

"I'm not—" Bonnie starts to say defensively, and then shuts up.

"I know you guys have kids," Alex says, stating the obvious. "But maybe you can get away for a week or something? I can fly to Chicago or Texas or wherever, and meet you guys, and we can drive from there."

Kevin mentally calculates Chicago to LA. How long would you need to drive there, with a stop-off at the Grand Canyon?

"And what am I supposed to do?" Bonnie asks. "Fly from Boston to meet you guys?"

"Yeah," Alex answers, nonchalant. "I mean, I'd be flying from London." She lets that fact sink in. "Or, you can *drive* from Boston, if you want."

"That's crazy," Bonnie says, almost automatically. Which is partly justified for any Alex suggestion.

"What's crazy about it?" Alex asks. "Rent a car. Get on the interstate. It's not that difficult."

"Alex, we can't just—" Kevin begins. Jobs and vacation time and getting the kids to school, all the stuff Alex doesn't have to think about because she's still not a proper adult.

"Alex, I have three kids!" Bonnie shouts. "Kevin has two. We can't just leave when we want."

"No," Mom cuts in, forceful. "You can do this. I had the three of you, and I managed to raise all of you, thousands of miles away from my own family, in a new country. With no extra help. Bonnie, you have Chris's family over there. Kevin, Jessica's mom is around the corner. They can all look after your kids. But where is your own mom? All the way over here. You think I don't miss seeing you?"

That shuts them all up. Mom always knows how to lay it on thick.

Kevin watches Bonnie rearrange her face into something corporate and diplomatic. "All right," she says. "I'll speak to Chris and see what I can do."

"Good, Bonnie, good," Mom says, like she's praising a loyal dog. Bonnie nods obediently but looks resigned. Kevin has to admit, there is a rare flicker of excitement inside him. A road trip. A whole week away from Jessica and the kids. The open highway calling, a welcome distraction from his current misery.

"See," Mom continues. "Do it for me. Make your mom happy, okay?"

For the second time on the call, Kevin wonders what exactly they owe their mom. Surely it is something; he just can't name it specifically. Could it be quantified? Repaid that easily through a single road trip?

That is the thing about debt (something that Kevin is now very familiar with). It accrues interest over time. It grows and grows, until it burns a deep, irreparable hole in your wallet and your bank accounts and your existence.

Sometimes, it is too late to repay.

A queasy jolt of excitement courses through Alex when her mom mentions the road trip. She would almost call it the adrenaline of excitement—what she normally feels at any mention of travel— but this time it is laced with something more apprehensive.

Of course, the Grand Canyon.

No one in their family has discussed it in all these intervening years, but it makes a terrible kind of sense.

She recalls with a surreal vividness the feel of the hot desert sun on her arm, as she rode in the back seat of their station wagon. The dust that filtered into the car's interior when they pulled into that gas station and she cracked the window open.

"So you can do it? We'll see you later this month?" Dad is asking now. Looking at his computer screen, expectant.

"Um . . ." Bonnie answers carefully. "The three of us will talk offline and figure out our schedules."

Did she just say "offline" in a family Zoom? Alex suppresses a snort. She can't remember how long it's been since Bonnie left her high-flying career, but the corporate speak still hasn't left her vocabulary.

"Should we do a deep dive and hammer out the timeline for you?" Alex jokes.

Kevin laughs. It's been ages since he's laughed at one of her jokes.

Bonnie rolls her eyes. "Ha ha ha, everyone."

Mom and Dad peer at them perplexed, oblivious to the joke at Bonnie's expense.

"So yeah, we'll be in touch," Bonnie reassures them.

They nod back—and for once, somehow, pixelated across each other's screens, the five of them seem to be in agreement.

When she clicks off the Zoom, Alex lingers for a moment longer in their bedroom. Nya is in the living room, most likely stretched out on their couch, watching some cozy reality TV competition about baking. Stroking her belly in that protective, maternal way that has become second nature to her in a matter of months.

Alex is relieved to have these moments of silence to herself, to contemplate what was said on the family call. And what wasn't. Her Mom could be dying. No one's mentioned it outright (her parents don't like to speak that candidly about things), but it was clearly there in the subtext.

Why else the request for this sibling road trip?

But a dark shadow undercuts that request, a crust of a memory that no one wants to acknowledge.

Alex stands up and peruses the travel guide books on her shelf. Decades' worth of Let's Go and the Lonely Planet and the Rough Guide, covering the Mediterranean, the Middle East, West Africa, Southeast Asia, the Caribbean . . . so many geographies comprised in the colorful spines of these books. So many places that she herself has eagerly set foot in. Except her own country. There is virtually no mention of the United States, save for a thin New York City guidebook from her trip with Nya four years ago.

Why hasn't she wandered her own country, with all those states that she's been accustomed to seeing on her flights to California — the broad, endless fields, the rugged mountain ranges, the dry desert expanses. All passing silently below her, unexplored.

She thinks about belonging. How increasingly, as the years went by, it seemed a foreign notion every time she set foot in America. Until she eventually stopped looking for it. Stopped expecting it.

Maybe it is time, she thinks. She can afford to leave the UK for a week or two. One final hurrah before the reality of parenthood sets in. Nya is nearly five months along, safely out of the first trimester, and still nimble enough to get around on her own. So they've got time.

When Alex thinks about her own mother, laid up in that bed in California, she realizes they still have time, too. But only just.